Contents

Chapter 1	
Chapter 2	
Chapter 3	23
Chapter 4	35
Chapter 5	43
Chapter 6	53
Chapter 7	74
Chapter 8	81
Chapter 9	90
Chapter 10	100
Chapter 11	109
Chapter 12	118
Chapter 13	131
Chapter 14	148
Chapter 15	162
Chapter 16	178
Chapter 17	186
Chapter 18	214
Chapter 19	223
Chapter 20	233
Chapter 21	241
Chapter 22	259
Chapter 23	269
Chapter 24	280
Chapter 25	291
Chapter 26	300
Chapter 27	310

Chapter 28	327
Chapter 29	360
Chapter 30	377
Chapter 31	386
Chapter 32	400
Chapter 33	407
Chapter 34	423
Chapter 35	427
Chapter 36	433
Chapter 37	439

Ireland 1983

David Crane watched through terrified eyes as the knife had been 'prepared'. A show had been made of carefully sticking two small scalpel blades together with a drip of Super-glue and clipping them into the machined aluminium handle. This, David was informed, would have the effect of cutting two parallel lines in the skin causing a cut to heal slowly and to leave a welted scar when it did.

"How's Moira Davy?" A thick Irish accent punctured the heavy air of the room.

"How's... Moira... Davy?" David Crane stayed still and silent looking down at the floor. *Don't let him get to you man.*

"And the kiddies, Davy. How are they? Not getting a lot of sleep these days eh."

Without warning, a fist thumped heavily into the side of David Crane's face. A man wearing a grey, hand knitted balaclava, then cut off the buttons of David's shirt using the glinting medical scalpel he had personalised. Sweat trickled slowly down David's forehead and into his eyes even though it was cold and damp in the vast space they were in. He wanted to wipe his hand across his face but his hands were tied securely behind his back and to the bentwood chair the three other men had manhandled him onto.

The apparent leader of the four, who were all wearing balaclavas, bizarrely introduced himself politely as Marvin. He was the one brandishing the knife. He was the one who'd thumped him in the side of the head.

"Did you ever see that film Davy?" Marvin walked behind the chair and prised open David's left eyelid with the thumb and forefinger of his left hand. He held the scalpel in front of David's wide-open eye with his right. The wool of Marvin's balaclava brushed the side of David's face, and his mouth was only inches away from David's ear.

"The one where they used a sheep's eye." Marvin slowly moved the blade from left to right an inch in front of David's eye. David was shaking, his whole body started to convulse.

"Calm yourself man." Said Marvin as he moved away from behind David. "We're not animals." He paced slowly round to stand in front of David and dropped the scalpel into his pocket.

"Left a scar on my subconscious. I'm telling you. I get nightmares...even now."

David knew where he was and he considered that little piece of information a bonus. They didn't know he knew. They had driven him around the lanes leading to this place for an hour or more, with a potato sack over his head, trying to disorientate him. They would have been more successful in that regard if they had taken him to a service station motel or somewhere equally faceless but they had brought him here. To a place he recognised even before they had taken off the blindfold. He could smell it. No other place smelt exactly like it. He used to play here as a boy and the smell brought back an instant recall.

It was once a silver mine. Not that he could remember anything precious coming from its midst. The room they were in was a vast concrete cube sunk into the middle of the hillside, the only entrance being a set of huge metal doors. It would be well hidden. It was thirty years or more since he had played here with his friends. It was remote so no one ever bothered them. They never used to anyway. Although he'd felt a sudden shock from the punch, it had taken a moment or two to turn into pain. His face was cut by the gold sovereign ring that Marvin was wearing on the middle finger of his right hand.

"I'm here to talk Davy." Said Marvin quietly as the same right hand landed another punch.

"Don't you want to talk?"

David sensed that Maurice or Marty or Marvin or whatever stupid moniker he had assigned himself, was enjoying his job.

David glanced up without moving his head and saw Marvin hold out his arm in the direction of one of the other three silhouetted figures that were standing half to attention to his side. He was thinking that this may be the end of it all, but he was somehow resigned. *If I get a swing from that pickaxe handle, it'll probably kill me.* Instead of handing Marvin the pickaxe handle, the other man leant it against the wall, opened a smart leather satchel that had been sitting on the floor and as if it had been rehearsed, passed across a buff coloured file.

"You were educated in England Davy. Weren't you?" Said Marvin as he opened the file. There were two sheets of closely typed paper inside. For a few moments Marvin read the words on the page to himself using a forefinger to help him.

"And you finished up at Oxford. Bright lad by all accounts. I hope not too bright for your own good." He scanned some more.

"That's where you met Boothe. According to this you were both political hotheads." Marvin was holding the dossier up with his right hand and appeared to be reading carefully, his left forefinger flicking between the paper and his chin as he did so. He began to pace around the chair.

You've got that wrong for a start. Eamonn may have been a bit of an orator but even he was only in it for the craic. We couldn't have cared less about your politics. "I'm going to ask you straight Davy. Are you working for the British?" David was not surprised by the question. He was of the opinion though, that nothing he did or didn't say would alter the outcome of the events here this evening. Marvin swapped the dossier to his left hand and picked the scalpel out of his pocket. He squatted in front of David. David could feel warm breath on his face. Marvin pushed David back on the chair so he was sitting upright and made a cut with the knife. A straight cut in the middle of David's chest, downwards, about three inches long. As the blade penetrated his skin, David Crane flinched but Marvin stayed steady with the knife.

"Did you sabotage the TPU's on the boat, Davy?" He asked but hardly waited for a response. Admiring his bloody handiwork with a sideways tilt of his head, he aligned the blade for another cut.

"You were both in port before the boat left Khoms Davy. Either of you could have done it. Do you know what it meant to us Davy? It's put us back twenty years. Do you know what the council will do to you if they find out you were in cahoots with Boothe?"

With a steady hand, he made another three-inch cut, one inch away and parallel to the first. The pain was not so unbearable. *So you've already put Eamonn in the frame,*

"They've asked me to put a little proposition to you Davy."

In the swing of his work now his next cut, three inches long crossed the other two horizontally one third of the way down.

"You see, they need to know that the boys on the ground, the foot soldiers, people like you and me Davy, they need to know that we are loyal to the cause. D'you know what I mean Davy."

Another cut, again three inches long was parallel to and one inch away from the previous one.

"They need to know who's loyal, Davy. They need to know who they can count on so's they can eliminate the one's they can't."

One inch cut, diagonal, starting top left and ending bottom right corner of the square formed by the four parallel lines.

"Just look up a second would you, for me Davy." Said Marvin as if he were cutting David's hair. David Crane didn't move his head. Marvin put the blade of the scalpel under David's chin and pushed slowly upward. David Crane saw another of the lieutenants search inside his black wax Belstaff jacket and pull out an automatic pistol. The lieutenant pointed it directly at David's forehead for a good few seconds enjoying his moment of power before he placed it on a bench made of old railway sleepers, to the side of them. The lieutenant then reached into another pocket, pulled out a magazine of ammunition and placed that next to the gun. Marvin walked over, placed the scalpel on the bench, picked up the gun, and clicked the magazine into position in the butt of the pistol.

"They want you to prove yourself, Davy. They want you to show them that you're a good man - someone they can rely on."

He checked the safety catch on the side of the gun before slipping it into a small Hessian sack he had taken from his own black donkey jacket pocket and dangled the sack in front of David's face.

"This is for Boothe."

His voice had lost its contrived gentleness. David felt physically ill. He knew he'd been playing a high-risk game and knew it would come with consequences but for some reason he hadn't bargained for this. How stupid and naïve he had been to get himself in this far. And for what? A few dollars so he could clear out of this God forsaken country and take his family to a better place. Marvin walked back over to the old wooden bench and unknowingly placed the bag holding the gun directly on top of some letters roughly carved into the bench top. Still visible after twenty five years, the letters EB sat two inches away from the letters DC. He picked up the scalpel again and put it back in his pocket. Marvin paced around the back of the chair. David could hear him jangling some keys.

"There's a car outside, Davy. Not much of a ride I'm afraid but you'll not be worrying yourself about that."

Marvin tossed the keys onto David's lap. His voice was loud and clear now.

"You're to get the Wednesday morning ferry from Belfast. Both of you. Drive down to London. There's three hundred pounds of explosives in the boot and under the back seats. The address to go to and instructions for the detonation are in the glove-box."

Marvin was pacing around like a schoolteacher. He swivelled on his heels.

"When you park the car, set the timer to go off at twenty-two hundred hours on Saturday night. Keep an ear to the radio, Davy. When you hear on the news that the bomb has gone off, that..." He pointed towards the gun on the bench. "...is for Boothe."

Marvin bent down again to stage whisper into David's ear.

"Don't go getting yourself any smart ideas Davy boy. We'll be watching you."

He stood up again and continued with his schoolteacher pacing.

"You've got forty eight hours after the blast to take out Boothe. If we see it's not been done in that time Davy, the boys will come for you."

His voice returned to mock softness.

"And with you gone Davy, who's to be looking after Moira and the kiddies?"

Marvin crouched again in front of David and picked the scalpel from his pocket.

"Make it messy if you can Davy. We don't want it to look like we did it. You understand."

An inch long cut starting on the top right of the square and forming a cross with the other diagonal inch long cut. He moved his head back and cocked it to one side again. He stood and leaned backwards.

"Just a little reminder, Davy. In case you're doubtin'."

Marvin bent forward again, his face just inches away from David's. He jabbed David on the forehead with an outstretched first and second finger, thumb sticking upwards.

"This isn't a game you can win."

For the first time David Crane noticed through his half-closed eyes that on the hand Marvin was using to mime a gun, there was no little finger.

2

David Crane and Eamonn Boothe stepped off the small stage to the applause and cheers of the mixed crowd gathered in the local pub.

"Can we go somewhere a little more private?" Said a young man in dark clothes and wearing a particularly conspicuous leather wide brimmed hat. Eamonn nodded at the landlord who was busy pouring pints. The landlord flicked his head back towards the end of the bar. Eamonn led David Crane and the Man-In-The-Hat through a door, along a narrow corridor and into a small room. Eamonn clicked a switch on the wall and the room was lit by a single unshaded light bulb. In the centre of the room was a wooden table and four chairs but no other furniture. On top of the table was a glass ashtray. Eamonn motioned for them to sit down. The Man-In-The-Hat placed the rucksack he's been carrying beside him on the floor and unzipped a compartment to pull out a roll of paper which he began to spread out on the table. He looked at his watch and said to no-one in particular,

"Eleven fifteen."

Eamonn and David were both sweaty from playing the second of two forty minute sets to their partisan audience.

David took a quarter bottle of whiskey from the pocket of his jeans, unscrewed the cap and took a big gulp. He put the bottle on the table to hold down a corner of the paper, which the Man-In-The-Hat was struggling to roll out, took a squashed packet of ten cigarettes from another pocket and lit one with a black lacquered lighter. He blew a plume of smoke up towards the light bulb, put the lighter back on the table by the ashtray and leant back on the back two legs of the wooden chair.

"Go easy," said the Man-In-The-Hat nodding toward the whiskey bottle, "You'll need your wits about you later."

The Man-In-The-Hat was still standing, still fussing with the curly edges of a roll of plain cream decorating paper torn to be half a metre long. On the paper was a map drawn roughly in pencil. Eamonn picked up the whiskey bottle and ignoring the advice of the Man-In-The-Hat, took another large gulp. He put the bottle back on the edge of the paper. Eamonn sat limp on his chair, his hands in his pockets and his head down.

The man in the hat sat on his chair and crossed his arms. He looked at the two men in turn.

"We don't have to do this you know." He said to them both as he leant across the table and picked up David's lighter. He turned it around in his fingers and nodding his approval said,

"Dunhill. Nice."

David and Eamonn exchanged a fleeting glance containing the slightest of smiles.

"I could just leave and you two could get on with the last few days of your lives. I wouldn't give you more than a week though. So it's up to you." He smiled at them both. He waited again and they both shuffled their chairs closer to the table.

"Good." Said the man in the hat and pointed at the edge of the map.

"We are currently here. This isn't to scale remember. The road leading to the ferry port is here." He pointed to the other side of the paper.

"After you leave here you drive seven miles towards the monument in Cluck. Then you take the big main road towards the ferry, which is about twenty miles away. Twelve miles further along the main road, just after the junction with the North road there's a tunnel." He looked at them both to see if they were paying attention. "Where's the car?" Asked Eamonn.

"It's still where you left it." Replied the man in the hat. "This tunnel," he continued, jabbing a finger into the paper, "This tunnel is where all the magic happens."

He reached down to his bag and pulled out a spiral bound reporters pad and flicked open the pages to a roughly drawn diagram. He took a pencil from behind his ear.

"The car they gave you was loaded with two hundred pounds of Czech made plastic explosives."

"He told me three hundred." Said David.

"Make of that what you will." Said the man in the hat

"We've added another fifty for luck. If they want to do a forensic on it after that explosion our guys will find it matches up with stuff taken from your lot..."

"They're not 'Our lot.' For God's sake. They wouldn't be trying to kill us if they were our lot." Said David softly.

"Well unfortunately you don't belong to us either. Not officially at any rate." He smiled at the two men again, looking for agreement. Neither Eamonn's nor David's expression changed.

"Shall we move on?" David and Eamonn reluctantly nodded. The man in the hat continued.

"Two hundred and fifty pounds of plastic explosive is enough to blow a hole in the road the size a two up two down. There will be nothing left of the car and nothing left of whatever or whoever was inside it. You chaps were supposed to board the ferry to North Wales, drive the old motor to London and detonate the bomb outside an address in St. James' Square. While you were there..."

The man in the hat looked toward David,

"You were supposed to make a messy job of eliminating Booth I believe."

Eamonn flicked his head quickly towards David. David nodded slowly in answer to Eamonn's unspoken question.

"You'd not told him that bit then I see." Said the man in the hat. "No matter." The man in the hat returned to the spiral bound notebook and pointed with his pencil.

"The steering lock has been modified to lock in the straight-ahead position. You just turn the ignition key forward a notch. If I were you…" He theatrically winked at them both in turn. "...I'd test that a few times before the final jump." David and Eamonn looked at each other and raised their eyebrows in unison. The man in the hat continued,

"The camber of the road could drag the car off the straight and narrow. At that time in the morning there should be little traffic about. We'll have to be lucky though." He reached down to his bag again and extracted a plastic box the size of a cigarette packet. He pulled an aerial from a corner.

"This is the detonator control." He flicked a toggle switch by the aerial and David and Eamonn automatically flinched.

"No batteries." He reached down and took an oblong battery from the rucksack.

"Just before you make the jump put the battery in here." He slid open a flap on the plastic box and handed it to David.

"If you put it in now and flicked that switch, your adoring fans would know nothing about it. But then neither would we. Don't worry too much though. Stuff's pretty inert without the detonator. Look. You got the car three days ago. They'll have been watching you pretty close since then. We're sure that the few hours we had it the ASU that was assigned to keep it in their sights was watching a lunchtime strip show in The Clock on Francis Street. We know because one of our lot..." He nodded towards David. "One of our lot is in that active service unit,"

He went back to the map and pointed again with the pencil.

"The tunnel is about fifteen hundred yards long and is dug through a hill. There will be an ASU following you at a distance. They're there to see you get on the boat. If they get too close, you're still good because of the slight curve in the start of the tunnel. Three hundred yards before the end of the tunnel is a metal door that leads to a neat double helix staircase. It's quite an architectural treasure actuallybut don't go wasting time admiring it. At the top of the staircase is a concrete bunker with a single door. Go out the door and walk towards the full moon. Five hundred yards directly ahead an armoured personnel carrier will meet you. They will drive you to the border where they'll give you the keys to another car. You drive to Cork where you get on a boat going to Southampton. Where you go from there is up to you."

Man in the hat reached again into his rucksack. He had two envelopes in his hand. He paused before continuing.

"This is it Gentlemen. You'll never be able to come back here."

The three of them sat in silence for a moment. Eamonn held out his hand first.

"Your name is Richard Starr. You'll find a British passport and one thousand pounds sterling." He passed over the envelope. "Good luck Richard Starr." Said the man in the hat. They both looked at David. After a brief pause, he too nodded his head and held out his hand.

"Good Man." Said the man in the hat and passed him the envelope.

"You are now Thomas Gates. Good luck Thomas Gates." The Man In The Hat went back to his notepad.

"The car's been fitted with a simple hand throttle in place of the choke cable just underneath the dashboard here." He indicated with his pencil to a sketch on the pad.

"When you flick the detonator switch there will be a delay of twenty seconds before it goes off. The car must," He made a special emphasis to this last word, "Must be outside the confines of the tunnel otherwise it won't matter how far up that spiral staircase you are, you will be torn apart by the shock-wave. If you are within fifty paces of the explosion, they'll not find a body. If the car is outside the end of the tunnel, you'll be fine. Might just want to cover your ears though."

"So let me get this right." Said Eamonn. "We have to drive a car load of high explosives from here to a tunnel on the main road later tonight and jump out of it while it's still moving in the hope that it makes the end of the tunnel relying on some Heath Robinson modifications 'you lot' have cobbled together, then detonate the bomb from a safe distance and make our escape up a spiral staircase where, as totally different people we begin new lives. Seems watertight to me. I mean what could possibly go wrong?"

"Well look." Said the man in the hat. "If you have any better ideas then I'm all ears."

"Why can't we just hide out for a few months?" Asked David as he took another slug from the whiskey bottle and lit another cigarette.

"Oh sorry." Said the man in the hat. "I hadn't thought of that. No. Unless they think you're dead, there'll be no hiding you. They'll find you eventually and god knows what they'd do to you then. Not to mention your family."

He looked at David whose expression was deadpan.

The man in the hat reached down to his rucksack again, pulled out a set of car keys, and looked at his watch.

"It's midnight." He said, again to no one in particular.

"The ferry will leave at six am. You'll need to be there an hour early so that's five. It'll take you an hour to get to the tunnel so I reckon you leave here in about two hours." He rose from his chair.

"Gentlemen. It's been a pleasure." He gathered the papers that were on the table and screwed them into a ball.

"Can I borrow your lighter?" He asked David. David passed him the lighter that was sitting on the table on top of his crumpled packet of cigarettes. He flicked the cover and rolled the sparking wheel over the wick and a small flame appeared. He watched the flame flicker for a moment then lit the papers in his hand. They burnt rapidly for a few seconds before he let them fall onto the bare floorboards. When they were all just cinders, he extinguished the last of the embers with his boot. David and Eamonn watched as he did this. The realisation of what they had just agreed to was sinking in. They really had no choice. As the Man-In-The-Hat opened the door and the noise from the bar filtered in. He turned and doffed his hat towards them and nodded. David and Eamonn both looked up slightly without moving their heads.

"I'll see myself out." Said the Man-In-The-Hat as the latch of the door clicked behind him.

David sat there in shock for a few moments rocking back and forth on his chair. He picked up the bottle of whiskey, unscrewed the top and swigged from it. He passed it to Eamonn who had stood up and was pacing around the table. Eamonn took it from him and drank what was left in the bottle.

"We can't give them any clues we're leaving you know." Said Eamonn. He had stopped pacing and was pulling a curtain to one side and looking out the window into the dark night. He could see a few cars parked down the dimly lit street but none he didn't recognise. David nodded in agreement, his eyes fixed staring into the middle distance through purple cigarette smoke.

"Moira and the little ones must never know." Said David. "That way they'll be safe. If this works tonight mate, and we manage to disappear we are going to have to stay dead."

"I'm sorry." Said Eamonn without much emotion as he sat down at the table again. He appeared to want to say more.

"What are you sorry for Aim? It's our own fault. We both took the shilling." They sat there in silence for a good few minutes. They each managed a thin smile when they heard the landlord ringing the last bell and calling time.

The tunnel that carries the A282 through Mayflower Hill, toward the ferry port in Belfast is lit at night by a single row of yellow sodium lights running along the centre of the semi-circular roof. Eamonn slowed the little car down and flicked on the full beam headlights. They had been the only car on the road for at least the last half an hour. During that time, they had not seen a car or lorry coming in the opposite direction and had not seen the lights of anything behind them. David sat forward in his seat looking for the iron door that The Man-In-The-Hat had described and it presently appeared in the beam of the headlights.

"Half a mile." Said David. "Can you see the end of the tunnel?"

"I can't see shit." Said Eamonn.

David leaned over into the back seat, lifted his cumbersome guitar case, and positioned it on his lap.

"Slow right down will you."

Eamonn raised his eyes to the roof and letting out a long exasperated breath slowed the car still further to a walking pace. David opened the car door and with a struggle dropped the guitar case as gently as he could onto the road.

"There it is." Said Eamonn. "The end is nigh. Put the battery in the detonator." David picked the detonator out of the glove-box and inserted the battery. He closed his eyes tightly as he made the final little clicked connection of the battery terminals. Eamonn had flinched too.

"We're still here." He said. "Twenty seconds from when we flick the switch it'll go off."

"Do I flick it before we bail or after?"

"After." Said Eamonn. "Are you ready for this?"

David nodded slowly. The car was crawling along at a walking pace.

"We're going to need it going a bit faster if it's to make it to the end of the tunnel in twenty seconds."

Eamonn adjusted the makeshift throttle control and the car bolted forwards. They both immediately jumped out and rolled over in the road before standing up to watch the car gathering speed. It was wavering toward the middle of the road but David was happy that it would make it.

"Twenty seconds." He said as he flicked the toggle switch. A little red light on the plastic box began to flash and the two men ran for their lives towards the iron doors. David snatched at his guitar case as he ran past it and in the process, the old worn handle came off in his hand. Eamonn was slightly ahead and did not see it. In fear and desperation, David left the case where it was. They both got to the recessed archway that held the double doors and Eamonn pulled at the heavy iron bolts. He pulled the door open and David ran through. Eamonn saw the guitar case sitting on the road twenty yards from where he was standing. He ran back to get it and had managed to shove it through the iron doors as the car exploded within a few yards of the exit to the tunnel. David was picked up by the shock wave and was thrown along the brick and concrete lining of the tunnel where he was slammed into a supporting arched buttress. The iron doors had slammed shut in the force of the blast and David fell against the treads of the iron staircase. The noise was truly deafening. In a moment he both cursed Eamonn and then himself for being so stubborn and bringing his stupid guitar. But Eamonn was right. If they left it out in the road, even if it was blown to bits, they would know that they got out of the car. That's why Eamonn had gone back for it and it had probably cost him his life. *Must do something.* David pulled himself up and went back out the iron doors. The explosion had smashed the lights on the ceiling of the tunnel for a hundred yards or more. The remaining lights cast a dim orange glow over the space. The explosion had ripped plaster and tiles from the surface and the whole place was full of a thick dust. David could make out Eamonn, a crumpled heap in a corner and ran the thirty yards or so towards him. Eamonn was lying face down in the dust. David turned him over. He was covered in blood and did not appear to be breathing. He pulled him up and heaved him onto his shoulder. He turned towards the iron door and with his free arm scraped up the thankfully still intact guitar case. He struggled with the iron door. He knew though that only a huge effort of will would get him to the top of this staircase carrying both Eamonn and the guitar. Without knowing how, he made it to the top of the staircase where he found another steel door. He pushed through it and dropped his cargo as gently as he could. He looked around him in the darkness. He was in a small clearing forty feet wide. He looked behind him and saw that he had emerged from a concrete cylinder eighteen feet across. Around the edge of the clearing were trees and bushes. To one side, thick black smoke was floating into the moonlit sky. He waited a moment catching his breath, crouching on his knees. He heard an owl call out into the night and then another. He looked in the direction of the full moon and saw the bushes come to life. Four soldiers appeared wearing full camouflage.

"This man is injured. Help. Please." The four soldiers sprang into action. The biggest of them picked up Eamonn and slung him over his shoulder just as David had done.

"Follow us if you will Sir." Said one of the soldiers. "We need to get you away from here." David followed him and the soldier carrying Eamonn. The two other soldiers walked backwards behind them, their machine pistols drawn.

Presently they arrived at a roadway. Two armoured personnel carriers were waiting. They approached the cars in silence and David was ushered into the first. Eamonn was carried into the second.

3

England, 2012.

Benson and Hedges sat waiting in the reception of a data centre. Data centres form the physical backbone of the information age. The invention of the internet required huge numbers of physically unassuming buildings like these to be placed around the world. They are the node points that join the copper wires, the fibre optic cables, the wireless transmitters and receivers that facilitate practically instant communication between computers that can be situated on opposite sides of the globe. Collectively, these buildings hold in their servers and hard disk arrays the memories of the human race. Memories neatly packaged into bite sized pieces that when encrypted, translated, fire-walled and de-coded make up the records, the text, the pictures or the web sites that are now regarded as being commonplace. The building is one of many similar faceless buildings on the site in an industrial estate forty miles or so from central London along the M4 Motorway. This one is four stories high and occupies about an acre of ground. Built from painted corrugated metal and breeze-blocks, there are no windows. It looks just like a large warehouse. It is similar to all the others but for one major difference. It is about as secure as a building can be. But it doesn't look like it - the thinking being that putting a big padlock on your garden gate gives the impression that you have something worth protecting. Although the building is designed to be protected from a physical attack, it is an attack from within the network of which it forms a part that was of most concern to the designers. This is where this particular data centre differs from most of the others. Government grade security systems keep the information it contains secret. Most of the time.

In the reception was an unmanned desk made of stainless steel and glass. An unmarked metal door hissed open and a suited young man in his late twenties approached Benson and Hedges.

"Gentlemen," he said offering them his hand. His accent was upper class English. Benson and Hedges rose from their seats and shook the man's hand in turn.

"Captain Pickering... at your service, we are honoured"

He continued slightly bowing his head.

Benson and Hedges said nothing.

"Yes, well gentlemen. If you'd like to follow me." He turned and began to walk toward the door he came through. Benson and Hedges picked up their black attaché cases and followed him. He stopped at the door and put his eye to a lens poking out of a steel box to the side of the door.

"A retinal scan gentlemen. Hope you don't mind." His voice was jocular and nervous. "Just so's we can check you are who you're supposed to be. Ha ha."

First Benson peered into the lens until a tiny green light blinked on the display and a bleep sounded. Hedges did the same. The door hissed open again and all three of them walked through. They started a walk along a long corridor lined with numbered doors. As they walked, Pickering talked nervously.

"We're very proud of our security here, gentlemen. Your clearance comes from the highest level. We don't get this sort of instruction very often. You guys are all very mysterious."

They walked to the end of the corridor to another solid metal door. The three of them in turn performed the retinal scan again and the second door hissed open. There was a small lobby with the same grey carpet, white plastered walls and white suspended ceiling. On one wall were the stainless steel doors of a lift with a single button control on the right hand frame. Pickering pressed the button and after a half a minute the lift door opened to reveal an area the size of a decent office. On the floor were twelve circles made up of the coloured concentric rings of the RAF. They were each about two feet in diameter. The three men stepped inside.

"I do apologise gentlemen." Said Pickering nodding towards the rings.

"The Co-ordinator of the last revamp was Ex RAF. If you'd just like to stand on one of them."

Benson and Hedges shuffled into position over the rings. Pickering did the same. The lift door closed. They all stood in silence for a moment before a shrill alarm rang and a red light flashed in the corner of the ceiling. Pickering tapped a long code into a keypad on the wall and the alarm stopped.

"Nothing to worry about gentlemen. There's no harm in you guys knowing given your clearance. The lift is equipped with new non-linear junction detectors." Pickering said this as if he expected the two men to understand what he was talking about. Hedges had read about them in technical magazines but Benson didn't have a clue.

"They're picking up on those." Pickering pointed towards their attaché cases. "It's to stop employees walking in and out with all the stuff we've spent so much money trying to protect."

Benson and Hedges remained silent. Out of sight of Pickering, Benson caught Hedges' eye and nodded imperceptibly towards the floor. Hedges returned the look and with the slightest of shrugs shook his head. The lift started to descend. For a full thirty seconds they travelled down until the lift stopped and the doors opened. "This way gentlemen. If you please." Pickering led them out into yet another corridor. This time just white painted concrete and rubber floors. Bright florescent tubes supplied the lighting. A twelve-inch diameter galvanised steel pipe ran the length of the corridor with venting grills every ten feet or so. They walked past another dozen white steel doors until they stopped at another retinal scanner.

"Well gentlemen, this is where my clearance ends. There's a red panic button just inside the room. Only use it if one of you is having a heart attack. Ha Ha. No really just in case of emergency. You're cleared for three hours so I'll be back to get you at..." He looked at his watch. "Sixteen hundred hours."

He proffered his hand again and Benson and Hedges shook it in turn with polite smiles and nods. As they entered the room, the harsh strip lights flicked on. The door hissed closed behind them and Benson let out a whistle of relief. He was about to speak when Hedges turned toward him, put his finger to his lips and pointed at his chest. Benson nodded in understanding when he saw the black half globes of the security cameras in the ceiling that Hedges was actually pointing at. Hedges took his attaché case over to a workstation and opened it up. The laptop inside sprang into life as he opened the cover. He tapped a few keys, nodded towards Benson, and mouthed the words 'one minute'. A green screen appeared on the laptop showing a number of bar graphs like the display of a graphic equaliser. After a moment or two, the bobbing columns settled down to their lowest level and a pop up window appeared with a coloured pie chart on it. The pie chart was pink for three hundred and fifty five degrees. A small slither of it was blue.

"Ok." Hedges said at last. "That's good enough. We're clear."

Benson was looking at him with a puzzled look on his face.

"You know as well as I do you can't be too careful. We built this stuff over four years ago." Said Hedges. "They were obsessed with security then, there's been a change in government since. You never know what they might have put in."

"No. Sure." Said Benson opening up his attaché case and pulling out his laptop. "That alarm in the lift freaked me out. Thought they'd rumbled us."

"They can't rumble us can they?" Said Hedges. "You said we'd got clearance from the top."

"You never know. There could have been a coup while we were on the M4."

"That stuff was never installed when I was here." Said Hedges. "The kit hadn't got that good. Non-Linear Junction Detectors. They detect printed circuit boards. Wonder what other gizmos were in that lift?"

The room was filled with rack after rack of blinking computer equipment. Twelve rows two and a half meters high and twenty meters long. At intervals in the ceiling between the racks were the cameras Hedges had pointed at.

"There's nothing transmitting out of this room so we're good to talk." Said Hedges pointing at the display on the open laptop.

"They are recording so don't do anything that looks suspicious."

"Like what?" Said Benson. "Given that everything we have done here so far is suspicious."

"Just behave like a computer technician would." Hedges was fumbling around in his attaché case.

"How does a..."

"Enough." Interrupted Hedges, "Let's get on with this."

Benson's laptop started up with a green screen. A blinking white cursor in the top left corner. He reached into his case for a network cable and plugged it into a socket on the wall behind the workstation. Hedges' opened a second laptop, which started up with a familiar blue window. He plugged both his laptops into network ports on the wall.

"The log on page should appear." Hedges said. After a few key strokes, a dialogue box appeared on Hedges' computer and a cursor prompt appeared on Benson's. There were two fields in the dialogue box. The third laptop changed to show a black screen at the bottom of which was a thin red line.

"Over to you Mate." Said Hedges.

"Type in user name RolandGarret," Benson told him, "Uppercase R uppercase G. All one word."

Hedges typed in the user name. Benson typed the same thing at the cursor prompt.

"Ok" said Benson. "Type in, and be careful. We get two chances apparently. The guys who set this up weren't anticipating dyslexics." He spoke the password one character at a time.

"Capital T, lowercase r, lowercase u, the number 5, uppercase T, uppercase N, the number zero, the number 1."

Hedges was waiting for more.

"That's it for this level."

Hedges looked around at Benson.

"Tru5tN01," he said to Benson, a sure-fire derision in his voice. "Top tier British government access password is trust-no-one".

"That's not top tier," said Benson with a nod of his head. "You just wait." Another box appeared on Benson's green screen with a flashing cursor prompt in the top left corner. Fifteen seconds later a blue window appeared on Hedges' computer.

"OK," said Benson. "Type capital T, the number zero, lowercase y, the number 5, capital T, the number zero, lowercase r and …"

"Lowercase y?" Hedges said. Benson smiled.

They counted down from three and pressed their return keys in unison. Benson's laptop immediately showed a green screen with a search box and a cursor prompt. Hedges laptop took more time but it too displayed a neat blue window with a white box in the corner containing a little magnifying glass.

"We are in." said Benson with a celebratory clap.

"Just look for the moment." Said Hedges. "When we find what we're looking for we'll need the mirrors to hide the deletions. I'll punch in the algorithm then. We'll need to do that in unison too." Benson looked at his watch. "Two and a half hours, yeah!" He looked at Hedges for agreement.

"Yeah" Hedges nodded concentrating on his screen. "The year was nineteen eighty four?"

"That's good. You go for time, I'll go place. Names change. We'll do them last."

"Just keep an eye on this screen." Hedges pointed at the third laptop. "It'll encode all our keystrokes so their log files will be worth zip."

The third laptop was scrolling a list of alphanumeric code just below the red line. Another bar graph appeared on the right of the screen indicating the success of the system. The coloured bars were only just visible and occasionally rose a little and turned from blue to purple.

They searched the time and place and got nothing. They started to search all the possible permutations given the information they had.

"Garret hasn't made it easy for us." Said Hedges after an hour of tapping their keyboards. "He would have access as good as anyone in the government."

"It's the civil servants who know where all the information is. Garret won't actually know." Benson replied. "That's why he asked us. Hold on. I think I've got something." Said Hedges after another fifteen minutes searching. A new screen came up in red.

MATERIAL SUBJECT TO THE OFFICIAL SECRETS ACT 1927.

AUTHORISED PERSONNEL ONLY.

Hedges pressed the enter key and the screen changed to a dense page of text with the first line in bold type.

Under the terms of the 1927 Official Secrets Act the Information contained herein must not enter the public domain until September 22nd 2013.

It then listed the authorities involved in producing the report. An icon indicated the presence of a graphic.

Hedges clicked on the icon and the royal coat of arms filled his computer screen. Raising his eyebrows, he minimised the graphic. There was a contents page, which listed witnesses, minutes of meetings and agent field reports, followed by the body of the report.

"This is what he wants Hedge. This is what is about to be published next year. My guess is that there's some pretty incriminating stuff in here."

The bottom of the contents page gave a clue as to the depth of the report. Fifteen hundred and forty-nine pages.

"What does he expect us to do with fifteen hundred and fifty pages? We can't edit the bad bits out." Said Hedges.

"He wants us to delete it." Said Benson. "Permanently."

Hedges shrugged his shoulders and started to tap some keys. The third laptop which had been flicking up a bar graph in blue and purple turned more purple than blue.

"So far we have just been looking. We've not made any changes. The system is detecting we want to make a change and has upped the priority. The moment we make a change that'll turn red." He pointed at the display on the third laptop.

"Ordinarily, they would be able to track that change and it would be traced back to our visit." Hedges pulled a data stick from his pocket and smiled up at Benson.

"Well they would be able to if it wasn't for our Korean friends." He waved the data stick in the air before plugging it into the USB port of the second laptop. A frame appeared with wriggling cartoon worm inside.

"Hold on a second Hedge." Benson too pulled a data stick from his pocket and handed it to Hedges. It had a yellow and black smiley face on the case.

"Make a copy... Insurance."

Hedges stopped his tapping and gazed at the screen shaking his head slightly, his hands limp in front of the keyboard.

"This was never on the menu, was it?" He said matter-of-factly.

"Not exactly, no." Benson replied with a smirk on his face.

"Benny, mate." Said Hedges, "I hope you know what you're doing." He took the stick that Benson had placed on the desk and out of sight of the cameras plugged it into the laptop.

"We've got to do this bit in unison or it won't work." Said Hedges. "If we weren't making a copy and we got caught we might get away with life. Making a copy means we're nicking it. We'd be hung. Or at least shot. So don't make a mistake."

The third laptop was still showing purple bars. Hedges tapped the keyboard again and issued orders to Benson. A black box appeared in the lower left corner of both their screens. A white cursor prompt was blinking.

"Type 'ENABLE' all upper case." Benson bent over the keyboard.

"No." Hedges shot at him. "One key at a time, with me."

Benson jumped back from his keyboard.

"I know. I know. Only kidding." He said.

"You weren't kidding Benny, I'm serious. Get this wrong and within twenty seconds we'll have a uniformed armed fucking battalion marching through that door." Benson took the reprimand and tried to control himself. It was a trait of his to be silly when the pressure and the stakes were high. They both went through the word one letter at a time.

"After three we press return. OK?" Said Hedges.

"One, two, three." They both pressed the return key and the purple bars on the third laptop went bright red and off the scale. Hedges rolled away from his screen on the chair.

"If that doesn't return to normal in the next five minutes then..." They both waited. Benson looked at his watch and counted down the seconds. A blue and white dialogue box flicked up on the screen informing them that there was insufficient disk space. Hedges blew out slowly through pursed lips. He glanced down at the little yellow and black smiley face.

"Just 256 meg?" He asked.

'Should be enough.' Said Benson.

"Well it's not." Said Hedges. "Have you got another one?"

Hedges nonchalantly removed the first data stick from the usb port of the laptop. Benson patted his jacket pockets.

"No," he said. "I didn't think we'd need another one"

"Well we'll just have to go with what we've got then," said Hedges.

"Wait." Said Benson as he patted the waistband of his trousers and pulled a small leather pouch around to the front of his belt. He opened a flap on the top where there were three compartments. From one he took out a small aluminium Maglite torch and unscrewed the knurled end cap.

Hedges, with one eye on his watch sat with his mouth slightly open and ever so slightly shaking his head as he watched Benson.

"Emergency back up." Said Benson smugly as he passed a small usb data stick hardly bigger than the plug itself across the desk.

"Might have a few pics of the Amsterdam jolly on it though."

Hedges took the stick from him, pugged it into the usb port and pressed the return key. Within a couple of seconds, the blue bar turned green and disappeared. The window that contained the jumping red bars looked like it was calming down slowly. Within another minute, the line at the bottom went flat.

"Okay. We're done here." Said Hedges as he pulled all the connection cables from the laptops, closed their lids and handed back the tiny data stick to Benson who took an unnecessarily long time to put it back where it belonged. He was still fussing about when Hedges, who had repacked the attaché cases in twenty seconds flat, had got up from his seat and was walking to the door. Benson had removed the leather pouch from his belt and was twisting the belt around.

"What are you doing?" Said Hedges.

"The belt is twisted. I hadn't noticed." Said Benson.

"Now?" Hissed Hedges. "Leave it Benny will you. We've got to go."

Benson ignored him and continued to adjust his belt as the door hissed open and Pickering appeared. His genteel smile momentarily turned upside down when he glanced at Benson hurriedly doing up his belt buckle.

"Hope you gentlemen got what you wanted." He said.

4

Benson and Hedges breathed a sigh in unison as the security guard at the gate phoned through to confirm their identities and the heavy barrier descended into the road to let them pass. Five minutes later and Benson, who always liked to do the driving, gunned the engine and shot across the road to the outside lane overtaking all the other cars on the M4 Motorway heading towards London.

"Steady mate." Hedges said quietly as he fiddled with his mobile phone. Benson took his foot off the pedal a little. The motorway was busy and the windscreen wipers were slashing back and forth in what was now torrential rain.

"Something's wrong Benny." Said Hedges, tapping the screen of his phone. He turned off the radio which was whispering away at a volume too low for them to listen to.

"Turn off the sat-nav." Benson flicked a switch on the column stick and a little blue box in the middle of the screen in the centre of the dashboard asked if he was sure he wanted to turn the machine off.

"Yes, Yes, Yes. I'm absolutely fucking certain." Shouted Benson at the screen as he flicked the stalk switch again. The little screen took a few moments to turn first dark blue and then black.

"All off." Said Benson when he was sure the device had powered down. "What you got?"

"You've got nothing in your pockets?" Hedges asked still looking at the screen of the mobile phone. Benson shook his head.

"You've not dropped a softball or something in here?" Benson considered for a few seconds and shook his head again.

"This is not the most accurate instrument in the world Benny but something is sending a... no, something is receiving a UHF signal." Benson reached into the inside pocket of his jacket and pulled out his own mobile phone. He passed it to Hedges with a condescending look on his face.

"It's not that you moron. Do you honestly think I wouldn't have thought of that?" Benson shrugged his shoulders.

"You did, didn't you Benny mate. I do this for a living." Benson said nothing in response to Hedges' exasperated outburst.

"It's not your phone. Okay? Something inside this car is receiving a signal." Hedges continued to concentrate on the screen of the phone.

"We got another little problem, Hedge old boy," said Benson peering at a blinking light on the dashboard. "It's telling me we're nearly out of fuel."

"That's not right. We filled it up on the way there."

"Your right. It's not right but that's what it's telling me and I doubt the gauge is shagged."

Hedges, sitting right up in his seat looked around them at all the cars close to them on the motorway. Nothing looked particularly suspicious but then that meant nothing.

"There's no such thing as coincidences, not in this game Benny boy." He said to Benson as Benson pulled first across to the middle lane and then on to the slow lane. The car was still running smoothly despite the fuel gauge reading empty. Benson clicked another button a few times on the stalk control and the readout from the trip computer was displayed on the sat nav screen on the dashboard between them.

"Distance till empty, zero." Benson read out the warning.

"There's a service station about five miles away in Reading. If the computer or the gauge or the sender unit *is* buggered we'll make it there and work out the problem. If it's..."

He was cut short as the big v8 engine miss-fired a few times, spluttered and died. The power steering and the brake servos died too so Benson struggled a little to bring the big car to a halt on the hard shoulder. He flicked the switch that operated the hazard warning lights.

"I'm concerned." Said Hedges trying to return his mood to being typically calm but continuing to look furtively around them.

"Mmm" mumbled Benson as he reached underneath the steering wheel and pulled out a glinting black pistol.

Hedges, who was looking out the passenger window surveying the terrain on the side of the motorway, turned and saw the gun. He raised his eyes and shook his head.

"We agreed Benny."

"I know we did Hedge, mate. But these are extenuating circumstances." He pointed the pistol at the headlining of the Mercedes and cocked it by pulling down the chamber on the top. A bullet from the magazine in the grip clicked into the chamber.

"I didn't sign up for this Benny. We're supposed to be able to do this stuff without those."

"Whether you signed up for it or not mate, you're in it now. This is just a precaution. Don't you go worrying yourself."

"I will go worrying myself, Ben, you don't even know how to use the fucking thing."

"Don't intend to actually use it Hedge, you don't need to actually use it. I find people tend to do what they are told when they have one of these pointed at them." He pointed the gun in Hedges direction. Hedges angrily pushed it away toward the windscreen.

"Are you fucking mad? Have you gone raving fucking mad? You've never pointed a real gun at anyone before. Who are you trying to kid?"

Their argument was cut short by a yellow flashing light blinking dimly in the interior of the car. It got slowly brighter as a breakdown assistance van pulled up behind them. They both looked back and through the rain could make out the three big letters of the RAC written in mirror writing on the front bonnet of the van.

"Put the fucking gun away Benny." Commanded Hedges. "This could be perfectly innocent."

Benson reluctantly complied and after making it safe placed it on the floor under the seat he was sitting in. Benson watched in the rear view mirror as a figure slid across to the passenger side of the van, opened the door and stepped out onto the hard shoulder of the road. Benson sat back in his seat and watched as the figure approached.

"There's definitely only one." He said. The figure walked along the passenger side of the car. They could hardly see out through the rain lashing down. There was a tap on the window and Hedges pressed the button and made the window drop two inches.

"Afternoon…" they weren't expecting a woman's voice and relaxed a little on account of it. She glanced in to see the two of them sitting there.

"... Gentlemen. Hell of a time to break down." She was shouting to get over the noise of the rain and the motorway traffic. "Nice car like this too." The rain was falling in through the window.

"What do you want?" Shouted Benson leaning over Hedges toward the window.

"We do this now Sir." She said pulling the hood of her huge blue and yellow hi-vis coat up over her head. "Never used to. They ask us to stop if we see someone stranded and sell 'em breakdown cover. Do you need it or are you covered?"

"Just a second," said Hedges as he closed the window.

He turned to Benson with a questioning frown.

"*Are* we covered?"

Benson shook his head slowly. He pressed the button on his own side to wind the window down again two inches and leant across Hedges.

"Have you got some ID?" He shouted to the woman.

"Sure." She shouted back and passed through a black plastic wallet.

"Waterproofing." She pointed at the wallet as it went through the gap above the window glass. Benson snatched at it and wound up the window again. He sat back in his seat and with his thumbnails cracked open the plastic clip. There was a short hiss as he opened it and the two men looked at each other in terror. Benson tried to slam the little case shut between his palms but it was too late. It took three seconds for them to inhale enough gas to make them both dizzy. They both tried not to breathe in but it was no good. Benson made a futile attempt to grab the pistol under his seat and Hedges was frantically trying to open the door but it wouldn't budge. Three more seconds and they were both slumped in their seats. The gun that Benson had managed to grab was laid neatly in his grip on his lap. Another twenty seconds passed and the woman waiting in the rain outside the car pulled open the flap of her big coat and tapped at a tablet computer. All four windows slid down as the central locking system unlocked all the doors A few more taps and the engine restarted, the fans in the dashboard went to full on and the boot slowly opened. A heavy clunk at the front of the car and the bonnet rose on its hinges two inches. The woman methodically picked out the two attaché cases from the boot, opened the rear passenger door, pushed them across the back seat, slid in after them and pulled the door shut.

She pulled out the tablet from the big interior pocket of the coat, tapped and dragged a few times, the boot closed, and all the windows slid shut. When she was opening the zip of a black nylon holdall, she noticed the gun in Benson's limp hand.

"Tut Tut." She said out loud reverting to her native accent. "I underestimated you boys."

One of the cases was locked with a combination lock, which she quickly forced with a thick bladed penknife she pulled out of a pocket. She put the three laptops into the black holdall and got out the same door she had got in.

She opened the passenger door and went through all of Hedges pockets. Nothing of any interest was there. She leant down into the foot-well and removed Hedges' black leather brogues. She examined the shoes. Nothing. She pulled off his socks. Still nothing. She sat fully on Hedges lap and repeated the inspection on Benson and found a data stick with a yellow and black smiley face in his jacket pocket. She tossed it into the holdall. She looked no further. Before she got out of the car, she took a pink lipstick from a pocket and using the rear view mirror laid on a thick layer. She kissed them both on each cheek.

"Thanks lads. You've been diamonds." She sat back on Hedges knees and looked at them both.

"Now listen." She spoke to the two comatose figures as if they were children.

"In the spirit of fair play, I'm gonna give you a fighting chance." She picked the gun from Benson's limp hand and having checked the chamber threw it into the holdall. She got out of the car and closed the door behind her. She opened the back door and dragged out the holdall.

She half zipped it up and left it sitting by the front wheel of the Mercedes. She went to the front of the car and lifted the bonnet. Inside the dense engine compartment, she unclipped a black plastic box with the Mercedes logo embossed on the lid. She unplugged a multi pin plug attached by a thick short cable to a machined aluminium cylinder the size of a can of deodorant. That too she threw into the holdall before closing the plastic box and the bonnet of the Merc.

She picked up the holdall and was about to walk back to the van when she dropped it again.

"Oh Mary." She said to herself out loud. "You are slacking." She opened the door again of the car and leaning over Hedges, fished around for her little gas canister. It had fallen between the seats.

Back at the services before Reading on the M4, the RAC man who went to the rescue of a single woman in her forties who had a problem with her hire car was struggling as he regained consciousness. His hands were tied together underneath one of his legs. The woman had parked her car in a quiet area of the services car park well out of the way of most of the other motorists and out of sight of the security surveillance cameras. He'd fixed her problem, a loose battery terminal of all things in the driving rain while she sat in the car. The last thing he remembered, having against company policy, climbed into the passenger seat to do the paperwork, was a sharp prick in his thigh as she leaned on him to get her glasses out of the glove-box.

    Now he was sitting there, trussed up, disorientated and missing his company overalls. He had no idea how long he'd been there. His van was gone, his keys were gone and his mobile phone was gone. He'd struggled hopelessly trying to free himself but his hands had been tied with a nylon cable tie which he could not shift. At first, the two security guards who released him some three hours later while on a routine tour of the car parks had found his predicament amusing. They didn't at first believe his story as he was sporting bright pink lipstick kisses on his cheeks.

5

Through green uniformed doormen, waiting queues of chauffeur driven cars with blacked out windows and the paparazzi photographers, Ian Whitting, carrying a light brown leather brief case, made his way unnoticed from where his cab had dropped him on Park Lane, across the crescent driveway and through the revolving doors of the Dorchester Hotel. Two minutes later, turning the heads and the lenses of a few of the paps, who couldn't quite work out if she was famous or not, Jill O'Keefe, heels clicking rhythmically, walked the same route.

"Who are they expecting?" asked Jill as she sat down opposite Ian on one of the couches that lined the long wide corridor that serves as the dining room.

"Some Korean rap star is playing the O2 on Friday." Said Ian. He wasted no time in getting to the point. "Why are we here Jill?"

"Good to see you too Ian." Jill said sarcastically.

Ian is a five foot ten ex paratrooper with the stocky physique of a rugby player. You'd hardly notice him though, slouched on the brocade sofa, dressed in a green sweater and sand coloured cargo pants. This apparent ability to, chameleon like, blend into his surroundings, served him well during his years as a British Army soldier and for different reasons serves him well now. Ian has written three bestselling novels based on his various experiences in the military from Northern Ireland, the Falklands and the Gulf. His name is well known yet his identity remains secret - giving his books an extra air of mystery. He appears though, to be stricken with writers block. Nothing more than a Christmas card, composed by the pen of the elusive master of the modern war story, has crossed the desk of his publishers for going on three years.

"I'm here to help Ian." Jill sat up like a mere-cat and smiled at a passing waiter. Ian slouched just a little further down in his seat like a rebellious teenager before replying.

"I've been doing some thinking Jill. Before you start banging on at me, I don't even know if I want to write any more, at least not the way I used to. I've come to a bit of a crossroads." Ian's semi aggressive stance had gone.

"Ok," Jill said very slowly. "Tell me more." She barely suppressed a smile. "What kind of crossroads?" Ian saw the look on her face.

"I'm not going to say any more, Jill, if you're just gonna take the piss."

She tried a more sincere smile.

"Go on, Ian. Tell me what's on your mind."

Ian finally sat up onto the edge of the couch and opened the flap of the brief case that was beside his feet.

He was about to open a zipped compartment when he paused.

"I'm out of here if you're not gonna take it seriously Jill." Jill gestured with another smile and an open palm for him to continue. He opened the pocket inside the case and took out a small Samsung notebook computer, placed it on the table between them and opened the lid.

"It's a letter, that's all Jill." Said Ian pushing the little machine towards her across the table. "A letter to my father."

"You've never spoken about your father before. Where is he now?" She said.

"Long gone." Said Ian. "But it's a letter I should have written years ago. Anyway it's the first thing I've put down on paper for years."

"You want me to read it?" Jill asked with a broad smile.

Returning the sarcasm Ian chided,

"Odd that a literary editor doesn't actually like reading. Course I do."

"Now?" She said, this time sounding just a little put upon.

"Yes Jill. Now. Five hundred words. That's all." He sat up a little on the couch and smiled. "Even you can do five hundred words before lunch?"

Jill was in the precarious position of never having actually read any of Ian's books all the way through. She had tried with the first of them that was about a disastrous secret mission behind enemy lines but she didn't get past the second chapter before finding the experience far too harrowing to continue with. She prevaricated.

"Listen, Ian. You love spending the money. You're spending it faster than it's coming in. Royalties this year will be a tenth of what they were five years ago. We need another book. We both do. You ain't gonna like being poor again Ian, I'll tell you that much for nothing."

"Please just read the letter Jill." Ian said still touching the top of the screen.

She had no choice. She let him sit there with his hand still on the top of the open screen a moment longer than was necessary.

"Please Jill." Ian said earnestly as he twisted the screen to face her. Jill, still playing games, delved into her handbag for some reading glasses. Ian's eyes slowly closed and his nostrils involuntarily flared. His head bowed a degree as his fingertips remained touching the top of the screen. Jill took more time than she needed to place her glasses on her nose and smiled as she pulled the laptop towards her. She nodded three or four times waiting for Ian's eyes to open and catch her eye. Ian didn't say another word but just shook his head slowly as Jill focussed and started to read.

Jill pushed the laptop back across the table and took her glasses off. Ian who had slouched back even further on the couch while Jill was reading looked at her expectantly. She raised her hand towards a waiter across the other side of the room.

Jill sat back into the couch too, mimicking Ian's apparently relaxed posture. She knew Ian was far from relaxed though.

"I'm not really sure what this is supposed to tell me Ian," said Jill after a moment or two.

"But I'm going to throw caution to the wind and take a stab." She was smiling again.

"One," she touched her left forefinger with her right. "You don't want to write war stories any-more. Two," She counted on her fingers. "You've read a newspaper for the first time in your life and discovered a world of misery corruption and hate..." Ian tried to interject but Jill waved her two hands in front of her, fingers still touching and continued.

"Three. You've realised that maybe you might have, at whatever meagre a level, contributed to that misery rather than helped alleviate it, and four, at the age of forty three that you're not the master of all you survey." She held up four bright red fingernails, and paused to think.

"Look Ian. I'm your literary agent and I think friend. As far as I'm concerned you are a writer. If I'm honest I never personally liked the war stories anyway. I know they sold well but Westlife sold loads of records. Doesn't make them any good. Write what you want to write babe."

Ian was suddenly filled with opposing emotions. On the one hand, everything she had said had been correct and on the other, he never knew she didn't care for his work and it came as a shock. Jill sat up again on the edge of the couch, her brief attempt at subtlety over. She looked up again for a waiter and waved a finger a little more vigorously than before.

"Where is that waiter...?"

It was a moment or two before either of them spoke.

Ian appeared to be mulling over her words until Jill continued.

"So what are you planning to do with this new found wisdom?"

"Something will come up." Ian's body language was defensive. He couldn't have got any lower on the couch if he tried.

Jill pulled out a brown envelope from her oversize handbag.

"Something *has* come up Ian." She looked him in the eye and passed him the envelope. She held it short of his reach so he had to sit up to take it. Inside the envelope was a miniature data stick with a black and yellow smiley face printed on the front.

A waiter handed Jill a menu. Without looking at it, she ordered a bottle of house champagne and Ian shot her a suspicious look.

"What are you up to Jill?" Said Ian as examined the data stick.

"I had lunch yesterday with Rick. He seemed even more wide-eyed and excitable than he normally is. He asked about you and told me he'd had a good idea. I dropped him back at the studios in the cab and as he was getting out he gave me this." Jill held up a small yellow data stick with a smiley face printed on the front

"Who's Rick?" Ian asked innocently as he took the data stick and plugged it into his laptop.

"Ricky Starr." Said Jill. "He doesn't usually like any of us talking about him. Likes to keep a low profile."

Ian still raised his eyebrows.

"What. *The* Ricky Starr. Starr Media? He owns the company you work for? He owns my publisher?"

"Three years ago Ian. He bought it three years ago."

"What happened to Pullman and Mrs. Phillips?"

"They were let go. I don't think they minded much. They were getting on and he paid them a good whack. Shows how much you get yourself involved, Ian. You hadn't even noticed they'd gone. Ricky bought the firm with you as the only author making them any money. That was then of course. It doesn't make much out of your stuff anymore either. Probably not enough to pay the rent on the offices and Bernice's salary. That's why we need a story Ian."

Whenever the conversation turned to money or Ian's inability to deliver, Ian tended to want to change the subject.

"He just gave you this did he?" Asked Ian, nodding towards the laptop.

"It was just as he was getting out. He didn't explain." Said Jill.

"So what's on it?" Asked Ian.

"I've no idea." She said shortly "It had a password. We couldn't read it." Jill's voice was getting softer, forcing Ian to sit up to be able to hear. However much he tried to disguise the fact, he was intrigued.

"Who's 'We'?" He said.

"Me and Bernice. We tried to see what was on it but it just kept saying 'You do not have permission to view. Contact the administrator'."

"Do you have Wi Fi here?" Ian asked the waiter as the champagne arrived.

"Of course Sir," replied the waiter pouring two glasses before pushing the bottle into an ice bucket. "I'll get you the details." Ian tapped some keys on the keyboard of the laptop.

The waiter came back with a slip of paper on a silver tray. Ian thanked him and reading from the paper, tapped again at the keys of the laptop.

"I'll just try something." He paused for a few moments while the laptop made its connections.

"It's a free download." He laughed, and turned the screen to show Jill what was happening. A stream of numbers filled a black box in the middle of the screen. One by one, a short stream of letters and numbers appeared in the bottom right corner of the screen.

"Look." Said Ian pointing at the screen and twisting it slightly further towards Jill. "You couldn't write this." Ian spoke out the letters and numbers of a password.

"Upper case F, the number 1, lower case I, lower case n, the number 5, lower case t, the number 0…"

"So what Ian." Said Jill.

"Jill. You don't understand. With a free download I've got past the security on this stick in what?" He looked at his watch. "60 seconds." He watched as the software completed the task.

"Flintstones. Jill. The password is Flintstones."

Jill nodding said "And?"

"Never mind." Said Ian, "Look. If Starr Media wants a story told. Why don't they tell it? He owns half the planet's TV stations for goodness sake. They could get it out in no time. I can't compete with a global media company."

Ian swigged from his champagne glass, winced from the dry bitter taste and pushed the glass away from him.

Jill was smiling and nodding.

"Not asking you to compete Ian. This part of the story's already been told...Somewhere." She pointed at the data stick with a bright red fingernail.

"This is just the back story. You're going to write what happens next and we're gonna get you right in the thick of it."

Ian smiled a sarcastic smile.

"An agent provocateur novelist. Has that been done before? Is that legal?" Ian's body language was at last giving him away. He sat up slightly further, waved his forefinger in the direction of a waiter, and ordered a beer.

"Everything has been done before for Christ's sake Ian and what do you care if it's legal or not. It's just a story, Ian. Fiction, you know that thing you used to do."

Ian frowned knowing that although this meeting was supposed to be an informal discussion, the outcome had already been decided. Jill knew that despite his prevarications Ian secretly liked her being the driving force.

"I've talked this through with Bernice and we love the idea. I've given us a nice fat advance to get things started too."

Jill took a sip from her champagne glass and with a confident smile stared into Ian's eyes. She knew he would try to appear uninterested and she knew he'd fail.

"They'll be looking for a winner though."

"How much?" asked Ian still trying to appear noncommittal. He was at rock bottom and in no position to bargain. He knew he needed something. As a novelist, his talent lay in embellishing the truth. A seed. He always needed the seed. He had never been able to create that seed and although this troubled him, he was resigned to his lack of true creativity. He saw himself as an elaborator, a teller of other people's stories. He'd never been able to just make them up. The waiter placed a frosted glass on the table and poured half a glass of beer from a Peroni bottle. Ian sat up enough to grab the glass and took a couple of large gulps emptying the glass. He refilled it with what remained in the bottle.

"Don't you worry about that babe," said Jill. "I got it all under control."

Jill was now looking at the lunch menu. Ian took another gulp from the beer glass and emptied it again. He glanced at the little laptop that had completed processing the memory stick.

"Isn't technology today wonderful?" He said as he tapped at the keys on the laptop. "So what happens now?" He continued, his defences broken.

"Does that mean you're in?"

"I never had a choice Jill. Did I?" The merest of smiles crept across his lips. It would only take a slight adjustment to the nuts and bolts of his subconscious to change grudging respect for this ballsy confident and not unattractive woman into something more.

"Yeah," said Jill. "Course you did. We've always got choices." A waiter came and stood by the table. Jill looked up from the menu over her reading glasses and ordered a club sandwich. She looked to

Ian who shook his head but smiling at the waiter pointed to his empty beer glass. He returned his gaze to the computer.

"I've made plans Ian. There are some people I want you to meet. People who'll be helping us. We'll get straight on with it after lunch. I presume you're available this afternoon? The ball is already rolling."

"I did have a pressing engagement with my sofa," said Ian, still looking at the laptop, his general demeanour changed, "but I suppose I could reschedule."

"Jill..." He said as she watched him like a mother. "Are you sure Rick Starr knows what he's doing." He paused and scrolled down the screen on the laptop.

"Are you sure you know what you're doing?" He turned the screen to face Jill again and she adjusted her glasses to read. In big red letters that you couldn't mistake easily read the words, MATERIAL SUBJECT TO THE OFFICIAL SECRETS ACT 1927. AUTHORISED PERSONNEL ONLY. Under this was the lion and the unicorn of the Royal Coat of Arms.

Jill read briefly and closed the lid of the laptop.

Neither Jill nor Ian was aware of the portly man in a creased-linen-suit sitting behind them, drinking whiskey, sweating and appearing to be playing a game on his phone. Stuck in the band in the back of his Panama hat was a yellow enamel pin the size of a five pence piece decorated with a black smiley face.

6

Ian signed the single page contract Jill had produced from her capacious handbag. Jill had been anxious suddenly to get out of the Dorchester and had rung a number on her mobile phone. Ian was still in two minds feeling distinctly uneasy with the events of the last few hours. On the one hand he was excited by the prospect of getting into what looked like an exciting project and on the other, the involvement of the British government worried him. He knew what it was like to have indiscriminate, uncontrolled, irresponsible power.

Meetings with Jill had never quite gone the way he expected them to. A chauffeur driven S Class Mercedes pulled up outside the doors of the Dorchester. A doorman opened the back door for Jill as she clicked across the pavement. Within twenty minutes, they were crossing the river towards the South London suburbs. The journey took them about an hour in which time Jill talked incessantly and excitedly about her plans for 'The adventure'. She seemed to keep talking as if she didn't want Ian to say anything. She had either forgotten or was deliberately ignoring the small matter of the official secrets act. Their destination this afternoon turned out to be a man's clothes shop. Forty minutes of back doubles and speed bumps later they arrived at a small parade of shops set back from the main road behind tall elm trees. They pulled up right outside this outwardly unimpressive frontage of a royal blue painted window frame and a cream painted façade with the name PORTERS sign-written in blue. Small brass letters by the side of this declared ' 1961'. The only clue to the value of the goods contained within might have been the amount of security employed which was discreet but not that difficult to see if you were inclined to look, which Ian was. Exterior and interior shutters made of heavy gauge metal obviously designed to deter more than just a casual drunk with a penchant for a nice shirt, hung rolled up underneath the fascia. Jill rang on the doorbell. A few seconds later a lock buzzed and they pushed through a thick hardwood front door. Inside the air-conditioning was clicking on and off noisily. There was only about four square metres of carpet. A meter cube walnut wood counter sat in the middle of the room and walnut-wood fittings lined the walls. There was not an inch of wall space not covered with shirt boxes or suits or trousers or ties or jackets. There were no displays, and the lighting was soft.

"It's a kiosk." Said Ian as footsteps emanated from a small staircase in the far back corner and a man dressed in a neat three piece camel coloured suit appeared, a cordless phone against his ear. He was talking in decent southern Italian.

"Appearances can be deceiving." Jill whispered as the man approached her, finishing his telephone conversation politely. He did not address Jill by name but greeted her cordially by holding both her hands and air kissing her cheeks.

"How was the holiday? Cuba wasn't it?" Asked Greg.

"Had a lovely time." Replied Jill. "Probably should have waited a month. The heat was unbearable." She wafted the collar of her silk blouse as she said this which for some reason annoyed Ian. Jill sensed his mood and got back to the matter in hand by introducing him.

"This is Ian, Greg. He's a client of mine." Ian shook Greg's hand.

"Pleased to meet you", Ian said. The look on his face contradicting him. Greg, having been in the business a long time had played this subtle game many times. He knew the look and seen these male power displays a thousand times. He ignored it. He knew where the power was.

Without another word, Greg pulled a random jacket from a coat hanger on a rail and motioned to Ian to remove his green sweater. He was wearing a white T shirt underneath it. Greg pushed the yellow checked jacket up over Ian's shoulders from behind, let him shrug automatically as men do when trying on a tailored coat then stepped around in front of him and pulled the lapels gently together. Greg and Jill both looked him up and down as if he were a mannequin. Greg then walked around him again and lifting the jacket off his shoulders, threw it over the tiny counter. He picked another from the rack. This time bright red linen and silk, buggy lined with white horn buttons. He repeated the procedure then inspected the fit more closely this time as if he was looking for flaws in a kitchen cabinet. Greg made a mark in tailors chalk on the sleeve of the jacket.

"They surely don't need shortening do they?" Ian raised both his arms up level in front of him and mimed holding a car steering wheel. The jacket sleeves retreated up his arms.

"They'd look ridiculous driving the Bentley."

Greg ignored him again.

"Anywhere nice?"

"Canaries." Jill replied before Ian could say no.

"Winter but warm." Jill continued and pulled a piece of paper from her bag and handed it to Greg who took it and looked it up and down. He pulled a pair of trousers from the rack and said to Ian,

"Do you mind?" Ian tried on the trousers in a curtained fitting room at the rear of the shop. He heard Greg asked what size shoe and Jill reply, "Forty two."

Ian struggled to do the waistband of the blue super 100 worsted trousers up as he pushed aside the curtain to the fitting room and stood again in the judgemental gaze of Greg and Jill.

"Fit fine around the arse." Said Greg as he moved in closely to Ian and undid the button on the waistband.

"Just need to let out the waist a little." Greg's expression was stern but Jill couldn't help a snigger. Ian was convinced, rightly, that Greg had purposely given him a size to small. Greg held the waistband of the trousers closed between thumb and forefinger and looked Ian in the eye. Raising both his eyebrows, he asked.

"How does that feel Ian?" Ian wanted to tell him that it felt fucking awkward but instead begrudgingly nodded wishing this ordeal would be over. Greg made another mark in tailor's chalk on the waistband of the trousers.

"That's all I need then." Said Greg. "If you'd like to slip them off."

"Can you be a love Greg and get them to the office for tomorrow?" Greg nodded his head as he wrote in an old-fashioned duplicate book.

"So, do you still do early doors in the pub?" Jill continued.

"Yeah we do." Greg looked at his wristwatch. "You and your boyfriend coming?" Said Greg as he continued to write in the duplicate book. "Still in Harley Street?"

"Still the same place Greg and he's not my boyfriend. I told you he's my client." Greg looked at her over the top of his reading glasses and smiled a gentle but condescending smile.

"I can't see why I need all these clothes." Ian said as they were strolling up the street toward the pub. Jill dipped her head and smiled towards Ian.

"You don't babe." She said. "You're the same size as someone else."

The pub was only yards away. Jill tapped on the window of the Mercedes and it slid down half way. The driver was sitting patiently in the car playing with his mobile phone.

"We're gonna be in the pub for a little while." Jill said to the driver. "Are you going to come in?"

"This is not on the plan Jill." Said the driver shaking his head. "Call me when you're ready to leave. I won't be far away." Jill could tell he wasn't pleased but she didn't really care. She raised her eyes as she straightened up from the window.

The pub had a saloon and a public bar. Jill took the left door through the lobby and into the saloon bar where the furniture was smarter. There was a roaring log fire in the middle of the far wall opposite the bar. It was five thirty in the afternoon and there were a few groups of drinkers already there. Standing at the bar a group of four men were going through the ritual of ordering their first round. They appeared regulars by the familiar way they addressed the young barmaid. Ian approached the bar and caught another, older barmaid's eye. He ordered himself a pint of Guinness and turned to ask Jill what she would like to drink and found her staring at the group of men at the other end of the bar. He stepped between Jill and the group of men blocking her view.

"Don't stare like that Jill. Didn't your mother ever tell you it's rude to stare?" He whispered as he nudged her elbow. Jill snapped out of the stare and lightly shook her head.

"Do you know them?" Ian continued.

"No. No I don't. Vodka Ian. I'll have a vodka and slim. Loads of ice."

Ian ordered the drink as Greg walked in. In the equal environment of a pub Ian felt more at ease. He saw Greg enter and remove a fancy coat with a fur collar. *What's with the big coat? He's only had to walk thirty yards* he thought.

Greg made a show of taking off the coat threw it over one of the unoccupied winged back chairs they were standing by.

"What'll you have Greg?" Ian asked graciously. Greg looked around the bottles and beer pumps as if this was going to be a hard question to answer. It looked though as if this was his own little ritual when entering a pub. His eyes fell on the Guinness settling on the bar. He nodded at it and said, "Well now. I think it would be rude not to be joining you. That's very kind." The tension that existed between the two men in the shop was dissipating now that they were on common ground. Ian ordered another pint of Guinness. As he turned to the bar Greg acknowledged the group of men standing at the opposite end that Jill had been staring at.

"Just pulled that off the rack have you Greg?" The tallest and fattest member of the group shouted good-humouredly across to them. Ian passed Jill her Vodka. She still couldn't take her eyes off the group of men at the end of the bar. Ian tutted quietly and handed Greg his pint of Guinness. Greg raised it saying quietly 'Cheers' to Ian. He then turned to the group of men and loudly called back, "There's one in your size waiting Ray. Shall I have it sent round?"

"Yeah right." Came the reply.

They went back to their conversation. Greg turned back to Jill and Ian.

"So come on Jill. What brings you down to the sticks in person?"

Jill was still preoccupied trying to listen in on the conversation of the group of men at the other end of the bar. She thought she was being discreet when in fact the opposite was true.

"Hello. Hello Jill." Ian said waving his hand in front of her face. "What's so interesting about that lot?"

Jill ignored Ian and turned to Greg.

"Who are those men Greg?" She asked, nodding in the direction of the little group.

"Same old Jill." Said Greg turning to Ian. "She's so bloody nosey." He moved a little closer to Jill and lowered his voice. Ian also drew closer.

"The big fellah," he said, looking over to see if he was being heard, "who shouted across to me, runs a market stall up at Borough. Ray Andrews. Tight as a tick. Never spends any money with me 'cept in the sale. The bloke standing opposite with the 'tash, that's Rob Winter. He's a solicitor. He's probably been in here since lunchtime and will probably be here at closing. You know the definition of an alcoholic is someone who drinks more than you do. I can tell you, he drinks more than you do."

"Who is the shorter bloke?" asked Jill.

"He's just moved to the area but I know him from way back. Name's Martin Farnham." Jill's eyes widened at the mention of the name. Greg continued.

"No idea what he does for a living these days but it obviously pays well. Pretty much keeps his business to himself. Spends a fortune though. He's in almost weekly and buys only the top end. You know him then?" asked Greg noticing the reaction to the name.

"Not at all." said Jill taking a sip from her drink.

"What have you got cooking, Jill. No. Don't tell me I really don't want to know."

A man in a creased-linen-suit, far too light for the season, was standing in the public bar sipping a tomato juice. Through the open door that separated the two bars on the serving side, he had an unhindered view of Jill and her little group. Having just finished sending a text message, he slipped his mobile phone into the baggy side pocket of his suit. He looked out the window to where a line of cars were parked and twitched his head backwards towards the four occupants of a blue Vauxhall saloon car. Three men immediately got out of the car. They were dressed in dark grey suits, white shirts and black ties. As they approached the door to the pub the driver of the car reversed out from the parking space and waited with the engine running on the side of the road. Inside the pub, the ambient noise level dropped to relative silence as the three men entered. Having made a brief appraisal, they approached Jill and her group. They arranged themselves around them in an intimidating ring causing Ian and Greg to stop mid slurp and look at them quizzically. The boss of the crew, a big bald nineteen stone bouncer, spoke in good English but with a slight eastern-European accent.

"Mrs. O'Keefe, we are from the Metropolitan Police. We believe you are in possession of stolen property, would you accompany us please." The other, younger but no less intimidating thug moved slightly to his right to indicate a direction of travel. Greg, who had been in at least a similar situation before stepped between Jill and the big Man.

"Can I see your warrant card, Officer?" He said with a false smile on his face holding his half-drunk pint against his chest and fixing his gaze on the big man's shoulder. The Big Man stared at him and slowly put his right hand into the inside breast pocket of his suit. Rather than pull out any identification he pulled out a clenched fist and punched Greg hard on the nose. Greg fell back onto Ian and their drinks went flying. The punch was neatly executed and in the commotion the third member of the gang violently ripped Jill's handbag from her arm, breaking the leather straps before walking without rushing to the waiting Vauxhall Car. His two accomplices followed. Jill, having finished her screaming fit tapped her mobile phone a few times and yelled into it. It went to answer phone.

"Stupid childish bastard." She yelled before bending to tend to Greg who was now sitting on the floor against the bar holding two bloodied bar towels against his nose.

"Get me out of here," said Greg, struggling to his feet, "before some idiot calls the police. My car's right outside."

Ian cancelled the call he was making. Greg, having gathered himself together ran out the door, followed first by Jill and Ian and then by a smattering of the regulars in the pub who hadn't seen anything as exciting as this in a long time.

"My Car." he pointed his key ring at a wine coloured Daimler sovereign double six - beautiful nick but a good fifteen years old. The car made a beeping noise and Greg jumped into the driver's seat.

"Get in quick or we'll lose them." He shouted to Jill and Ian. They both slid into the white leather rear seat. Greg smashed the big V12 into reverse and swung it out onto the road. Jill and Ian never saw it because they were being tumbled about on the slippery leather of the back seat but a wry smile slipped across Greg's bloodied face as he did something he'd always wanted to do but for reasons only known to himself he had never done before. He dropped the clutch at four and a half thousand revs. The old Daimler behaved exactly as Greg had hoped it would and they were launched towards the traffic lights at the crossroads four hundred yards ahead.

"They went right." Called Ian from the back. At a reckless speed Greg turned off down a slip road and slamming on the brakes, came to another cross-roads that intersected the main road. He floored the accelerator pedal again and hared across the road into a small gap between two buses. The bus behind angrily sounded its horn. The heavy traffic was moving at a walking pace.

Their view of the road was obscured by the bus in front of them. None of them could see if the blue car was anywhere in the traffic ahead.

"Are you sure?" Greg called into the back as he pulled into the middle of the road and roared down the outside.

The oncoming traffic was swerving car by car onto the pavement as they lost the little game of chicken Greg was playing with each of them. Ian and Jill were hanging onto the straps in the roof lining. Ian was attempting to fasten his seat belt as both he and Jill were being sloshed about on the slippery leather back seat as Greg weaved in and out of the line of traffic enacting out a fantasy that had been lurking in his subconscious for years. They rounded a curve in the road and they could see that the traffic led all the way up to the major intersection that led onto the main route towards the motorway that circled London.

"Can you see them?" Greg called again into the back. Jill was now squeezing herself over the centre console between the front seats. Judging by the look on her face, she was enjoying this. She slumped herself down into the bucket seat and buckled her own seat belt. She looked ahead and in a moment pointed through the windscreen at a blue car some five hundred yards ahead of them.

"There they are." She shouted. "They're in the traffic. They don't think they've been followed." Greg stood on the brakes and attempted to cut into the line of traffic.

"If they don't know they've been followed, we'll keep it that way for the time being." Said Greg. He was stuck out in the wrong lane much to the noisy disapproval of the oncoming traffic. None of the cars going in their direction would let him cut in. Jill pressed the button that wound down the window and attempted a smile at an elderly man in an old cream coloured Ford Metro beside them. As politely as she could with just gestures she asked if they could slip in front of him but he was having none of it and with his eyes staring forward stuck closely to the car in front of him.

"Too late." Said Ian from the back seat. "They've seen us." The blue car had pulled out of the traffic and was charging up the wrong side of the road. Greg floored the big engine again and the rear wheels span. He fought with the steering wheel to keep the car in a straight line as it snaked forward smashing into side of the little metro as it did so. Greg twisted his head to one side and grimaced.

"In for a penny," he said closing his eyes tightly as he made for a gap that would have been a mile too small to get through at any other time. The chrome wing mirror on Jill's side was knocked clean off by the rear corner of a black pick- up truck. The blue car had made in onto the roundabout intersection and had turned right onto the dual carriageway. Jill, whose phone had not left her hand, was madly tapping the screen with both her thumbs.

"Can't you leave that damn thing alone ever?" Said Greg as he swerved again to avoid two more angry motorists.

He too had reached the roundabout and had screeched around the bend onto the ramp that took them down to the dual carriageway.

"There's a junction four miles up," said Greg looking suspiciously like he drove home like this every night. "If they take it, there'll be solid traffic up there and they won't be able to go anywhere." Jill was still busy on her phone.

"What's this road called?" She said to Greg who shot her a maddened glance.

"What are you doing, woman?" He said. "It's the A20. Why?"

"Just seeing if there's any help around." She replied still tapping away at her phone.

"Excuse me." Said Ian from the back. His doubts about getting involved in Jill's little scheme growing stronger. "What are we going to do if we actually catch up with them?"

A frown of realisation spread across Greg's face.

Jill's reaction was somewhat less understanding.

"You're an Ex Para Ian. Thought you might think of something." She shouted back at him. The understanding of the male ego cut into Greg's thoughts. He saw fleetingly in the rear view mirror Ian's face and it told a long and complicated story in a half a second flat. What Greg wanted to say was 'Is he?' Instead, he said in a comradely fashion.

"He's right Jill. There are at least three of them in that car. I don't mind an even fight even these days, but is the bag worth it."

"What are you two?" Jill screeched as a blue flashing light turned all their attentions in a different direction. They had pulled briefly onto the inside lane, the Jag's engine purring away beneath them like a hair-dryer disguising the fact that they were doing over a hundred and twenty miles an hour. The police officer's face in the car next to them was red and veined. An angry finger jabbed in the direction of the hard shoulder of the road. Greg shook his head as he stood firmly on the brakes. The police car appeared to jump forward. It took a little bit of too-ing and fro-ing for the cars to align themselves as the police officer wanted with the police car behind.

"Looks like we're not going to get to find out." Said Ian.

Greg slowed and pulled the car over. The police Volvo estate, with its yellow and silver grey reflective decals pulled up behind. Greg stayed where he was and watched in the rear view mirror as the officer in the passenger seat got out. Banging on the glass of the window, he seemed most anxious to talk with Greg. In a spirit that most generally law-abiding individuals who pay their taxes, Greg would be apologetic, remorseful and cooperative. He knew that ordinary police officers, (whose main qualification for acceptance into the service, as it was now called, used to be, being in excess of five foot eight inches tall, but even that wasn't required now,) have been given by statute, extraordinary powers to completely ruin your day if they chose to use them. This didn't mean you couldn't take the piss if you could get away with it.

The red-faced copper rapped on the window hard again.

Greg pressed the button on the door and the window slid down.

"Get out of the car." Said the officer with no attempt at false pleasantries.

"Was I doing something wrong, Officer?" Greg said through the open window. He could not resist a smirk and was also in the process of showing off. The officer was having none of it.

"Sir," he said. His voice sounding outwardly calm but his eyes telling a different story.

"If you don't get out of this car now I will assume you are obstructing a police officer carrying out his duties and I will take great pleasure in pulling you out." Greg thought for a second or two about his options and decided, probably correctly, that the best thing to do, for the sake of his suit at least, would be to do as the officer had asked. It turned out the officer wasn't interested in what Greg thought and he needn't have bothered too much on his suits account. He'd got no further than one shoe on the tarmac when the officer grabbed his tab collared lapels with two big hands and in what must have been a practised movement pulled him violently out of the car, slung him around, slammed his head on the roof and held his head down with his right hand. His speeding up the A20 didn't seem somehow to Greg to warrant the force being used and years of always cow towing to unearned unwarranted or unnecessary authority welled up in him. Not to mention the fact that the sound of tearing cloth indicated that the brute had all but ripped off the lapels of his suit. Greg calmed himself a moment to calibrate his spatial awareness by taking slow and deliberate breaths through his nose and out his mouth as the officer was struggling with his left hand to extract the handcuffs from his ridiculously over-burdened utility belt. Churches shoes are made from stout leathers. In the few moments that he had, Greg noticed that the officer, though technically with the full power of British law behind him as well a colleague sitting in the patrol car who seemed to have a disapproving look on his face, was standing behind him with his legs apart and as such was vulnerable. He seized the moment as it were and kicked the heel of his right shoe upwards with as much force as he could muster. Greg was aware that it was a high risk strategy and the consequences of him missing the target would mean more degrading treatment at the hands of a man who undoubtedly would have joined the police precisely so that he could enjoy the odd moment like this where his power over his fellow man was absolute. He needn't have worried as possibly more by luck than judgement his heel contacted the target. It didn't need a great deal of force. Greg could feel the officer press down harder on his head briefly before easing the pressure. The policeman's almost three quarter length high visibility jacket had denied his colleague in the patrol car a good view of what Greg had done and he was only alerted to his power hungry friend's loss of control of the situation as the officer fell to his knees clutching his bollocks.

But alerted he was. But so was Ian who was pulling at the handle of the back door. Nothing was happening. The door would not open. Ian could see the top of the cap of the officer who was kneeling on the tarmac through the side window but could also see the other police officer frantically struggling to get out of the car.

"Child locks." Ian shouted. "Stupid fucking child locks." Jill's face was in her hands and she was peering through her fingers at the unfolding events. She pointlessly pressed a few of the rocker switches on the dashboard of the car. Ian could see the police officer in the car behind them was half way out, impeded by his own array of modern police equipment that was attached to him. Ian dived through the narrow space between the front seats and out the open driver's door. He sprawled onto the road but swiftly gathered himself up. He straightened up to a height that Jill was surprised and impressed to see. He stood for only a second like this, flicked his chin up and down and twisted his head from side to side. Out of nowhere, he produced a green beret which he slid onto his head. He walked purposefully past the police officer who was now gently writhing on the road next to Greg who had turned with his back to the car. Ian caught Greg's eye and lowered his head in a nod of appreciation towards him.

"Get back in the car Greg. Jill in the back. I'll be driving." He said as he passed. The officer that had been watching from behind was fully out of the car now and was drawing his euphemistically named defence baton from its holster. Jill, from the front seat of the Daimler, looked on through her fingers, which were covering her face. She was panting from being short of breath. Ian strode towards the officer who shouted aggressively waving his stick before taking a swing at Ian's shoulders. Ian turned slightly parrying the blow and with his right hand grabbed the officer's yellow reflective coat. He deftly used the officer's own momentum to lower him slowly to the ground. In a flash faster than the officer could believe, his hands were fastened behind his back with a pair of handcuffs Ian had taken from the officers own utility belt. Ian left the officer on the ground, wriggling and shouting.

The traffic passing had been slowing to see what was going on and behind the police car, an old cream Ford Metro and a black pick-up truck had parked up.

"Gentleman." Ian shouted to the elderly man and the shaven headed geezer in shorts getting out of their respective cars. Ian was walking into the middle of the road with his hand held palm forward toward the oncoming traffic.

"Gentleman." He commanded. "We have a situation here." His left hand still purposefully palm up towards the traffic, which had slowed to a stop.

"Gentleman. This is a matter of national security. Would you please pull your vehicles over here." He motioned with a sweep of his right hand across the road.

The elderly man immediately got back into his car and under Ian's direction drove it across to the faster of the two lanes. The shaven headed geezer took a few seconds more to comply but he obeyed and blocked the road with his pick-up.

"Thank-you gentleman." Ian shouted at the top of his voice. "Your nation owes you."

Ian walked calmly back to the car where he slipped into the driver's seat. The engine was still running quietly. He dropped the handbrake lever and pushed the gear lever forward into first gear. He gently let out the clutch and accelerated slowly. He pulled the door shut as the car approached thirty miles per hour on the now empty road. Greg was sitting in the passenger seat looking even more dishevelled. He had blood on his face, was shaking slightly and was sweating. He was running his fingers over the ripped lapels of his jacket.

"Bloody Philistine." He said. "Totally ruined."

The car was doing in excess of a hundred miles an hour again. Jill was sitting in the back seat looking up at the two men in the front between tapping away on her phone. Ian caught her eye and despite the tension and the violence of the last ten minutes, she had a big smile on her face. "What you so pleased about?" Ian said. He was still breathing heavily and she could see his hands shaking as he gripped the steering wheel.

"Nothing." She said. As a text message came through. "It's from Benson. He says take the next junction and head for Eynsford. Pub called the Pied Bull. He'll meet us in the car park."

"Listen Guys," Greg piped up from the front seat. "Had a lovely time. It's not often you get the opportunity to be assaulted twice in the space of half an hour and one of those times by a copper, that you get to wreck a perfectly respectable old motor not to mention a perfectly respectable whistle and then be driven to a pikey pub in the middle of nowhere."

He was beginning to rant, as was his wont on occasion.

"Calm down, Greg." Said Jill. "We'll have you home in no time. Sure Benson wants to get back to his bedsit or whatever it is anyway. He won't keep us long."

"Hold on." Said Greg, his brow furrowed. "How the hell does this fellah know where we are or where to turn off for Chrissakes?" His mind was working slowly probably due to the bump on the head. He was about to continue but didn't. Ian turned to look at him as if he were going to say more. His brow was furrowed in questions and he had an agitated look on his face. He was shaking his head as he turned through the back seats. His demeanour had changed from a being slightly excited by what was going on and happy to make a joke of it, to being mildly angry.

"Who the fuck is Benson anyway." He said at last as they drove into the gravel car park of the Pied Bull.

The only other car in the car park was an S class silver Mercedes. Leaning against the side of the car was a man wearing a cheap grey chauffeur's suit, his arms crossed tightly in front of him.

"That is," said Jill.

Ian pulled the car up alongside and lowered the window. Benson leant down still with his arms crossed.

"Evening." He said. He nodded at Greg sitting in the passenger seat. Greg politely nodded back. No one else saw the conspiratorial look that passed between them.

"Looks like you've had a little prang." Benson inspected the dents in the bodywork. "Still nothing a little elbow grease won't sort eh?" They were all too weary for his lame jokes. Benson pointed at the back seat.

Jill was sitting up, her knees almost between the front seats. She shuffled along the seat as Benson opened the back door behind Ian and slid in.

"Nice interior." He said as he looked around. "Don't make 'em like this any-more, do they?"

"Sadly not." Said Greg.

They sat there in silence for just a moment. None of them knew where to start.

"Now I know you are thinking that I haven't been doing my job." Said Benson shortly. He was holding his own phone between his thumb and forefinger and almost nervously twisting it back and forth.

"I'd noticed the four goons in the car. They stuck out worse than sore thumbs. Their operator was in the bar on the other side from where you guys were. A fat man in a cream suit. Didn't manage to get a tail on him. Guess where the car went when it lost you guys?" Benson held his phone steady in his hand, tapped the screen and started to slide his finger across the face.

"Recognise this?" He showed around a picture of a large house.

"That's a business centre." Said Greg. "I take stuff there sometimes."

"That's right. Well done." Said Benson. "And in that business centre are the offices of Brideshead Security. They specialise in the ugly end of the euphemistically named security trade. Anyone know who this is?" Benson then tapped his phone again and showed them a picture of a fat sweaty man in a cream linen suit taken in the public bar of the pub. It wasn't a great shot and was in profile only but his face was clearly visible. All three shook their heads.

"He's the boss of Brideshead. Used to work for both the British and the IRA in the eighties. Has a reputation these days of paying peanuts and getting monkeys."

"Listen chaps," piped up Greg from the passenger seat and simultaneously tapping at his own mobile.

"Lovely as it's been meeting you," he nodded toward Ian and Benson still tapping. "And Jill, exciting as ever, really... I'm going home now." He tapped a few more times and waited while the phone performed the task he had given it before replacing it in the inside breast pocket of his suit. He continued.

"My wife will already be wondering where I am and I'm going to need a moment or two to explain this." He turned his palms toward himself thumbs pointing upward. "I'm not the best man to be doing this kind of shit."

"I'm not sure that would be a good idea, Gregory old boy." Said Benson as he scrolled down on his phone again. He turned the phone towards Greg. A picture of Greg standing in the pub filled the screen.

"I think you're on the list now too."

7

"It's a gig." Said Benson. "Pay's good. I've heard that business hasn't been so lucrative recently."

"Business is fine Benny." Replied Greg. "Do me a favour. Don't let my business ever again concern you."

"Come on man. This is meant to be. I mean she came to you."

"She came to me Benny, because she too might recognise something good when she sees it. I am not, by the way, expecting you to even begin to understand."

"Look," said Benson ignoring Greg's derisory and condescending tone, "a week in Lanzarote in the best hotel on the island all expenses paid. That cannot be bad. Might even ease the pain of the, ahem, altercations the other day."

Benson winked. Greg took a deep breath. "Come on Man." Continued Benson before Greg could talk. "It'd be like getting the band back together."

"It's nothing like that Benny." Said Greg as calmly as he could. "In the spirit of honesty and integrity, concepts with which I know you are unfamiliar, I have to declare an interest and I need to level with you on a couple of points. I'm going to ask that you listen and I'm going to ask that you don't just ignore what I'm saying like you usually do."

"Shoot Gregory Old Man." Said Benson as he hoisted his rotund arse up onto the small counter top.

"One. I've never liked the childish way you do things Benny." Started Greg. "Your silly computer passwords, your lack of empathy and your hubris. I understand that it's all a defence mechanism to make up for your general personality defects not to mention the very real possibility that you have figuratively and maybe literally a small penis which fucked you up to start with. Part of me feels a certain sorrow for you, but only a very small part." Benson sat with his arms crossed and the same smug smile on his face. He thought Greg was mucking about but he wasn't. This wound Greg up even more.

"Two." He started again. "I've already been asked on this gig and so it's not on your account that I'll be there. So there'll be no throwing your weight around and if you lift up your hand while I'm talking just once I'll arrange to have you shot." Benson nodded with the same smug smile on his face.

"Three." Greg went on. "It won't be the first time that I've been to this particular hotel. I've worked it before."

Throughout Greg's speech, Benson had his arms crossed in a relaxed way. A smug benevolent smile water-coloured onto his face. Benson pushed himself off the counter and paced towards the door. He turned around and held his hand up in front of him even though Greg had stopped talking. Benson stopped short of using the full definitive flat hand gesture and more pointed at Greg with his fingers outstretched.

"What do you mean? Worked it?"

Greg got up and walked towards Benson. He closed one eye and peered into Benson's left ear. He mimed taking aim with a gun and shooting him.

"Whoops. I missed." He said. "That's because there's nothing there. I'm genuinely saddened by the fact Benny that I have the misfortune to occupy the same space and time as someone as obtuse as you. But I have no choice. Fate has dealt me a joker and to some extent, it's up to me how I play it. Regardless of my personal feelings towards you, Benny, a job is a job. I have been asked to attend the said hotel on the days you mention to perform."

"Perform?" Said Benson in a high-pitched voice. "Perform what?"

"I can't say I'm afraid." Said Greg turning away and unnecessarily tidying a pile of shirts.

"You have to tell me. We are on the same team."

"No I don't Benny and no we're not."

"Oh come on man. You can't do this to me. What do you mean you have been asked to perform?" Said Benson sarcastically emphasising the last word. "And who by?"

"I'm not going to tell you Benny so stop asking. All I'll say is you don't know the half of it."

Benson was finally if only temporarily and mildly offended. He changed the subject in an effort to regain some control, which according to him he did.

"Have you got the information you've been asked to provide?" Said Benson in his corporate-speak voice. Greg nodded with a satisfied smile and leant under the counter and produced an A4 buff coloured envelope.

"Before you ask," said Greg. "Yes. It's as comprehensive as usual and no I've left nothing out. Not even the smallest detail. Given your attention span, I think I'd better go through it with you."

"Thanks." Said Benson as he put out his hand to take the envelope. "I'll be fine." Greg pulled the envelope back slightly, ignoring Benson.

"The hotel is built on a honeycomb of tunnels and caves created by volcanic eruptions that occurred as recently as 1850. The volcano on the island is technically still active. The present owner bought it as a barren plot of land twenty-five years ago. Paid cash. Took two years to build the hotel and it has remained pretty much unchanged since then except for some alterations around ten years ago."

"You're good Gregory old boy. I'll give you that. But I'll run with it from here." Said Benson as he reached forward again to grab the envelope. Greg pulled it away again. Benson raised his eyes and turned away.

"What kind of alterations?" Benson asked after a pause.

"Benny," said Greg. "Things are looking up. You were listening. Lifts." Said Greg.

"Lifts." Repeated Benson.

"Lifts." Said Greg again as he opened the loose flap of the envelope, pulled out the contents, and put them on the counter.

"What like elevator lifts?"

"Knowledge is power Benny boy". Said Greg ignoring Benson's question. "You know that. Knowledge is power."

He started to unfold several sheets of A1 plan paper that were dog-eared and yellowing. In the lower right hand corner of the sheet was the name of the architects. Benson was immediately interested.

"Where the hell did you get these?" Benson said in a high pitch voice again, his eyes growing wider. "RSA Architects." He read aloud the name on the lower right hand corner.

"What do you know about them?"

"Apart from the POBox address nothing at all." Said Greg.

"These drawings are over twenty years old. They're done by hand in ink. I have a sneaking suspicion that the RS stands for Ricky Starr."

"So it would be Ricky Starr Associates."

"I'm guessing that but I don't know for sure."

"Ricky Starr never trained as an architect."

"As far as I know Ricky Starr never trained in anything Benny. The clue is in the name. The people who do the work are Starr's associates."

"What else do you know about Ricky Starr?" Said Benson. The tone of his voice giving away the fact that he was more interested than he was letting on. Greg, ignoring Benson's question again, unfolded the plans completely and smoothed them out so that they covered the entire counter. He twisted them around so that they faced Benson and pointed at an elevation.

"The hotel was built on three floors. As the land falls away behind the sheer cliff face here." He pointed. "Two of the three stories are visible from the land side. You take a flight of steps up to the open area on top of the cliff. Below that is the huge and elegant ballroom that looks as if it has been hewn from the volcanic rocks. In fact, it was created naturally during the last volcanic eruption. The interesting bit is that directly below this room is another that is identical in every respect. In the lower room the windows are all fake and there is only one real entrance and exit. This door leads on to corridors that access every other part of the hotel."

"Why is that interesting?" Asked Benson.

"I don't know." Said Greg. Benson thought he detected a note in Greg's voice when he said this. He thought Greg was lying.

"Are you not telling me something?"

"No." Said Greg curtly.

"You do know why that is interesting."

"Well. It is. It's as if the whole place has been designed for a big game of Cluedo. If you were playing Cluedo there," He tapped the plans with his finger. "This would give you the advantage wouldn't it?"

"It all just looks like a bit of a folly to me." Said Benson

"There are a total of thirty two guest rooms in the hotel. They can all be accessed via secret panels and hidden staircases. Three of the rooms, or should I say suites," Greg unfolded another plan and smoothed it out before pointing to three places where concentric circles were drawn.

"Whether he intended to emulate Indiana Jones I don't know but these three rooms all contain a stone staircase. When lying flat it just looks like a pattern carved into the stone. A circle about a foot wide and then another surrounding it about six feet in diameter. Between the inner circle and the outer circle are sixteen segments like flower petals. When activated the stones fall downwards one by one creating a spiral staircase. Technically a single helix. This gives access to all the lower floor connecting corridors."

Benson's look was flustered. He was having trouble keeping up with the possibilities. His face at once was quizzical and judging.

"What kind of person has that sort of thing in his place?"

"I don't know." Said Greg. "I think the owner has a rather unusual sense of fun."

"Who is the owner?"

"His name is Tom Gates. He is originally Irish going by his accent. The records office in Arrecife have no records of him, no previous address, nothing before 1986.

He turned up on Lanzarote and stayed a while working on construction jobs in the developments at Porta Calera for two years. According to the official records a total of four jobs working around the construction sites. They mustn't have been the only jobs though. There must have been other stuff going on because the land registry in Madrid has him buying this plot of land two and a half years after he surfaced on the island. Back in nineteen eighty six he paid fifty million pesetas, the equivalent of about two hundred and fifty thousand pounds. In cash."

"So Tom Gates suddenly came into money."

"Looks that way. Yes"

8

The Thames clipper had just left Westminster pier and was heading across the river toward the London Eye. It was halfway through an autumn afternoon and the boat was busy with tourists and commuters. Roland Garret had sat on the furthest seat but one at the back on the riverside as instructed by Ricky Starr in a curt text message earlier that day. Ricky had got the same message from Roland and he wondered as he was waiting in the queue to board the boat if he'd show up. As it was, he joined the queue only three behind where he was standing. Roland hadn't recognised him in his wide brimmed black hat, false beard and glasses. It amused Ricky greatly that it was so easy to change your appearance and in such a clichéd manner. *A hat and a false beard.* Ricky waited for Roland to sit down and for the boat to cast off before he removed the hat, glasses and the beard and put them in his satchel. He walked across the boat and sat down next to Roland who was gazing out the window. Ricky shuffled about in his seat. He couldn't help it. The little boy in him was making light of what otherwise would be a serious grown up encounter. He shuffled some more crossing the invisible dividing line between them. Roland uncomfortably shifted toward the window and Ricky filled the space he had left.

"For God's sake man. Do you want to sit here?" Said Roland without looking at Ricky at first. Then he realised who it was with a jump. Ricky was grinning.

"For mercy's sake Starr. This isn't a pantomime."

"Keep your voice down Roland." Said Ricky.

The boat was making a tight turn towards the opposite bank.

"You fucked up Starr." Said Roland without any further pleasantries. "You said it'd be a breeze. You said you'd handle it and now look."

"You start a fight Roland. You gotta know that there is gonna be a winner and a loser."

"Don't give me any of that shit." Said Roland. "I pay you good money to handle my public relations and you might as well have just had me shot."

"We weren't exactly handling your PR Roland. You engaged us to do a highly illegal job hacking into a government data base and removing information that would end any ambitions you had of being anything other than the black-heart you are."

"Whatever." Said Roland with a dismissive wave of his hand. "You said you had people who could do it. You got paid a tidy sum and you didn't get it done."

"We got it done all right. Have you noticed any of the usual suspect hacks who would normally be out for your blood on account of the fact that you are a lying bastard, asking for a statement? No. No Roland because that information does not exist in the public domain any more. Someone knew we were doing it though. Someone with a distinctly Irish twang to her voice." Ricky emphasised the word 'Her'. Roland positively took a comic double take and turned noticeably pale. Ricky noticed immediately.

"What's wrong Rolley old boy. You look like you've seen a ghost. Is there something you want to tell me?"

Roland was temporarily lost for words. He knew who the woman was with the Irish accent. *It won't take much for her to get the gist of what was on that data stick. And if she knows, every fucking hood and assassin will be wanting a piece of me.*

"I think you've got out of your depth on this one, Starr. I think maybe we'll have to call it a day." At that, a voice came from behind them. Polite and quiet.

"Morning Gentlemen." Ricky and Roland both turned around to where the voice was coming from between their shoulders.

"Sorry to interrupt." Roland looked the strangely dressed figure up and down trying to take him in. He was wearing a black and white puppy-tooth check suit with a matching double-breasted waistcoat with lapels, a black and white check shirt and a checked tie. The article of clothing that made him stick out though was the grey milled worsted cape, in the style of Sherlock Holmes. Roland tried unsuccessfully to pigeonhole the stranger into one of his predetermined stereotypes but couldn't.

"Fuck Off." Said Roland loudly, turning the heads and drawing stern looks from a few of the commuters. The man remained where he was, leaned forward slightly and quietly said,

"Now now Mr. Garret. That's really not the way I'd expect a minister of the crown to greet a loyal subject." The way the man spoke gave both Roland and Ricky the impression that he was not sitting behind them by chance. Although Roland Garret was a high profile politician, and was always being interviewed on television and had even taken part in topical quiz shows, the man had something else to say other than "Aren't you the man off the Telly?"

Roland turned back slightly towards Ricky.

"Is this one of yours? If you're..." He trailed off as he saw Ricky had anticipated the question and was slowly and gravely shaking his head. Ricky turned around and offered his right hand over the shoulders.

"Rick Starr. At your service." A polite but Pan Am smile on his face. "And you are?" The man shook Ricky's hand but didn't answer the question.

"I know." He said putting on a voice that sounded like an adoring fan that is on the verge of becoming a stalker.

"You're famous in our house. What luck I've had seeing the pair of you here and on such a lovely day." Roland was getting agitated. He looked about to explode. The man leaned forward again and whispered between the heads of the two men in front. This time his voice took on a sinister sound.

"For the moment, at least, you two are going to do exactly as I say," and sat back in his seat. Ricky and Roland both turned again and saw a glinting gunmetal pistol that had been covered by the man's cape.

"Now turn around and sit there quietly. In case you're wondering if I will shoot you in cold blood in front of all these people..." The man thought for something appropriately threatening to complete the sentence but instead said, "well that's your decision."

The clipper pulled alongside the north Greenwich pier.

Some of the passengers got off and some others, fewer, got on. Ricky Starr and Roland Garret appeared to be obeying him but the man had been warned not to get complacent. They were both 'clever and conniving' according to a report he'd studied. But he hadn't really needed the report to tell him that.

"Can we have a little chuckle to ourselves gents? Like I just told you a funny story." Said the man leaning between them again. The two men stayed still.

"Maybe you didn't understand me," he said. "I'd like it very much if you pretended to laugh a bit."

"Ha Ha." Said Roland in a monotone. Ricky attempted a false laugh himself slightly better than Roland.

"Oh dear." Said the man. "You don't want to play my game. Never mind." He paused and said louder now so anyone who wanted to hear could.

"You are both going to love what I'm gonna say next." With this he slapped the two men lightly on the back. "Now let's just go back a moment to where I was suggesting that you may be thinking about whether or not I'd shoot you if you just got up and said to the captain 'Arrest this man. He has a gun'." Roland kicked himself for not thinking about it. "Well that might have been the best course of action then. As it happens it's not now." He tapped the two men on the back where he had patted them a moment earlier. The boat was half way to its next stop at Blackfriars Bridge.

"Gentlemen," He said. "Attached to your respective backs are specially designed fabric patches. They are stuck using a type of self-curing super glue for fabric. I am reliably informed that the glue was developed alongside Velcro by the chaps at NASA. Unlike Velcro, it doesn't come undone. There are four other elements inside the cloth pouch. A high frequency receiver, a detonator and an incendiary. It works rather like a car remote locking system. You press this little button here... No stay where you are. Do not look around. Act normal. You press this little button here and the pouch emits a single beep accompanied by a little vibration."

He pressed a button on each of two adapted key fobs and the two men one after the other heard a beep very similar to a car alarm being activated and felt a vibration in the middle of their backs. Just like a mobile phone vibrates.

"The beep serves the single purpose of alerting you to the fact that the device is armed." The man continued as if describing the construction of the sleeve rope in a handmade Italian suit.

"The vibration does two things. It alerts you to the fact that the device is primed and ready for use if for some reason you can't hear it and it shakes the phosphorus and the mercury together. This forms a highly volatile compound that can be detonated by the tiniest electric current. If it should go off the results are spectacular. The cloth itself is impregnated with a flammable liquid and it positively sparkles when ignited. Your hair will probably go first, what there is of it eh!" He poked Roland Garret gently in the back.

"And then the phosphorus and the mercury burn for about eight seconds at upwards of three thousand degrees centigrade. The flammable liquid flows down your back where it will continue to burn for a further 30 seconds under its own steam. That is if it doesn't catch the clothes you're wearing alight which in your case Roland, you might just be ok. That's a Huddersfield cloth if I'm not mistaken. Bullet proof that stuff. You're probably not so lucky though Mr. Starr. I wouldn't go near a naked flame wearing what you're wearing. Still I'm side tracking. There are just another couple of things you need to know. Inside the pouch is a small movement detector. It's set to rough. We're all quite lucky that it's a calm day on father Thames today eh? Anyway, any sudden movement like getting up and trying to follow me will result in the detonation of the incendiary. So best no hanky-panky eh? Last thing. When you hear two beeps, the device is disarmed. You still have to be careful because the mixture is still volatile like nitro-glycerine was in the westerns. Has a tendency to go off when shaken so take your coats off before you go for a run. Now I don't want to frighten you unduly. Just take it easy and wait for the two bleeps. You'll be fine. Last thing. And I promise this will be last. Mr. Starr, been a pleasure meeting you and I'm sorry to draw you into our little meeting."

The Man directed his voice towards Rolland Garret and continued in a voice that seemed more rehearsed than before.

"You'll be wondering who I am, who I could be working for and what it is that I want? Well I'm hardly about to tell you who I am. It's for you to work through your past to discover who I'm working for, if it isn't myself. What I want is detailed in this envelope." The man handed through two envelopes. Neither of the men lifted a hand to take the envelopes so the man dropped them onto their laps.

"Don't trouble yourselves too much. It's only extortion. Nothing important. Bon chance gentlemen."

With that the man rose from his seat, his cape flowing and stepped off the boat as it docked at north Greenwich. Roland turned towards Ricky very slowly. He waved the envelope lightly in front of Ricky.

"If you're fucking with me Starr I swear..."

"I know nothing about this Roland. Remember you text me the message." Ricky pulled out the mobile phone from his pocket and showed Roland the text message as the boat made its way further east along the river. "Here." He said. "I thought you wanted to harangue me about the stick."

"I didn't text you. You text me." Roland checked his own mobile phone and showed Ricky the screen. Roland opened the envelope he had been given. Inside was a plain sheet of paper containing lines of numbers. Both men knew what the sheet of paper was but tried to disguise the fact from the other. Ricky was more successful at this than Roland whose political acumen and innate ability to make people believe him and that he had no ulterior motives for what he was saying, left him and almost involuntarily he said, "What day is it today?"

Ricky, knowing why he'd asked, said, "Why?"

Roland caught himself and shaking his head still slowly said, "No reason," and then continued. "What do you make of this?"

The boat was heading at a frightening speed towards the pier at Wapping. Ricky heard two beeps from behind his head and let out a flow of breath from between pursed lips.

"No idea Rolly. Have you been upsetting people? Think this is my stop though Old Boy. You look after yourself. Call me on this number." He gave Roland a plain paper card with a telephone number printed on it. "The other one's been hacked. Don't ring me on yours." He left Roland still sitting rigid in his seat. Ricky could see that he was shaking slightly. Was that fear, anger or Parkinsons? He thought.

As Ricky crossed the gangway and stepped onto the pier, he carefully removed his coat as he was walking and examined the patch stuck to it. He pulled at the cloth and it came off instantly. A smile slipped across his face.

He ripped open the patch to find a simple circuit board. Nothing.

"I thought as much." He said out loud, and chuckled to himself.

He realised he didn't have a clue where he was. Somewhere in Woolwich. He'd never been here before. He walked up from the pier to where there may be some life but there was no-one. Eventually he came by what was the first of many convenience stores that served as off licences, newsagents and grocers. He went in and bought a single cold can of Tenants Super Strength lager and a crummy all day breakfast sandwich. Before sitting on a bench at a bus stop lit by a single street lamp to ingest them, he reapplied his glasses beard and hat. Not because he thought he might be recognised but because he thought it was funny.

Roland fared less well. He got into an altercation with a ticket inspector. He had been on the boat waiting for the two bleeps that hadn't come for two entire circuits of the boats route. He was attempting to remain still while remonstrating with the staff trying to explain that he couldn't get up without telling them why. Eventually they manhandled him off the boat putting his behaviour down to him being drunk despite his protestations to the contrary. He could hardly use the 'do you know who I am?' tactic as he was completely happy that they didn't. A distinctly angry, embarrassed and tired Roland Garret walked up Villiers Street having eventually got off at the same place he had started six hours earlier. Before going into the pub and ordering the first of many pints of Guinness, he stopped at a news-stand and bought a copy of Private Eye a notebook and a pencil. *The day was Friday.*

9

Portcullis house is a building designed and built to impress the great and the good in the world of politics, law making and power. The interior walls are lined, at great expense by acres of unnecessarily hand finished oak veneer panels. In the central atrium there are six mature lime trees, imported again at huge expense to the taxpayer and amid not a little controversy from a Mediterranean island where they grow in abundance. In their unnatural setting, they look elegant and serene but not as elegant as they do in their natural one. The most distinguished architects and interior designers will be proud of what they have produced and of having once again excelled themselves with their 'tax payers paying' budget. And so they should. Nothing is too good for the men and women who selflessly put themselves forward to govern the British Isles. In return for a life of sacrifice to the cause these selfless citizens have built themselves a highly secure, virtually bomb proof palace of work with coffee shops, swanky bars and elegant restaurants all subsidised by the ever accommodating Great British Tax Payer.

In hardly a more appropriate setting, Roland Garret MP and Secretary of State for Northern Ireland sat waiting for his lunch guest in a private room on the fifth floor of the building. His table overlooked, through a bullet proof, floor to ceiling window, on one side Waterloo Bridge and the huge slowly revolving London Eye and on the other the Houses of Parliament themselves in all their majestic glory.

Thirty years ago, Roland Garret was commonly referred to by the law enforcement agencies of both the United Kingdom and Northern Ireland, the British Army and the press as a terrorist but has, by a peculiar combination of fate, guile, luck and downright bullying, found himself in the position his wildest dreams could never have predicted when he was setting off car bombs thirty years ago. Powerful, respected and hugely well paid both officially and unofficially, Roland Garret is finally in his element. Before he came to England he wouldn't have known a Claret from a carrot. He would have seen as bourgeois anyone spending the amount of money he was about to spend on a bottle of expensive French wine. Very expensive French Wine. Yet here he is flicking his fingers as if he were asking for more butter. Even taking into account the specially subsidised prices reserved for staff, a cleaner, working in the same building would have to work two entire weeks to pay for the bottle he has ordered. Rather than fight the establishment, Roland Garret has embraced even some of the finer details and works hard to preserve the illusion that it has always been this way. His suit, a too heavy tweed three piece, is stretched around his overweight frame and is creased and scruffy. It is quite new but new suits are frowned upon in the reaches of the British Establishment that Roland Garret wants to be accepted into so he has made deliberate efforts to make it appear as if it belonged to his father. Just like the others do. Saville Row have this look down to a tee for a price and Roland Garrett can afford it now. Not that his act fools many of the genuinely ridiculous establishment figures. He has no friends in parliament and acquaintances and colleagues are generally polite and respectful towards him because of what he has made his business to know about them. He wields his power with little finesse but he doesn't care. His bullying and aggressive tactics have stood him in good stead over the years and he is not about to change now.

The wine waiter arrived with the wine shortly followed by another immaculately dressed waiter leading a woman to the table.

"Mr. Garret, Sir. Your luncheon guest has arrived." The waiter gently dragged a high back, richly upholstered, chair away from the table, the portcullis logo of the House of Commons embroidered in gold silk on the seat. An attractive red headed woman dressed in a black tailored suit and knee length black suede boots sat down as the waiter gently pushed the chair in underneath her. She nodded toward her host as they were both handed a menu.

"I'll be back shortly to take your order." The waiter told them as he backed away.

"I'm glad you could come, Mary. At such short notice." Said Roland with a condescending smile and tilt of his head.

"Look at you Garret," said Mary as she took a compact mirror from her neat black clutch bag and checked her makeup.

"Pappy would be turning in his grave."

"My dear, your father would approve of what I am doing and if I may say so, that's rich coming from you."

"He wouldn't approve, Garret, and for the record neither do I but I'm sure you'd not be letting that bother you now. Why am I here Garret?"

"Let me pour you a glass of wine. It's very good stuff you know." She made no effort to refuse so Roland half-filled a huge round wine glass. She took a couple of big gulps that all but emptied the glass.

"So a pint of the black stuff's not good enough for you anymore. Doesn't impress me Roland. Now cut the crap. Why am I here?" She leaned forward and in a slightly lowered voice said,

"Security in this place?" She saw Roland's face flicker into a smile.

"I'm not kidding, Garret. This is the fucking lion's den." Roland remained calm, controlled and condescending.

"Did you have any problem at the airport or at the door here?"

"None at all."

"There you are you see. If I can't do it. It can't be done. This room is swept twice a day for bugs and I had my own guys go over the table an hour before I got here so we're safe." Mary picked up a menu and cursorily looked it over. She raised her eyebrows as the waiter approached the table again and with one hand behind his back and his feet together he refilled the wine glasses emptying the bottle. Roland pointed at the bottle.

"Could we have another of those, Reynard. Excellent. Excellent stuff."

"Certainly Sir." Said Reynard. "And are you ready to order yet sir?"

Roland looked across to Mary who was shooting him a look saying *get on with it*.

"Yes Reynard I think we may be." Reynard turned to Mary, "Madam?"

"I'll have the roast beef." She said as she handed the menu back to Reynard.

"And how would you like it done Madam?"

"Just as it comes man. I'm not fussy."

"As you wish Madam and for you Mr. Garret, Sir?"

"Would you recommend the Monk Fish Reynard?"

"Absolutely. Fresh in this morning. Excellent choice Sir."

Roland Garret nodded as he handed back the menu. When Reynard was out of earshot Mary chided.

"Hook, line and fucking sinker. I can hardly believe my ears."

"Look Mary." Said Roland getting just a little infuriated with her attitude, "I don't need nor want a lecture on the nature of right and wrong from you. As much as I was a good friend of your late father and we were brothers in arms, times have changed. I've just changed with them."

"Not changed that much as far as I can see. If you had I wouldn't be here." Mary bit back.

"You're here for a job interview and that's all."

"Well I've never heard it called that before." She laughed, taking another very unladylike gulp from her wine glass. "What job? Where?"

"I've lost something." He said and paused to hear her reaction which he pretty much predicted.

"Go to the police. Lost property is not my field. What have you lost?"

"Information." Said Roland. "Information that I thought had ceased to exist."

"Roland." Her tone was at once gentler but more frustrated. "Don't talk in code. What have you lost and why have you called me? I've not heard from you since Papy's funeral, and that was ten years ago."

"I'm sorry for that, Mary. Truly I am." Mary almost believed him.

"You were only a small girl. Thirty years ago or so, there was a government enquiry into an arms smuggling operation that went wrong." Roland's voice trailed off as Reynard arrived with the food.

"My Goodness Roland. There's no hanging about in here is there." She gestured toward the plates of food.

"This is a busy place, Mary and we are busy people. We don't like to be kept waiting." Roland waited for Reynard to finish serving.

"Excuse me for being thick Roland, but wasn't all that pretty common knowledge. Papy even talked to journalists. I've seen books written about it."

"Well everything that was published then is known. Except thirty years have passed since the end of the enquiry and there was plenty of stuff then considered far too sensitive for the public to stomach. What was never revealed was that it was an inside job. The old boat carrying the arms was meant to be scuppered if it got discovered so as to hide the source and not to jeopardise any further shipments but someone, person or persons unknown, from within our organisation, sabotaged the fuses on the limpet mines that were attached to the hull of the boat so the British, via French customs, got the whole lot. They knew where it came from so were on their guard. Gaddafi was livid. He threatened to cut us off completely."

"And so...Forgive me. I am being thick."

"And so thirty years have gone by and all the documents that were never released at the time will soon enter the public domain."

"Surely if there is anything in those papers that implicates you, it's too late. It's out already. And anyway, Roland, you did your time at her majesty's pleasure, as Papy did. You're legitimate now. You're a fucking British Minister."

Roland looked curiously guilty for some reason, thought Mary. But the expression switched back quickly to the more familiar grave and concerned, as if he really believed he was talking about the greater good.

"My position affords me certain powers, some of which I abuse terribly I know. Of course I knew these papers were to be released and I had the records doctored as any self-respecting corrupt politician would. Cost me surprisingly little. Anyway I should have paid more for a decent job.

You know what they say about buying cheap. The records have been erased from the government database and that would have been the end of the matter except for one small problem."

Mary, who had been tucking into her roast beef while Roland was talking put down her knife and fork. For some reason something was amiss with Roland's story. Not the story exactly but the way he was telling it. He was almost trying to convince her of something and he had no need to. "One small problem?" She repeated.

"Yes. One small problem. The people who did my little job for me got a bit busy and for reasons only known to themselves, made a copy of the material. It exists on a data stick."

"Surely it makes no difference if you get it back or not. If the information on it puts you in the shit, whoever has an interest to do it, they'll just make a copy. You're done for already in my book."

"Well maybe but the stick is protected. You can read it but you can't copy it."

"I reckon that's bought you maybe twenty four hours. When did it go missing and who do you think has got it?"

Roland Garret reached into his inside jacket and extracted a folded piece of paper.

"Two days ago. Someone was very well informed." He unfolded the piece of paper and passed it across the table to Mary. It was a photo copy of the front page of a Private Eye Magazine.

"Ever seen this man before?" Mary shook her head. "Your father knew him. I had a copy of the magazine posted to my home address. Nothing else with it. Just the magazine. Thirty years ago two men were accused, at least by our side, of sabotaging a mission. He was one of them. At that time he was known to us as David Crane and we were fairly certain, although we could never prove it, that he was playing for both teams."

Mary took a long look at the photograph. "Who was the other man?"

"His name was Booth. Eamonn Booth. They were both supposed to have been killed in one of our car bombs that was meant for London two weeks after that bust. Even now I'm not sure. No body was found. Not that there is ever much to find. All the resources my position affords me and I've not come up with an answer. He's either clever, lucky or dead."

Mary was still looking at the photograph.

"If he's not dead and he's not lucky..." She passed back the photograph. "What makes you think I'll do the job?"

Roland reached again into the inside pocket of his jacket and slid a fat sealed envelope across the table.

"Here's twenty five thousand reasons on account."

Mary's face gave nothing away as she took the envelope and ran her fingernail through the seal. She flicked through the wad of fifty pound notes inside the envelope. She deftly counted out twenty notes and removed them from the envelope and put them folded into her clutch bag. She slid the envelope back across the table.

"Have you ever heard of the Peter principle?" She asked as her elbows moved onto the table either side of her hardly touched roast beef. She picked up her wine glass, put it to her lips and took another gulp. Roland raised his eyebrows and sat back in his chair.

"No I haven't but I'm sure you're about to tell me."

"A theory about hierarchies." A smug smile appeared on her face. "By a fellah by the name of Doctor Peter. In a hierarchy, Roland, every employee rises to his level of incompetence and there they remain. Very interesting idea. He wrote a book. I'll lend you my copy."

"Don't you go taking the Mick, Mary. I was born at night but it wasn't last night."

"Love," Mary continued with her condescension, "You know what year we're living in. They'll search my bag on the way out for a start. It would only take some new boy on the security team, not yet aware of your munificence, to find twenty five thousand,"

"Twenty four thousand." Roland interrupted.

"Twenty four thousand pounds..." Mary nodded. "In grubby used notes about my person and they would start asking questions. No Roland. This is a modern world and envelopes full of cash are so eighties."

"They've always seemed to work OK for me," said Roland.

Mary was picking around in her bag for a business card.

"This is a holding company based in the Cayman Islands." She took a Biro from the bag and wrote on the back. "Twenty five into this account." She pointed at the numbers she had written on the back of the card. "I'll want that on account, and twenty five more when the job is done." She got up to leave and kissed him on the cheek.

"Mary." He said as she was stepping away from the table. He was suddenly talking to her like he wanted her vote. "I trust you. Your father and I went back a long way. Don't let me down." Mary was confused. *Was that a threat or a plea?* She thought.

"I'll call when the job's been done." She said as she walked toward the lift and pressed the call button. The doors slid open and she stepped inside removing her compact again from her bag. Without a look back she selected the ground floor. The lift was lined in mirrored glass. She noticed the dome of a security camera in the corner of the ceiling but ignored it. As the lift descended she touched up her lipstick looking in both her compact and the mirrored walls of the lift.

"Who does he think I am?" She said out loud to herself, squashing her lips between her teeth and then checking the results with a wide smile.

10

Across the river from portcullis house, on the top floor of St Thomas' hospital, in a room cluttered with black ABS plastic flight cases of various shapes and sizes,

Hedges, wearing a white doctors coat, was sitting on a chair with one eye peering through the viewfinder of a telescope that was set on top of a heavy tripod. Next to him sat a laptop computer showing columns of numbers that seemed to be constantly changing. Next to the telescope and pointing in a similar direction were two more instruments set on their own, even bulkier tripods. All three were connected by cables to a rack of electronics in a black flight case. A triple knock on the door of the room and Hedges got up from his chair to unlock the door to let Benson in. He was wearing a similar white coat but with the addition of a stethoscope draped around his neck and a pair of black rimmed glasses.

"It's today. Soon." He said as he walked toward the telescope and stooped to peer through the viewfinder. "Kit worth the trip?"

"See for yourself." Said Hedges.

Hedges lifted the laptop from the table and scrolled the cursor with his right hand. He tapped the touch pad twice. They both peered at the screen of the laptop as the column of numbers changed to a picture. For a few moments it was a static image but as they kept looking the pixels resolved themselves into ever smaller squares until a regular video picture appeared.

"You ain't seen nothing yet." Hedges tapped the laptop again. "They said we could be up to five clicks away on a clear day if we had line of sight and we'd get the same resolution. I didn't believe them when we were there but I do now." Benson smiled and nodded with an 'I told you so' look on his face.

"Don't give me that look." Said Hedges. "We got lucky OK!"

The picture on the laptop was moving.

"You are recording?" Said Benson. Hedges leant to press a button on the rack of electronics.

"I am now.'" He said as he replaced the laptop on the table and watched the screen. Benson moved toward the window and peered across the river to the object of their attention.

"You're right," he said, "we did get lucky. Their engineer said if the atmospheric pressure was too low the particulates in the air would scatter the signal. But." He sang, "It's a beautiful day for spying."

The door handle rattled and a knock at the door caused the two men to jump.

"You said we were good for the day." Hedges whispered.

"Thought we were." Said Benson as the knock was repeated followed by a male voice.

"Security." They both detected an accent. Possibly Eastern European

"Can't be routine. I'll hold him off. You get the handshake." Benson said as he quick-stepped towards the door.

"What if there's more than one. They mustn't see this kit." Hedges called anxiously.

"Get two handshakes. Pass one to me." Benson stood at the door his hand gripping the handle. Hedges lifted a black holdall onto the desk. He turned the lights out before tentatively unlocking and opening the door. He stepped outside the room and closed the door behind him. There were indeed two men dressed in black. He put a finger to his lips.

"Gentlemen." He said in a hushed voice. "A little decorum please. We are conducting important and..." before he could finish, the larger of the two men grabbed Benson's arm, pulled him forward in a swift movement and held him tight in a full nelson wrestling hold. The other shorter and lighter man punched him once, hard, in the stomach. Inside the room Hedges, having extracted two handshakes from his black holdall, decided to pick out a Jockey also. He carefully removed their vacuum foil packs. He slipped the Jockey and the second handshake into the back pocket of his jeans. He could guess what was happening outside the door and was being given fair instruction by Benson who was shouting theatrically

"Okay man, okay. It's just me here today, okay. I'll do whatever you say. I'm sure the three of us can come to an arrangement."

The bigger of the two men who was holding Benson in an arm-lock nodded to his accomplice. They were being careful not to say anything. A professional tactic. Not because they wanted to appear cool but because talking would give away clues as to who they were. The smaller man turned towards the door and pushed down on the handle. The big hospital door slowly opened and he tentatively stepped through. Hedges had closed the curtains enough to allow the surveillance scopes to see through the window and the room was in semi-darkness. Hedges remained motionless lying prone beside the skirting board by the door hidden from view underneath a hospital bed. He carefully and silently placed a 'handshake' which was the size of a fifty pence coin, in the palm of his right hand and armed it by squeezing the edges together between his thumb and forefinger. A tiny needle sprung out of the surface. The door shut behind the skinny man. Benson heard a click as the skinny man opened a four inch switch blade knife. He stood with his back to the door. His boots were only a foot away from Hedges' head. Hedges slowly reached out from his hiding place and slammed the 'handshake' into the skinny man's calf. The effect was not quite instant. For a moment or two the skinny man tried to compute what had just happened but did not come to a conclusion before the nerve toxin in the handshake rapidly travelled through his bloodstream. He released his grip on the switch blade and with a low pitched thud it fell to the floor beside Hedges' head. Before the skinny man could fall, Hedges rolled out from under the bed and stood smartly. The skinny man was losing control of the muscles in his face and his eyes were glazing over. A second later he fell to the floor helped to land quietly by Hedges who then grabbed him by the feet and pulled him away from the door then searched through his holdall again and pulled out a packet of large black cable ties, bit open the plastic packet and extracted four.

Rolling the unconscious man onto his stomach he tied two of the cable ties around his wrists behind his back. Noticing a Casio digital watch on the man's left wrist he took it off him and altered the time ahead twelve hours before replacing it. He then tied the man's ankles together with another of the cable ties.

Hedges brushed himself down and straightened his white coat. He stepped toward the door palming another of the handshakes in his left hand. He opened the door to the brightly lit corridor to see Benson still being held in the same hold with a look of disgust and anger on his face. Benson was a good few stone overweight and the blow to his solar plexus was well timed and accurately targeted and he was winded.

"Morning Sir." Said Hedges as if nothing was amiss, to the big man holding Benson in a headlock. The man swiftly ran through his options. He obviously wasn't the brains of the pair. He was standing holding Benson in a headlock with both his arms. Benson knew that unless he literally had something up his sleeve he was not going to come out of the encounter victorious. A second later the big man performing the headlock, realised this and pushed Benson roughly forward. Rather than pull something from his sleeve, he deftly pulled a pistol from a holster slung under his arm.

He waved it in a haphazard manner towards the two men.

Benson and Hedges raised their hands in surrender. The big man was sweating profusely and it was obvious that he was still considering his next move. He was silent apart from his heavy breathing. A half a minute passed with an apparent stalemate. Benson and Hedges stood motionless and expressionless. The big man had decided what to do. He took three paces back to put a little distance between himself and Benson and Hedges, then turned tail and ran down the corridor. He almost got into a stride. Hedges, in a wild west draw movement pulled the Jockey from his back pocket, flicked off the plastic safety cap and threw it with some force at the running man. With an accuracy that the namesake of the device would have been proud, the dart penetrated the Big Man's back around the area of his kidney. After rebounding off the corridor walls where his momentum was pushing him but his legs no longer were, he fell with a hell of a noise into a corner.

"One hundred and Eighty." Shouted Benson clapping his hands above his head in victory. Hedges looked at him and shook his head.

"We're in trouble." He said. "Big trouble." Hedges trotted toward the fallen man.

"Quick" he hissed to Benson. "Let's get him back in the room before anyone comes." Hedges pulled out the Jockey and picked up the pistol that had slid along the floor. They both grabbed a trouser leg and dragged the man back to the room. Hedges trussed him up as he had done the other man.

"They were twenty fives." He said to Benson as he was at work. "They'll be out for four hours I'd guess." He took off the man's watch and altered the time as he had done with the other man. Benson, who was peering through the telescope again glanced back at him doing this and shook his head.

"No idea why you insist on doing that." He said.

"Old habits." Said Hedges. Benson had his eye fixed to the telescope eyepiece.

"You're gonna wanna see this." Said Benson. "I can just make it out. I think he just handed her a wedge and she just gave it back to him." Hedges, having finished his job of tying up the big man got up to look through the telescope.

"Are you sure you pressed record?" Benson asked.

"Yes. I'm sure I pressed record." Hedges replied.

Benson looked through the sight again, "Looks like they're saying their goodbyes. Give it a few minutes and we'll see if our investment has paid off. What shall we do with these two?"

"They were obviously trained by someone." Said Hedges.

"They're not privateers. The skinny one only said one word, sounded Eastern European to me. What did you think?"

"Possibly." He said. "Not much to go on though."

"We won't have long." Hedges said. "We need to wrap up here. Grab some gowns from one of those cupboards." He pointed to a row of white cabinets underneath a stainless steel worktop. Hedges picked up the gun and pulled the ammunition clip from the butt.

"Russian." He said. "But that doesn't tell us much." He pushed out a round. "Live too. They meant business." Benson had found two hospital gowns and he threw them onto one of the beds. Hedges put the ammunition clip into his black holdall and bent down to pick up the switch-blade that was still sticking into the vinyl floor. He looked it over before throwing it also into the black holdall.

"Give me a hand with the big lad." Hedges said to Benson motioning towards one of the beds. They shifted the big man onto a bed.

"Leave these two to me." He said. "If they've finished across the road then start packing up the stuff."

Benson peered through the telescope.

"They're gone. The waiter's clearing up." He began to unplug the two heavy scopes. Hedges jumped up and pressed a blinking button on the rack mount and tapped the keyboard on the laptop.

"Careful Man. We're new to this." He threw him a frustrated glance and then a 'carry on' gesture. Benson raised his eyes a fraction.

"Thought I was the control freak." He said under his breath and continued packing up the equipment.

Hedges had undone the cable ties and was rummaging through the big man's pockets.

"No ID, nothing." He said. "Except..." He pulled a card from the hip pocket of the big man's jeans. "Except a strip club card. They're professional but not that professional."

He turned and smiled toward Benson.

"It's got a name and number on it." He put the card in his own hip pocket. He continued his work pulling off the big man's clothes and replacing them with a surgical gown. He laid him on his back on the bed and placed the gun on the table by the bedside. He then started with the skinny man. Altogether an easier job. The skinny man's pockets revealed nothing. Benson was finishing packing away the equipment. The big man and the skinny man lay peacefully in adjacent beds. A pistol between them on the bedside table. The gear was packed except for the flight case containing the racks that were still blinking and the laptop.

"We can't be seen here with these guys." Said Benson.

Hedges sat at the laptop and tapped the keyboard. An image appeared, pixelated at first in squares.

"We can do this when we get back." Said Benson.

"Just give me a second. I want to know if we got anything."

The picture appeared sharp as a pin but the sound seemed out of sync. Hedges clicked the mouse on the screen and a window appeared.

"They are clever bastards." He said slightly turning his head. "They... are... clever.... bastards." He repeated as the image and sound fell into sync.

They both watched the twenty minute encounter. It took almost the same amount of time it had taken them to deal with the two men who were now lying unconscious next to each other on hospital beds. When the clip had finished, Hedges turned to Benson.

"Was that the same woman...? Did you know it went this deep?" Benson shook his head while still looking at the screen. There was a look on his face Hedges hadn't seen before.

"No." He said. "How strong's your stomach. Hedge? I think maybe it's a little more complicated than I thought."

11

The smile that Greg generally reserved for high rolling customers turned to a very suspicious frown as Martin Farnham held open the door for a man he recognised. All that morning, Greg had been attempting to arrange that friends of his in the trade look after the shop for a while. He'd got home the previous night and had parked his car in a neighbour's garage. He was expecting a fight with his wife which he duly got. Greg wasn't the philandering type and his wife knew it but he was never going to get away without a hard time. As it happened she was more sad than angry. The last time he had fallen foul of the law the six months he was away were difficult for her to say the least. She didn't want to have to go through it again but she knew he was a good man so, although not altogether forgiving him she had at last relented and saw that actually he needed a bit of care. Much to his horror though, she threw away the torn suit and the blood covered shirt.

"Morning Gregory." Said Martin. Greg heard a tone in Martin's voice that was unfamiliar.

"I've brought a friend of mine Gregory Old Boy. He thinks maybe it's time he smartened up his act a little." Greg forcibly removed his frown like he had wiped a damp flannel over his face and walking past Martin with his hand held out in front of him greeted Martin's friend.

"Mr. Starr. Good to see you again. And so soon." Said Greg. Ricky had a big smile on his face as he too held out his hand. The handshake was slow and long as each of the two men attempted to gauge as much as they could from the moment. When they eventually let go of each other's hand, neither was any the wiser.

"I absolutely loved it." Said Rick beaming a smile that told Greg so much more than the handshake did. Or at least he thought it did.

"Whose idea were the old remotes? Went better than I'd hoped." *Go with your instincts.* Thought Greg. T*hey're all you've got.* Ricky looked around him taking in the shop. "I was going to say that you are in the wrong job but this is just fabulous too." He shook his head in mock disbelief.

"Well I'm glad you like my humble little establishment." Said Greg who imagined that Ricky wouldn't notice him looking him up and down. Greg clocked the training shoes and the three-quarter length trousers, in November? The crime with the trousers wasn't that they were being worn out of season, no, that could be excused. The real crime was that the man wearing them was between fifty and sixty five years too old. These things were designed for five year old boys or mid-western AmericansAside from that most heinous of sartorial crimes, Ricky was wearing a sweatshirt worn under a plastic Puffa jacket. The name displayed across the front of the shirt was of a brand that had started life in a sweatshop in Indonesia. Greg knew that for some inextricable reason that that same sweatshirt, bought in one of London's marble halls, when packaged in an expensive paper bag, cost more than one of Greg's two ply cashmeres. Unforgivable. Ricky scanned Greg's face. After a second or two, as if reading Greg's mind, Ricky said, "Show me what you've got then." Ricky had a big smile on his face and sensing Greg's cynicism, nodded, "Really."

Greg had nothing to lose. He didn't miss a beat and started talking before he moved.

"You're a man who knows a good thing when you see it." Started Greg. "You're good with other men. You're more interested in women than they are in you. You don't need a suit to tell others who you are. You are confident in yourself but there is a 'but'. The 'but' is, you are in two minds. You are two different people. You know who you are but you have convinced yourself you are the person you would like to be."

"Very good." Said Ricky. His smile hadn't changed. "Do go on." He said even though Greg wasn't looking for permission.

"I know a little about you on account of your fame and fortune. Much of this is common knowledge and you'll perhaps think it cod psychology but you'll recognise something. You'll recognise the fact that due to your position in the world, people rarely tell you what they think. They just tell you what they think you want to hear. This is because you have the power, or at least they think you do, to make their lives, better or worse. In fact only they have this power."

Greg reached into a rack of jackets and motioned for Ricky to remove his. He held the coat from the rack in one hand and held out his other for the Puffa jacket. Greg roughly threw the coat up under Ricky's obedient arms where he had turned with his back to him but as soon as it had reached Ricky's shoulders, Greg pulled it back down again.

He walked to the back of the shop. A distance of five meters and picked a white shirt from hanger.

"Best loose the sweatshirt." Said Greg as he stepped back toward Ricky. Martin had sat down on a leather tub chair and was concentrating on looking nonchalant and pretending not to be interested in what was going on even though nothing could have been further from the truth. He was leafing through a book of old Norman Parkinson photographs.

"None of this stuff," Greg twirled his forefinger around three hundred and sixty degrees, "makes any difference. If you're happy with how you appear to the world then you should wear..."
He stopped and theatrically paused, "Small boys trousers."

The smirk on his face was now becoming obvious and he wasn't trying to hide it. Martin raised his eyes from the book and glimpsed Ricky's face. Ricky was having fun too.

"You can't half come out with some bullshit Greg mate." Martin mumbled.

"Not bullshit my friend. Hard won experience." Said Greg. "I've got something you'll love too, so prepare yourself." Ricky had taken off his sweatshirt and was replacing it with the white Egyptian cotton shirt Greg had handed him. Greg slipped the jacket back on Ricky's shoulders. Ricky shrugged a few times looking at himself in the standing mirror next to where Martin was sitting.

"Too tight." Said Martin.

"Listen," said Greg, slightly put out. "I don't interfere when you're doing your job. Don't interfere when I'm doing mine."

"I hear you got yourself in a spot of trouble with the Old Bill." Ricky said as Greg was taking the coat from his shoulders. Greg casually threw the jacket over the shop counter.

"Oh! OK. I get it. Why do I get the distinct feeling I'm being shafted. With respect, Mr. Starr..."

"Call me Rick." Ricky interrupted.

"With respect Rick, what's it got to do with you and…"

"It was one of my people who got you into it I'm afraid."

"I see." Said Greg "I see." He pointed at the jacket on the counter. "I'm wasting my time?"

"No No." Said Rick. "Not at all. 'Bout time I got myself a new disguise. No really. Do your worst." Greg picked another jacket from the rail and pushed it back up onto Rick's shoulders. The dynamic may have changed but Greg was still on the case.

"Super one twenty Loro Piana cloth from Southern Italy. Hand made in a factory on the outskirts of Florence where there are no sewing machines. So which one of them was one of your people and what was in the bag that was so important?"

"Jill O'Keefe works for me. She's a good sort. I hear you are old friends."

"I wouldn't exactly say that." Said Greg. "She used to sell me advertising in a local paper. Whenever she met a new geezer she'd bring him in here to change his appearance. Unfortunately for her, in most cases it was more than their appearance that needed changing."

"She's asked if there is anything I can do to make things better." Said Ricky. Greg glanced at Martin. "Do you know her?" He asked. Martin shook his head still reading the photo book.

"Never had the pleasure I'm afraid."

"I'm still confused." Said Greg. He pointed with the forefingers of each hand at the two men.

"Martin does some freelance work for me too." Said Ricky anticipating his question. Greg nodded slowly still not quite understanding.

"See I think maybe you are going to need some help. That record of yours won't go down too well when the law catches up with you. Now show me that first one again." Greg nodded his head and looked at Martin who was avoiding his stare.

"I thought we all agreed never to talk about that. First rule of Ford. Never talk about Ford. So I'm being stung again. Well and truly fucking stung."

"Hold your horses Greg." Said Ricky. "It's not what you think." He walked toward the door and held a sleeve up in the daylight.

"Nice. I like it. I'll have one of these. What are the strides like?" Ricky continued to look through the small panes of glass in the front door.

"Greg." He said slowly as Greg was sorting out the trousers to the suit.

"Think maybe they've caught up already." Two uniformed policemen were walking purposefully towards the door from where they had pulled their car up on the opposite side of the road. Ricky looked around for his mobile phone that was in the pocket of his Puffa jacket that was lying in a heap on the floor. One of the policemen rapped heavily on the door.

"Sorry gentlemen." Said Greg. "I'll have this dealt with shortly." He stepped past Ricky in the narrow gap up to the front door and opened it. There was a kerfuffle as four men tried to get into a space only really able to accommodate two. They all retreated into the floor of the shop. Martin remained looking at his book. A fact that annoyed the smaller of the two policemen who believed like a has-been soap star that everyone should stop doing what they are doing when they walk into a room. For not too dissimilar reasons, none of the three men had any respect for the police.

"What can I do for you Officers?" Said Greg.

"Are you Gregory Isaacs of 12 Bough Road Chislehurst?"

"I am Officer, yes."

"Are you the owner of a red Jaguar 4.2?"

"No I am not Officer." The officer flashed a puzzled look. Greg continued.

"It's a Bordeaux Daimler, Officer." The smaller of the two policemen drew his baton.

"I'm arresting you for assaulting a police officer. You do not have to say anything…"
Ricky who had been tapping at his mobile phone interrupted the officer.

"Excuse me officer Dibble, I have someone here who wants to talk to you urgently." He offered his phone to the policeman, who snarled at him,

"Fuck Off." said the policeman and started his speech again from the beginning. Rick butted in again holding out the phone.

"I really think you should take it." Said Ricky. The policeman ignored him and raised his voice a little continuing his speech. Ricky put the phone back to his ear and just as loudly said into it, "I'm afraid he doesn't want to talk to you Sir." He emphasised the last word. The policeman turned towards Ricky, "Yes. Yes I will," said Ricky and held the phone away from his ear with his hand over it.

"The Commissioner says that if you really don't want to talk to him then you won't have a job when you get back to the station." Ricky was smiling a broad and smug smile and doing a 'whoops' expression with the bottom of his cheek.

The officer relented and took the phone.

"Hello." He said at first still unsure if he was being scammed.

"Yes. Yes it is…yes Sir." Martin and Ricky looked at each other while suppressing a laugh like little boys in church. Greg was looking daggers at the copper with the baton in his hand and the copper was looking back at Greg.

"Yes Sir." The first policeman said again. Behind his back, Martin mimed the words 'yes sir' while rocking his head from side to side. "Yes I will, Sir." The policeman said for the last time and handed the phone back to Ricky. Ricky put the phone to his ear but there was no-one on the line. He smiled at the policeman.

"I don't know who you are or what you've just pulled," said the policeman, "but mark my words all of you. You've not seen the last of me."

"Or me." The copper with the baton said, attempting unsuccessfully to be menacing with these two little words and merely causing all three men to further suppress giggles.

"Come on." The first policeman said to his colleague.

"Someone here has friends in high places. Let's get out of here." The two policemen left with their tails between their legs. As soon as the door had clicked shut behind them the three men inside cracked up with howls of laughter that could easily be heard from outside. As often happens with nervous laughter of this kind, when it subsided none of the men knew what to do next. There would be a transition period of a few moments while they returned to the serious business they were conducting before the intervention of the policemen.

"So Rick." Said Greg eventually. "That was obviously your part of the bargain. What's mine?"

"We're square Greg. I wouldn't want a man with such obvious theatrical talents to be bothered by the boys in blue on my account. Now, how about a nice pair of boots to go with that suit?"

12

Paul Finch had just finished his day, hand making fancy doors in a swanky flat, just to the south of Saville Row.

He'd been paid in cash seven hundred and forty five pounds for his efforts. The money was currently burning a hole in the hip pocket of his work trousers and he was feeling rich. Having money in his pockets made him feel rich even though it was all spoken for. He was not a carpenter though. Paul Finch was an artist. He was only working as a carpenter because he had found he had a bit of a talent for it and needed to do something to keep the wolf from the door while he started whatever it was that interested him. He never actually finished anything that he started though, much to the chagrin of all those close to him. It was beginnings that interested him. He would say that the creative process isn't a process at all without a beginning, the birth of the idea. Finishing is the easy bit. Finishing is logistics. In the meantime though, it just happened that carpentry was the only thing anyone would actually pay him money to do. But Paul Finch had finished his work for today.

'Scholastic a' he'd say to anyone who would listen or to anyone who asked that he work overtime.

'I am relieved of labour.' He wasn't in any way certain that this was an accurate translation from the Greek but he thought it unlikely he'd come across anyone on a building site who would contradict him. He would tell anyone who would listen that the root of the English word scholar comes directly from the Greek. If you use your mind, you didn't have to labour. Paul Finch's mind then, was not as sharp as he would have liked to think it was because at the age of fifty he was still labouring.

'A work in progress' he'd say.

Half–way along lower St. James's is an expensive and very pretentious bar fitted-out in cream leather, chrome and mirrors. The brass plaque by the plate glass door bears the name 'Laskeys' and nothing else. Its décor, its staff and its prices could be designed to discourage the likes of Paul Finch. There were many places in London where his hard earned cash would not be good enough and he took a peculiar delight in finding them and breaking their pretentious rules. He brushed all the dust he could from his deliberately saw-dust coloured clothes, swaggered through the door and along a ten metre long corridor lined with unframed modernist paintings, into the bar. He mounted a stool and ordered a large Jim Beam with ice from the polite and efficient barman who, if he had formed an opinion about Paul on account of his appearance, he was at least professionally and possibly graciously, not letting Paul know. Paul was aware that he didn't fit in to this place and aware that the clientele would be altogether different from him, but he liked that. Besides, there was nothing waiting for him at his tiny flat in Pimlico. Paul left the change from his tenner on the little chrome tray as a tip.

An act that did not go unnoticed by the young barman.

After the second large Jim Beam with ice had been carefully placed on the cardboard mat in front of him together with some cashew nuts in another tiny silver bowl, Paul Finch saw reflected in the mirror behind the bar a tall, slim, heavily made up woman with short bleached blond hair. He guessed she was in her mid-forties. She was in the process of perching herself on the bar stool next to his. Dressed in a grey woollen, figure hugging dress, her lips, nails and high heeled shoes were all the same shade of pillar box red. His first assessment of her was that she was a prostitute. As she settled herself on the barstool her mobile phone rang. She looked briefly at the screen, silenced the ringing and placed it on the bar on top of another cardboard bar mat. She dropped an oversized handbag containing papers and magazines on the floor beside the stool and asked for a Jack Daniels and diet coke. Paul glanced at the papers sticking out of her handbag. *Not on the game then.* He thought. *You don't generally carry paper work with you in that job.* Paul looked at her in the mirror behind the bar as he swirled the ice around in his drink. He hoped she would notice how suave he was when he nodded at the Barman and without saying a word got a refill. After three quarters of an hour and four more rounds, Jill O'Keefe had become positively exasperated by Paul Finch's complete failure to make any attempt at conversation. Not to mention a little tipsy. She was doing all the right things. *After forty five minutes you'd have thought he'd say something to me. We're the only people in here for chrissakes and I sat right next to him.* Jill had never had a problem attracting the attention of men in bars and she wasn't about to lower her batting average on Paul's account. *Sod it.* She thought, looking at him in the reflection of the mirror, she waited until he caught her eye and asked lamely,

"So you are what, a carpenter or something?"

Although Paul had been checking her out from the moment she had walked through the door, had wondered what kind of woman she was, whether she was on her own or if she was meeting someone and among a mass of other questions if she might be on the game, he would never have made the first move. Paul Finch thought it was rude to invade a woman's personal space without an invitation. But now he had an invitation.

"No" He said. Looking back at her in the mirrored bar back. "What makes you think I'm a carpenter?"

"Because you're covered in sawdust. I'm surprised that he let you in here." She said nodding towards the barman.

"Appearances can be deceptive." He replied. Still conducting the conversation through the curiously playful third party that was the mirror. "It's been a long day."

Something about this woman was familiar. Nothing about her appearance though. It was her voice, he decided. He'd heard it before and he tried to place it but he couldn't. Their glasses were empty so Paul, without asking, ordered another Jim Beam and another Jack Daniels and Diet Coke.

So he has been paying attention. Jill said to herself and smiled.

Now she knows I've been paying attention. Paul said to himself and smiled. For a second or two they were both unintentionally grinning at each other in the mirror.

"If you're not a carpenter then what are you?" Said Jill, giving the comment a little twist of flirtatious body movement by twisting on her bar-stool slightly towards him.

"That's a question I often ask myself." He said, clinking the ice cubes around in his glass.

"Do you ever give yourself an answer?" The drinks were put in front of them and another till receipt was placed under Paul's silver tray.

"I like to write."

"Really?" She said. "It's a hobby, right. You make your living as a carpenter." Jill said this as a matter of fact and immediately regretted doing so. There was a momentary silence. *Oh God, why would I say that? I'm supposed to know nothing about this man.* She was relieved when Paul answered her assuming it to be a question.

"I suppose that sooner or later I'll have to acknowledge that that is the case, yes." For the first time Paul turned to face Jill and smiled a longer, charming, resigned, and worldly smile. Jill was slightly taken aback. She wasn't expecting that and she spent just a moment too long looking at his face. There was a warmth in his eyes that surprised her. She reached down towards her voluminous handbag and struggled to pull it up onto her lap. She searched inside and while doing so, let a folded copy of Private Eye fall onto the floor. Paul had to get off his stool to retrieve it. As he picked it up he knew what it was and he became excited as a kid at Christmas.

"You're a reader?" He asked, putting the magazine on the bar.

"I get it from time to time." She said. "I'm a bit of a lightweight I'm afraid. I like the Celeb cartoon and the lonely hearts."

"Listen." Said Paul with a big smile on his face. "I've got a confession to make."

"You're gay?" Blurted Jill. She was smiling and she couldn't help it. It just fell out. Helped along the way by Jack Daniels. Paul's head retracted on his neck and his lips went tight.

"No." He replied. The pitch of this little word going from low to high. Jill was on the verge of giggling. "Is that what you thought?" He said.

"Well you sat there for ages without saying a word to me."

"So any geezer who doesn't try to chat you up is gay then is he?" Paul is faking his indignation.

"Keep your hair on kid. I's only joshing. Anyway I knew you weren't. My gaydar is usually bang on."

"I didn't talk to you because…" He paused.

"Go on" She chided him, intrigued and amused in equal measure thinking she might know what he is about to say.

"I thought you might be a professional." He blurted out.

"So any single female in a bar is a hooker now?" Jill was faking her indignation nearly as well as Paul had.

"Keep your hair on Kid" Paul mimicked Jill's response. "I was only joshing."

"No you weren't." She said. "You really thought…" She was cut short by Paul calming her with a wave of his hands.

"No. Look." He said "No-one with all those papers…" He pointed to her handbag, "could be… could be in…in that field."

As soon as he had said it he knew he was digging himself into a hole. He should have just kept his thoughts to himself but in his case Jim Beam was providing the encouragement for him not to.

"So you thought I was a business woman who looks like a prostitute? That's good. Makes me feel a whole load better."

"No," Said Paul. "In the time you were sitting there I thought a lot of things about you. You looked very…. interesting." He knows this is lame. He knows she knows this is lame so the last word was drawn out longer than it needed to be to let her know he knows that she knows.

"Oh yeah" Said Jill, not letting him off the hook quite so easily. "What kind of interesting?"

"Well funny thing is," he said doing a poor but passable impression of a theatrically camp redcoat. "Funny thing is I was wondering," he couldn't keep it up and came out of character, changing to a serious face and moving his head a tiny bit towards hers. "I was wondering if you were a Private Eye reader."

Jill saw an expression of mirth on Paul's face but she suddenly felt a pang of guilt. She knew loads about this man. Well loads of facts anyway but the reports had not prepared her for this. She doesn't read the damn Private Eye, she'd just been told about Celeb and the lonely hearts by Benson and Ian.

"That was going to be my confession before you started to question my sexual persuasion. It's sad I know but... I'm what they call a private Eye completest. I've got every single copy, well nearly. All except for three editions from the early days and one elusive copy from the seventies.' Jill had to feign interest. What she really wanted to say was 'Yes I know' but she couldn't. What she said was,

"You must be one sad bastard." Jill was shaking her head slowly and the vaguest of smiles told him she liked him. For reasons that later she would not be able to explain she tapped her smart phone a few times severing the private connection to Benson who was waiting in a car parked in a taxi rank around the corner. Paul would have had no idea that those party to their conversation up until that point were not restricted to the occupants of the bar. She tried to think how to get back to the script but she needn't have worried.

"Listen." Said Paul, emboldened by her and still with a big smile on his face. "We all have our crosses to bear." He shuffled on his stool. "Private Eye is a distillation of all I hope for. All the anger and outrage is there, hopes I have that things will change and get better are there, nothings masquerading as somethings that might just be exposed as nothings are there. Then they've got cartoons that say really important things in such a glib and noncommittal way, and it's all printed on cheap paper and you can be party to their labours, party to their fruitless cause twice a month for a quid a time. They are the underdogs. They'll never win coz they don't toe the line." Paul paused his lecture and swivelled on his bar stool and smiled at the barman, who had been listening to the conversation. The barman quickly resumed appearing to be busy. He didn't have a clue what Ian was banging on about. He was only a youngster. He'd never heard of Private Eye.

Jill had told Benson, that on this occasion she didn't want close surveillance. She'd handle this part of the operation. She was glad she did. Her knowledge of the 'The subject' was based on information provided by the services of Benjamin Hall Associates. The information contained in the report was quite detailed and personal. In the short time she had been in his company, this 'opinionated and possibly deranged self-obsessive' though, seemed nothing like the person Benson had described. Neither Benson nor Ian had liked the idea of her going it alone. They had an idea where Paul might end up because every day, for two weeks previously, regular as clockwork, he had left work at 4pm. According to Benson's reports he'd walk up St James's street and along Piccadilly, past the Ritz to the tube at Green Park, travel the two stops south to Pimlico and go straight into his local for early doors. There had been no mention previously of him popping into Laskeys for a quick one and it would have been the last place they would have imagined he would go. So Jill, as soon as she got the call from Benson, had to change her clothes from the casual look she'd prepared for a local pub in Pimlico to the look she wanted in a fancy west end bar. Ian had wanted to be close too, 'for research purposes,' he'd said. She'd immediately vetoed that suggestion too. The previous morning, Benson had shown her a particularly good impression of an American tourist complete with checked trousers and a rucksack and tried to convince her that he could easily blend into the background in a London pub but Jill was having none of it.

In the end they compromised with Benson loading up a listening ap on her iPhone. The phone would appear as if it were in sleep mode but would covertly be transmitting whatever was in ear shot to whoever had rung the number. It would continue to do this until it was switched off or the battery died.

Two and a half hours after Benson had dropped her off, Jill returned to where the car had been waiting around the corner and asked Benson to drive slowly along Piccadilly towards the entrance to the tube. She wanted to see that Paul Finch at least made it that far.

"Why did you turn off the baby monitor Jill?" Said Benson before starting the engine.

"Did I?" She said in a deliberately recalcitrant tone. "Sorry I didn't notice." Benson carefully pulled out from a parking space in the side street before turning onto Piccadilly.

"You know Benny," said Jill, turning her head to watch Paul Finch drunkenly but competently take the final few steps on the flat pavement before ducking down the stairs to the station, "Your report was very thorough." She paused a second wondering if she should continue.

"I hear a 'but' coming." Said Benson as he accelerated along Piccadilly.

"It's just odd," she said. "That's all. Odd that the facts never tell the whole story."

"I did warn you about this you know. If you're going to indulge yourself in this kind of skulduggery, be prepared to hear things you don't want to hear." He said.

In the few weeks she had known Benson, she had come to understand that the relationship would not be an easy one. Among his annoying traits, Benson had a need beyond anyone she'd come across before, to be right. Down even to the most insignificant details. He had an inability to listen to what was said to him, as if his own world was the only one that mattered. Ask him a question, and he'd answer a different one. The one he wanted to answer. He would interject in the middle of a conversation by raising his hand like a traffic policeman and rudely stop a discussion in its tracks. Jill wanted to slap the top of his balding head when he did this.

"No Benny, I've not heard anything I didn't want to hear. I know his family history better than he does including his real name. I know the state of his finances. I know about his personal habits." She stopped briefly again suddenly conscious of the fact that the drink may be doing too much of the talking. She continued all the same. "The camera in the bathroom may have been a step across the line."

"With respect Jill," Said Benson, meaning with no respect whatsoever, "You stepped across the line the moment you asked me to do the job." his tone was belligerent. He was obviously smarting from her going against his rules. Jill threw him an angry look which he didn't see. He was looking right at a junction and was thinking that it didn't really matter what he said to her or how he said it. She wouldn't remember in the morning. He was as wrong about that as he would be about many things in the weeks to come. She decided to play him at his own game and continue as if he'd not said anything.

"I'm saying you're in no position to be passing judgement." She said.

"Well whatever. If you ask me, which I thought was one of the things you're paying me for, I thought he was a loser."

"We're paying you to provide information. Not opinions. But that's what I mean. You've never actually met him. You've only seen him through a lens and yet you've formed such strong opinions."

"Fair point, well made." Said Benson in a voice that only he would not recognise as being patronising. Jill had had enough of him this evening. She wasn't sure if she'd done the right thing in engaging him. Ricky had been very convincing telling her that he was the best in the business and that he would be able to obtain any information about anyone and that he was someone who you definitely want on your side. She knew Ricky had some strange friends and employed some even stranger people but she mostly trusted Ricky's judgement. They all needed a way to get Paul Finch to play their game. It was decided unanimously though, that in order to preserve the authenticity and the spontaneity Paul Finch must not know that he is the player in their play. He should not know of the plan. None of them should. None of the players should know. Paul and the others must be drawn in without knowing. It must appear to be their idea. So when the first report from Benson contained the snippet of information that he was an avid reader and collector of Private Eye, they decided to put an ad in the personals. In fact the idea to place an ad in Private Eye came from Ricky. The first one elicited no response. At least not from Paul Finch. He saw it though and it was just as well they had persevered. The second Ad worked. He had responded with a curt note and it was time for Jill to call him and put a proposal to him.

"Where are we going?" asked Jill as they drove up Park Lane towards Marble Arch.

"Your boyfriend's waiting back at the office. He wanted a de-brief." Jill shook her head. "No, No. It's far too late now. Take me home will you I'm tired. We'll get together in the morning...and he's not my boyfriend."

"As you wish." Said Benson flicking the stalk control on the steering column and activating the mobile phone. "He'll be disappointed." The phone rang on the car's hands free. Two rings and Ian answered.

"Hi Man," said Benson. "We're aborting the de-brief for tonight. The boss is tired and emotional."

"Ian, Babe." Jill butted in. "It's late. I'll see you in the office in the morning."

Benson made a U-turn and returned down Park Lane. Twenty silent minutes later they were outside Jill's house in Wandsworth. Without another word to Benson, she pushed the door of the Mercedes shut and climbed the four steps to her front door. Parked across the street unnoticed by her, in a line of parked cars, was a black Chrysler voyager. The two occupants were only just visible in silhouette through the windscreen as Benson pulled away up the street.

13

"The car is registered on a diplomatic plate. Jill," said Benson, the following morning, in a condescending –I told-you- so manner. "Attached to the Libyan Embassy. Anybody like to tell me why that might be?" He was stepping around the boardroom apparently trying not to stand on the joints between the carpet tiles.

"Would you mind keeping quiet 'till this thing's done its job." Hedges, who was sitting at the head end of a boardroom table, said without lifting his head. He was tapping at the keys of an open laptop. "Two minutes."

Jill, sitting on a leather high backed office chair at the other end of the table continued to leaf through a copy of Hello Magazine. A heavy knock on the door made them all jump a little. The visitor didn't wait for an invitation.

"Coffee everyone," said Bernice, as she pushed through the door of the room. Hedges slowly shook his head and raised his eyes to the ceiling before getting up with a smile and taking the tray from Bernice.

"Let me help you with that." He said.

"Everyone," Said Jill with a sigh, "Meet Bernice, my secretary." Ian, Benson and Hedges all nodded a polite hello.

"Wow." said Bernice. "Serious faces in here."

"Yes" Said Jill. "Bernice. Would you see that we're not disturbed... by anyone." She threw her a confirming nod.

"Certainly will." Said Bernice as she made back towards the door. She turned around to further examine the strangers in the room, looking them up and down quickly.

"Just call if you need anything."

"Will do," said Jill "Thank-you Bernice."

"Oh it's nothing." She said. Smiling at each one of the men in turn. Before shutting the door behind her. It was Jill's turn to slowly shake her head.

"Okay." Hedges called, having returned to look at the screen of the laptop. "Looks pretty clear in here. We've just got to watch the WIFI Jill. I'll need to get on to your server before we go. Make a couple of changes to the security settings." He went to the tray and picked up a large cardboard cup of coffee.

"As I was saying." Benson continued. "Libyan Embassy anyone?" He was looking directly at Jill.

"I've got no idea why a car from the Libyan Embassy would be parked outside my house. This is the middle of London. Could just be coincidence."

"Could be but I doubt it." Said Hedges picking up the laptop and walking round the table. He placed it in front of Jill and turned it around so that she could see the screen. Ian woke from his daydream and got up from the black leather couch he was sitting on and strolled toward the table. All four of them were leaning over the laptop. The screen was filled by an aerial photograph. As Hedges pressed the keys that magnified the image Jill and Ian became aware that the picture was of the building they were in. As the image zoomed in Hedges moved the cursor to a black oblong shape sitting by the curb opposite the side entrance to the building.

A blinking red dot singled it out among the other dark oblong shapes.

"Is that in real-time?" Asked Ian. Benson nodded. "How the hell do you do that?"
Benson didn't answer the question. Jill was beginning to think that the smug look that was on his face was the only one he had.

"When I saw the car in the road last night, Jill, It looked suspicious for some reason. Don't ask me why. They always do. They stand out like sore thumbs to be honest. They're a bit like kids who go shoplifting. They just don't look like real punters and they're the only ones who can't see it."

"You saw the car, did you? I didn't see anything." Said Jill, immediately regretting it.

"That's why I do this and you do what you do." He pointed at his eyes with two fingers in a vee shape. "Anyway, I parked up along the street and went back. They just assumed I was a cab I suppose. They paid no attention to me. I knocked on the window to ask for a cigarette. Just flicked a softball in through the window."

"A softball?" Ian repeated.

"Our own design." Benson said proudly nodding towards Hedges and flicking a small furry ball onto the table. "Stands for Sort of Furry Transmitter. Clever name don't you think?"
It rolled towards Ian who picked it up between his thumb and forefinger. "It's a short range locator bug. Enough battery to last for 24 hours in darkness. More if it falls into direct sunlight then it can fire itself up again. Photoelectric cells underneath the fur."

"So is the same car that was outside my place... here?" Jill pointed at the blinking dot on the screen... "Now?"

"I believe," said Benson walking towards the window and loving the performance. "I believe that the little furry ball I flicked onto the back seat of that Chrysler last night is still sitting there." He looked down from the third floor window and pointed towards the street. The three others all moved towards the window and looked down.

A black Chrysler was parked across the street.

"I don't know what either of you is going to tell us shortly, but…" Benson started. Ian Butted in,

"Don't include me in that, I've not got a clue."

"Let me tell you what we do know." It was Hedges' turn to take the floor. He stood with his arms crossed and with his back to the window half sitting on the window sill.

"The people in that car are interested in you for some reason but they've not got that interested yet because if they were and they were doing their job properly, they'd know that a bug is transmitting their location from inside the car. The tools for detecting something as old school as that are cheap as chips. So, we can surmise that they imagine they are looking at what we in the business call a 'neet'. An innocent mark. Someone who is unaware they are being watched. It's the opposite of a 'Teen'. A 'Teen' is someone who imagines that they are being constantly watched and takes appropriate precautions. Everyone in the business should be a 'Teen'. Our friends downstairs in the car are not doing their job very well. They should be 'Teens' but they are lazy. They have assumed we are 'Neets'. Anyone who is in the game," he gestured toward Benson, "should always assume that they too are being looked at. It's just the nature of the beast." Hedges looked around at the other three. They all had puzzled looks on their faces.

"Can you see what I'm getting at?" He asked. They all nodded their heads but the puzzled expressions didn't change.

Benson took over.

"Last night when I left you. The car in question," he gave an exaggerated thumbs down sign, "stayed where it was for maybe an hour. For all I know they were monitoring your internet browsing or your mobile phone calls. Did you make any calls last night Jill? Did you surf the net on your laptop?" Jill shook her head. "Anyway after about an hour it pulled away and I followed at a distance. It went to a large house in Belgravia. The house is a mysterious one. According to my sources it is owned by the Libyan government. Can you think of any reason why the Libyan government would be interested in you, Jill?"

"No." said Jill. "I can't and I'm beginning not to like this. "Maybe we should just call off the whole thing. We'll get Ian to write a book about something else."

Hedges looked at Benson with a quizzical look.

"A book?" He said. "Is that what all this is for? A book?"

Jill pointed at Hedges while addressing Benson.

"You haven't told him why we are doing this. Have you?"

"Better get on with it," said Hedges, "otherwise I'm out of here."

"They're writing a book." Said Benson apologetically.

"A book." Hedges repeated. "You're using us to write a book." He tried to weigh up the consequences of this.

"This is Ian Whitting, he wrote Seven Days in Iraq and several others." Jill informed Hedges. Hedges looked at everyone in turn. They were all looking at him waiting for a reaction. A wry grin spread across his face.

"What and 'The Western Connection' and 'Bog Rats'?" Said Hedges.

"That's me." Ian nodded, trying to hide his self-pride at someone knowing of his work. Hedges kept looking around at each of them.

"So let me get this right. We've been engaged to provide security for you while you write a book?"

"Not exactly." Said Jill.

"What exactly then." Said Hedges his tone well short of belligerent but a long way from his calm measured self.

"Well more of a research nature. We'd been told that you are the best in the business at what you do." Said Jill.

"Do you know what we do? No. I'll rephrase that. Do you know what it is that I am supposed to be best in the business at?" Said Hedges.

"Spying." Said Jill innocently with a shrug of her shoulders, "information. Getting hold of information." Hedges shook his head. He walked over to the table and picked up a coffee cup.

"Who put you on to us Jill? Who put you on to me?" Before Jill could answer Benson butted in.

"You know better than that Hedge mate, I've done some private work for the publishers before, that's all we need to know." Hedges could tell there was more to it. True, he never normally needed to know who the paymaster was. He was just for hire. But that was when the paymasters were big business or government or military. This was different. These people were civilians, and it was obvious they knew nothing about what they were getting themselves involved in. As it happened neither did he. Yet. But he was sure that the Libyan Secret Service were not going to get themselves involved if Jill O'Keefe hadn't paid a parking fine.

"Jill." Said Hedges. His tone gentle. "In my experience of these matters, which is... broad," he said without sounding boastful, "if a government agency has got you in their sights, it won't be you who can 'call the whole thing off." Hedges walked towards the window flicking a forefinger towards Benson for him to do the same. He whispered in Benson's ear so that Jill and Ian could not hear.

"Sure you know what you're doing?" He said. Benson nodded.

"Rates as normal?" Benson smiled and pushed his own mouth closer to Hedges' ear.

"Better." He whispered. Hedges turned and headed back to his employers.

"Okay, so we're writing a book. Great. Still work is work." He clapped and rubbed his hands together. "And we're in charge of... getting information." His tone was brighter. Maybe falsely brighter but the serious and formal façade he had been hiding behind had dropped off a little to reveal a happier and less tense Hedges. He stepped forward a pace or two to where Ian was sitting back on his high backed office chair with his hands behind his head. He took Ian a little by surprise. They hadn't really been introduced.

"The elusive Ian Whitting eh." Said Hedges. Holding out his hand. Ian had to abruptly sit up in his chair and hold out his hand which Hedges grasped. "I'm a big fan," he said. "Big fan." Ian smiled broadly again. Hedges returned a little to his earlier self.

"So let's get on with this?" Hedges said to the three of them. Including Benson in his gaze, "I don't know how much you know, how much they know," he pointed to the window, "or how much you want us to know." He nodded towards Benson. "What I do know is that information is the valuable commodity here. The more we know about what you know the better we can do the job you are going to ask us to do." He nodded at them all for agreement. "Yes?"

Looking bemused again Jill and Ian slowly nodded in agreement at Hedges' prompt. "So tell me what you know."

"I've got the bones of a back story here. That's all." Said Jill. "I'd rather not go into what that story is about if you don't mind, but Ian here is going to write the 'what happens next'. That's about it." She pulled a file from her handbag and slid it across the table towards Hedges. "This is the summary of what has happened so far." Hedges opened the file and saw on the top a copy of Private Eye. There were five or six pages of copied paper beneath the magazine. He closed the file again.

"Can I take this?" He asked. Jill nodded a 'yes'. Hedges turned to Benson. "Do you know what's in this?" Benson also nodded a 'yes'.

"We need to move on to what happened before all that last night." Benson said. "With Finch." Ian had moved back towards the window. "In view of the changed circumstances."

"Can we refer to him as Paul and what change of circumstances are you talking about?" Jill interrupted. Benson who had been stepping between the joins of the carpet tiles swivelled on his heel.

"Jill, have you not been listening." He pointed to Hedges who was back in front of the laptop. "The situation has changed slightly due to the intervention of the Libyan Secret Service." Jill nodded in a tired way. Ian who was standing by the window surveying the street below piped up. "Children." He said referring to everybody in the room.

"Three blokes have just got out of that car." Benson and Hedges bolted to the window. They both got there to see three men looking distinctly sinister, all dressed in dark clothes, standing on the pavement looking furtively around beside the car. At the nodded command of a small thin man who got out of the front passenger seat they split up. Two of the men walked towards the front of the building and the other two walked across the road into the side entrance.

"They're not going to fall for the same tricks again." Said Benson.

"What d'you mean fall for the same trick?" Asked Ian.

"Is there something you're not telling *us*?" Benson and Hedges were agitated.

"C'mon." Said Hedges ignoring Ian. "We've gotta get out of here." He turned to Hedges. "Escape plan?" Hedges shook his head.

"Never thought they'd be that keen." He replied.

Hedges turned to Jill.

"Do you know of any other way out of here other than the lifts and the main stairs?" Jill shook her head.

"There's a fire exit on the other side of the building." She suggested.

"There are four of them. They'll have done their homework. They'll have all the ways down covered." Said Hedges.

Benson was beginning to panic, Jill could see it in his eyes. There was definitely something they had not told them. Hedges remained looking calm.

"Listen, it may be just us they are looking for. I can't think how they would know about you guys but we can't take any chances. We all need to get out of here now. Any suggestions seriously considered." Jill had an idea.

"I know." She said, "All these buildings are on a terrace. They are doing some renovation work in the Royal College of Surgeons. It's three buildings along and covered in scaffolding. We'd need to get on the roof."

Ian shook his head. "You never go up when you want to go down." He said as if reciting from some kind of training manual. "You just narrow down your options." Hedges shook his head and quickly returned to the laptop. He zoomed the picture out to encompass the tops of the surrounding buildings.

"Ok." He said. "Quick review. We either narrow down our options and go up to the roof and hope there is a route down." His finger traced a line on the screen. "Or we stay here and fight those four goons with..." He looked furtively around for something... anything. "These pencils." He picked up a pencil from a holder on the big table.

"Up." Said Benson. "How do we get there?"

Jill rushed towards the door. "This way." Outside in the glass walled corridor they all ran towards an emergency exit. Bernice who was sitting at her reception desk eating a pastry looked up. Hedges stopped as he passed her. She looked at him with a mouthful and attempted to smile through the whipped cream.

"Bernice." He said calmly. "Lovely to meet you. Do us a favour. If four men dressed in black come looking for us could you tell them that no-one's been in all morning." Bernice who had temporarily stopped chewing nodded affirmatively.

"Thanks." Said Hedges. "Oh and thanks for the coffee." These last words made him stop in his tracks. He shouted to the others who had opened the door to the fire escape.

"You go ahead. I'll catch up." He rushed back to the meeting room and gathered together the cardboard coffee cups and the laptop. He once again rushed out of the office and dumped the cups in a waste basket in the hall and as he passed Bernice's desk passed her the laptop.

"Look after this will you?" He said with a wink. "I owe you." Bernice took the laptop. She still had the remnants of her pastry in the corner of her mouth. She smiled again with her mouth closed but said nothing. Hedges ran to the fire exit and gingerly opened the heavy door. He stepped through and heard the sound of footsteps below him on the white concrete stairwell. Then he heard the hiss of static from a two way radio. He looked carefully over the banister in the middle of the stairs. He could see nothing. The static on the radio was quickly silenced but he could still hear the faint footsteps coming from below. *He must be only on the floor directly underneath,* He thought. *Can't go up now. He* stood still and silent against the white concrete wall listening for movement on the staircase below. He went through his options. If the guy was one of the two that they had come across in the hospital he would be extra wary. Not to mention pissed off. If it wasn't one of them, but it was an associate, he'd have been well briefed about what to expect. Hedges still hadn't a clue as to why they were being followed. Why Jill was being followed. What did they want? His question was answered at least in part by the unmistakable wisp of a silenced firearm. The bullet was not so quiet though as it ricocheted around the concrete walls of the stairwell. It appeared, spinning, on the floor by his feet, its energy absorbed by the hard concrete walls. He had intuitively covered his face and eyes and crouched to form as small a target as possible the moment he heard the sound from the gun. It was a random shot. It must have been. Not very professional. The bullet must have bounced around the walls half a dozen times but the space was once again quiet. He tried to regulate his breathing by blowing air slowly out of his lungs. This was proving difficult as a random bullet ricocheting around your head tends to raise the heart-rate somewhat. He stayed where he was and listened. He listened for any discernible signal but there was nothing coming from below him. Had the gunman left, disguising his footsteps downward with the shot. No.

He couldn't justify that scenario. He hadn't heard anything more than the whisper from the muzzle of the gun and the six or seven, yes, he counted them through in his mind, seven ricochets. The time taken from the moment the gun was fired to the bullet coming to rest at his feet was two maybe three seconds. He was five floors up. The gunman could not have run down without him hearing. Each flight would have taken two seconds to complete. Shit Shit Shit he thought. If he was not still below, which he might have been, he must have just slipped out the door to the staircase on the floor below. His mind suddenly turned to Bernice the secretary. She must have heard the noise of the bullet rattling around the stairwell. She was a nosey type. She would want to know what was going on. She could appear at the door at any moment. The gunman could feasibly still be standing just feet below him and have a good line of sight to the top of the door. Bernice would be shot at if she were to poke her head through to see where the noise had come from. It had been forty seconds since the shot was fired. Her curiosity could get the better of her any time now and even if she cautiously opened the door it would be a signal for the man below to make a move. He could be doing exactly the same as he was. Just waiting for a signal. The faintest sound that would give him enough information to know what to do next. He estimated a minute had now passed since the shot. As quietly as he could and still crouching he turned his back to the wall. The door to the offices was on his right hand. He lifted his arm and grabbed the long tubular steel column that was the door handle. The door opened outwards. He would lock it with his arm. Hold it rigid against the door-frame. He crouched in this position for a further minute. He noticed again the bullet on the floor six inches away from his left shoe. He carefully touched it to test its temperature. Although it was still hot it had cooled enough for him to pick it up and put it in the pocket of his black Harrington jacket.

Another minute passed. He almost counted it out in heartbeats. His breathing had steadied to a slightly less frantic pace. His mind was no less frantic though. What of the others? Had Benson led Jill and Ian to safety across the rooftops like they planned? He would have to take the initiative soon and get them help. Benson just thought he was good at this stuff. He'd read too many stories, but it wasn't like this in the stories. Bravery and instinct and courage and strength were no match for training and experience and skill when you were actually dealing with a man with a real lethal weapon in his hands. He slid slowly up the wall keeping a firm hold on the door handle. He'd give it thirty more heartbeats. What he would do after thirty more heartbeats he hadn't a clue. It occurred to him that in the heat of the moment no amount of training, experience and skill had prepared him for this and that he was relying on bravery and instinct for a clue as to what he did at the end of those thirty heartbeats. He made a mental note to be easier on the oaf that was Benny Wright. He liked this last thought a lot. It showed he still had some confidence that he would get out of here. He was listening so intently to any sound that might be coming from the landing below him that a second or two passed before he registered noises coming from the offices behind the heavy door he was holding shut. Muffled screams and the sound of furniture being thrown over. He was right. At least in one of his conjectures. The geezer had gone down and come up another way. He turned and yanked open the door. Another wisp of the silenced gun and this time a bullet bored a neat hole on the entrance side of the two inch thick fire-door and exploded out the other side. He dropped to the ground and pulled the bullet out of his jacket pocket and tossed it on the floor as the door was closing shut on its sprung loaded closer. The bullet acted as a door-stop and wedged the door firmly about a foot from being closed. He looked out from as low a vantage point as he could manage. He could see below the reception desk two pairs of feet. A pair of silver stiletto heeled shoes over black nylon tights and a pair of black training shoes and black jeans. He had to act now. Muffled but hysterical screaming told Hedges that the gunman had grabbed Bernice with his hand over her mouth. He could also see by their feet that Bernice was putting up a fight. Hedges shouted at the top of his voice.

"Leave the girl alone. We can talk." In the background he could hear there were other people. Other workers in the offices were starting to panic. Female screams, the sudden movement of chairs and furniture, male voices barking orders of 'get down'. Hedges showed himself an inch at a time. He knew he'd have only fractions of a second to take in the situation and make a move. As it happened the move was initiated by Bernice. She really couldn't have timed it better if she had been coached. He saw the gunman's eyes close briefly as Bernice simultaneously stamped one stilettoed foot hard down onto the man's instep and ferociously bit the hand that was unnecessarily, Hedges thought, clamped over her mouth. The gunman's aim in the general direction of the door-frame was compromised by Bernice's actions and another high velocity bullet shattered the Perspex ceiling panels and took out a concealed light fitting. Hedges took his chance and in the half second or two it took him to leap the four yards toward the reception desk he reverted to his original view that training was better than courage. He kept his eyes wide open, focusing on the gun and the man's eyes. He wanted to apologise to Bernice even as he was in mid leap across the desk. His left hand was going to grasp the wrist of the hand the gun was in if it was the last thing he did.

    To his relief he fulfilled at least this objective.
    Bernice, showing more natural timing, ducked the six inches she needed to avoid the full force of fifteen stones of Hedges arching above her. Hedges eyes were still wide open up to the moment his forehead impacted with the forehead of the man with the gun. Behind the reception desk was a coloured Perspex wall that held the three foot high letters that made up the name of the firm, PPS. The letters were lit from behind by LED lights. The two men crashed violently into the wall. The force of Hedges flinging himself across the reception was enough to temporarily overpower the gunman. They landed on the nylon carpeted floor and against the Perspex wall in a random heap except for two hands, Hedges right locked around the gunman's right. Much to Hedges disgust he landed with

his mouth on the man's right ear. He could feel the stubble of at least a day's growth. He hated himself for it but as he was taught long ago, needs must as the devil drives, and bit the man's ear hard. He had the upper hand in more ways than one and in a move that was familiar to him grasped the man's bollocks with his free hand and squeezed. The gunman let out a high pitched squeal, like a teenage girl would when opening a present. Hedges held on fast with both his hands and his teeth. The two men writhed about on the floor beneath the coloured Perspex wall when Hedges heard a dull thud right next to his ear. The gunman took a second or two to go limp, the energy in him ebbing slowly away. Hedges found himself lying on top of what he thought might be a dead body. He didn't release his grip on any part of the man though. Just in case. As the seconds rolled on he tested for further indications of the man's condition. He could still hear a heartbeat but there was no movement. He released his jaws from the man's ear first and turned his head slowly round. He saw two feet. One in a silver stiletto shoe and one just shod in nylon tights. A round red tube lowered itself to the ground beside his head. He looked upwards from his prone position on the floor on top of the gunman to see Bernice standing there slightly lopsided with one hand holding the top of a fire extinguisher and the other tightly covering her mouth. Her make-up had ran around her eyes causing black streaks to run down her cheeks and the neat tight bun that her hair had been rolled into had half fallen off the top of her head. Hedges smiled at her. It was all he could think of to do and behind her hand she smiled back a reactive frightened smile. Hedges watched as the gun fell out of the gunman's hand and drop the three inches to the floor.

14

The Crystal Hotel on the north eastern outskirts of the city of Casablanca, Morocco is a cube of white concrete and glass. It sits in a position overlooking the Atlantic Ocean, directly under the flight path of all the tourist jets that bring holidaymakers to the airport less than four kilometres away. An inch thick plate glass wall runs around the entire building to a height of four storeys. In front of the hotel on the ocean side is a swimming pool surrounded by a landscaped embankment. The embankment and the heavy planting of Palm trees attempts to disguise from visitors the fact that they have booked to stay in a hotel popular with plane spotters. To the side of the swimming pool is a car park. At 7.15am and timed to coincide with the sun shining on the hotel's glass façade, thus obscuring the view inside, Ricky Starr, dressed in deck shoes and yachting clothes stepped out of a blue long wheel-base Iveco panel van on the road outside the hotel. He walked the hundred and fifty or so meters past the swimming pool and the palm trees to the two story high, revolving glass door entrance to the hotel. In the car park a silver Mercedes Vito van, with black glass, was parked and looked as if it had been there all night. The sun would soon fill the sky with warmth and bright light. Two minutes after Ricky Starr had entered the hotel the blue Iveco drove into the car park and pulled up twenty paces from the silver Mercedes.

Starr quickly orientated himself and strode toward the reception desk. At the other end of the atrium, fifty paces away from him and bathed in a shaft of early morning sunlight a man sat alone smoking a cigarette at a white marble bar with a small coffee cup in front of him. He was dressed in a beautifully cut navy blue business suit and an open necked white silk shirt. Although the two men were the same age, in a favourable light, Ricky Starr could have passed for being ten years younger. Ricky asked the receptionist for some notepaper and scribbled a brief message. He took a twenty Euro note from a tight roll in his back pocket.

"D'you mind terribly taking this to the man sitting at the bar?" He asked a smartly dressed porter and handed him the note and the money. "The man in the blue suit."

"Si Señor." Replied the porter, nodding, who took the note and the money and walked smartly over to the bar. Ricky watched as the porter passed the note over. Ricky pulled a bleeping smart-phone from the pocket of his gilet, tapped at the screen and immediately looked up and around to the silver van in the car park. Two heavily built if not overweight men had emerged from it. He looked back to the bar where the man in the blue suit was still sipping his coffee. Ricky watched with growing concern as the man, having read the note, didn't appear to react to it. The two men from the Vito were walking purposefully toward the revolving doors of the hotel. Ricky tapped the screen of his smart-phone again and held it to his ear.

"Now." He said quietly. First one of the men appeared to trip and fall to the ground where he rolled down the grassed embankment and came to rest a foot short of the swimming pool. The other man, having broken into a run, veered from his intended path, collided violently with a palm tree and he too fell to the ground. Ricky walked quickly over to the bar.

"Thank heaven for small freedoms." Ricky nodded toward the cigarette as David Crane took a last drag before squashing it into an ashtray. David turned and slid off his barstool in one movement and held out his hand.

"Good morning." He said, looking the stranger up and down. "I hope..." David stared into the stranger's eyes as they shook hands.

"I thought..." He said, hesitating, trying to work out what was happening. "I thought I was meeting..." Again his sentence trailed off in confusion.

"You thought you were meeting a real estate agent Davy." Ricky finished the sentence for him.

"Yes." Said David. "Yes but my name is Gates. Tom Gates." There was something about the stranger now. Something David recognised. Ricky let the cogs slowly turn in David's head but was all too aware of the men outside. They wouldn't have long.

"Yes Davy. It's me. Eamonn." Ricky smiled. They were still shaking hands slowly. "Well. It's Starr these days. Ricky Starr. Remember?" David's grip seemed to tighten and his jaw was hanging open. He had turned pale as if he had seen a ghost. He looked deep into Ricky's eyes. It took what seemed an age but eventually David Crane's face indicated the fact that maybe he was beginning to understand. The expression was still confused but Ricky noted a glimmer of realisation. He couldn't wait any longer.

"C'mon" Ricky nodded his head towards the front door. "Time we got you out of here." He started to walk toward the door.

"You're dead Eamonn. It's been thirty years. Is that all I get?" Rick turned slightly and put a forefinger to his lips.

"Later Davy. C'mon. I'll explain later." He continued walking and David Crane reluctantly followed. Ricky tapped the phone again and whispered 'Go' into it. The blue van parked in the car park started up and drove along the approach ramp towards the doors of the hotel. Several anxious hotel staff were fussing around the entrance having noticed the two men lying like rag dolls in the grounds. As Eamonn and David passed through the revolving doors the van drew up and the side door opened. The attention of the staff was concentrated on the two prostrate men. Ricky motioned for David Crane to get in the van. David briefly turned to see what the cause of the commotion was and saw the two men. Just visible under the chest of one of them he made out the shape of a pistol. Not for the first time in recent weeks fear appeared to drain the blood from the usually ruddy face of David Crane.

"Get in Davy." Ricky whispered again. They both jumped into the dark interior of the van. The electric side door slid smoothly shut as the van turned and made a sedate and unremarkable 10mph down the ramp. The back of the van had two cloth seats along one side in front of a bench made of four by two timber and MDF along the other. Littered throughout the back were the various tools and materials of a builder. These included a stack of breeze blocks by the back door and half a dozen scaffold poles held in place by cable ties lying in a rack in the ceiling. A girl who appeared to David to be no more than nineteen was sitting on one of the seats in front of a laptop computer. There was a bulkhead behind both the driver's and the front passenger's seats. Between the bulkheads was a gap just wide enough to squeeze through. David Crane sat on the nearest of the seats in front of the bench next to the young woman with the laptop. Ricky squeezed through the gap into the front passenger seat.

"Good morning Mr. Gates." The girl closed the lid of the laptop, placed it in a black rubber cover on a shelf under the bench top and pulled out another from the same shelf and opened the lid. The second laptop blinked into life showing a satellite image of a road network.

"Morning," David replied not a little confused. Now he's being called Gates again. He'd been stunned into silence by the sight of the pistol and was in a daze. The van swung around a tight curve onto a main road. The two lane road was busy with the morning traffic but was moving at a fair pace. Through the tinted rear windows of the van David Crane watched as they joined a long line of traffic.

The girl clicked a wireless mouse a few times and the picture on the screen of the laptop zoomed-in to a line of coloured rectangles. In the centre of this line was a blue rectangle a little bigger than most of the others. A small red dot flashed in the middle of it. She clicked the mouse again and the image zoomed-out. The red dot remained in the centre of the screen. Another click and the image zoomed out further. On the edge of the screen another red dot appeared in the centre of a grey rectangle.

"We only got two kilometres on 'em." The girl called through to the front of the van. Ricky's voice came back through from the front.

"That was fast. You only used five didn't you?"

"Five." The girl called back, nodding.

"They were both big men. Ten would have done them no harm and would have got us out of range." Ricky's voice was tinged with frustration but he kept his tone measured.

"Would someone like to tell me..." David started finally as he gathered his thoughts but was cut short as the van swerved out of the slow moving traffic and onto an exit ramp.

"You might like to put on that belt Mr. Gates." The girl with the laptop motioned towards the seatbelt on the rear of the seat. "Katie's a great driver but it doesn't feel like it if you're in the back." Ricky's voice called through from the front again.

"If they follow us up here, we're wired."

"I'll do another sweep." Said the girl with the laptop pulling a black ABS plastic case the size of a shoebox from a ragged looking toolbox under the bench. She opened the box and took a hand-held device that looked like a hairdryer fitted with a diffuser, from its foam padding. She pressed a few buttons and a regular audible bleep started to sound.

"Nothing." She shouted through to the front after a few seconds of waving the instrument around. She looked back to the screen on the laptop.

"They turned onto the exit Dad. They're on to us somehow." Ricky poked his head through the gap.

"How did that happen love? We're supposed to be good at this."

"No idea but we are bugged somewhere. It's gotta be in the upper frequency. I said we should have upgraded this piece of shit." She waved the hair-dryer about in the air.

"Will you be minding your language in front of my friend here Nana." Ricky had squeezed into the back again and crouched on the floor to rummage through a holdall.

"I was saving this for your birthday my darling." He handed her a gift-wrapped six inch cube. David Crane's mouth hung slightly open and he was involuntarily shaking his head. The girl's eyes flicked with excitement as she took the box and ripped off the wrapping paper.

"Let me get this right Aim..." David was straining against his seat belt as they took another curve on what seemed to him to be on two wheels.

"It's Rick or Ricky if you like David." Ricky nodded his head in the direction of the young girl.

"Rick then." Said David. "You hustle me out of a perfectly safe hotel lobby past two dead guys lying on the ground. We are apparently being followed by someone who has planted a bug in your... your builders van here and you're handing out birth...." David was stopped midsentence by a shriek of delight.

"Daddy you are one cool dude. Rhode said this was only a prototype. It's not supposed to be on the street yet." Nana had ripped open the box and having inserted the frame of a tiny umbrella into an instrument the size of a mobile phone pressed a button.

"Give us a hug honey." They both went to hug as the van did another two wheel swerve and the two of them fell heavily onto David Crane. The instrument, still in Nana's out-stretched hand started to make an obviously alarming noise. The three of them attempted to reorganise themselves as the van straightened up.

"Wow Dad, is that saying what I think it's saying." Ricky became suddenly serious.

"Slow down Kate." He called through to the front. The van slowed to a relatively sedate pace.

"No point running now girls. We have to find that bug or they'll follow us home. Get onto it Nana." Ricky called through to the front again.

"Keep a regular forty Kate. Let them catch up. It's time to deploy a bit of Irish tech." Ricky smiled at David.

"It wasn't safe at all Davy and those men are very much alive. C'mon, this'll need your help."

Ricky picked up one of the breeze blocks and with surprising ease threw it toward the side door. He stacked another on top of it. He glanced out of the tinted rear window and saw the silver Mercedes recklessly overtaking cars about a quarter of a mile behind them.

"Davy, press this button when I say so." He motioned toward a red button that operated the sliding side door.

"They're getting closer Dad." A voice came through from the front.

"They mustn't get ahead of us Kate. I need them to try to overtake us on this side."

"No worries." The voice called through. "They're six cars behind. There's a clear stretch up ahead Dad, they'll do it then." Ricky flashed David a proud wink and nodded his head toward the front of the van. A half a minute later the silver Mercedes was approaching fast from behind. The blue van swerved across the dual carriageway to stop it from overtaking.

"Right behind Dad. Soon as I pull across they'll try to overtake."

"Ready yourself Davy, and be sure to hold on."

"Five seconds Dad."

"Okay Davy." David pressed the button and the side door slid open frustratingly slowly, the wind and noise from the road filled the back of the van. The blue van pulled over and the silver Mercedes appeared by the side door. Kate dropped down a gear and accelerated. The Mercedes was left briefly behind but the sound of its engine said the driver had also dropped a gear and it was now storming up to the side door again. Ricky lobbed the breeze blocks one after the other out of the door onto the road and the silver Mercedes rocked as in quick succession the breeze blocks impacted with the underside of the van. The sump of the Mercedes appeared to take the blows and this caused engine oil to trail smoking over the road. The van slowed and gradually came to a halt on the dusty shoulder.

"That's gonna need a service." Katie shouted from the front. Ricky pressed the button that closed the side door and the three of them sat in silence for a moment as gradually the roar from the wind and the road disappeared. David was gripping his seat with both hands and had turned pale. Nana was once again waving her early birthday present around the roof space and the machine was responding by emitting a higher pitch than before.

"It's somewhere up here dad. According to this it's transmitting at 38gig. That's a government frequency."

"We need to pull over and find it. We don't know who else is looking at us. Take the first exit you can Kate."

Ricky called through to the front.

"Check out the black Chrysler 'bout six cars back Dad."

Ricky slid toward the rear windows of the van. A look of frustration and disapproval wrinkled his face.

"They are just so obvious." He said to no-one in particular.

"Rick or Eamonn or whatever you call yourself, what in heaven's name is going on? Who are so obvious?" David Crane's impatient voice filled the back of the van and the woman who was waving the detecting device looked around at him and frowned. Ricky bent down to whisper in David's ear.

"We are being followed, Davy, by some not very pleasant people. No. Correction, Davy. You are being followed by some not very pleasant people and if they get you Davy they will kill you and they'll probably not stop at you. Now please just sit there and be a good boy. And Davy. It's Rick Okay." He raised his eyes toward Nana.

"Who are they?" David couldn't resist.

"Later Davy," Ricky snapped. "Not now."

The voice from the front called back,

"The black Chrysler didn't follow us."

"Don't think we're out of the woods girls. Kate. Take us up to the next town we need a place to look over this thing without being seen. Maybe we can try out the new toy."

They drove through a residential area towards the town of San Carlos. At an intersection they stopped at a red traffic light. Opposite them waiting at the light was another black Chrysler Voyager.

"Stay cool everyone. If they look like they are making a move Kate, floor it, otherwise don't do anything suspicious." The lights changed and the blue van and the black Chrysler passed each other slowly and deliberately.

"There's a bus depot up on the right Dad." Kate's voice came through from the front again.

"If they are out of sight pull into it." Said Ricky. They pulled into the bus garage.

"Over there Kate," Ricky stepped halfway through the bulkhead and pointed to a corner by an office. "And Nana, you jump out and find that bug." Nana opened the side door and jumped out of the slow moving van. The garage was virtually empty of buses and there was not a soul to be seen. Ricky knocked on the office door and went in re-emerging seconds later shaking his head. He jogged to where the van was parked.

"No-one in. Swiftly now. Let's get this sorted. Have you found it yet?" He shouted up to Nana who was now crawling around on the roof of the van with the scanner bleeping.

"It's in the roof-rack tube." She called back. She unscrewed the end of a powder coated steel tube and pulled out an object the size of an AA battery.

"It's only a 3G locator Dad, but it's expensive. If I took it apart I could hack the SIM card."

"No leave it running Nana, take it with you and get on a bus or two. Get to know this town a little for a couple of hours. I'm gonna show my old friend our new toy and we'll meet you back at the boat."

"No worries Daddy." Nana jumped into the back of the van and gathered a small rucksack and a baseball cap and put the battery bug in her jeans pocket. She kissed Ricky on the cheek and waved at David.

"See you shortly." She shouted as she looked carefully up and down the street before disappearing.
Ricky looked at David with the same look of pride as before.
He returned to the side door of the van. "Kate, let's look at that new programme."

David saw for the first time Kate emerge from the driver's seat of the van.

"Hi Mister Gates." She held out her hand. David was a little taken aback as he shook hands with a girl who was the spitting image of the one who had just left.

"Close your mouth Davy. Kate is about four minutes older than Nana. They have their mother's dominant gene." Said Ricky.
David was still staring at Katy and held onto her hand longer than necessary.

"Nice driving." He said.

"Davy," Ricky called from the side door of the van. "Come and see this."
Ricky had opened the lid of yet another laptop computer and was waiting for a programme to load.

"Kate, you're better at it than I am." He handed her the laptop. She tapped a few keys and turned the screen to face the two men. On the screen was a detailed line drawing of the van they had been riding in.

"It works wirelessly from here." Ricky said.

Kate tapped a few more keys and six pictures appeared of the same van, each in a different colour. "Which colour would you like Mr. Gates?"

David looked at the screen.

"Don't call me Mr. Gates, Kate. It's..." He paused. No one had called him David for over thirty years. "...It's David. OK?"

"OK David. Which colour would you like?"

David pointed to a Ferrari Red. Kate tapped at the keyboard and within seconds the entire blue painted surface of the van changed to a bright shiny red.

"Show him the Lennon Rolls that Nana did." Ricky was now in the back of the van starting a small diesel electrical generator. Kate tapped the keyboard again and the van changed colour to the psychedelic paint job of John Lennon's famous Roll Royce.

"It's pretty authentic too." Said Kate. "You can manipulate the artwork in the programme."

"Power's the only drawback," called Ricky from the inside of the van.

"Draws a lot of juice but we're working on that. Now we've got two hours in disguise. C'mon Kate. Make us into a UPS van and we're out of here." Kate tapped again at the laptop and the van changed to a dirty brown colour with the distinct and precise logo of UPS on the side. Even the licence plates were miraculously transformed.

"Pretty cool stuff eh Davy?" Ricky said as Kate drove the van carefully out of the bus garage wearing a beige peaked cap. Ricky and David were perched on the side bench seat in the back.

"Make for the Marina now Kate. I think we're safe." Ricky said.

"We'll find out soon enough Dad." Kate called back from the front. "Bogeys right behind."

Directly behind them the now sinister shape of a black Chrysler Voyager with all round blacked out windows had appeared seemingly out of nowhere. Ricky and David exchanged a knowing look. Maybe it was because he'd run out of options but for the first time since they had met again after all these years Ricky looked terrified. It would have been half a lifetime previously but he'd seen the look before.

"Just keep it cool Kate." Ricky whispered through to the front of the van. The Chrysler began to overtake and draw level with the newly liveried UPS delivery van.

"Cool's my middle name Dad, you know that." She replied. For what seemed an age the sleek black car stayed alongside glinting in the sunlight before turning left down a side street. All the occupants of the van let out an audible sigh of relief.

"We need to pick up some provisions." Said Ricky to no one in particular.

"And I need to know what the hell just happened." Said David Crane.

15

Kate drove the UPS liveried van up through the secure gates of the marina entrance nodding to the guard who opened the barrier without making them stop.

"I'm going to tell Ramon we're leaving, Kate." Said Ricky. It was now mid-afternoon and the sun was high in the sky. "Start getting this stuff out will you Davy."

Ricky got out of the van and walked towards the glass doors of the main marina building.

David, now weary from the drive climbed out. He started to unload the provisions that had been stacked among the builders rubbish. Ricky returned dragging behind him two wheeled trolleys. Ricky's mobile phone rang. He touched the screen and put the phone to his ear.

"Yeah. Hi love...Good...are you sure. Yeah... We are here... Yeah sure... See you in a mo." He touched the face of the phone again and put it back in his pocket.

"Nana's just got here. The bus stops at the end of the road. She'll be here in ten. We'll meet her at the boat." When the trolleys were all loaded Ricky flicked the lock on the van. It turned back to its original blue colour. They started walking along the wooden decking of the marina. Moored to a hammerhead at the end of a long pontoon was an eighty five foot Blue and White Beneteau sailing yacht. "May I introduce you to BabyDove." Said Ricky.

David nodded his head in approval. "Nice little toy Aim. Now what do you propose we do?" Eamonn looked around to see if Kate was in earshot before leaning close in to David,

"Please Davy, call me Ricky. And it's more than a toy Davy." Ricky said. "It's a full on ocean sailing yacht. We could cross the Atlantic in this if we wanted to and make respectable time. But don't worry. We'll not be going that far." Katy, who was dragging one of the trolleys raised her eyebrows.

"David. You go aboard. I'll throw up these supplies." She said.

"Off about six Davy," said Ricky. "We'll catch an evening breeze first. We should be able to run with it for a few hours. Might even get the spinnaker up."

David pulled Ricky aside by his elbow as he passed him and whispered so as Katy couldn't hear.

"I don't want to put a damper on it Aim or Ricky or whatever it is you call yourself, but I want to know what's going on. I've got things to do. The business doesn't run itself."

Ricky smiled at him as Nana skipped down the pontoon towards them.

"How did you get on Nana?" Said Ricky ignoring David's questions again and giving Nana a big hug.

"I put it in a rental scooter in the old town. Bunch of lads on a jolly. They'll have loads of fun chasing it around town."

"Good girl Nana. You and Kate get the boat ready to go. I'm going to take Mr. Gates up to the Marina shop get him some stuff. We might have a cheeky half while we're at it."

Nana and Katy both tossed Ricky a stern look. "We'll need a hand on deck later dad, so go easy." Said Nana.

"She's like a schoolteacher sometimes." He said to David raising his eyes with a good natured tut, "Come on Davy. Follow me." Ricky started to walk away from the boat.

David eventually followed.

"Ramon, this is a friend of mine," Ricky said as they walked through the reception. "We'll be leaving about six. Katy will be up with a passage plan later." He winked at Ramon conspiratorially and they went through to a well stocked and plush Chandlers. Ramon nodded dutifully and smiled at David as they walked past. David nodded a curt greeting.

"You're going to need some stuff for the journey Davy." Said Ricky as he approached a display of deck shoes. "What size foot are you?" Ricky strolled around the shop picking up shirts and shorts and a pair of sunglasses. Davy stopped him by grasping his elbow again.

"This is going too far Aim. I need to know what is going on." Ricky looked him in the eyes for a second or two checking his expression. Checking his demeanour. He turned and walked toward the shop counter and placed all the stuff that was in his arms on the countertop. He smiled at Ramon who had come into the shop.

"Put these on my account Ramon. And could you take them to the boat? Me and my friend here are going into the bar." He turned and paused. "The shoes David?" David shook his head wondering what he meant. "The shoes, David. What size shoe?" David was bullied again into an answer as Ramone was looking on.

"Eight." He said. Ricky turned to Ramon and translating, pointed at the shoes. "Those in a forty two." He said.

Ricky led Davy through another set of glass doors into a modern bar. There was a wall of sliding glass doors half open leading to a terrace overlooking the marina. Chrome café tables, teak chairs with green canvas cushions, all shaded by green canvass umbrellas, filled the terrace.

There were a few other groups of yachting types all dressed in the international uniform of a marina bar out drinking and enjoying the afternoon sun. Ricky nodded a greeting to a party of three sun wrinkled couples then led Davy toward a table well out of earshot. They sat and a waiter approached. Ricky ordered two large beers. David pulled out a battered packet of cigarettes from his trouser pocket. His crisp white shirt was no longer crisp and white and his smart pressed suit trousers, were creased and dusty. He lit his cigarette with a scratched and worn old fashioned gold Dunhill lighter. He took a long drag before putting the lighter on the table. Ricky picked the lighter up and looked it over carefully. He looked at David and David nodded.

"It's the same one." He said, answering the question Ricky was about to ask. Ricky smiled. "I left with practically nothing you know, Aim."

"I know," said Ricky. "I know." The waiter arrived with the beers on a silver tray. "Can you bring my friend here an ashtray?" He said to the waiter. "He has a cavalier attitude towards life." Ricky smiled and nodded towards the cigarette.

Davy took a long and welcome gulp from the frosted beer glass. He waited for Ricky to start talking as the waiter went to fetch the ashtray.

"Davy, I really, honestly do not know where to start... but yes, I suppose I owe you an explanation." He pulled from the hip pocket of his jeans a piece of folded paper and slid it across the table. "But then perhaps you owe me one."

"What's this?" Said David as he unfolded the sheet of paper. Ricky watched his reaction.

"I was rather hoping you'd be able to tell me." He said. On the photocopied paper was a recent picture of David Crane in the centre of a Private Eye cover, looking tanned and fit. The headline said 'Lord Lucan Found'. David looked at the picture for a moment.

"I don't get it Aim." He stared at it some more. Ricky said nothing still trying to gather something from David's reaction but he was getting nothing. David took another drag from his cigarette and squashed it into the ashtray. A look of annoyance formed on his face. *Funny how expressions are like voices or gaits. They never change. No matter how long it's been.* Ricky noticed the change. He'd seen it before. A long time ago. David put the paper on the table. The afternoon sea breeze tried to blow it away so he put the ashtray on top of it.

"What are you up to Eamonn?" His voice was hostile.

"Don't shoot the messenger, Davy." Said Ricky. "Are you saying you know nothing about this?"

"Yes Aim." David's voice was still hostile. "I am saying I know nothing about this." The sea breeze was picking up. "I took a hell of a risk getting here Aim. If I've done that so you can play games at my expense, then I made a mistake." He took a long gulp of his beer, pushed his chair back and rose to leave.

"Sit down Davy." Ricky said as if talking to a child. "Those men earlier…They would have killed you. It wasn't me they were after. They are still close by. You won't get far from here alone." David sat back down on his chair. He picked up the cigarette packet and lit another.

"Davy," Ricky continued pointing at the paper beneath the ashtray, "Three weeks ago, a copy of that magazine was delivered to my house in Chelsea. I keep the place very secret. I have to in my position. There was no stamp, no postmark, just a plain brown envelope. It looked like an original back copy from eighty two except for that front page. It was printed authentically. Made to look real." Ricky was interrupted by an agitated Katy trotting towards them.

"Katy, Love. What's up?"

"We gotta go Dad. The bug's come into range, what's wrong with your phone. We've been calling." Ricky pulled his smart-phone from his Gillet pocket.

"Damn. Battery's dead. How far?"

"Ten K maybe. They might have just got lucky."

"Have you filed the passage plan?" Ricky asked as he rose from his chair.

"Gibraltar then Malaga."

"Come on Davy. You need to trust me."

David stayed where he was for a moment, considering his options.

"Davy, C'mon. If they find you here they won't take prisoners."

Reluctantly David got up to leave with them and they all walked back through the clubhouse towards the pontoons.

Nana was waiting on the rail of the boat. The engine was running and Nana was leaning over the side checking the exhaust. They all climbed aboard.

"I've done the slips." Nana shouted to them. "Kate, you take the forward line and slip it. The wind will blow us off the pontoon. We won't need the thruster. Dad. Slip the stern when I tell you." Nana was standing behind one of the two huge wheels in the cockpit. The prow of the big boat slowly floated away from the pontoon. When the stern was six feet away from the pontoon Nana, who seemed in complete and easy control told Ricky to slip the stern line. Kate was already rolling the bow line onto a loop.

"Gun that engine Nana." Ricky called to Nana. "If they're coming we need to be out of sight when they get here."

David had been watching the proceedings from a vantage point in the cockpit and was admiring the slick way they had operated.

"We'll get clear of the Marina Dad. Then we'll take it up to full. We don't want to spill everyone's gin and tonics."

Kate jumped into the cockpit from the mid deck.

"Well David," she said. "How do like our little home from home?"

"I'm most impressed." He replied, smiling generously, hiding from the girls as best he could that fact that he was feeling used and abused and distinctly ill informed. But he was along for the ride now so he sat resigned in the cockpit and watched as firstly the pontoon then the inner harbour wall got smaller and smaller behind them.

"I feel as if I should be doing something." He said to Kate. "What can I do?"

"Nothing for the moment David. It'll get livelier once we get a bit further out and there'll be lots to do then. Sailing is mostly long periods of doing nothing interspersed with short periods of frantic activity. Here," she handed him a tube of lotion. "Put some of that on. The sun can be evil out here, even at this time." Nana reached across to two chrome levers on the control console between the two five foot diameter wheels and pushed them forward as far as they would go. The noise of the engines doubled and the boat lurched forward. As they passed the line of the outer wall of the harbour the swell noticeably increased, the bows of the boat crashing into the water in great smashes. They were shouting at each other now to be heard.

"What speed we making Nana?" Ricky yelled. He was standing on the rear deck of the boat.

His arm wrapped around the back-stay and peering through a pair of rubber binoculars toward the shore.

Nana glanced at the instrument panel. "About eight knots, Dad. Heading about due north."

"When we get level with the head over there," He let the binoculars fall to his chest on their lanyard and pointed to a head of land only just visible through the heat hazed air. "Steer a course about two two five degrees." He yelled over the combined din created by the engine at full bore and the wind and the waves. "We should catch a south easterly on the beam if we're lucky and we'll do some sailing." Katy rose from her seat in the cockpit next to David.

"Thought we were going north Dad." Katy said casually then grabbed David's hand. "Come on David, I'll show you below." She made for the hatch of the companionway. "Mind yourself down here David. We'll find you something more appropriate to wear."

David followed carefully down the companionway his leather brogues slipping on the polished wooden steps, and entered a whole new world. He steadied himself against the pitching and rolling of the boat by leaning on the saloon table. A big oval slab of American cherry wood.

"Do you suffer from seasickness?" Kate asked him as she rummaged through the shopping bags that they had brought on board and were lying about untidily and precariously on the saloon couches. One of them had fallen on the floor. She lent to pick it up.

"No idea." He said, "I've never been in a sail-boat before." Kate looked at him as she would look at a small child. It was her mothering instinct.

"Well you'll know soon enough." She said. "The winds are never that heavy this time of year but it'll get feisty later." The boat pitched heavily and David saw the water submerge the port hatches.

"Is that supposed to happen?" He said. Kate smiled.

David slumped down onto the couch held safe by the table.

Kate had pulled out the pair of deck shoes Ricky had bought in the chandlers. There was a couple of long sleeved shirts and some shorts.

"Try these." Said Kate. "If we can get you looking the part, maybe you'll get your sea legs quicker." David obediently started to undo the buttons on what had been a beautiful white silk shirt. He slipped a pink canvass rugby shirt over his head. He then pulled off a pair of cashmere wool trouser that formed part of the blue suit he had dressed in earlier that morning. The cloth was never supposed to have been treated like it had. The events of the previous few hours had taken their toll on him as well as the suit and he suddenly felt tired. Kate noticed the look on his face.

"Listen David, if you'd like to get yourself some sleep, feel free." She pointed towards a door on the port side of the boat. "Make yourself at home in there. You can do the next watch with me if you like. Should be a breeze."

David was pulling on a pair of canvass shorts. "Unless there's a drastic change in the weather we should be on the same tack all night." David was struggling putting on the shorts behind the saloon table and stopped in his tracks.

"What d'you mean - all night?"

Katy leant against the galley sink as the boat listed hard. She was filling a kettle from a slim chrome tap.

"Oh dear." She said shaking her head. "I've asked him before not to do this. He hasn't told you how long has he?"

She turned to look at David.

"Hasn't told me how long what?" He said. Kate was hesitating thinking what to say. "Kate. What hasn't he told me?" His tone was trying not to be aggressive, he knew it was nothing to do with her and he was more than curious as to what it was Ricky hadn't told him. David had gathered that whatever the explanation was behind their very unorthodox first meeting in thirty years, he was trying to keep it from the girls.

"David," she said. "We'll be at sea now for three days at least. The next stop, if he doesn't decide to follow the coast down, which I doubt if we stay on this course, will be the Canary Islands." David took a moment to take this all in. He hadn't spent three hours out of contact with his business before, let alone three days. Kate saw a temper rising in him.

"We are sailing back to the Canaries and it'll take three days?" David asked, his voice rising in pitch. Kate nodded as David angrily made for the companionway steps and stumbled up into the cockpit of the boat. Nana was at the helm concentrating hard. The boat was heeled at a frightening angle and a huge mainsail towered above. David looked furtively around, his politeness had dissipated. Nana could tell by the expression on his face what he wanted. She nodded towards the front of the boat. Ricky was standing on the foredeck, up past the mast on the port side wrestling with an aluminium pole twelve feet long and three inches in diameter. Around his feet was a mass of billowing purple sailcloth. There was a rope attached to the life-jacket he was wearing. David climbed out of the cockpit and headed towards Ricky who had his back to him working in the pitching and rolling of the boat on the spinnaker.

"Eamonn." David shouted at the top of his voice. He crouched on the deck not confident enough to stand upright. There was little to hold onto to steady himself apart from the ropes that seemed to be everywhere. He grasped at a loose rope hanging from the mast. He attempted to pull himself up with it. The rope held firm for a moment but as he straightened up it ran in his hand.

"Eamonn." He shouted again as he tried to balance on the deck. The boat, pitching under him, briefly gave him the false impression that he was stable and upright. Ricky heard him shout and turned to see David glaring at him angrily. The boat pitched back the other way and David went with it, he grasped hand over hand at the free running rope to try to steady himself. Genuine horror spread across the faces of both men and Nana screamed as David fell over the guard rail and into the waves. Nana immediately pressed two buttons on the console. The engine started, the mainsail began to roll into the mast and the foresail began to furl on its stay. Nana screamed for Katy to press the man overboard button on the radio by the navigation table below. Ricky countermanded this with a roar.

"Do not touch the radio." He yelled in a primal scream.

"Nana. Can you see him?" Katy tried to look over the stern while pulling the two chrome throttle levers all the way backwards. The boat lurched as the engines fought against the forward momentum. Katy had come up from below and was now up high on the aft deck holding on the backstay.

"I can see him." She screamed, in tears now. She knew the odds were not good. She could see a small pink bundle already sixty or more meters behind them.

"Just keep pointing Kate." Shouted Ricky unable to take the panic out of his voice. "Whatever you do don't lose him."

Ricky had made it into the cockpit.

"Why not the radio Dad?" Nana yelled at Ricky who ignored her as he yanked furiously at one of the big wheels.

"Take the wheel. Fast." He shouted. "Pull us around." Nana did as she was told and continued to roll the wheel causing the boat to start a reverse turn. "Just don't lose him." He shouted up to Kate who was on tip toes hanging on to the back-stay with one arm and pointing with a straight arm with the other at a little pink dot in the ocean.

Ricky was tying a thin nylon rope to the clip on his own life-jacket. He stumbled up towards the bow again. "Full throttle towards him Nana." He shouted back. He tied the other end of the rope to a deck cleat and flicked it three times around a winch.

"I can see him Dad. I can see him." Nana screamed through panicked tears. Ricky had got past the mast and onto the foredeck. "Head straight towards him full throttle." He shouted. He stood up on the foredeck and saw the pink bundle. Thankfully it still looked to be moving. He guessed they only had seconds to get him back.

He looked to be flailing. *Just keep calm man.* Ricky caught himself saying. *Conserve your energy.* Slowly, so slowly, the distance between them shortened. Ricky was pointing now, with a straight arm, indicating to Nana the direction she should steer.

"When I say, put it into reverse." He yelled. David was twenty feet away slightly off the port bow.

"Now." He shouted. The boat lurched again. Ricky just hoped he'd judged it right. The huge boat slowed. God. It's a long way down. David was twenty feet away. Ricky jumped. Katy screamed again. This was definitely not the way they had been drilled for a man overboard. Nana handed Katy a lifeline and clipped them both onto a jackstay.

> "Best we don't all go in." She shouted to her sister. Katy was crying and shaking her head.

"Come on sis. We can do this." Said Nana, sure-footedly making her way to the port side of the boat where Ricky had jumped into the water. He looked as if he had managed to grab David who now appeared lifeless. Ricky's life jacket was just about supporting them. He had a hand under David's chin. Both their heads were being rhythmically dunked below the surface.

"He's got him." shouted Nana back to Katy at the helm, and pressed the button on the electric winch.

"Turn off the engines." Katy turned a key on the control console and the noise of the engines died away leaving an eerie calm after all the commotion. A slight whirring sound came from the winch as it took up the slack in the rope.

"There's no way we'll be able to pull them up." Nana shouted at Katy. "Best chance, get them around to the bathing platform. We'll winch them." Ricky had clasped his arms around David's chest. The two men were face to face now. Katy saw that David's face was blue.

"God no," she said. "Please God no." The rope holding the two men was pulled taught over a guard rail. The rail was strong enough she was sure but they were now almost underneath her bobbing along the side of the boat still ten feet away from the platform at the back which would be their only hope of getting them back on board.

"Katy. Release the winch a little. I'll try to move the rope over to the back." Nana pulled the rope up with all her strength, using the pitching of the boat to help her. It took them working together to manipulate the rope into a position that might just get the men onto the bathing platform. Both the men were quiet. Their lives were in the hands of the two young women. They worked as quickly as they could. They would have to time the winching carefully. Finally the two men were lying on the narrow ledge of the bathing platform held fast by the rope but they were still a dead weight. Ricky looked up. The look of determination on his face turned into a soft barely noticeable smile.

"I got him." He said.

There was still the problem of hauling them up the four feet or so into the safety of the cockpit.

"Give me the spinnaker halyard." Ricky shouted. "Quick as you can. I don't think I'll be able to hold on to him much longer." David was lying limp in his arms. He saw the frightened look on both their faces looking down at him.

"He's still breathing. Come on now. Chop Chop." They looked at each other and understood. Katy went back up towards the foredeck where the pile of purple sailcloth lay and undid the shackle that attached the halyard to the sail. She flicked it around the mast and brought it back along the cockpit. She shook it and it went all the way to the masthead. The other end was still wound around one of the four electric winches in the cockpit where Ricky had previously been preparing to raise the spinnaker.

"Tie a big bowline in it." He shouted. "We'll do David first." Katy tied the bowline and passed it down to Eamonn. He struggled to place it under David's arms without letting go of him. They slowly winched David upwards. He cleared the guardrail and the two girls held onto his sodden clothing as he swung like a hanged man back towards them in the cockpit. They lowered him on the winch and guided him to lie on the port cockpit bench. Katy immediately left Nana in charge to repeat the process with Eamonn but he was clambering exhausted up the ladder from the bathing platform.

"I'm ok." He said as Katy grabbed him and hugged him tightly. Nana sprang up from tending to David and did the same thing.

"I thought you were gone." She said. They were all crying.

"It'll take more than that to dispatch a couple of wily old Irishmen. Look. Come on now." said Ricky. "I'm fine. Let's see to this old man."

"I've only ever done this on a plastic model." Said Katy as she sat astride the prone David. Nana was holding his wrist.

"There's a pulse but it's intermittent." She didn't hesitate in her next move. She held David's nose closed with the forefinger and thumb of her left hand and taking a deep breath blew slowly and positively into his mouth. She could taste salt water, tobacco and beer. She lifted her head and nodded towards Nana who was poised with her hands, one over the other, on top of David's chest. Nana pushed down firmly six times. They repeated the procedure and after the third attempt, David spluttered and coughed out a good pint of seawater.

16

"We kept each other awake Dad by singing." Katy said as Ricky emerged from the companionway hatch blinking into the early morning. The sun was a foot above the horizon. Ricky smiled another proud smile. He suddenly felt a tear well up inside of him. The boat was under full sail in a strong breeze. It was as if nothing had happened. The decks were cleared and the two girls were sitting beside each other on the topside. Katy had one hand on the wheel deftly making slight adjustments to the course.

"You were right," said Nana. "We've been on this tack all night. The plotter says we might make Lanz by tomorrow evening if we keep this speed." Ricky was speechless. He pulled himself up and wriggled down to sit between them. He put his arms around both of them and they snuggled into him.

"God, I'm a lucky man." He said still suppressing tears.

"You certainly are," said Katy. "Since when was that in the textbook?"

"I'm sorry girls." He said. They were all quiet. All gazing at the wide open empty ocean. None of them would rather have been anywhere else. Ricky pointed across the deck at the horizon.

"La La La La La America, La La La La La America, Everything free in America, For a small fee in America," the two girls sang in unison.

"How's the casualty?" asked Nana after a while.

"I looked in on him earlier. He looks like he's having a good sleep. He could be a natural sailor if falling overboard on his first time out in a force four without a life-jacket doesn't put him off."

"Dad." Said Katy. "Why does he keep calling you Eamonn?"

"It's a long story." Said Ricky.

"It was never a force four." Said Nana.

"It'll be more than that when we tell the tale." Ricky said as from the companionway hatch David emerged blinking into the sunlight.

"Here he is. How you feeling?" Asked Ricky not sure of what to expect.

"I had this odd dream," said David. His annoyance and anger obviously subdued by his experiences. He pulled himself up the companionway steps and steadied himself. He seemed strengthened. "Dreamt I was abducted by a ghost and two angelic helpers then I fell into a watery grave and while all this was happening all I could think was when's lunch. I am Hungarian." They were all smiling at him.

"Ok ok I get the hint," said Nana. "I'll do slave." She got up to make her way towards the galley.

"Oh Nana," said Eamonn. "Come on. I'll do it. You guys must be whacked." He didn't make any attempt to move though. Nana looked at him as she would a child again as she shuffled past David.

"Come on Sis. Let dad take the wheel." Said Nana. "Let's go and get them something to eat."

"Only if we can be sure they'll both stay in the boat." Katy said, grabbing Ricky's hand and pushing it around the wheel. "Keep it steady Dad."

"Eye eye Capt'n. I'll try." He replied. The two girls disappeared down the companionway steps.

"You're a lucky man Aim." Said David as he sat down in the space the girls had left. Ricky shuffled along the bench and lifted his head to check the bearing but he didn't need to. As long as he kept the sun on the quarter he'd be heading in the right direction.

"We both are." Said Ricky. They both sat there looking at the empty ocean. David this time pointed with a straight arm at the horizon.

"Everything's free in America, something for me in America," He sang with what he thought was a Latino accent. Ricky joined in the second time round. The two men chuckled to themselves and sat back and watched the empty blue ocean almost seamlessly melt into an empty blue sky.

"It was thirty years ago Davy." Said Ricky eventually. David nodded. "They want to get you Davy." David's expression didn't change. He just nodded again. "And it's my fault I'm afraid."

"Until yesterday, Aim. I thought you were long dead. I thought you died in that tunnel."

"I did. Davy. At least Eamonn Boothe died in that tunnel. I was reborn. As another man."

"I suppose you got lucky." Said David. "I was warned that if I ever returned it wouldn't just be me. They're all the same you know. Both sides."

"I know." Said Ricky. "I know." The two men sat in silence again until David spoke.

"It was all a long time ago."

"Maybe so. But it's come back to us." Ricky replied.

"Us?" said David.

"Ok so it's come back to haunt you. You know who I am Davy, don't you. You know what I've become?"

"I thought I knew who you were Aim. Not sure I know what you've become."

"Didn't the money make you think?"

David nodded slowly, his eyes fixed on the horizon. He took a while to answer. A smile soon crossed his lips and he blinked away from staring at the horizon and turned towards Ricky.

"That was you?"

"Who else did you think it was?"

"You were dead Aim. How could it have been you. I thought maybe The Man in the Hat had organised it. Frankly I didn't ask. It took me a month before I realised there was something in the guitar. I picked it up to play it one day and it sounded dead. Your guitar Aim. The guitar of a dead man. I was so scared it was a trap I buried the money in the garden. Didn't touch it for ages and then it took me a year to make it legit, so as I could do something with it." David turned his body to face Eamonn who was making slight alterations to the course to keep the tell-tales on the sails horizontal and the sun on his cheek.

"Where did you get the money from?" David asked.

Ricky knew this would be one of many questions that David would ask and he would find difficult to answer.

"I stole it." He said still looking at the horizon.

David was unmoved and he too stared out at the ocean again.

It was as if nothing Ricky could say now would surprise him.

"Who from?"

"Now that's a tricky one." Said Ricky. "Some think the Libyans and some think the Irish. Then there's the Liberians and then there's the CIA."

David let out a long whistle through pursed lips. He put his feet up on the wheel housing and slouched down on the bench seat putting his hands deep into his pockets.

"The Liberians?" He paused, Ricky nodded. "And the CIA? Where they the ones following us through town?"

"Dunno exactly." Said Ricky. "That could have been any one of them." David sat there contemplating for a few minutes.

"Who were the two men at the hotel." He asked.

"We thought they were freelancers working for the Irish but to be frank I'm not yet sure about them either."

"Bit of a mess." Said David after a while.

"Yep" said Ricky letting out a long quiet breath. "A bit of a mess."

The girls reappeared at the hatchway carrying two mugs of tea and big plate bacon sandwiches.

"You two are Angels. Truly." Said David beaming them a big smile and sitting up. He unhinged a teak table that sat between the seats in the cockpit forward of the wheel binnacle. The girls put the mugs and the sandwiches down in front of them.

"We're going to get a bit of kip. Will you two be OK on your own?" Said Katy. The two girls turned and gave the men a little wave before slipping down the hatch again.

"What became of Garret, the sneaky little fuckwit." Said David after three or four bites from his sandwich.

"When I re-emerged I spent a while reorganising. I went back home and bought the Galway Herald. Do you remember it? That turned into the business I run now. I'm Rick Starr, David. Starr Media."

David turned towards Ricky and looked him in the eyes still just chewing on his sandwich. He nodded his head as if the information was slowly seeping into his brain. His face remained expressionless. Ricky continued.

"I had always kept a close eye on Garrets ascent up the slippery pole and it was serendipitous that he came to my firm to run his public relations. He had absolutely no idea who I was. And why would he. No-one ever twigged it was me, not even..." Ricky stopped suddenly. David appeared too deep in thought to notice. "I'd always wanted to get even but I hadn't thought of a way to do it. Then he gave me the idea. He asked me to arrange, if I could that some information be removed from government records and..."

"Is that even possible?" Asked David.

"Yes it is. It's not easy. But it's possible. I own a little euphemistically named IT company. Only two guys but they are the most..." Ricky searched his mind for the word. "The most dysfunctional, no that's not fair. They are good at what they do - clever as hell. It's all about information today Davy. It's the most valuable commodity there is."

"It's thirty years Davy. Thirty years since it all happened. After thirty years, Davy, all the sordid secrets get released."

"Hence why it's all kicking off now." Said David. Ricky nodded.

"And you're dead. The only fellah in the frame for all the shit you did, is me. Right?"

"Well you and Garret."

"Garret?"

"If the Irish find out what he really did back then, he's a dead man."

"What did he do?"

"He was the traitor Davy. He ordered me to sabotage the mines on the ship in Khoms. He said if I didn't he'd kill you. I know we were treading a fine line Davy but ours was an altogether more innocent game."

"But the stuffs not been made public. No?"

"Well no. Not exactly public. It probably never will. It doesn't exist any-more. It's been erased. The guys I got to steal it had it stolen from them." David nodded some more as he picked up another bacon sandwich and took a bite.

"On a data stick." Ricky continued.

"Why does it exist at all if it's been erased?" Said David.

"Because my guys thought they'd be clever and make a copy. It was the copy that got 're-stolen'."

"Who by?"

"Not entirely sure." Said Ricky. David nodded and chewed some more.

"You don't know much." He said.

"Thought I did." said Ricky. "Thought I did."

"Listen," said David. "What speed are we doing?" Ricky was a little flummoxed. He looked at the log on the binnacle.

"About eight knots."

"How much faster will it go with that big sail up?"

"A little. Not much. It's a spinnaker."

"What say we put it up anyway. I've always wanted to sail in the ocean with the wind in my... What do you call it…spinnaker?" They both jumped up and Ricky, after handing David a life-jacket and line with a wink sprang onto the fore-deck and within fifteen minutes they were sailing the ocean with the wind in the aft quarter, filling the huge purple sail. The motif sewn into the sail was a thirty foot high white dove.

17

"Davy you devil-child you, you're a fast learner." Ricky shouted across the cockpit to where David, with a huge smile on his face was grasping the five foot diameter port-side wheel. The boom of the mainsail was almost at ninety degrees to the centre line of the boat. The foresail was set back to the opposite side and the spinnaker, like a hot air balloon cut in half, appeared to be effortlessly dragging the huge hull through the waves.

"This is called running with the wind." Said Ricky. "We probably don't need all this sail but it looks good doesn't it? Feels like we could fly."

"I feel like I am flying." David replied.

Ricky squinted through his sunglasses at the screen of the plotter on the instrument binnacle.

"Another two hours of this and we should see land again. First thing we'll spot will be a huge lump of rock on the starboard bow."

"That's this side yeah?" David lifted his right hand.

"Yeah. That's right." Said Ricky. He squinted at the plotter again.

"Funny, it's not named on this chart."

"It's called The Rock of the West. Some of the locals call it Inferno."

Ricky looked across to David who had taken to his new role rather well.

"You forget I've lived here for thirty years. It's uninhabited but you can go hiking on it. It's been ten years since I've been there but there's a most spectacular cave system you can only get to underwater."

"Really." Said Ricky. "If we sailed towards it could you show me where the caves are?"

"Why?" Asked David. A little sneer in his voice.

"I just like caves, Davy."

"No you don't Aim."

"How do you know I don't? I like boats."

"How can those two things be related?" Said David with an amused twist of his head. They fell back into silence for a while as presently a land mass appeared on the starboard quarter.

"So you can scuba dive can you?" Asked Ricky, breaking the silence.

"Eamonn," said David with a slightly patronising tone, "everyone in the Canaries can scuba dive." He paused. "Why are you interested in an underwater cave on an uninhabited island?"

"Don't really know. Quite interesting though."

David let his mistrust of Ricky's motives pass, "I think I'd remember where it was but it was a long time ago. You know how your mind tends to make up its own pictures."

"Come on." Said Ricky. "It's not far away. We might even need to change direction a bit and put in a couple of tacks."

"Are you serious Aim. After all you've told me. Don't we need to get back to sort things out?"

"We do Davy but we're ok. Not everyone's there yet. Besides we need to have a strategy meeting before we do anything."

David looked across to Ricky.

"A strategy meeting?"

"Yes David. We all need to be reading from the same script."

"Is that part of the problem here Aim?"

"What?"

"You think this isn't for real. You think this is all made up. Like a film."

"No I don't Davy but we need to prepare for a bit of a fight. There's a lot at stake and I just don't want to take any unnecessary chances. I'm going below to wake up the girls. Keep the boat steady will you?"

David nodded a 'yes' as Ricky disappeared down the companionway steps. Suddenly he was all alone again up there behind the huge wheel of an ocean going yacht. He was in control of this monster and in command of the wind and the waves and his anxieties and fears temporarily left him. He smiled inwardly to himself and he found himself thinking of the future with a positive mind. For the first time in years he felt as if he were coming to a springtime having spent years in winter hibernation. Suddenly self-conscious he looked around thinking that someone must be watching him. Someone must be near, about to cool his heightened mood but there was no-one. Just the wind and the waves. His peace was short-lived but it was curtailed by the pleasant sound of Katy and Nana talking and giggling below. They appeared shortly, blinking into the afternoon sun.

"Wow." Said Katy. "You look like you've got the hang of that David."

For just a moment David took a double take on his own name again. God this is strange he thought to himself.

"I could get used to it." He said with a smile.

"All change now though." Said Nana who followed Katy up the steps. "I've never sailed further or for longer on the same tack. Did you know that in the days of wooden ships, if they sailed for too long on the same tack, the wooden boards that were out of the water," she pointed to the side of the boat that was highest, "would dry out and shrink and if you weren't careful they let in water when you dunked them again. Anyway time for a bit of action. Dad wants us to plot a course for a position north west of where we were going."

She pressed buttons on the console of the plotter on a binnacle between the wheels. Katy had gone up forward and was fiddling with various knots and ropes. Nana saw David's inquisitive expression and as it was her desire to share her knowledge she said,

"We're going to lower the spinnaker. We can't tack with it up. Keep us on the same bearing David while I pull in these sails. Used to be a whole load of work but it's not so hard now."

She winked and pressed a button by a cylinder of chrome plated steel sticking out of the wall to the cockpit.

Wrapped around the chrome plated cylinder four times was a purple rope three quarters of an inch in diameter. The boom slowly retracted towards them bringing the mainsail with it as the electric winch turned. Nana had completed her preparations and had taken a position just behind the main mast.

"David, will you press this button here when I say." Said Katy pointing up towards the spinnaker. "The big sail up there will start to come down. Do it slowly and we'll gather it in as it comes down. We don't want it to fall in the water as we do it."

The three of them completed the operation without fuss and David managed to keep the boat on an even keel while doing it. Nana finished packing away the big sail into a surprisingly small sail-bag and Katy stood beside David and studied the image on the plotter.

"We've not done this yet David. It's called gibing. When the wind is coming from behind and you want to change direction from here to here," Katy indicated two directions with an out-stretched arm, "you sail through the wind. The boom goes from this side to this side. See that sheet there."

She pointed at a rope. David couldn't see a sheet.

"The ropes that control things on a sailing yacht are called sheets." She said to clarify.

"Does everything have a different name to the one I know?" Said David.

"Practically," Katy answered. "You'd be surprised how much sailing talk has got itself into the English language." She paused briefly for thought.

"The course we need to steer, as calculated by our Skipper, who must be obeyed, is two seven two degrees."

Katy tapped the numbers into the plotter. "He can be very peculiar sometimes." She said as she tapped at the screen. "He loves all things new and high tech. But still likes to work all this stuff out long hand. On paper for goodness sake. With rulers and pencils." She tapped again and looked at the plotter display. She smiled and shook her head.

"He got it right though. The electronics say two seven zero." David Laughed.

"Don't be too hard on us. You youngsters don't know what it's like not to have a complete set of faculties. If we don't use 'em, we'll lose 'em." Katy smiled a slightly patronising smile towards David. She didn't mean to. It was almost a default position of kindly young people. David had thought that he'd earned the right to be treated like one of them. He was not ready for old age and never wanted to be. If he'd have died when he went overboard yesterday, he thought, he'd have been none the wiser. His high mood was ebbing away. Katy noticed nothing. She continued with her tuition.

"See this is the bearing you've been keeping us on." She pointed towards a point ahead of them that was in the general direction of where they were going.

"And this is where we want to go." She swung her arm through forty five degrees. David nodded dutifully.

"The wind," Katy continued, "is blowing from over there." She pointed again with her arm and looked to the top of the mast where a little wind cock was flailing about. She adjusted the direction she was pointing in a little.

"So the wind is blowing on the sails here." She used both hands this time to demonstrate.

"So in order to sail in that direction," she pointed, "we need to set the sail here," she pointed again, "so the wind blows us here." Two hands again. "Do you understand?" She asked David finally.

"Absolutely." He said with his tongue in his cheek. "That's the theory. Now for the practice." She said.

Nana jumped into the cockpit with them.

"Ready to make a turn everyone?" She said.

"We need first to pull in the boom." Said Katy. "Now, this is an important bit here David. You must hold the course while we do this because if you turn the boat too early the wind will take this boom here," she pointed to the huge mail-sail boom hanging four feet above their heads, 'and blow it violently across to here." She motioned with her arm again. "It's called an accidental gybe and it's not something we want to happen. The forces involved break stuff. So what we do is slowly bring it in close to the centre line if the boat." She pressed the button on the winch and the boom started to move inwards. "At the same time Nana will ease out the fore sail and it will go limp and floppy." Katy stopped the winch controlling the boom and turned to David.

"See it's not one thing after another. It's kind of all at the same time. We have to work together. So as I pull this in, when it gets to about here... you start turning onto the new course. You okay with that?"

David had been concentrating hard.

"We're going to do this now are we?" Said David, a note of anxiety in his voice.

"Absolutely we are." Katy replied. "Here we go." She pressed the button on the winch control again and the boom moved closer toward them.

"Ok," said Katy. "Start the turn." David slowly turned the wheel. The boom had reached the centre line of the boat. Nana had released the fore sail sheet and it was flapping about at the prow. David continued his turn and began to straighten up in the direction that Katy had indicated. The main-sail filled up with wind again as did the foresail but on the other side of the boat. Katy pressed the control button on the winch for the boom and Nana pressed the one for the foresail. A few moments passed and they were under way again, the commotion of the change all gone. David glanced at the compass and the readout on the instrument binnacle. They were both reading Two-SevenZero degrees. He nodded to himself. The two girls gave him a little round of applause. They sailed together as a team for the following two hours and performed the same manoeuvre two more times without really needing to. Towards the middle of the afternoon a lump of rock appeared on the horizon and as they approached it two more appeared behind it. They sailed up to within a half a mile of the rock where Katy took David through the process of anchoring a large sailing boat. The sea was calm. Ricky appeared from down below.

"Katy been showing you the ropes? Literally." He winked at David.

"She's a very patient teacher." Said David smiling at Katy.

Ricky was holding a small aluminium cylinder the size of a hand-torch and was screwing an end cap onto it. The boat was rocking gently on the water.

"Come with me." Said Ricky and led David out over the cockpit. Ricky knelt on the teak deck, turned a recessed chrome latch and lifted the lid to a locker the size of a large car boot. David recognised immediately the bright yellow of the oxygen cylinders. Next to them were two machines that David had never seen before but had read about. Sub aqua scooters. Straight out of a Bond film.

David smiled and shook his head.

"You certainly like your toys, Aim." He leant into the locker to pull one out. They were connected to the wall of the locker by a cable.

"Rechargeable Lithium Ion batteries." Said Ricky.

"They're incredible. They're good for an hour on a single charge at full tilt. More if you take it easy. That's longer than you've got in the air tank."

David was impressed and excited. He'd wanted to have a try with these ever since he first learned to scuba dive but like so many things he'd denied himself because of the thought of it being extravagant or unnecessary. He was resolved now to try as much as he could.

"I've got wet suits below." Said Ricky. "What say you we go and find that cave?"

Katy and Nana couldn't help but laugh as the two old men wriggled into their tight rubber wetsuits. It was a mission that neither of them found easy. They eventually made it into the water.

"Jesuuuuus." Shouted David as he resurfaced. "Has it got colder since I was last in here?"

"No." Shouted back Nana from the bathing platform of the boat. "Just that the last time you went in you had something else on your mind." David trod water trying to acclimatise to the temperature. He was at the top of his breath. He knew he'd have to calm down before he started to use the oxygen otherwise it would last no time at all. It had been a while, perhaps ten years since he had done any diving. He thought that maybe he'd overestimated his abilities. He soon shrugged off this idea. '*What has become of you?*' He said to himself. It wasn't that he had to keep proving his physical prowess to himself or anybody else. It was just that all his life he'd thought that the doing is in the mind. But his body was letting him down. He was seriously weakened by falling overboard yesterday and now here he was bobbing up and down in the Atlantic again. At least this time he was wearing a wet suit and an aqualung. Ricky bobbed up beside him.

"Ok?" He asked. He didn't appear to be suffering the cold as badly as David. David nodded a yes.

"Take your time." He said. "How long has it been?"

"Ten years or more." Said David. "I'll be fine."

Ricky blew out his face mask and put the regulator in his mouth. David could have done with a few more moments but did the same. Ricky waved to Katy and Nana on the deck and they lowered the two underwater scooters into the water. They were two hundred meters from the rocky shore line. The machines took them that distance in no time.

They resurfaced close to the shore. The swell was noticeable but it wasn't going to dash them onto the rocks just yet. David had a big grin on his face.

"That was incredible." He said. "Like flying again."

"Is rather good." Said Ricky. "Do you recognise anywhere?"

"No way Aim. It was a long time ago."

"Let's go and have a look." Said Ricky. "You go first. I'll follow. Try and keep each other in sight."

David's body had got used to the cold. He dived below the surface and the quiet world returned. The world of just his solitary breathing and the low hum of the little electric motor of the scooter.

He remembered how much he enjoyed the peace and quiet and the feeling of isolation. He switched the toggle on the scooter to slow, looked behind him to Ricky who had given him a thumbs up and started to travel along the rocky coast-line. Perhaps there was more than one cave on the island. In fact now he came to think about it the likelihood was that the place would have dozens of them. It wasn't long before he came across a dark water inlet. The water coming out of this, he could see it streaming out, bringing small amounts of sand and debris with it, was warm. Very warm. David beckoned to Ricky to follow. Ricky pointed at the front of the underwater scooter to a light. The switch was near the speed control. David switched it on and a beam of light lit up the narrow corridor ahead of them. Behind him Ricky had switched on his own light and it surrounded David in an eerie blue shroud. The water had become the temperature of a warm bath and was getting murkier but he could still see some distance. There seemed to be a bend up ahead and he could make out the faintest of lights. David was excited as hell. When they dived around here all those years ago he must have done the diluted tour, the tour designed for the lowest common denominator.

This was a different thing altogether. As he turned the corner in the pipe he turned to see Ricky was keeping very close. They stopped together for a moment. David noticed the water behind Ricky was pitch black. The lights from the scooters lit where they were kneeling magically. David could see the obvious excitement in Ricky's eyes through the clear glass face mask. David motioned for them to continue, turned again and rolled the control thumb wheel slowly forward. The machine dragged him towards the faint light. Ricky followed closely behind. Now the light had travelled a little towards them but the source looked to be some thirty metres away. The temperature of the water was getting warmer and warmer. David rolled the thumb-wheel up a couple of notches and a little green indicator light moved to halfway along its register. He was flying again.

The visibility was not so good now but he could see the source of the light now not so far away. He looked at his depth gauge. They were 15 meters below the surface. The water, still very warm was clearer now and they could see they were in a bowl of sorts. Ricky pointed upwards and they swam towards the surface. They both pulled off their masks. They were in a round crater maybe half a mile across. They looked around for a place to land and saw some low rocks jutting into the water behind where they had come from. They swam over and one by one scrambled up onto the rocks and pulled their underwater scooters with them. They were both relieved to remove their oxygen tanks. Ricky looked at the gauge on his tank.

"We'll have to be careful on the way back." He said as David was looking for a place to perch himself and rest on the black volcanic rock. He sat on his haunches admiring the black prehistoric looking landscape.

"Why have you bought me here Aim?" Said David eventually breaking the silence.

"It wasn't me." Said Ricky. "You led all the way."

"No Aim. You know what I mean. To a remote uninhabited Island."

"I do have a reason." Said Ricky, his head held downwards. He didn't look at David when he said this.

David nodded in understanding.

"Thought you might," Said David as he sipped from a water flask. "Are you and Garret in it together?"

Ricky turned his head as if he were trying to listen to a very faint sound from a long way away.

"Davy," He said. "You have added up the numbers wrong."

"Have I?" Said David. "I'm the only man alive who knows who you really are Aim. I could come clean myself couldn't I and that would be the end of your idyllic life of Reilly."

Ricky nodded.

"I see what you mean now." Said Ricky in a sarcastic tone. "I'd never thought of that. Yes you do hold rather a lot of power over me don't you." His voice went back to normal.

"Come on Davy. Think about it. If I'd have wanted you out of the way why didn't I just let those goons in Casablanca have you or any of the others that have been chasing us?"

David thought for a moment. He suddenly felt a bit silly but he still wasn't sure.

"What's in that tube Aim?" He said pointing to the Aluminium tube that Ricky had brought with him from the boat.

Ricky looked down to the aluminium cylinder.

"It's just a beacon Davy. In case we get into trouble. They can locate us."

David nodded again slowly towards Ricky. The explanation about what was in the tube seemed plausible.

"I'm really not sure about you Aim. Show me."

Ricky tossed David the aluminium tube. David unscrewed the cap and saw a blinking green LED light inside. He screwed the cap back on and threw the cylinder back to Ricky.

"Davy, I'm your friend."

David nodded.

"Let me just recount. Maybe, me falling overboard was planned. You let me live in exile for thirty years. Is that something a friend does? Why Aim. Why didn't you tell me?"

"I don't think I know why Davy. There's a lot to tell you though Davy. Really. A lot, but why? I'm not entirely sure I know why."

"Have a go Aim. Have a go."

"I don't know why I didn't tell you Davy. You know where we both started Davy. It wasn't in the gutter like so many people like to make out. We were lucky boys, Davy. Who before you in your family ever went to university for goodness sake? We were given everything and yet we were kids. We wanted excitement and risk. We wanted more."

"Don't bullshit me Aim. I've tried to put two and two together over the years and I've never been able to make four. I want to know the truth."

"When we were recruited by the English fellah with the hat, Davy, we both thought it pretty cool to be players. I was never really sure who you were or what side you were on."

"I didn't even know there were sides."

"Whatever your motives were, Davy, we were both taking the shilling. Back then Roland Garret was a young thug who'd done his time in the IRA at the dirty end. He got wind, I don't know how, of me supplying the British with information. He saw he had an angle. He threatened to expose me to the council and I'd have become just another body to be found in a ditch somewhere with a single bullet through my head. Garret proposed a little deal to me. The arms from Gaddafi were supposed to make the difference Davy. That's what they were saying. Unknown to them Garret had other ideas. He knew that the British were in the ascendant. He knew that the people didn't really have the heart any more. They were becoming richer, slowly maybe but richer. The feeling was it was time to move on and they didn't want their young men to die for the cause anymore. Garret saw a way to get onto the winning side. The mines were a safeguard for Gaddafi. They were one of his conditions of supply. He didn't want Britain to know the arms were coming from him. If the operation were to become compromised the crew would evacuate on the RIB and then scupper the boat with the cargo."

"So he ordered you to sabotage the limpet mines" Said Davy.

"He not only did that, he told the English where to look for the boat. As it happened a French customs boat was sent, the shipment was seized, as a result no more shipments would be made, end of party. It really did signal the beginning of the end. At the time there were all sorts of rumours about who was having secret talks with the British. Well it was Garret. He did a deal with them that kept his involvement out of the public eye and kept it from the Council. He played a cool game for years. Thing is, thirty years have gone by. The story is about to become public knowledge. The secret files detailing the findings of the public enquiry are about to be published."

"Garret was the IRA Mole?"

Ricky nodded "He has the most to lose from the information becoming public. He'll last days at most if the current council get wind. Even with his personal protection."

"So there are still people in Ireland who hold a grudge?"

"You bet there are."

"So where is this information now?"

"Part of my company deals with public relations. My media company has a worldwide reach and is practically a monopoly. High profile people come to us to handle their public relations. This is a euphemism for paying us to either publish good stories about them or paying us not to publish bad ones. This is of course tantamount to blackmail but there you are. I'm not necessarily proud of it Davy, but I really do have the power to make or break anyone. Not all publicity is good publicity contrary to what you might have heard. Anyway, Garret came to me. It was strange all these years later sitting across the table from him. After a few months of us handling his affairs he thought he could trust me I suppose and he asked me if I knew anyone who, given the appropriate codes could hack the government database and delete the files that he didn't want being made public."

"And you knew of such a person."

"Brace yourself Davy. That person was your eldest son."

"Martin?" Said David in a high pitch. "I thought he was a builder."

"No Davy. He's not a builder. Least not in the traditional sense."

"After the explosion I spent eight months in a military hospital. To all intents and purposes I was dead. You'd left Ireland later that same day. No-one knew where you had gone but then that was the idea. They rebuilt my face and after about two years I decided to take the risk and return to Ireland. No-one recognised me so I stayed a while."

"What, not even your family? Not even Moira?"

Ricky shook his head.

"Tell me about Martin. I want to know about the boys."

"I'll get to them. But Davy, it's a long story."

"It's a lovely afternoon." Said David looking up at the sky. He pointed to where the sun was sitting above the ridge of the crater. "We've probably got an hour before it gets a bit gloomy in here."

"I'm going to go back to before the bomb. Davy. To before that first shipment of arms was intercepted by the French coastguard. I was in Khoms negotiating with the Libyan authorities about the shipment when I met a fellah called Said Barrachat. Barrachat was recently assassinated at his home in North London by a pro. The bullet used was from that original customs haul. You wouldn't do that by choice would you? You'd use modern ammunition."

"I've no idea Aim." Said David looking confused.

"I became the broker in a deal between the Libyans and the Liberians. There was a civil war going on in Liberia secretly financed by the CIA."

"Wo-Wo," said David. "Slow down. I thought you were joking when you said it could have been the CIA."

Ricky nodded his head before continuing.

"The CIA couldn't be seen to be dealing with the Libyans even if it was underground so they used me. I was in the right place at the right time and I always thought something was going to go wrong but to cut a long story short I hauled in six million dollars from the deal. Back then I took it by boat across the Med to Italy and drove it up to Switzerland. Quite a hefty suitcase. Those days no one was that interested in where the money came from. That was about a month before that last night we played in the pub and the bomb blast."

"This is not getting better Aim. You had six million dollars sitting in a bank account, and you didn't say anything to me." He thought for a moment. "Explains the money in the guitar though."

"I'm not entirely sure why I didn't say anything to you Davy. I'd like to think it was for the right reasons but I'll never know that now. I was crapping myself I'd be caught. As it turned out it was probably better you knew nothing about it. At least it was then. In the transcripts of the inquiry, I was named, well Eamonn Boothe was named and was recorded as being deceased. You, I'm afraid

Davy were scapegoated and named as the double agent. All the details about you and the man you became after that time are catalogued in that document. Although the information hasn't reached the public attention yet, it has got into the hands of the intelligence community. This is a euphemism for a rather tight knit club of professional assassins and agents working for a diverse selection of employers from sovereign states to terrorists. We are not talking about divorce and cheating wives."

David was looking at his feet trying to take in what Ricky was saying. Ricky continued.

"Your eldest son Martin is a member of this club."

"So my son was trying to kill me yesterday?"

"No Davy. Martin was the man I used who arranged for the incriminating information to be deleted from the government database. As of now everything that happened back in '84 and that was discussed and documented at the enquiry, didn't officially happen. What happened yesterday is because the two guys Martin employed to do the job took it upon themselves to make a copy. I wasn't aware of this but in their game it's apparently standard practice. That copy was subsequently stolen by another freelancer who is loosely speaking employed by me also. I'd asked her to keep an eye on them."

"Loosely speaking employed by you?" David repeated.

"I've kind of made it my business over the years to get these people on my side. Better the devils you know. Apparently she's something of a Kaiser Soze figure. Her reputation for being a ruthless psychopath is as well-known as her lack of discretion and within forty eight hours of her getting hold of the stick, the Irish, the Libyans, the Liberians and the CIA all knew about the leaked papers and you are now on a wanted poster."

"So who were those people yesterday?"

"Like I said, I'm not sure. It could have been any of them."

"So why are the Irish after me?"

"Because according to the enquiry transcripts you were a double agent working for the British and they still regard this as a heinous crime."

"And the Liberians?"

"Unknown to me the arms we were buying from the Libyans and I was selling to the Liberians through the CIA were sub-standard to say the least. Practically nothing worked. They felt short changed."

"This is obviously part of the problem Aim. You sell some duff guns to terrorists and call it 'short change', and the Libyans?"

"I effectively stole those consignments from Libya. I'm dead Aim. You got the blame. These are the people who are the most dangerous. Well together with the Liberians. They really take it personally. They want everyone to pay."

"What does that mean?"

"It means they will go after anyone close to you. They are happy that the child pays for the sins of the father. That means your family. These people are gangsters Davy. They will hurt anyone close to you if they think it will hurt you."

"But I don't have a family any-more. Aim. Not since I left."

"You do Davy. You do."

"You said that in a very strange way Aim."

"Davy, I said it was complicated and it is."

"Keep talking Aim."

"I'd returned to Ireland as a different person. I was free and rich but I was guilty. You were exiled from your family. Do you remember what we agreed that night in the back room of the pub? No-one must know. Well nobody does know. Yet. I decided that as you had had the rotten luck and mine had been half decent…" David wagged a finger at Ricky aggressively.

"Hold on now Eamonn. Not sure you can put all this down to a bit of rotten luck. Don't you dare start saying you had nothing to do with this."

"I won't Davy. I won't. I know I can't bring back the past but I can try to make the future happen like it should."

David was shaking his head.

"I think I might have had enough of this. I'm thinking maybe you don't have the answers. You just think you do."

David picked up his face-mask and stood up.

"Please Davy. Sit down. At least hear me out." Said Ricky. David reluctantly re-settled himself on the rocks. Ricky waited a moment before continuing.

"I vowed I'd look after your family. Make sure they all did ok. Your eldest, Martin, he was a difficult one for a few years. Got involved in a fraud scam and went to prison for a brief spell. That's where he met all his colleagues in the business. I couldn't stop that from happening. I wasn't yet powerful enough."

"Do you mean you could now?" Said David still with a slightly angry tone to his voice. Ricky nodded without embarrassment or conceit. Ricky continued.

"When he came out I employed him to do some technical work. I've no idea where he learnt it but he's a formidable engineer. He doesn't know who I am. At least I don't think he does. Paul was different. Is different. He lives alone now in a little flat. He has never accepted help however well I've disguised it. He is fiercely independent and appears to live in his own little dream world."

"What happened to Moira and the girls?" Asked David.

"I looked after them Davy."

"You looked after them." Repeated David. "Those two girls, Katy and Nana. Are they who I think they are?"

"Yes Davy. They are." Ricky waited. Expecting a reaction. David remained calm.

"But they call you Daddy."

"I married Moira Davy." There was a silence between the two men for a few moments.

"You really did the whole nine yards. With a friend like you a man really doesn't need an enemy. Where is Moira now? Is she OK?"

"She's fine Davy. She lives in St Tropez. We don't really get along anymore." Said Ricky. The silence returned for a few more moments until Ricky nervously spoke again.

"It just seemed to happen, Davy. I didn't plan anything."

"You don't need a plan to do the wrong thing Eamonn."

David shuffled about on the rocks before pulling down the big nylon zipper on the front of his wetsuit.

"Do you know anything about the man who did this?" He said indicating towards the welted scars on his chest.

"Of course I do." Said Ricky glad that David had moved on. "He was a British agent deep under cover in the IRA. These days he runs a security firm in south London. He has recently got involved with this business."

"How would that have happened?"

"Kaiser Soze probably. She would have told someone who told someone who got him," Ricky pointed at David's chest, "one the job. Which brings me to another delicate point. A piece of information that may shock you." David shook his head at the irony.

"I hardly want to tell you to continue." Said David. "But to be honest in the last twenty four hours…" He shrugged.

"Your eldest isn't Martin, Davy. Your eldest is a girl, well hardly a girl, an independent, intelligent woman called Jill. She runs a publishing company."

"Don't tell me. A publishing company you own."

"Well. Yes actually. Anyway, she had her bag stolen by your man's gorillas. They were looking for the stick. They thought she had it."

"The stick?"

"Well one of them. The guys who did the job on the database decided to copy the data onto a memory stick. Except they didn't put it all on one. Half is on one stick and half is on another. A little yellow plastic usb memory with a smiley face on."

"Did she have it?"

"She had one of them."

"Did they steal it from her?"

"Yes."

"So they've got half the information. Who has the other half?"

"I do."

Ricky nodded in a slightly embarrassed way and David nodded along with him.

"Aim, I've known about Jill her whole life. I ran away Aim. I was eighteen. Surely you can't think I didn't know about her. My idiot logic said she was better off without me and from what you are saying she and the rest of them might still be better off without me."

"She was better off without you or you were better off without her?" Said Ricky immediately regretting it.

"Don't you start preaching to me." Said David angrily again. "I'm a hairs away from losing it."

"I'm sorry Davy." Said Ricky. "I'm no-one to judge. She's fine though. I've a feeling you'll be seeing her soon."

"I don't like being manipulated Aim." David glanced at the diving knife sat in a rubber sheath strapped to his calf.

"Maybe I should just slit your throat and let you slide beneath the waves."

"Maybe that's a good idea for us both. But it wouldn't end there Davy. I have responsibilities. However right or wrong the reasons you do too. I have to protect these people. I have to protect them from the consequences of mistakes I made in the past."

David thought for a while trying to take it in. Trying to rationalise.

"If the report incriminates Garret then why not just let it be published. Garret will get his comeuppance."

"I think it's better that the information in the report remains private." Said Ricky.

"And why would that be. I didn't do anything. You did."

"That's not entirely true now Davy is it. You spied on the IRA for the British. If it becomes public then you'll be dragged out from hiding and probably sent to jail that is if you're not killed by the Irish, Libyan or Liberian contingent first."

"But then Garret gets off Scott free."

"Well maybe not. I happen to know that your son Paul is what is called a private eye completest. He has a collection of Private Eyes."

"I used to collect them." Said David. "I had an original number one. We used to use them for…"

"The coded messages." Ricky finished his sentence. "Yes I know. The fact that your son Paul collects Private Eye magazines and the fact that you used to as well are not unconnected."

"Why."

"One of your friends sent him your collection after you went. Don't really know why. They cleared out your house, found a stack of magazines and thought that maybe they should give Paul something to remember you by I suppose."

"Why Paul and not Martin."

"Don't know. I think Paul was easier to find at the time."

"Why would this change things with Garret."

"You must remember Davy. Because like an idiot you tallied up all the coded notes and left them in the magazine they referred to. That wasn't really the idea with a secret code."

"And you think that there is enough there to incriminate him."

"More than enough. There are messages ordering me to murder you, details of the car bomb including addresses of targets. All stuff that was in the enquiry but if the transcripts get deleted could not be known in any other way."

"And how would that work then. How would we use it?"

"Do you remember the man in the hat?"

"We never knew who he was."

"When I was in hospital he came to see me. He said that I would come out looking significantly different to when I went in and that for a while I'd not look too pretty. He was the one that suggested that I return to Ireland. I'm fairly certain that he knew about the deal I did with the Liberians but I really to this day don't know about his motives for helping me. We've remained friends of sorts all these years although we rarely meet. He has become the commissioner of the metropolitan police. He is a powerful man. We exchange information from time to time. I am able to find out things through my unofficial network that he can't. Through my papers and media companies I manage, again unofficially his public relations and it was at least partially down to me that he became the commissioner. He knows something of my little scheme. He's helped me put it together."

"Your little scheme Aim? There you go again. It's all just a game to you. So all this is not just coincidence."

"No Davy. Far from it. If I'd have let events take their course then the wrongs I did earlier in my life would just keep having consequences. I had to do something to stop that happening. If I hadn't become a rich and influential man Aim I wouldn't have been able to do it. But I am so I can. The Man in the Hat approached me a year ago to tell me that something needed to be done. He said that the British government was never going to expose Roland Garret but they would have sacrificed you. To them you are disposable. The Man in the Hat told me about the official secrets act and the thirty year rule."

"Why didn't you just have the documents erased if you could do that and be done with it?"

"That was the original plan. It would all have just disappeared slowly. If Martins guys had done as they were asked instead of getting busy making copies then we would not be here now. But they did and we are and I thought that maybe that's how it was meant to be. Maybe this is the only way to put the balance back. If we didn't, Garret and his ilk, get away with it. The bastards and the bullies win again. I didn't want that to happen. There was more to it though Aim."

"More to it?"

"I've got to a time, Aim. A time where I want to be forgiven. A time when I want to do the right thing. I wanted to get the family back together. Your family back together. I feel I was the architect of its demise so I could put it back again. I wanted to reunite you with your kids Aim. It's the least I could do before,"

"Before what? Before I die. Before you die? Before what?"

"Well yes I suppose. I'll not live forever and neither will you."

"But I'm not dead yet."

"I know that Aim. But the years are going by and…"

David had a tinge of impatience in his voice. He was thinking that Ricky was sounding melancholy as if looking for sympathy.

"Your little scheme. Aim. Continue with that."

"I'd watched over the kids, all of them as if they were mine. I've tried to keep them out of trouble and tried to keep them employed. They don't know who I am. Or at least who I used to be. They don't know I'm an old friend of their natural father. Jill knows me as Ricky. She and I see each other because she runs the publisher I own. She has no clue. Some years ago she went to Ireland in search of information about you. As far as I am aware, when she returned she did nothing with whatever information she had gleaned. Martin works for me sometimes as I said. I've got an idea he knows more about you than he lets on. Fairly certain he knows nothing about me or our connected past. Paul was a difficult one. He gets by, just. I've tried to throw some work his way but it never comes to anything. Katy and Nana do not know. I've never had the heart to tell them. They're good girls you know. I had this stupidly elaborate idea. I thought if I could get everyone together in one place. On their own accounts you know. As if it were their ideas then I might just initiate a reunion. This is how I thought it might work. Jill runs the publisher Phillips and Pullman. They practically have only one writer on their books and that is Ian Whitting. He and Jill need a good story. I thought they don't get better than this. I gave Jill a scaled down version of the report and the use of two of Martins men to do some investigations. Involving Paul was more difficult. I added to the report saying that he was your son and that he should play a part. We decided that Paul should not know why he is to go to Lanz because if he did he wouldn't go."

"Lanz. Is that where they are all going? Is that where we're all headed. To my place?"

"Yes it is."

"We set Paul up using the private eye small ads. Jill and the writer are going to get a story."

"So will the writer write the story?"

"Not if you don't want him to."

"Paul is at your hotel posing as a rare book dealer. I imagine he thinks you have some Private eyes to sell."

"Martin. Why is Martin there?"

"The Man in the Hat and I arranged for him to be very theatrically shot. Not literally you understand. They missed. I like elaborate displays. They make better news stories. My people were on the scene hours before anyone else. The Man in the Hat assigned a real hot shot detective to the case. Given the clues they have taken the bait big time. Did you know Martin has a house on Lanzarote?"

"No I didn't. Where?"

"Not that far away from your place."

"And you are on a sailing holiday with Katie and Nana."

"That's right."

"So there you are Aim."

"You get us all back together and what then. We are all supposed to just have big hugs and all is forgiven."

"Something like that."

"Well I can't see it happening like that."

"How can you see it ending?"

"I've no idea but we'd better get cracking."

They gathered up their things, put the air canisters on their backs. Davy slipped into the water. The sun was about to dip down past the ridge of the crater. Ricky passed down to him the two sub aqua scooters. As Davy was putting on his face-mask, Ricky wedged the little aluminium cylinder firmly between two sharp rocks.

18

A round of polite applause rose from the thirty or so seated gentlemen assembled for lunch in the elegant member's dining room of Chislehurst golf club. Martin Farmer was due to address the weekly Monday lunchtime meeting of the Orpington Rotary club. These days he is a wealthy and highly respected businessman. The assembled pillars of the community would be gracious in his presence but would remain ignorant of the real story of Martin Farmer's past. They would have invited him to talk at their lunch even if they were aware of the truth as it was every bit as interesting as what he had planned to talk about. In the past 18 months or so he'd been asked to speak a dozen times about his life and he had invented for the purposes of being accepted into this community of mostly honest middle class men, a story about his early days that was pure fiction. He liked the storyline he had created. He almost wished that that was how it was. The more he told the story the more he began to believe it himself.

The members had finished their main course and two matronly ladies were serving the desserts. The chairman of the meeting, a man in his sixties who ran a newsagents, tapped a spoon on the side of his glass and in a voice inappropriately quiet for the job, called for some silence and introduced Martin Farmer. There was a definite atmosphere of anticipation in the room. Martin Farmer wasn't like anyone else that had spoken at the lunchtime meetings. He was wealthier than anyone there for a start or at least it appeared that way. He was dressed as if he were on his way to a photo shoot in an obviously expensive suit and the Bentley he had arrived in was driven by a chauffeur wearing a chauffeurs cap. All very impressive stuff. He was standing as the applause subsided and a wag from the back of the room heckled.

"Stand up Martin, we can't see you from back here."

There were harrumphs of laughter. Martin Farmer, noting the culprit, theatrically stood on his chair to another smattering of applause and good humoured laughter.

He acknowledged the applause with a bow of his head and waited a few seconds for the room to become silent which it did quickly.

"Gentlemen," he began, loving the attention. (If things had been different he would have been an actor.)

"Gentlemen," he repeated, "I may not be the tallest man in the room here but I'm a great believer in using whatever resources you have available to you to your best advantage."

He paused again for effect then continued and pointedly singling out the wag from the back of the room raised his voice just a little.

"Can you see me now, Sir?"

The atmosphere in the room turned chilly with Martin's distinctly aggressive tone and his obviously false and belligerent smile. The wag, a cumbersome scrap metal dealer from South London with the social skills that matched his physique took a swig from his wine glass and pointedly refused to meet Martin's stare.

"Well can you, Sir?" The atmosphere went from chilly to cold. After a few seconds Martin continued, raising his hands. The room warmed a little as Martin's face changed to a broad, less contrived, smile. There was to be no more heckling. Martin liked to be in control and now he had laid out his ground rules it would stay like that. It would for the next two minutes.

"I thank you gentlemen for inviting me today. But I must confess to never quite understanding your organisation."

Some of the audience raised their eyebrows. The less conservative among them were enjoying this distinct alternative to the usual lunchtime address where middle class businessman get a chance to stand up and tell their peers about what it is they actually do. (Which in nine out of ten cases turns out to be incredibly boring.) Even those more conservative would be a little shocked at what was about to happen and on account of this Martin Farmer would be unlikely to receive another invitation to talk at a Rotary Club lunch, however interesting his story was, let alone an invitation to join their ranks.

In the grounds thirty meters away and directly across the raised eighteenth green a figure wearing khaki shorts and a green fleece was lying prone on the ground secreted by the bank and a covering of thick undergrowth. Through the cross-hairs of a Hecler and Koch telescopic sight the back of Martin Farmer could be seen standing on his chair, framed in the foreground by a tall box sash window and, forming the background to the picture, a huge crystal chandelier, the centrepiece and focal point of the elaborately decorated room. It would have made a great photograph. The optics in the sophisticated sight in conjunction with low bright sunshine on this clear November day, had the effect of framing Martin in the centre of a kaleidoscope.

"Who does he think he is?... prick." The prone figure whispered slowly out loud.

The sight was attached to a Russian made Dragunov assault rifle equipped with a sports silencer.

"Talk about putting yourself on a pedestal." The figure said even slower and in rhythm. The figure was wearing earphones attached to a mobile phone which was lying in the grass just in eye-line.

"You're a worldwide organisation with many important and influential members. The power you could wield if you were to work together could be immense." Inside the members dining room Martin Farmer was in full rant. Much to the almost universal chagrin of the audience who to a man liked their club just the way it was.

"I'm ready when you are' a voice whispered into the phone lying in the grass. 'Just show me the sign."

"And yet you call yourselves a-political." Martin Farmer continued.

The mobile phone bleeped with an incoming picture text message which took a few seconds to appear on the screen. It was a 'thumbs-up' symbol. The gun was re-aimed and the trigger squeezed. The gun thumped backwards but barely a whisper was heard from the muzzle of the gun. The sights were checked. Further action was considered but thought unnecessary. The job was successfully completed. The gun and telescopic sight were disassembled and packed into a black rucksack. Sideways a meter and down a bank towards a small clearing around an electricity substation a royal mail postman's push-bike was waiting. A red postman's jacket was pulled from the rucksack and put on over the green fleece.

The rucksack was placed in the red and yellow post bag that was sitting in the wire framed basket over the handle bars. A whistle could have been heard if there was anyone there to hear it, which there wasn't as the assassin freewheeled down the long hill that is the private road that borders the south side of the golf course. At the bottom of the hill a small van was driving at a snail's pace under the arch of the railway bridge that crossed the road. The assassin, peddling lazily, followed the van into the short tunnel on the push-bike. Only the small van emerged from the railway arch. A canny getaway indeed as when the police made enquires along this road, not a single householder, not a gardener or a tradesman saw anything unusual that day. Posties often ride their bikes down this hill.

    Back in the members dining room the bullet had smashed through the old glass of the upper sash of one of the tall windows that overlooked the eighteenth green. Rather than leaving a neat hole, as the plan had imagined it would, the bullet fragmented the old brittle glass and it exploded into the room. Martin Farmer caught the majority of the debris as he was standing on a chair only feet from the window. Several shards lodged themselves in Martin's back, totally ruining a brand new midnight blue bespoke cashmere wool three piece suit. After the bullet had shattered the glass it passed within six inches of Martin's left ear and made its way toward the chain holding the centrepiece chandelier. The chandelier held onto its mount for perhaps three seconds and then fell to the ground from a height of sixteen feet. The supply cable broke and caused the RCD to trip. All the lights on the ground floor went out. The afternoon sun streamed weakly in through the tall, narrow, box sash window. Within a second of the bullet hitting the glass everyone in the room except for Martin Farmer were underneath the tables. When, two seconds later the huge chandelier fell to the floor the noise was loud enough to make the Rotarians believe that they were under a full scale attack. As the dust subsided a few of the braver ones poked their heads out. They saw that Martin Farmer, having been thrown onto the top of the table he was standing on a chair in front of, was starting to gather himself together. A small amount of blood goes an awfully long way and mixed with half eaten bowls of sherry trifle can give the impression that things are a lot worse than they actually are.

As it was, no-one in the room sustained physical injuries severe enough to require any more than a sticking plaster but emergency services were called just in case and this provoked what some of the Rotarians described, rightly or wrongly as 'an over-reaction.'

The circular gravel driveway that held an elaborate water fountain at its centre was, within minutes filled with three police cars, a police van and three ambulances. Within fifteen minutes a STARR MEDIA television news crew was setting up its outside broadcast van and the occupants of the member's dining room were being evacuated to the men's locker room. Within the hour a police forensics team had arrived wearing white coveralls and the police had commandeered the member's bar to set up a temporary incident room and no-one was allowed to leave without being questioned personally by detective inspector Sarah Quinn who had assumed control of the investigation.

"Are you sure you feel up to this Mr. Farmer?" Asked the detective to a dishevelled but otherwise seated and calm Martin Farmer. "Can we get you anything?"

"Yes. Yes, I'm fine," replied Martin. "But seeing as we're in a bar you could get me a brandy. Is this going to take long?"

The detective nodded at the uniformed constable who was standing half to attention with his hands clasped together in front of him, guarding the door to the room. The officer went behind the bar and scouted about for a brandy bottle.

"There's been a very serious incident here this afternoon Mr. Farmer. It'll take as long as it takes. We're treating this as attempted murder. Have you any reason to believe anyone would want you dead?"

Martin Farmer laughed a false laugh that made his shoulders bob up and down.

"My dear," he said in his most patronising manner, "I could give you the names and addresses of half a dozen or more people who would like to see me dead but I'd be very surprised if any one of them would have the balls to go through with it."

The officer getting the drink, only a very young man, placed an obviously expensive, unopened bottle of brandy and a glass on the table in front of Martin Farmer. Sarah Quinn's nostrils flared as she tried unsuccessfully to hide her frustration at the officer's complete lack of common sense.

"If you'd be kind enough to go through that list with my colleague shortly, I'd be obliged." Said Sarah Quinn, squirting the young officer a furious look.

"Couple of things," said Martin, "A window I'm standing in front of..."

"Standing on a chair in front of, apparently." Sarah corrected.

"A window I am standing on a chair in front of," Martin continued, "For no apparent reason, shatters and then a light fitting falls to the ground. Why do you think it was anything to do with me?" Martin pulled his chair forward towards the table and ran his thumbnail around the seal of the Brandy bottle, pulled the cork out with a twist of his wrist and sniffed it.

"OK. Mr. Farmer," It was Sarah Quinn's turn to be patronising. "It's clear that neither you nor any of your colleagues..."

"I wouldn't describe any of them as colleagues." Martin interrupted, "I was giving a talk at a Rotary Club Lunch for goodness sake."

"Neither you or any of your... audience?" She nodded at him for approval and he shrugged his shoulders in reply.

"Neither you or any of your audience realise that the commotion...? Yes. Shall we call it that for the time being, the commotion here this afternoon was caused by a rifle bullet." She paused a moment to see Martin's reaction but she got nothing. She was pleased with herself all the same. She continued. "A nine millimetre round of the kind usually used to kill rhinoceros was found lodged in the ceiling by the chandelier. Forensics estimated from the glass fragments where this might have come from and found a patch of ground on the other side of the eighteenth green that had been trodden down recently. If the bullet had come from there and you were standing on your chair where your friends say you were standing on your chair, we estimate the bullet missed the back of your head by mere inches."

She had got Martin Farmer's attention and she knew it. He knew she knew. He was pouring the brandy into a glass as he nodded at her.

"Your boy's got taste." He said. "You having one?"

"Yes," she said surprising herself. "Yes I will."

19

"A single bullet to the head, Sir. The victim was of Libyan origin but had been living in London for the past thirty years. Male. Seventy two years old. Wife died two years ago."

Detective Inspector Sarah Quinn was sitting across the desk from the commissioner of the London metropolitan police.

"The bullet used in the attempted assassination in South London three days ago was the same type that was used to kill the Libyan, Sayeed Barrachat in Marylebone last month. The thing that forensics found most odd sir, is that these rounds haven't been manufactured in over twenty years. They are of Russian origin and the last time they were used in any quantity was during a military coup in Liberia in the early Eighties. Rebel troops used them against the government forces." The Commissioner was listening intently to Inspector Quinn's account.

"Why have you brought this to me, Quinn? It's not that unusual for old stock to turn up on the street." Sarah was taken aback by the question. He had summoned her to this meeting. With a slightly puzzled look on her face she continued.

"According to the records the rounds match a batch seized in 1984 in a joint operation by British and French customs."

"I remember the operation." Said the Commissioner. "Ok so there's a connection between the two incidents. Again, why are you bringing this to me?" He was leaning forward across the desk staring at her.

"Well I..." She didn't really know what to say. She looked around her looking for a clue as to why the situation felt so strange.

"You summoned me, Sir." She said and then suddenly doubting herself. "Didn't you?"

The Commissioner appeared to be trying to communicate something with his expression, like he was playing charades but Sarah couldn't think for the life of her what it could be. She continued tentatively.

"I have come across security clearance issues when I try to access files. Even Martin Farmer, the intended victim of the attempted assassination at a Rotarian lunch doesn't seem to have much of a past and I've been 'access denied' on security grounds on both him and Barrachat. I suppose if I'm to do my job properly, I need access to the information."

The Commissioner stood up from his desk and moved to gaze out of the window as if deep in thought. He eventually turned around.

"DI Quinn. Leave this with me will you. I'll be putting you on leave from this afternoon. You've been working hard on this I can see. You need a break." He sat down at his desk again.

"But..." Sarah Quinn tried to protest but the Commissioner raised a finger to his lips to stop her from talking. He opened his desk drawer, pulled out a pad of lined paper and started scribbling on it. He continued talking in a theatrical manner that was different from the way he had been talking moments before, as he was writing.

"Yes, now Sarah." He glanced up toward Sarah briefly with an anxious expression. "Do you mind if I call you Sarah?" He continued his frantic writing.

"Yes, Yes." It took an age for these two little words to come out of his mouth. "Yes," he said again slowly.

"I'll contact your station later this afternoon. See if we can't swing a month. You'll need time to sort out those personal problems." Sarah was shocked.

"But I don't…" The Commissioner raised his hand again. He carefully tore the top three pages from the pad and folded the first of them into four. The three blank pages he fed through a shredder under his desk. Again he raised his finger to his lips. He stood up and Sarah Quinn did the same.

"Yes, leave this with me for the moment Sarah." He said and pushed the paper across the desk. Sarah slipped it into her handbag.

"Thank-you Commissioner…" Said Sarah not sure at all what had been happening, "for your time, Sir." They shook hands and he opened the door for her to leave. The Commissioner gave her a long hard stare as he shook her hand.

Sarah Quinn walked quickly to the police car pound and slung her bag onto the passenger seat of her silver-grey Ford Mondeo. As she drove out of the police station she saw a black Mercedes panel van parked illegally across the street. Her first instinct as a police officer born out of long years in the traffic section was to report it but it went out of her mind as she saw it pull into the road behind her. She drove towards Parliament Square and then over Westminster bridge. Ten minutes later she was on the Old Kent Road and heading back to the south London suburbs. At a red traffic light she stopped and reached into her bag for the piece of paper the Commissioner had given her. The handwriting was as legible as a doctor's handwritten prescription. Before she got a chance to read what it said, the lights changed and she put the piece of paper back in the bag on the passenger seat. She noticed a black Mercedes van directly beside her in the left hand lane. *Was that the same one that was parked outside the police station?* She was in stop start traffic now and the black Mercedes was keeping up with her. She picked up her mobile phone from her lap and dialled a number.

"Martin. Sarah...Martin, Hi, I know this is very unusual, Yeah I'm good thanks. I need to see you. Now."

She listened.

"No. I don't care. This is important."

She listened again.

"Where are you?...Something odd is going on...I'll be there in..." She looked at her watch, "thirty minutes."

She pressed the button that ended the call and glancing to her left saw the black Mercedes take a left turn away from her. She drove on in the traffic towards Bromley and arrived shortly at a house in a leafy suburban unmade road. She tooted her horn as she approached the gates and while waiting in the driveway for them to open, picked the piece of paper from her bag again. It took her a few moments to decipher the scribblings. She shook her head and stared into the distance before tossing the paper back into her bag as the gates swung open. She pulled her car around the crescent shaped driveway and parked behind the Bentley that was sitting outside the front door. As she walked past the car she felt the bonnet. It was cold. It had not been driven recently. Martin opened the door. He was dressed in a lightweight grey suit and an open neck shirt and looked like he was about to go somewhere.

"Well well," said Martin, a broad smile on his face.

"So soon."

She walked into the marble floored hallway and through the double smoked-glass doors straight ahead of her, through a small sitting room and into a double height kitchen the size of a squash court. The glass roof seemed a mile above and was letting the November midday sun stream in. Martin shut the front door and with a raise of his eyebrows followed Sarah through.

"I can't see a hat." He said. "Who are you going to be today, cop or robber?"

"This is not official Martin." She said as she perched herself on a stool by a marble breakfast counter. Martin nodded as he took a plastic pod from a chrome rack, placed it in a little red coffee machine and pressed a blinking green button.

"What is it then?" He asked.

"I'm taking a big risk coming here, like this Martin."

"Why is that?" He said as he swapped the pod in the coffee machine for another one and pressed the green button on the side again. "I can hardly be a suspect."

"No... You're not." She said. Martin noticed a nervousness about her. She was almost reluctant to talk. The coffee machine finished its job and Martin handed her the cup.

"No sugar, yes?" He said. Sarah Quinn nodded her head. She took a sip from the cup as Martin began to repeat the process for himself. Sarah picked out the piece of paper from her bag.

"Since we met the other day, after the incident..."

"Sarah," Martin interrupted. "If you're not here on police business then you don't have to speak in cop-speak. Relax."

"I wrote a report when I got back to the station. Really basic, some names, times, what we already knew, and I filed it the next morning just as I'm supposed to. I got a copy of the forensics report later that day. I'd done some poking around in the police records and as I was about to leave I got a call from the Commissioner in Scotland Yard. At first I thought someone was having a joke. He was ever so polite. Like a dad. He asked if I could come up to his office. That's where I've been this morning."

"Forgive me," said Martin. "But this is unusual is it?"

Sarah continued nodding. "It never happens. It was like something out of a film." She was holding the piece of paper in her hand.

"They've put me on leave, Martin. They don't want me looking at this case." She looked at him suspiciously, trying to read his face. She liked him. He was charming but she knew men like him didn't get to have all of this without telling a few lies.

"You haven't got any idea why that might be, have you?"

She tried hard to ask sweetly and with a smile on her face but she couldn't do it. It came out as an accusation. Martin wasn't flustered though. He sat down on the stool next to her with his cup of coffee and put his hand on her knee. She was shaking. The look on his face told her that he was sincere. It only took a fleeting glance.

"It was as if someone was listening in." She said.

"What's on the paper?" Asked Martin. She gave him the piece of paper and he took a few moments to read it before she continued.

"He kept on talking as he was writing this and shredded the paper underneath it." Martin listened.

"Anything else?" He said.

"He wouldn't let me speak. Just kept holding his finger to his lips."

"Where is your passport?" Martin asked.

What kind of question is that, thought Sarah as her doubts about him returned. Martin could see it in her face.

"Do you know something Martin?" She said. "Do you know something you should be telling me?" She had reverted back to her police inspector voice. Martin got up from his stool. He realised that the smug smile he had been wearing since she had arrived was no longer appropriate. He liked her. It was unexpected to say the least that she would stay with him that night. He laughed to himself briefly at the irony of him taking a shine to a police woman. They couldn't have been more different.

"I don't think he's taken you off the case." He said as he stood up from the marble bar top. "I think he's put you in deep." He pointed at the scribblings on the paper.

"An address and the names of five people." The smug smile was gone and was replaced by a worried frown. "Did you call anyone else other than me on your way here?" Asked Martin.

Sarah was shaking her head saying 'no' but also because these were not the questions that she was expecting Martin might ask. At least they weren't if he was the completely innocent party he was claiming to be.

"No I didn't." She replied "but," Martin stopped her short and asked another question that threw her further off balance.

"Did anyone follow you here?" Ok Now she was getting angry. Why would he ask that? She slid off the stool she was sitting on.

"Martin, you're not being straight with me." Martin had turned his back to her, his hands on the marble worktop either side of the piece of paper.

"I'll tell you all I know and believe me that may not be much." He walked away from the marble top a few paces, before turning again towards her.

"Sarah, I'm fifty years old, I'm well off and I live in a pretty fancy pile of bricks." He gestured around him. "I have no family, no life really except the business I do which on the whole is…" He shrugged. "Well…business. I met you the day before yesterday and although I'm not a man known for jumping the gun, I like you…"

"Thanks." Said Sarah, not trying to hide the sarcasm in her voice. Martin, although getting her little chide, continued.

"I have nothing to hide from you, or the police for that matter. I did do some time, it's true but that was twenty years ago. I have no reason to lie."

Not giving in so easily, Sarah hit back. She had been the victim of charming men before and was not going to let it happen again if she could help it. It didn't surprise her either that he'd been a bad boy in his youth. She made a mental note to pursue that line of questioning another time.

"Then why ask me if I was followed or if I used my phone."

"Well I can hardly say 'let's call the police,' can I?" He said with a little smirk on his face which he couldn't resist. His face returned to being serious when he saw that Sarah was in no mood for jokes. He stepped back to the counter top, picked up the paper and went over it again.

"There are five names on this paper." He said. "One of them is mine." Sarah looked quizzically at him. Her head pulling backward on her neck causing her chin to dip into her chest. She reached out for the paper.

"No it's not." She said 'Your name is Martin Farmer.' She didn't like where this might be going either. *Oh God.* She thought. *He uses a false name.* She looked again at the piece of paper, not that she needed to. Martin's name was not on it. Martin saw her struggling to understand and didn't want to keep her in the dark any longer.

"I was born Martin Crane. I was adopted into the Farmer family when I was three months old. I have a brother who I have never met and have no particular intention or desire to. My mother died giving birth to me. As far as my father is concerned I had an inclination to trace him some years ago, got nowhere except to know he was born in Lifford, a border town in Ireland."

Sarah let him finish what he was saying and felt a little guilty for thinking the worse about him. His short synopsis of his life brought out the mothering instinct in her and she looked on him kindly. He wasn't the sort of man who sought sympathy and he could see a little of what was going on in her mind.

"Don't give me that look." He said. "It's one of the reasons I keep it to myself."

"I'm not giving you any look." She replied unaware that she was. "What are the other reasons?"

Martin, ignoring her question, pulled down a monitor screen from underneath a wall cupboard and opened a top drawer containing a keyboard and a mouse. He tapped the space bar on the keyboard and a google search page appeared on the screen. He started tapping keys.

"My father was involved in the IRA." He blurted out without being prompted. "I got an idea he'll be at the address the Commissioner gave you."

Sarah Quinn was gradually putting two and two together although she was not coming up with anything close to four.

"It was over thirty years ago." Said Martin while concentrating on the computer screen. "I think we should go there."

"Go where?" Sarah asked lamely not believing he could mean to the address on the paper.

Martin pointed at the paper on the counter-top.

"There." He said, looking at his watch. "There's a flight out of Gatwick North to Arricefe at six fifteen this evening." Sarah heard the muffled sound of a printer coming from somewhere. Martin opened a lower cupboard door and pulled out two pieces of printed paper.

"They're not boarding passes. We'll have to check in."

Martin grabbed the coffee cups between thumb and forefinger and walked over to the sink. He ran them under a stream of water. As he was doing so he turned to Sarah and smiled her a big smile. She was sitting there on the stool a little dumbfounded by events. Her jaw was hanging open a touch.

"Come on." He said. "If we're going to catch these," he held up the printed papers. "We'll need to leave now."

20

They arrived at Arrecife on Lanzarote and were out of the airport a little after midnight. They were both wearing the clothes they had been wearing earlier in the day. They had no bags so were the first out of the terminal and into a taxi. Martin gave the taxi driver an address on a card. The driver looked at it and nodded as he opened the back door of the car. Thirty minutes later they turned off the main road. The roads appeared to get narrower until they disappeared completely and they were being bumped about in the back on dusty dirt tracks. Sarah, who had fallen asleep in the back under Martin's arm was awoken by the bumps. She could see nothing out of the side windows of the car.

"Where are we?" She asked.

"Not far now." Replied Martin. He said something to the driver which Sarah did not understand and they made a left turn along another narrow lane before stopping at some high iron gates. Martin pulled a key fob from his pocket, pressed a button and the gates swung apart. They drove through and along a neatly tended driveway towards a white house with a blue domed roof. It looked tiny. Like a shrine. The car swung round in front of the building and as it did so bright security lights flicked on. They both got out of the car. A strong wind blew in from the blackness on the other side of the house. As soon as they had closed the car doors the car drove off again. Martin led Sarah to the disproportionately large front door and fiddled with his keys in the lock till the door opened. He switched on the lights inside. There was marble everywhere and in the middle of the space was a double sided staircase going down. Three huge abstract pictures, in, Sarah thought, not very tasteful frames hung on the walls of the surprisingly large stairwell.

"This way." Said Martin. "Let's get ourselves a drink." He started to walk down the curved marble stairs and as he did so small lights automatically flicked on. As they walked down Sarah could see her reflection, seemingly miles away in a glass wall four stories high. Behind that was a swimming pool, blue and shimmering. Three sides were lit by underwater lights and the fourth finished somewhere in the blackness beyond. Around the pool the garden was slowly flicking into view as more lights blinked on. Sarah was excited and tired. She stopped briefly at the top of the stairs.

"Martin. Where have you brought me?" She said. Martin continued to walk down the stairs.

"Come on. Make yourself at home. It's my little hideaway." He said without turning around. Sarah walked down the staircase after him, gazing around her like a schoolgirl. The place was immense. The floor they walked onto was open plan with furniture arranged into groups of styles. Martin would not have liked it but Sarah thought it looked like a hotel lounge. Martin disappeared around a corner. Sarah followed to find Martin standing behind a bar, like a landlord of a pub, picking two glasses from a rack above his head.

"What'll you have? Maybe a Brandy?" He said with a smile and wink of his eye. Sarah smiled with him.

"You are the devil you are." She said. He poured two very large brandies into the glasses and leaned down into a fridge below the bar top and took out an ice bucket. He grabbed some ice in his hands and plopped the cubes into the glasses. Sarah, who had perched herself on a bar stool pulled one of the glasses toward her and eagerly took a sip.

"Mmm," she purred. "I think I needed that." Martin took his drink and stepped toward the side of the bar where a small light blue illuminated panel was set into the wall. Beside it, hung on a cradle, was a plastic rectangular box with its own little screen on and a round plastic toggle button.

"Twenty two degrees." He said as he pressed a switch on the box. "Can you believe it? In November."

Sarah turned to see the huge glass wall, all four stories of it, open in the middle and start to slide apart like a pair of curtains. She sat on her bar stool watching with her mouth hanging open.

"Aside from the people who built it, you're the first person to see this little marvel of engineering actually working." He said. As soon as the wall had parted a stream of balmy night air started to fill the room. It was scented by the sea and the garden outside. Although the wind at the top entrance had been strong, down where they were it was gentle and refreshing. The walls had parted enough for them to walk through.

"C'mon." Said Martin beckoning with a flick of his head. "It's beautiful out here."

Sarah slid off her barstool and picked up her drink. She had a smile on her face. She walked out through the slowly widening gap between the glass walls. In spite of the hour and her dog tiredness she couldn't remember a time when she had been more excited. Martin sat at a thick topped round wooden table on a chrome and teak chair. Sarah ambled toward the edge of the swimming pool and kicking off one of her shoes put her toe in the water. The water was the temperature of a warm bath. She walked towards the table

Martin was sitting at and before putting her glass down took a large gulp. She started to slowly undress in front of him. Martin sat there watching. A slight and contented smile on his face. She removed all her clothes in quite a long performance that included things she had never done in front of a man before. Martin reached out his hand to touch her but she seductively walked away towards the steps into the pool. She felt like a film star as one by one she tip-toed down the steps of the pool into the water. She let the water support her and swam. It was bliss. Martin got up from his seat where he had sat being happily entertained and took off his clothes. Within half a minute he had dived into the deeper end of the pool.

Four hours later Sarah was woken by sunlight, diffused by white linen curtains, streaming in through the window. Martin was still sleeping soundly next to her. She swung her legs out the side of the bed, stood up and stretched like a cat. She was naked. She needed something to wear.

All her clothes were embarrassingly now, in the bright light of day, around the perimeter of the pool. She opened a shiny gloss painted door to a fitted wardrobe ostensibly looking for a robe or something similar to put on. She found a thick white towelling robe in the second door she opened. She pulled it out and put it on. She continued to look in all the other cupboards and drawers although she had found what she was looking for. Maybe it was the detective in her. At least that is what she told herself. This had nothing to do with her job though. She was looking for evidence of another woman. She found nothing. She put on the thick towelling robe and checking that Martin was still sound asleep she ventured outside the bedroom. As she crept out of the room, Martin, who was snoring very lightly opened one eye. Very little of what Sarah saw tallied what she remembered from the previous evening. The glass wall was there, the pool was there. She didn't remember the corridor she had just come from and she didn't remember the huge kitchen she had just walked into-all stainless steel, like a catering kitchen with purposeful rather than pretty stainless steel cabinets. A huge central island containing a six burner industrial gas hob and above that an extractor unit that would not have been out of place in the police canteen. Everything was pristine and new as if it rarely if ever got used.

Such a shame. She thought. One of her secret passions was cooking and she was good at it even if only in her own opinion. She hardly ever got the opportunity to cook and she couldn't remember the last time she had cooked for a man. On one of the counter-tops sat a Gaggagia coffee machine. Not a domestic watered down version. No. This was the kind you'd see in a cafe in Florence- all chrome and brass pipes. She saw that a small red light was indicating that it was ready for operation. *In all that commotion last night did he remember to switch it on?* She can't remember seeing him do it but that doesn't mean he didn't. Or was it on from the last time he was here. How long ago was that? Maybe he has someone that comes in before he gets here and does things like that. Changing the beds and putting ice in the freezer. She opened a big industrial fridge and found it full of various brightly coloured produce. She went back to the coffee machine and looked over the controls. She felt the top and it was hot as hell. She took one of the coffee presser handles that was sitting on top of the chrome grill and filled it with ground coffee from the grinder next to the machine. She patted it flat, locked it into the holder on the machine and pressed the button beneath it. She took a cup from the top and placed it under the spout. The coffee took a few moments to start to splutter into the cup. While it was doing so she looked around her again. She noticed a digital keypad on the wall between the fridge and a steel door. There was a tiny blinking yellow light on the keypad. Next to it in small electronic letters it said ACCESS CODE. She pushed in four zeros and a red light appeared against the words ACCESS DENIED. She waited for the light to turn back to yellow and tapped in 1234. Again the machine indicated ACCESS DENIED. Frustrated she pushed at the chrome handle of the door and it swung open. As she stepped through the doorway the lights flickered on in the windowless room. It was the size of a double garage and could not have been in starker contrast to what she'd seen of the rest of the house. There were desks around three sides all strewn with papers and files and newspapers and all sorts of mess. Pencils, old flight boarding passes, three or four flick over calendars all showing different dates, pamphlets, newspapers, catalogues and books everywhere. A tower computer stood on top of one of the desks next to a wide screen monitor. On the wall behind this was a huge flat screen television.

There were year planners lining the walls from years ago. A confusing place. One of the desks seemed to be empty. A leather office chair sitting neatly in front of it. It seemed that the mess could not be contained on the two desks alone and was creeping slowly onto the relatively tidy one. She walked in and got closer to the desks. There were at least a dozen ring binder pads and various yellow post-it notes by three separate telephones as well as a cordless handset. As she strolled barefoot across the carpet trying to make some sense of this she was stopped in her tracks by the sight of her name, at least the name Sarah, written on a reporters pad poking out from under a magazine for optical equipment. With mild curiosity she moved the magazine and had to slump down on one of the chairs as she saw the name written down. It was her name. Sarah Quinn. Next to it was her mobile telephone number. A hundred questions started to formulate in her mind. Some of the hypotheses she came up with in those first few seconds, and there were many, were not very pleasant. She tried hard to think of a rational explanation as to how or why he would have her name and number written down here. In this room. A thousand miles away from home. An eerie chill went through her 'But No' she determined it couldn't be that. Not again. Martin was different. She just didn't get the weirdo vibe from him. But then in truth she hadn't from any of the other obsessive possessive control freaks she'd known. They'd all seemed pretty normal at the beginning.

She'd let him answer. That's what she would do. Her thoughts suddenly turned back to the coffee machine. She swivelled in the leather office chair and nearly jumped out of her skin. Her hands covering her muffled scream and both her knees sprang tightly up toward her chest. The office chair rolled backwards before banging into the cluttered desk. Martin was holding a cup of coffee in his left hand and, wearing only a pair of grey checked boxer shorts, was leaning against the door frame. He could have been there for a while. She must have looked genuinely terrified. The expression on his face was innocent and carefree. With his right hand he pointed to himself.

"Martin. Yeah. You were like... sleeping with me... not so long ago... over there." He pointed along the corridor towards the bedroom.

"You frightened me." Said Sarah her hands still covering her mouth. She didn't know if she should laugh or cry.

"Never mind Charley." He said weirdly putting the coffee cup down on a coaster on the cluttered desk. "I'm going to do us some breakfast. I've got some explaining to do." He kissed her on the forehead. A very un-sexy gesture but she somehow didn't mind. He walked out into the kitchen.

For some reason those last few words separated him from the others. Like he didn't believe his own hype, like he had a self-awareness she had never really seen in other men. Nothing she had seen she didn't like. Even if there'd been some deception on the way. *We all do that a bit don't we? Anyway. It's all about to become clear.* She thought and jumped out of the chair.

"No let me do it." She called.

21

"Sarah." Said Martin at last after they had laughed and joked their way through the process of cooking and eating breakfast. Half of Sarah's jokes were designed to elicit some small insight, some piece of information but then so were half of Martin's. Their mood was high though.

"Sarah," said Martin again. "You are wondering why your name and number is written on a piece of paper in an untidy room in an otherwise scrupulously tidy house belonging to a man you only met three days ago. Even though he is aware of your name and number he has not had opportunity to write it down on a piece of paper in that room over there. Or has he now? No he hasn't. Since you arrived he has not been out of your sight except maybe when you were sleeping but then why would he get up and go and scribble your name on a pad when it's already programmed into his phone. Any ideas?"

Sarah didn't miss a beat. She enjoyed being challenged.

"The hand-writing is not yours. The room is untidy because you are not in control of it. Someone else uses that room. Actually more than one other person works in that room. The tidy desk is yours, obviously. Given your need to be in control, as soon as you met me the other afternoon you phoned here. You phoned because if you'd have sent a text the person sitting here wouldn't have written it down. This is not a regular place of work though. All the documents and charts are in English. But we are on an Island a long way from England. And there is no natural light. You couldn't be expected to do a full days work in there."

Martin had raised his eyebrows and they had stayed raised while Sarah had been speaking.

"Why would you ring here," Sarah continued "and ask someone sitting at that desk to take down my name and number? The answer is that you wanted to know more about me. I'm not flattered by that. I think you just like to know who you are dealing with." Martin tried to interject but Sarah wouldn't let him. She was on a roll and she wanted to impress.

"I think we have been thrown together so to speak by my commissioner. I've no idea why but I'm hoping that what you are about to tell me will at least throw some light on why. Not that I'm complaining you understand."

"Wow." Said Martin. "I'd not seen it as being that obvious. But then now I look at it, it is."

"It's not obvious Martin. Not everyone sees the clues. They're always there though."

"You are one regular Sherlock Holmes. Sorry. I didn't mean anyone could do it." There was a short silence between them. Martin got up from the table.

"Do you want another cup of coffee?" He asked.

"Martin." Said Sarah reproachfully. He knew what she meant. He started making some more coffee. He was trying to work out where to start.

"I don't really know where to begin." He said.

"I'll help." She said. "What is it that you actually do here?"

"I provide a number of services to industry that are not necessarily recorded in their annual reports."

"Martin please." Said Sarah. "Just tell it like it is."

"Sarah. You've got to understand that much of what I and my colleague's do, while not exactly on the wrong side of the line isn't exactly on the right side either. Sarah. You're a policewoman. You play for the other side."

Sarah's expression changed. She was offended. She thought that Martin had taken her in to his confidence already but she was wrong. She got up from the table.

"Martin. It's obvious you don't trust me. Something is going on here but frankly I don't really care. I couldn't give a shit about your little boy games. The only problem with little boys playing with fire is that one day they get burnt. It's like this Martin." She was angry now. "I'm either in or I'm out. Make up your mind and make it up now."

She went to leave the room.

"Sarah, Sarah I'm sorry. You're in Ok. Come and sit down." Sarah turned and sat down again. She hoped she'd made her point.

"Ok." She said. "I'm listening."

"I'm an industrial spy if you like. One of the reasons we tend to talk in euphemisms is because there isn't really a simple description for what we do. We get asked to do all kinds of stuff."

"Tell me what kinds of stuff."

"I don't really get involved with the fieldwork. I leave that to the other two."

"Who are the other two?"

"Their names are Ben Wright and Terry Hall. Stage name Benson and Hedges. You're right. They are the other people who use that room."

Sarah hunted through her memory banks for the names but nothing came.

"Where are they now?"

"To be honest I don't exactly know. One of my customers asked if I could supply some labour. They are on a job somewhere undercover."

"Who are your customers?"

"I have a few." He hesitated.

"Listen Martin. I'm not looking to nab anyone but I'd like to get to the bottom of why the commissioner thought it prudent to give me those names."

"My biggest," he paused again. "My only customer is Ricky Starr."

"Of Starr Media."

"One and the same."

"So you work for Starr Media."

"Not exactly," he said. "I'm freelance."

"I'm not talking about how the Inland Revenue categorises you."

Martin shrugged his shoulders. Sarah noticed a change in him. It was as if the need to be male had seeped away. The natural instinct to have everything you say agreed with without question had gone. The bravado, the arrogance the conceit which all can carry some attraction had gone. She found herself having a weird thought. *I liked this Man when he was full of himself. I don't really like the gentle thoughtful empathic version.* She was staring at him. He hadn't noticed. He turned to meet her eye and she shook her mind out of the stare.

"The day you were shot at, a Starr Media outside broadcast van arrived on the scene even before the ambulance."

"Did it?" He said.

"Martin. Did you know that the day before you were shot at in South London a man of Libyan origin was shot dead in Marylebone in what appears to have all the characteristics of a pro hit? Do you know anything about it?"

Martin shook his head. Sarah knew he was telling the truth.

"There's a connection?"

"The bullets used were the same. From the same batch."

"How does that work? How do you know that?"

"It wouldn't normally work. We'd normally only be able to tell where they were made and when, but these were different. They were the same type of ammunition seized thirty odd years ago by customs on an arms smuggling raid."

Martin nodded slowly as if someone had just revealed the secret to the origin of the world and he understood.

Sarah saw it in his eyes. Martin laughed.

"What, I tell you that and now it's all clear?"

"It's not all clear but it's maybe starting to make some sense."

His demeanour had changed again. A bit of the lad had returned.

"Listen," He said. "Where would you start if you were investigating whatever, whatever this is?" He suddenly realised that they had nothing to actually investigate. But something was happening.

"Listen." He said again. "The commissioner obviously gave you a lead to something. He gave you a lead unofficially otherwise you'd have received outright orders, yes? That makes you unofficial. Like me. It makes you freelance. So where would you go first now you are in Lanzarote?"

"Well it's obvious, I'd go to the address on the paper."

"That's where we'll go then. Lunch at the Moridaira hotel then."

"Martin. You dragged me hear wearing the clothes I was standing in. I need to get some things. I'm not going anywhere until I've got some clothes to wear."

"No problem." Said Martin. "Put on what you've got." He looked at his watch. "We'll drive to Tesique in the hills. It's a great place. I know a shop there that will be just what we need. You'll love it."

"Martin, you've avoided telling me anything again. I'm going to want you to level with me."

"I will. I promise. Come on we'll talk while we're driving." He was very persuasive. He disappeared through the corridor into the bedroom.

"I feel like a rag doll." Said Sarah as she walked down some white concrete steps into a lower level garage.

"You'll be fine." Said Martin as they entered the cool dark space. Martin flicked the button on a remote control and a roller garage door started to rise up into the ceiling. As the light flooded into the garage a big smile appeared on Martin's face.

"My little plaything." He said. Sarah's face had lit up also. To one side of the garage next to a big silver car of indeterminate make sat a gleaming red convertible Ferrari Dino. Sarah walked up to the car and stared at it. Martin opened the passenger door. "Come on," he said. "Get in."

"We're not taking this are we? It's not what you'd call inconspicuous."

"Let's not worry about that. It's the perfect day for it."

"How old is it? Is it still ok to drive?" Said Sarah still standing by the open door. She was touching her chin with the fingertips of both her hands and her mouth wouldn't quite close.

"It's over forty years old." He said. "And yes 'course it is. It drives like new. I've had some modern upgrades fitted. Come on," He said flicking his head towards the passenger seat, "daylight's burning." She slipped into the car and Martin closed the door. He trotted around to the other side and settled himself in the driving seat. They both clicked on their seatbelts as Martin pushed the key into the ignition on the steering column and twisted it with a slight look of apprehension on his face. The look changed immediately into a broad smile when the v6 engine fired up first time and roared as he blipped the accelerator pedal. He put his foot on the clutch and flicked the gear lever into the first slot of the chromed gearbox gate. He eased up the clutch and they were out of the garage into the midday sunshine. He drove up a concrete ramp with high walls either side that sloped upwards for a hundred yards or so. They came to an empty tarmac road and Martin accelerated away, the engine wailing. Sarah looked behind her. There was no obvious sign of a house from this perspective. Sarah was enjoying this but Martin would have known that any conversation would be difficult in the car due to the noise of the engine and the wind and the road. She decided to let it drop for now. They approached an intersection where there were many more cars on the road.

She had never been in a car that drew so many admiring looks. It was exactly the car you would need, she thought, if you absolutely wanted to get noticed. As they drove, the traffic got a little heavier but in the sense that they saw a car every minute instead of every two. Martin shouted above the engine.

"See that mountain over there." He pointed over the windscreen towards a black mountain emerging from the land.

"That's the volcano. We're going into the hills." Sarah just nodded. She was holding onto her hair which was being blown all over the place. She needed a headscarf. *They look pretty* she said to herself, *but they're not very practical.* They drove on for twenty minutes and presently came to a town square of sorts. The place was busy now with cars and people. Both tourists and locals by the look of what they were wearing.

"I think it must be market day." Said Martin. "I didn't think they held it on a Sunday." They could hear each other now with the engine noise on tick-over. Martin pulled up outside an old stone built house. The front door and the shutters were open. He tooted the horn and within a few seconds a young boy appeared.

"Good morning Mister Ferrari." Said the young boy.

"Morning Ramon." Said Martin as he switched off the ignition. The sounds of the market coming from around the corner could be heard. Someone was playing pitch pipes.

"How are you today?" He said as he got out of the car and walked around to open the passenger door for Sarah. He helped her out.

"I'm OK thank you." Said Ramon lazily. Martin fished around in his trouser pocket and pulled out a single note and gave it to Ramon. Ramon took it and put it in his own pocket.

"You haven't lost the phone have you?" Asked Martin. Ramon who was leaning up against the frame of the open door to the little sand coloured house grinned and pulled a mobile phone from his back pocket.

"No." He said. "But I could do with an upgrade. All my friends have Galaxies." Martin grinned.

"Really." He said. "You still got my number?"

Without saying anything Ramon pressed a few buttons and Martin's phone rang. Ramon touched his phone again and the ringing stopped. Ramon lifted his chin towards Martin.

"We won't be long, you know the drill." Ramon nodded and smiled. Martin took hold of Sarah's hand and led her unhurriedly back towards the town square. They walked past what the town hall that was hosting a wedding fair. Brides and grooms were littered all over the place. Martin seemed to know where he was going and after four or five turns through different alleys all lined with market stalls and tourists they arrived at a doorway. Around the doorway hung mainly white or off white clothes. Shirts, dresses and skirts for men as well as women. Sarah satisfied herself with the explanation that Martin would know this place because he had bought himself some clothing here. She looked for the first time at the shirt he was wearing and yes it was a sort of off white cotton. Martin walked straight through the door and into a series of small rooms. The assistant didn't appear to know him but recognised him as a customer and was polite. She spoke immediately in English with a Spanish accent.

"Good morning Sir, How can I help you today?"

"My friend here needs some nice things." He said.

"Certainly." Said the shop assistant looking Sarah up and down. "What kind of things had you in mind?"

Nervously at first but gaining confidence quickly Sarah began trying on clothes in the changing room. Martin having suggested a few pieces that he saw hanging on the rails soon gave up and sat on a wicker chair by the old painted wooden table that served as the shop counter. Slowly a pile of clothes started to appear on the counter. Sarah was not proud. He had dragged her here so she would buy clothes for a week.

"I think that will do me," she said to the shop assistant when she thought she had gone as far as she should, "but I need shoes." The shop assistant shook her head.

"My Brother." She said. "I show you."

"And." Sarah hesitated. She didn't know how to put it. She turned her back so that Martin couldn't see and pinched a bra strap from underneath the new blouse she was wearing.

The shop assistant nodded knowingly.

"My Aunt." She said. It took her fifteen minutes to pack away all the purchases and when they had done Martin paid the bill with a credit card. The assistant called out to the back of the shop where another young woman appeared.

She said something that Sarah didn't understand in Spanish to the other young woman.

"This way," said the second young woman to Sarah as she walked out the shop door. Sarah and Martin, both laden down with shopping bags, followed. They struggled through the now denser crowd in the cobbled alleyway outside. The shop assistant led them to a corner, along another alley and down a side street where the crowd had thinned out.

"My Brother is down there on the left." She said, "And my Aunt has the shop just next door to him."

She nodded graciously and went back the way she had come. Martin lead the way and they repeated the performance albeit to a lesser degree in both the Brother's and the Aunt's shops. They started walking back towards the car.

"We just need one more thing." Said Martin as they passed a colourful display of silks billowing in the warm breeze. Martin pointed at a bright red square with a gold printed lattice work design and paid the man cash from his side pocket. They got back to the car and Martin opened the boot and the piled in the packages that filled the little compartment.

"Here." Said Martin handing Sarah the silk. Sarah smiled and took the silk square and walked around the car away from Martin and stood resolutely beside the driver's door of the Ferrari. She grinned. Martin slowly shook his head.

"No." Said Martin. "Absolutely not."

"Oh come on Martin. I'm police trained." She said with a cross between a big smile and a demanding look on her face.

Martin let out a deep breath, raised his eyes in his head and opened the passenger door. Sarah excitedly got in the driver's seat and began to tie the silk scarf around her head. Ramon appeared and walked around the car to where Martin was sitting.

"Mr. Ferrari." He said.

"Hi Ramon," said Martin, "anything wrong?"

"Not really Mr. Ferrari Sir." Said Ramon as Martin handed Sarah the keys.

"Big Black Car." Said Ramon as Sarah started the engine.

"Big Black Car." Ramon repeated shouting this time above the engine noise, "very interested in this." Sarah was anxious to get going, she'd put it in gear and was moving off. "I took a picture." Ramon shouted as Sarah revved the engine a little too vigorously not quite used to the clutch.

"Send it to me." Martin shouted back as Sarah moved the car off down the street.

Within a few minutes they had reached a two lane road of black tarmac. It looked new.

"After the circular intersection take the second exit and follow the road for about six miles north." Martin shouted over the din. "There's a great road after that. Could have been built for this car. Switchbacks to and fro up the hillside and back down the other side towards the coast. The Moridaira Hotel is somewhere up on the north-west coast."

"You've never been there before?" Shouted back Sarah looking cool and in control and now she had control she was loving the noise the engine made. She was getting used now to the rather less than responsive controls she was used to in modern cars.

"No." Shouted Martin. "But I've got a pretty good idea where it is."

Martin's phone vibrated in his pocket. Sarah had one eye on him as he pulled the phone out and touched the screen. A puzzled look came over his face. He held the phone forward so that Sarah could see it without taking her eyes off the road. She glanced at it and shrugged. It was a picture of a Black Chrysler Voyager stopped in-front of the, by comparison little Ferrari. The front window was rolled down and the silhouette of the driver could be seen.

It was just a silhouette though. The camera on Ramon's phone was not good enough to pick out the contrast. After staring at the picture for a moment or two Martin decided it meant nothing. Just another admirer of the car probably.

He put the phone down as Sarah shouted across to him.

"I don't believe in coincidences Martin." Her eyes were flicking up to the rear view mirror more than normal.

Martin crouched a little so as he could see behind in the small round passenger door mirror. Perhaps four hundred meters behind them was the same shiny black Chrysler Voyager that was in the picture Ramon had sent him.

"So they like Ferraris." Shouted Martin.

"Maybe." Said Sarah. "But for some reason I don't think that's why they are behind us."

"Why? Did you pick up some clue that I missed?"

"No." She said. "And don't take the piss. I've got a feeling. That's all. Female intuition."

"Shall we put it to the test?" Said Martin. "Your intuition. How fast are we going?"

"Sixty five." She said.

"Well they'll be doing the same. Don't speed up. Slow down to forty five. They'll have to do something."

Sarah eased off the accelerator. The noise of the engine dropped as did the wind noise. The Chrysler appeared not to change its speed.

"There you are you see. So much for your intuition." Said Martin as the Chrysler came slowly up behind them and pulled over to the other side of the road to overtake.

"Quite innocent."

The driver of the Chrysler, hidden behind black glass, reduced speed so as to match that of the Ferrari. Sarah was furtively looking quickly between the big car and the road ahead.

"This isn't innocent Martin." She said as the passenger window started to lower. Fast as the Ferrari might have been forty years ago, if she dropped two gears and redlined it now and that big old bus of a Chrysler wanted to keep close it probably could. She could hear the rumble of a straight six or a V8. It was a long straight road for as far as she could see. Sarah was waiting for her moment. The black window of the Chrysler had dropped two thirds. It was still aggressively sitting by the side of them. Martin leaned towards the passenger glove-box. This movement seemed to provoke a response from the Chrysler. The window dropped to the bottom and a grey metallic cylinder appeared. Before Martin could shout any warning he had been thrown forward against his seat belt and then violently flung first against the door panel and then Sarah's shoulder. He heard the sound of a gunshot. Sarah had jammed on the foot-brake suddenly. The Chrysler had continued going for a second or two but the driver reacted quickly and jammed on the brakes as well. Forty meters had been put between them but she'd left inertia in the little Ferrari. She simultaneously yanked the steering wheel down and pulled the chrome hand brake lever upwards on its ratchet.

She trod on the clutch pedal with her left foot and was revving the engine with her right. She left the ratchet on the hand brake lever to hold the back wheels still while the car skidded in a one hundred and eighty degree arc. At about ninety degrees around she deftly dropped the gearstick into second gear and glanced at the rev counter. As the car approached one hundred and thirty five degrees she checked that the revs were close to the red line and with a good deal of force pressed the button on the end of the hand-brake lever and released the back wheels. She let her foot fall off the clutch pedal and the result of this was a spectacular display probably never before attempted in a vintage Ferrari. To give it it's due the fat tyres smoked and the engine screamed as the back wheels spun and the car snaked away from the Chrysler which was performing a similar manoeuvre albeit much less spectacularly. Sarah shook her head as they raced away. If she didn't know better she'd have sworn she'd heard the Ferrari screaming with delight. Martin was sitting in his seat his arms straight by his side gripping into the sides of the seat.

He had a grimace on his face and his eyes were closed.

"Martin." Sarah shouted. Martin remained locked in his position

"Martin." Sarah shouted again. Martin opened his eyes and stared straight ahead. The expression on his face was as if he was about to cry.

"Martin." She shouted again. He seemed to hear her this time. "Martin. What's in the glove-box?"

At first Martin didn't understand. Then as if waking from a dream he shook his head and returned to the present.

"Did you just do a handbrake turn at forty five miles an hour and then drop the clutch at five and half thousand revs in a forty year old Ferrari? My forty year old concourse Ferrari?" He almost screamed.

"Well yes." She yelled. "I suppose I did. Martin, what's in the glove-box?" They were racing now back up to the circular intersection. Martin tried to pull together his battered senses.

"Where's that fucking Black car now?" He shouted as he bobbed his head around trying to see in the little round side mirror.

"Behind about a half mile. It's fast Martin."

"This thing may be old but it was way ahead of it's time. The Chrysler will have us on the straight but we'll piss on 'em through the bends. Go right round the circle and back up the road we were on. We'll get a hundred and twenty out of this. We've got six miles to go before we can lose them."

Sarah was beside herself with excitement. In all her years of training she'd never done anything that came close to the manoeuvre she had just completed and it had gone brilliantly. In a bright red Ferrari. She could hardly conceal her joy. She thought to herself a moment. A little bit of inner dialogue. Odd. The most excited and joyous she's been that she can remember and someone's pointing a gun at her. She too had to flick herself out of her reverie. She did as Martin told her and with the revs high and the gear low she drifted the back end out around the circle of tarmac that took her back onto the road she was on before. The Chrysler was going up the ramp to the intersection as she was going down. The Dino had a six speed gearbox before many of the sports cars of the day had five. Sarah raced up through them and pinned the accelerator to the floor as she shifted into sixth. Martin was quiet in the passenger seat. Sarah got the impression that he was having his own inner dialogue brought about by the extreme conditions.

"How far are they behind?" Shouted Martin. Sarah could barely hear him. At a hundred miles an hour the idea that an open top sports car is fun is plain wrong. In truth it's a very uncomfortable place to be. Sarah and Martin gritted their teeth as they approached their top speed. They envied in a perverse way the occupants of the modern car that was chasing them who, for all they knew could be playing Scrabble.

"Half a mile." She shouted. "Your little car has more in it than you thought."

Martin did some mental calculations. He looked at his watch.

"At sixty miles an hour you do a mile in a minute. At one hundred and twenty that mile goes by in thirty seconds. Six miles will take just three minutes."

He looked at his watch again.

"Time flies when you're having fun. Take the next exit." He shouted.

Sarah didn't ease off the accelerator until the last moment then put the brakes to the test. They did fine. The big black strip of tarmac turned into a narrower road that snaked upwards. The lack of a roof afforded a view of the road as it turned back on itself almost completely but at the last moment turned again and went upwards. The road could have been used in the film 'The Italian Job.' The Ferrari seemed to take on a life of its own. Like an old dog that's been shown familiar fields. Although Sarah was driving, it was like another force was willing them along. They were going slowly, relatively. The engine was revving up through the range and Sarah was changing up and down the gears like a demon. They could no longer see the shiny black Chrysler behind them but they both knew not to get complacent. Sarah drove on as vigorously as ever. Until they reached a point in the road where they could see below them. The Chrysler had stopped at one of the hairpins and was parked in one of the viewing areas. They were a mile away as the crow flies. She pulled the Ferrari up to a wall surrounding a similar viewing space. Leaving the engine burbling away they both got out of the car and carefully peered over the wall. The Chrysler was turning around. Martin turned to Sarah and gave her a bear hug and then kissed her. In the confusion of her fear, excitement and mixed up emotions the thing that stuck in her mind the most was that Martin walked back to his car, his pride and joy, his mistress, his weakness and symbol of manhood and got in the passenger seat. Sarah, after retying her red silk scarf got into the driving seat.

22

Ireland. 1997.

Jill felt increasingly anxious the nearer she got to the small border town of Lifford. She had half an hour to spare before her appointment with the registrar. The Taxi driver had not stopped talking from the moment she had got in the cab, speaking in a comic but easy on the ear southern Irish lilt. It was as if he had been trained by the tourist board.

The journey had exhausted her and she thought that maybe something a little stronger than coffee would be appropriate but decided it was too early. She walked into a coffee shop on the street where the taxi had dropped her. Although she was born in Ireland, Jill had never been back.

Brendan and Sheila had left with her to seek their fortune in England when she was just a baby. She may have been imagining it because she thought she should but she had a relaxed feeling about the place. She felt as if it could be her home. The taxi driver, although annoyingly talkative, had that Irish charm that people speak about and the woman behind the counter in the coffee shop also had a way of making her feel comfortable. It was a long way from the impersonal and irritating London she was used to. She didn't mind at all telling the coffee shop owner, who seemed genuinely interested, why she was there and while she was talking, it occurred to her that, of course, if her father was from here, she would have relations here too. In all the years that her attentions had been focused on knowing who her real father was, it was the first time it had dawned on her that there would be others. They were Irish Catholics after all and stupidly she'd never thought about what might be of the rest of the family.

"You'll be havin' that on me." Said the woman behind the counter, smiling a broad and generous smile as Jill approached the counter to pay. "Good luck with your searchin'. I'm Carmel." She held out a hand towards Jill and they exchanged a feminine handshake.

"Jill." She said introducing herself.

"Don't be too fussed about Bernie." Carmel called after her as she was walking out the door. "She's my brother's wife. Bark's worse than her bite. Takes herself very seriously." Jill turned around and nodded.

"Thanks." She said.

The registry office was a short walk from the coffee shop. Jill checked her watch. *Five minutes. Good.*

The last time she was in a registry office it had turned out to be a mixed affair as her marriage lasted only a few months. She was only young and it was a rash mistake. The registrar had started the proceedings as if they were some kind of celebration but they had turned very quickly into an officious interrogation. She thought at the time that it was hardly worth the effort. As it happened she should have gone with her instincts. What would this encounter be like?

"Good morning to you my dear." Said the registrar who appeared after a few minutes in the beige council waiting room. "My name's Bernadette Caffrey, and I'm the registrar for the county. You've come from London this morning?"

"Yes." Said Jill. "Morning to you." Jill found herself falling just a little into the Irish vernacular. *My God,* She thought to herself. *I nearly said 'Top o' the morning to ya.*

"If you'd like to come with me Miss... O'Keefe, wasn't it?." The registrar held open the door to a corridor and Jill walked through. "Second door on the right's mine." She said.

The room was only a little more comfortable than the waiting room. There was a desk with an office chair behind it and two vinyl upholstered chairs in front. The registrar directed Jill to take a seat and took her place behind the desk.

"Well now Miss O'Keefe," said the registrar opening a blue paper file on her desk, "what's it like to be coming back home?"

Jill was slightly taken aback. She was on her guard on account of her previous experiences with officialdom and authority, but she needn't have been. The registrar noted the look on Jill's face.

"I'm sorry my Dear." She said. "Did you not know you were born here?"

"I thought my father might have been from here." She said. "I actually have no idea exactly where I'm from." She felt stupid saying this as well. It occurred her that she had never asked herself the question. She knew she had been born in Ireland but never knew where.

"We've been given certain powers in the last few years. Well not powers exactly, I mean some of the rules, or at least the way we do things have changed." The registrar continued.

"Ireland is a very different place to what it was fifty years ago. The sisters provided a valuable service then but we like to think that our policies these days are a little more transparent." Jill smiled appreciatively. The registrar handed over an official and quite old looking piece of paper printed with red and black ink.

"You'll be pleased to know that you yourself were born here too." It was a copy of her Birth Certificate. Jill read the names on the certificate. Father: David John Joseph Crane. Occupation: Student. Mother: Barbara Edith Moine. Date of birth 9th December 1958.

Jill was shocked. She was expecting to just glean some information about her birth parents. The sight of her own birth certificate and the strange handwritten names contrived to bring a tear to her eye. All her research had suggested that this mission of hers was going to be long and painful and that she would come up against barrier upon barrier on bureaucratic insouciance and official ineptitude. But she had breezed in here and as if they had been waiting for her the registrar had produced the document that showed who her birth mother and father were and that she too was born here. Surely it couldn't be that simple. It was that simple though. The registrar was very comforting.

"I'm sorry." She said, "there's never a good way to tell these tales."

"No." Said Jill delving into her bag for a packet of tissues. "No I suppose there isn't." The registrar continued.

"Have you brought your adoption papers?" She asked.

"And I'll need your passport or some form of identification." Jill rummaged through her bag again. "I should have asked for them first," the registrar confessed. "But I could tell, the moment I saw you, you were Davy's kid."

Jill was shaken a second time and began to regret her decision to come. Her thoughts turned back to Brendan and Sheila, her adopted parents. They were her real parents.

Who was she trying to kid? They were the ones that had given her so much love had been so kind. Being here was almost tantamount to a slap in the face for them. Brendan hadn't seen it like that. He was a pragmatist and had told her to do whatever she needed to do. He was confident enough about his love for her that it didn't concern him. What was important to him was that his daughter, his little cherub was happy. If she was happy then he was happy. The registrar was shuffling the papers in the file.

"There's something else." Said the registrar, almost waiting for permission to continue.

"Something else?" Jill repeated.

"Yes." Said the registrar. "Under these circumstances, we are able to pass on to applicants such as yourself details of any information we might have about close relatives."

"Close relatives?" Asked Jill. The registrar was opening another buff coloured file that was beneath the first.

"Yes Mrs. O'Keefe." She handed over another piece of paper. This time not so official looking. "Again," she said and paused before continuing, "There really is never a good way of doing this." She let Jill read the piece of paper.

"Is it saying what I think its saying?" Said Jill after scanning over the piece of paper.

"If you think it says that you have two half brothers, then yes. It is." Jill appeared nonplussed. But appearances can be deceptive. She was attempting to work out how she felt about this further revelation.

"Do you know of any other family I might have around here?" Jill asked. The registrar put her elbows on the desk. A slight smile crossed her face. She flicked her eyebrows up momentarily.

"I may do." She said, "except I'm not at liberty to say." She paused. The slight smile broadened. "At least not in my official capacity." Jill caught a hardly disguised wink.

Outside the registry office Jill took a deep breath and began retracing her steps back to the cab rank. She'd have a fair wait at the airport but better to get there early than miss the plane. She was full of tangled feelings but decided to let time play its part in straightening those out. As she walked up the street past the coffee shop, Carmel called to her from across the narrow street as she was locking the wooden door of the shop.

"You know." Said Carmel as she walked quickly across towards Jill. "I thought I saw something in those eyes." Jill just smiled. Carmel continued. 'Come with me,' she said not giving Jill a choice. "I've someone you need to meet."

"I've got a plane to catch." Jill protested. Carmel continued to walk.

"We'll make sure you catch your plane, don't you go worrying yourself now." She said. "Finbar's got a good fast car. He'll take you."

Jill reluctantly followed her. They walked past where the cab had dropped her off, turned a corner and went through the front door of one of the small houses in the street. The only thing that would set it apart from the others was a sign on painted black wood over the door. The lettering, at some point in the past, may have been yellow or even gold but was now a faded brown. You could only just make out the name. O'Keefes.

Oh Right, thought Jill. *Could this place get any more like a horror film. That cannot be a co-incidence.*

They went inside to find a room larger that the outside would suggest. An old wooden bar was against the back wall furthest from the door. The floor was bare untreated wood that had been worn down into a shallow miniature mogul field of bumps. To the left of the bar was a stage area only eight feet square and a foot high. It was half-way through the afternoon but a couple of young men were setting up a small PA speaker system next to the stage. The room although not full was busy with drinkers sitting either on barstools or on wooden chairs at plain wooden tables.

"Come along now, My Dear," said Carmel, noticing her apprehension at walking any further into the bar room. She grabbed Jill's hand and strode towards one of the drinkers sitting with his back to them on a stool to one end of the bar. The way the old man occupied his position gave the impression that this was his little patch and woe betide anyone who would trespass upon it.

"Albert." Said Carmel, firmly putting her hand on the man's shoulder. Albert turned around. He looked at Jill and tilted his head.

"Well now Carmel, m'darling, who have we here?" Without waiting for a reply he got off his stool and grasped her hand and forearm with both his hands.

"You should be flattered my Dear," Said Carmel. "Albert doesn't get off that stool for no good reason." Albert continued to shake Jill's hand. He was looking her in the eyes as he was doing so. "Can you be guessing who this is?" Carmel continued. Albert had a look on his face as if someone had just asked him a trivial pursuit question and he was sure he knew the answer.

"She reminds me of someone, that's for sure." He said, shaking his head. "But for the life o' me..." Carmel couldn't hold back any longer,

"It's Davy Cranes girl. Can't you see?" Albert's face looked as if he had just been told the answer to a trivial pursuit question that had been on the tip of his tongue.

"Of course." He said still shaking Jill's hand. "Of course." Jill was not enamoured with this attention. She was regretting more than ever coming here. She was not Davy Cranes kid. It had only been an hour or so ago that she had heard the name for the first time. *If they know David Crane then they must know that he left me to be adopted into another family, that he disappeared out of my life. I've no desire to be Davy Crane's kid.*

Albert, sensing an unease, finally let go of Jill's hand.

"What'll ya have, my dear." He asked. Jill was actually relieved.

"Very kind of you Albert," she said. "I'll have a vodka and tonic."

"And what'll be yours?" He asked Carmel.

"See what a pretty face can do to the most financially cautious of men." Carmel gave the old man a smile. A young barman was now standing in front of them on the other side of the bar. "I'll have my usual." Carmel said, addressing the barman.

"VAT and a Port and lemon." Said Albert "And start another one o' those will you lad." He pointed at his own half full glass, turned back to Jill and grabbed her hand again.

"Well now my dear, you are certainly a sight for sore eyes." He pushed her away gently and looked her up and down.

"Let me be getting a good look at ya." He said. Jill was confused but tried not to let it show. Albert continued, "What made you decide to return after all this time?"

Jill tried to remain light hearted.

"Oh well. You know. Thought it was about time I came back to my roots." The pub was full of wafting cigarette smoke. The door opened and Bernadette from the registry office walked into the bar and directly up to them.

"Bernie," said Carmel. "Another long day at the office?" Jill automatically looked at her wristwatch. It was just after four in the afternoon. The two lads had finished setting up their gear on the stage - two huge speakers and two microphone stands.

"You can hardly be one to talk now Carmel. Business must be good for you to be able to shut up shop for the afternoon." Replied Bernadette.

"It wouldn't be polite of me to let the return of the prodigal daughter go unnoticed now would it Bernie." Carmel turned to Albert at the bar.

"Get your sister a drink you skinflint." She chided.

"You'll not be wanting the family thinking we're mean."

Albert ordered another port and lemonade from the barman.

Jill was standing there with a polite smile on her face feeling distinctly out of place. She was staring into the middle distance. The realisation slowly dawning that they were all talking about her. She felt stupid that she had not seen it before. Albert was the first to see her ill-disguised discomfort.

"Oh goodness." He said to the group and more directly to Jill. "Oh Goodness." he repeated again. "I'm so sorry. We thought you knew." He turned to Bernadette and fixed his eyes on her. He lifted his head up silently asking her the question. Bernie answered the unspoken question defensively.

"It would be more than my job is worth. Rules are rules." Albert shook his head.

"Anyone would think you were English Bernadette." He turned back towards Jill. "I am so sorry my dear. We thought Bernie would have done the necessary before we bought you in here."

"Now that's not..." Bernadette tried to object but Albert interrupted.

"No matter Bernie." He said handing her a glass, "see if that will put some sense in that official head of yours." Jill felt more awkward than ever. And Albert could see it. He said a little hesitantly. "Maybe it's time I made some proper introductions."

23

Two young men stepped onto the little back painted stage. One of them sat down on a bar stool with his guitar over his knee and the other, a guitar strapped over his shoulder, stood in front of a microphone. After a short instrumental introduction from the guy on the stool the singer started a song Jill didn't recognise. Jill found herself staring at them. She'd finished her drink and was nudged out of her stare by Albert handing her another. She didn't object. If she stayed to finish this though she'd not make her flight no matter how fast Finbar's car was. She was resigned to let the afternoon, *God it was still only afternoon,* take its course.

"You know your dad used to play here." Said Carmel leaning in towards her. "He and his friend Eamon. These two remind me a lot of them. That was before they left of course."

"Before they left?" Jill questioned.

"You're assuming too much Carmel." Albert butted in before turning back towards Jill.

"You'd have been about eighteen. My brother adopted you and left for a job he had going in England when you were a year old."

"So you are Brendan's brother?" She asked incredulously. "My..." she hesitated.

"Your uncle. Yes." Albert could see she was unsure.

Adopted uncle She was about to say but didn't. Albert looked perfectly happy to be just her uncle.

"And this is my wife Bernadette and my sister Carmel. So I suppose they are your Aunts." He continued.

Carmel smiled a wry smile and twisted her head to the left having sipped her drink.

"Well I'm more..." started Bernadette but was cut short by Albert.

"There you go again Bernie, getting all technical. We're all family Jill." He said.

Bernadette slapped him playfully on the arm and repeated the wink she had given Jill in the registry office.

"Didn't the sign over the door give you a hint. You really didn't know?" She said. Jill wanted to cry again. She didn't know why. This was all getting too much. Carmel and Bernadette were standing looking at her. They could see her distress. Carmel put a comforting arm around Jill's shoulder. This had the opposite effect to the one intended and Jill burst into tears. Albert's answer to this was to bark at the barmen for more drinks. This time an Irish whiskey for Jill. He thrust it toward her as the other women were fussing around in their handbags for tissues.

"Get this down you girl. There's not much it won't improve." Jill swigged down the whiskey as ordered and the burning liquid made her splutter and cough. The tears of sadness or whatever they were turned into a little laugh and the four of them all laughed with her.

"Why didn't Brendan ever tell me about his family over here?"

"Your family over here." Said Carmel.

"Brendan had big ideas when he married Sheila and when he did, that was it. They were off. They were like so many of the Irish. They wanted to go somewhere else. Anywhere else." Said Albert.

"She never really liked us though." Said Bernadette.

"Looked down her nose at us."

"There's lots more." Said Carmel "If you want to hear it."

Jill waved to the barmen and pointed at the four of them in turn.

"My round." She said. "So what happened to David Crane?" She was not comfortable calling him her dad. After bickering about whose round it was where Carmel and Bernadette insisted that it was theirs by which they meant Albert's, Albert continued.

"Davy and Eamon were playing on that stage there." He pointed to where the two lads were now singing an Irish sounding version of Come on Eileen. Some of the audience were beginning to join in. *At five in the afternoon. This is a strange place. I like it though.* She thought to herself as she sipped more carefully this time at another neat Irish whiskey.

"They weren't youngsters like these two. I remember 'cause I was serving behind the bar. A tall fellah, never seen him before, wearing one of those leather wide brimmed hats walks in and watches them as they finish playing. The whole pub was singing along with them. Don't remember the song. It'll come to me though." He thought for a moment. "No still don't. The three of them go out back. We thought that maybe he was some kind of record company agent or something. David and Eamon both had stern looks on their faces. That night there was a huge explosion just outside the Connaught tunnel on the port road. They said it was IRA. No official word came back that they were in it and Bernadette here would have known if there was. She keeps her ear to the ground if you know what I mean. No-one ever saw them again."

"So he died in that explosion did he? With his friend Eamon?" Asked Jill.

Albert and the two women all changed their expressions.

They wanted to talk but something was stopping them.

"Come on." Said Jill. "It was over twenty years ago. I never knew him." Bernadette was the first to speak and she did have an official air about her.

"Your dad..." she started, "Davy Crane was never much liked around here. As a young man he was a terrible womaniser and had a way with the ladies." Carmel laughed and elbowed her.

"No." Said Bernadette. "That's not fair. He was a lovely looking boy I'll not deny, but he never touched me. Not for want of trying though." She brought out another wink from her bag of them.

"Other way round the way I saw it," said Carmel. "It was embarrassing, the way you flaunted yourself in front of him."

"That's not true, Carmel O'Keefe and you know it."

Carmel took over.

"Davy Crane had an arrogance about him that some people didn't like too much. That's all." They thought they had evaded the question but however amusing and slightly creepy it was, these two woman talking about her father in this way they still hadn't told her what was so difficult to tell her.

"So is David Crane still alive then?" She asked. Again their expressions changed. This time it was Albert's turn.

"What do you know about the politics around here?" He said in a serious tone. Carmel tutted.

"She'll not be wanting to go into that you old buffoon." Albert shot her a look that shut her up. She might as well have hissed at him in response. Jill answered the question after Albert turned back to her.

"Only what I read in the papers." She said.

"Well, you shouldn't go believing all you read in the papers as I'm sure you know." Albert glanced around them, shifted on his stool and lowered his voice.

"It was rumoured that David and his friend Eamonn were spying for the British. They may have been recruited when they were at university together," Jill nodded trying to work out the implications of this revelation. Albert continued. "Now whatever your particular position on the matter, Unionist or Republican, Protestant or Catholic, everyone managed to get along fine around here. We were not constantly at war with each other as the papers would have you believe. The English weren't great. No-one thought they were. But no government is. There were many, myself included who thought the IRA and their particular brand of bullying politics ten times worse than what the British were throwing at us."

"Come on Albert," said Carmel. "Get off your soapbox." Jill was still waiting for an answer to her question. She was coming to realise that getting a straight yes or no was going to be difficult. She'd finished her drink again. The whiskey wasn't making her feel tipsy like she normally would have felt but it was doing something. It seemed to make her feel alert. Like an upper. Albert ordered another round and as he did so Carmel and Bernadette exchanged a conspiratorial glance. Jill noticed and the two sisters noticed she noticed. Bernadette shook her head, leaned toward Jill and in a stage whisper said, "It's just that he's usually notoriously stingy." She pulled another wink out of the bag. Jill smiled with them and made a point of thanking Albert with a kiss on his cheek as she took her glass. She winked back at Bernadette.

"So?" Jill said looking at them each in turn. "What happened to David Crane?"

"We don't know." Carmel piped up. "We don't know if he met his maker that night. All Albert was trying to say is that on account of his nefarious activities there is a possibility that he had to leave and never come back. But we just speculate. The Irish are a hopeful bunch."

"There were some clues though." Said Bernadette. "Bear in mind it was the main talking point of the town for months and all sorts of wild tales were made up and told as if they were the truth by many a blarney kissed poet."

"David's guitar." Said Albert. "He'd had it since he was sixteen. It was a rare type with an odd number of strings. He'd take it wherever he went. A forty year old man carrying a guitar around all day. He was known for it. Well that went too. No trace. Not in his little house. Nowhere. But Eamonn left his guitar here the night they disappeared. It hung around out back for months. I eventually hung it on the wall over there behind where the boys are playing." Albert pointed to the stage. Jill, brought out of her concentration realised they were playing a Celtic sounding version of an Elvis song. She saw no Guitar on the wall.

"Where is it now? I'd love to see it." Said Jill.

"So would I." Said Albert. "Occasionally it got played a bit in here. I think it was quite a valuable instrument. At least someone thought it was. It got nicked."

A round of applause rose from the now quite full pub room. Jill turned to see Bernadette stepping up onto the stage. Oh God Jill thought to herself, *she's going to make an announcement.* She was wrong.

"Watch this," Said Albert. "She's quite good."

Bernadette counted the two boys in. They started a word perfect rendition of Bohemian Rhapsody complete with backing vocals and guitar solo incongruously performed without any hint of irony in the delicate operatic soprano of an elderly Irish registrar. Jill could not believe her eyes or her ears. So much so she looked at her empty whiskey glass and shook her head. When she had finished, the audience clapped loudly with a whistle or two and Bernadette returned to the little group as if she'd just been to the powder room. Jill's mouth was hanging open looking at Bernadette.

"I...have...never...seen anything like that before in my entire life." She said to her. "...That was amazing."

"Get over." Said Bernadette. "You should hear my Stairway." She lifted her glass from the bar, which only contained a teaspoon of liquid, drained it with a slurp and all but slammed it back down. "Come on Albert." She said loudly, obviously invigorated by her performance. "Don't want us girls dying of thirst." She winked again at Jill.

"So where were we?"

You only hear the truth from drunks and children, thought Jill. She'd heard that from Brendan and she accepted another, of what was turning out to be an easily acquired taste, from Albert.

"We'd got to the bit where the guitar was stolen." Said Carmel as if she'd been taking notes. Jill got the idea that this tale had been told many times before. Again the three of them turned silent. The atmosphere changed again. It was as if they had more to say but didn't want to say it. This was a pub after all. You are supposed to drink and forget in an Irish pub. Supposed to just chew the fat.

"Come on guys." Jill said. The whiskey revealing hidden powers. "We're family. What are you gonna tell me that can be worse. Finbar's got a fast car and Oh! He's also your brother." The three remained silent. Jill detected a slight shaking of each of their heads.

"No Finbars I'm afraid." Said Carmel at last. Jill was past being surprised at anything. She may take her time in the morning to work out what went on, *God the morning, I'll need somewhere to stay*. She almost panicked but the air in the pub wouldn't let her.

"If no Finbars, then what?"

"David was a ladies man." Said Carmel.

"I've gathered that."

"As well as your twin half-brothers which I told you about, you have twin half-sisters." Bernadette rose to the occasion. "There. I've said it. Now can we move on?" Jill nodded slowly.

"I've got twin half-brothers and twin half-sisters." She repeated. They were all looking at her.

"Told you there was no good way of saying it." Said Bernadette. Albert mounted his soapbox again. He looked poised to reveal all.

"Your daddy... David Crane went to university in England with his friend Eamonn. They both came from here. Eamonn about ten miles up the road. They were boyhood friends and both fish out of water in England so it was natural that they'd stick together. They were bright kids. Selected from the vocational college on a scholarship. David was home for the summer in fifty eight when his charms drew in your mother and you were the result. David didn't even know. He went back to England and didn't return for a year. At the time you were born I'm sad to say some of the old ways in Ireland still persisted. You were the product of an unmarried woman and you were taken away by the nuns at Saint Valerie. That's when my brother and his wife, who couldn't have children herself adopted you and left within the year for England. As you know, Brendan was a groundworker. He had a touch when they were building a tube extension or some-such. He did well for himself. When David returned from university the town decided for better or for worse not to tell him. He hitched up for a while with a wild thing whose father owned Wrigleys, the department store in Cork. The lad had something because twin boys were the result of that union. He dropped her like a hot poker though and the boys were taken in by the church. The girl joined the convent soon after. David would have nothing to do with them and it was this behaviour that didn't exactly endear him to the town's folk."

"And what happened to the boys." Said Jill. "Surely you know where they are. They must be just a little younger than I am."

"The boys were named Martin and Paul." Continued Albert. "Martin was adopted into a family by the name of Farnham. They lived in the far north. Technically still southern Ireland. I think the old man made substantial contributions to the church coffers. They left as well when Martin couldn't have been more than three years old. I don't really think they wanted to. It's just an odd situation. The old school in Ireland has very strange ways."

"And Paul?" Said Jill.

"Paul was adopted into a family of what you might call 'Hippies' they were very forward thinking. I don't know what kind of favours the dad might have bestowed upon the convent but there it was. He too went to England for much the same reason his brothers new family did. I kept in touch with them. They were named Finch and he was a carpenter. When we cleared out David's little house, probably two years after he left, there was a stack of old magazines. Some of them looked old. Private Eyes I think they were. Carmel and I bundled them all up and had them sent, at huge expense I'll have you know, to an address I had for Paul's mother and father in north London somewhere."

"How long ago was that?" Asked Jill.

"Fifteen years or so."

"Is he still there?"

"No Idea."

"What about Martin."

"He went Awol a long time ago. I've no idea where you would start to look if you wanted to find him."

"We're not through yet." Said Carmel. "Go forward eighteen years to the year he disappeared. He'd been with Moira Carlin, another local girl, for four years or more. Two weeks before the night he went, she gave birth to twin girls."

"What happened to them? They can only be in their twenties." Said Jill.

"About three years after they disappeared, Moira, who'd had a hell of a job keeping the two girls, hooked up with and quickly married a fellah who was in town looking to buy a house or business or something. Funny looking bloke as I remember. I think they might still own a house around here somewhere. The rumours were that he was a bit of a high flyer from England. We've not seen them either for years."

Jill checked her watch. It said eight fifteen. She looked around for a clock to double check but there didn't seem to be one anywhere in the pub. *That was ten minutes* she said to herself. *Not three hours*. She genuinely had a concern for her sanity. *Three hours*. She shook her head. *Three hours*. She hadn't noticed that the boys on the stage had gone so she clapped loudly when they reappeared.

Bernadette came out from the ladies. She had done herself up in scary make-up. Completely inappropriate, Jill thought, for a village pub. But then time had moved on. Moved on without her it seemed. She looked around to see an altogether different clientèle.

Before, she and her two new aunts were the only woman in the place but now it was an even split. All the girls were made up as if they were going to a film premiere. Tight dresses, pouty lips and hooker heels. Bernadette didn't look out of place at all. She had to negotiate her way around quite a crowded bar to return to where they were standing. She swigged back, in one, a whiskey that Albert had ordered for her, brushed down the sides of her skirts and with another of her winks for Jill she turned and weaved her way through the crowd of punters to the stage. Jill watched with a mixture of admiration and incomprehension as Bernadette sang an extended version of Stairway to Heaven in her operatic voice. The two boys were note perfect on their guitars.

24

Among the old take-away cartons and empty beer cans on Paul Finch's kitchen table, a copy of Private Eye had lain open at the page on which the ad appeared for going on three days. Paul had read it, what there was of it, again and again.

Eye Guru wanted by near completest.
Must have passport. Discretion required and assured.

It was accompanied by a PO Box Number. Could this be the opportunity he'd been waiting for? He'd often imagined the key to a different life might be contained in something that had been right there in front of his nose all these years, and maybe his collection of Private Eye magazines were that something. A similar ad had appeared in the previous issue but although he'd read it over many times, he'd done nothing about it. Paul Finch was a Private Eye collector. He had been collecting them for years. He had gone to great lengths to acquire copies that he had missed.

He always studied the classified ads in the back as they were as entertaining as anything else that was in the magazine. From Eye Love to Eye Want. Did people really give money to an ad that said 'Need ten grand to finish studies. Can you help?' These used to have a PO Box number attached but now they just put an account number and a sort code.

Lazy he thought.

But Paul had replied to this one. It was the first time he'd ever replied to an ad despite his best intentions. He'd thought about it many times but somehow he had never got around to it. *The PO Box thing was the right way to do it though. Something that seemed so old-fashioned in this modern world of emails and text messages as a classified ad in the Eye should at least warrant the effort of a reply to a PO Box number. Who says you have got to move with the times?* He had posted a little hand written note three days ago.

There was no work today. His workshop was in urgent need of some reorganisation but it had been in urgent need of reorganisation for months. It could wait a little longer. He'd spent the previous evening in his local pub with a bunch of semi alcoholic bores who thought they were funnier and more interesting than they actually were. It was coming up for eleven in the morning and Paul Finch was still lying in his bed. He'd been half awake since the traffic started to get heavy on the main road outside hours earlier. He was slipping in and out of one cinematic wide screen dream to another. He is watching himself looking up at a huge cathedral complete with flying buttresses and Gothic gargoyles. He can hear the bells ringing from the top of the cathedral tower. The bells get louder until he wakes and realises that the sound is his mobile phone ringing. He turned over and pulled a pillow over his head.

If it's the people in Mayfair, they can swing.

"The Ad," he shouted out loud to himself. He jumped out of bed and ran to the kitchen where his phone was lying plugged into a charger on the worktop, banging into the walls while his inner ear caught up with his brain. He missed the call just as he picked up the phone. He looked at the screen. Number Withheld. *Shit. Shit. Shit.*

He walked back to his bedroom and pulled on an old pair of jeans that were lying on the floor where they'd dropped when he'd taken them off the previous evening. He walked back to the kitchen rubbing his eyes then began shoving three days of single man detritus into a black plastic bin bag. The phone rang again.

He picked it up and saw the number was withheld again.

He pressed 'answer' and in a most unlikely of voices said, "Finch"

"Good morning Mr. Finch." A woman's voice he thought. Forty or thereabouts he guessed. American accent. Possibly.

"We got your note and feel you might be the perfect person for the position we have available."

"Well I'm flattered you thought so." Paul answered.

"Do you have a passport?" The woman on the other end of the phone asked without any further pleasantries and Paul was now convinced that she was putting the American accent on.

"Yep." Replied Paul tapping the left back pocket of his jeans. He raised his eyebrows in self-congratulation.

Convincing himself that you had to be positive about these things, he had put the passport there when he posted the reply to the ad.

"Can you be ready in half an hour?"

Paul was completely flustered by this. *Half an hour.*

That doesn't give me time for anything. It's a test though, he thought. *If I say yes then I'm too eager. Don't show weakness though. Negotiate.*

"Give me an hour will you?"

"That's cutting it a bit fine Paul." The accent is falling by the wayside now. "The plane leaves at three."

"What plane? Where?"

"The plane you're booked onto. All will become clear in due course. We do need absolute discretion and commitment Paul."

The two continuously battling sides of his character started their familiar inner dialogue. *Am I sure I want to do this? - Should I pull out of this ridiculous scenario now? Come on man. This is an adventure. You have absolutely nothing to lose. What if it's illegal or something. What if I get arrested at the airport? What if these people are smuggling drugs? What if? What if? What if?*

"I'll be ready in half an hour," he said and ceremoniously flicked his left shoulder. "What will I need?"

"Paul. You just need yourself. *Everything* will be provided." The woman on the other end of the phone gave special emphasis to the word everything.

"Just take a shower, Paul, and be downstairs in thirty minutes."

The phone went dead. He looked at the display on the mobile phone. The caller had rung off. He did exactly as he was told and jumped into the shower. *That was a curious remark* he thought as he was drying himself down. *How did she know I hadn't already had a shower?* The thought gave him a little shiver. *Hold on. I've not told them where I live either.* The two sides in his battling subconscious resumed their fight but he flicked his shoulder again and for good measure shook his head as if to shake out the unwanted thoughts. They wouldn't go away that easily though.

"Look." He said to himself out loud. "This is all wrong...Every bit of it...but I really don't care."

A man and a woman sitting in an executive business lounge at Gatwick North Airport terminal were both crouched on the low sofas looking at the screen of a laptop that was sitting on the table. In unison they gently nodded their heads, turned slightly to face each other and smiled.

Half an hour later, Paul Finch looked out of the window of his flat and saw a silver Mercedes pull up outside and toot the horn. He walked down the stairs and opened the street door to the flat. He felt he was opening the door to a new life. A man in a black suit, aviator sunglasses and a chauffeur's cap got out from the driver's seat and opened the back door of the Mercedes. Another man dressed similarly got out of the passenger seat and stood by the car with his hands clasped in front of him like a mourner at a funeral.

"Good afternoon Mr. Finch. I trust you are well. My name is Hedges, Sir, and this is Benson." He raised his arm toward the other man. "Your driver, Sir. It is our pleasure to be escorting you to the airport, Sir." The man's voice and his tone, thought Paul, was that of a call centre worker going through the motions of having to do a boring repetitive job. Hedges, as it happened would have been more than happy with this appraisal.

Paul stopped before getting into the car to look at the two men and a grin skulked across his mouth.

"You're 'avin' me on right." Paul said with one foot on the sill of the car and a hand on the roof.

"How do you mean, Sir?" Hedges asked politely.

"Benson and Hedges." He said, his grin getting wider. "Have you made that up?"

"I assure you. Sir, I am making nothing up." Hedges said convincingly without so much as a glimmer of a smile.

"Okay," replied Paul nodding. "Sorry." He slid onto the black leather rear seat of the car. On the seat next to him were a number of bags and packages that looked as if they had been left there by a previous customer who had been out on a shopping spree. Benson and Hedges slid into the car and shut the doors in unison. Hedges started talking immediately after the car had settled into the afternoon traffic.

"I do hope you don't mind sir, we are on a bit of a tight schedule if we're to catch the plane. There are some things on the seat beside you that my employer has asked if you'd mind putting on. It'll be about an hour before we get to the airport sir, if you could be ready by then. Oh and can I have your passport, Sir?" Hedges' tone and manner had become altogether friendlier bordering on the obsequious. "We've just one short stop to make on the way."

He continued. "Your phone, Sir." Hedges turned again through the seats. "I'll look after that if I could." He sensed Paul's unease at giving up the phone. "Don't worry, Sir, we'll not leave you incommunicado."

Paul, resigned, intrigued and excited, handed his passport and his phone through to the front seat where Hedges took it from him with a nod of the head. He assumed the passport was to speed up the formalities at the airport. He'd heard that this was the kind of treatment first class passengers got. He couldn't think of a good reason why they might want his phone though. Hedges began to fiddle in the glove-box of the car.

"Where are we going?" Asked Paul as he started to root through the packages.

"I believe you are going to the Canary Islands Sir. Very lovely this time of year if not a little breezy. We're going back to Camden. Don't be shy Sir. I won't look. Promise." Paul is holding up a pair of tight fitting briefs.

"What everything?" He asked.

"Everything." Said Hedges adjusting the rear view mirror which had been angled toward where Paul was sitting. Paul could now see the expressionless face of Benson, his own face reflected in Benson's mirrored sunglasses. In the back of Benson's peaked cap, Paul noticed but paid little heed to, a sort of hat pin the size of a five pence piece decorated with a yellow and black smiley face. In the executive lounge at Gatwick North, the two people looking at the laptop nodded again in unison. One of them said what the other was thinking.

"Benson and Hedges?"

The bags contained various items of clothing. A neat pair of grey lightweight trousers a navy blue silk and mohair blazer and a beautiful white cotton shirt. He struggled in the confined space putting the whole lot on. The shoes were a burnished brown brogue and were accompanied by a matching belt with a gunmetal buckle.

"There is a black bin bag in the foot-well next to you, Sir. You can put your old things in that." Hedges motioned with his thumb to behind his own seat. Paul is slightly put out.

"You'll look after them!" said Paul. "Only these boots have sentimental value." He was removing a pair of brown suede Chelsea boots that were well past their prime.

"Course I will sir." Hedges lied.

Paul emptied the pockets of his jeans onto the back seat. A wallet, the keys to his flat and an old Swiss Army pen knife. He started to load up the pockets of the new clothes. These objects together with the silver watch he was wearing, had practically never left his person for years.

The Mercedes turned into an industrial estate and through the gates of a health club.

"Ok. Mr. Finch." Hedges leant between the front seats as Benson pulled the car to a stop in front of the steps leading up to the doorway. "We've not got long Sir."

"What are we doing here?" Paul asked, a slight note of concern in his voice.

"Don't worry Mr. Finch." Said Hedges as he led him up the steps and through the automatic sliding glass doors of the health club. "It's just a hair-cut." At the reception desk a smart, heavily made up girl, with blond hair tied in a tight pony tail and dressed in a grey mandarin collared uniform, greeted them.

"Appointment for Mr. Finch." Said Hedges as he motioned towards Paul and then took a step back.

"Good morning Mr. Finch. We've been expecting you." Paul, with a big smile on his face repeated what she had said in his bond villain voice. The receptionist, not quite getting his attempt at humour, looked up from the computer screen and said,

"Sorry?" Still with a big smile on her face.

"No nothing." Said Paul. "I'm only kidding." The receptionist resumed studying the computer screen as if he'd not said anything.

"Sedoko will be looking after you this afternoon Mr. Finch." and glanced to one side where two more glass doors slid apart to reveal a hairdressing salon. Sedoko was standing in the doorway.

"This way Mr. Finch. Don't be scared. I won't bite."

"I'm not," said Paul as he swaggered through the glass doors. "And I was rather hoping you might." Sedoko giggled as the glass doors slid closed behind them. Hedges looked to the ceiling and as he was caught in the act by the receptionist, gave her a big smile.

"I'll be waiting in the car." He said and walked out the door.

"He carries them surprisingly well. Better than I thought he would." The woman in the executive lounge at Gatwick North Terminal said to her companion who shrugged his shoulders in response but actually had to agree that she was right.

A different man arrived at the airport in the silver Mercedes. At least a distinctly different looking one.

Hedges opened the back door and as Paul Finch got out he put on a pair of designer sunglasses that were at the bottom of one of the bags, even though it was a bleak and sunless November afternoon.

Paul Finch was in a film. He was convinced of it. That could be the only explanation. He looked around for suspicious people or for people with cameras or funny hats or newspapers held up in front of their faces but was disappointed that he saw no-one like this. Hedges handed him an envelope and with a full on wink slipped a new smartphone into the side pocket of his jacket.

"The departure check-in is through there." Hedges pointed with one hand while flicking a remote control towards the car with the other. The boot lid opened. He pulled out a glamorous leather suitcase and put it on the floor at his feet.

"They'll ask you if you packed it yourself so best you have a rummage." Said Hedges as he looked at his watch. "You're in good time. Make sure you're happy about everything."

"Well thanks for err" Paul didn't quite know what to say. He held out his hand for a handshake, "Thanks for driving me here."

Hedges shook Paul's hand with a smile in which the paranoid portion of Paul Finch's mind saw condescension, pity or smugness.

He bowed his head towards him. He was about to get back in the car when Hedges turned back.

"Goodness me," He said, "I nearly forgot." Delving into his inside jacket pocket. "You'd be going nowhere without this." He handed Paul back his passport. "Your name is Roger Penrose. All your details are in the welcome pack," He pointed to the envelope. "Good luck, Sir."

Hedges got swiftly back into the car. Benson flicked through the menu on the car phone and called a number. The phone rang twice before it was answered.

"On his way." Was all he said.

"See you here." The reply came through the car's loudspeakers. Benson clicked the phone off on the stalk control. He drove the car to the filling station around the corner from the airport, picked Paul Finch's black plastic bag from the back of the car and threw it in a rubbish bin and continued to the long stay car park. After parking the car they tossed their black jackets and peaked caps into the boot and pulled out a large black holdall and two smaller wheeled cases. Benson took a brown leather jacket from the holdall and put it on as Hedges did the same with a longer grey overcoat. The two men hurried to the bus stop and waited for the bus that would take them back to the terminal. When they arrived at the terminal they went directly to the men's toilets in the main hall. They emerged minutes later wearing different clothes.

In the executive departure lounge at the North Terminal the woman tapped her mobile phone.

"He'll be on the 15.50 from London. Arriving 20.05 your time. Take him the long way round would you?"

Paul Finch stood for a minute or more watching the silver Mercedes disappear along the exit road. His mouth was hanging slightly open. He opened the envelope Hedges had given him. Inside was an Easyjet ticket to Arrecife airport. One way only. "Oh my God" He said quietly to himself. "What have I done?"

25

It had been a while since Paul Finch had been through Gatwick airport or any airport for that matter. The last time he travelled, the north terminal at Gatwick hadn't been built, so it took him a while to orientate himself. Everything seemed like a mirror image of how he remembered it to be. The budget airline was a disappointment. He really thought he might be travelling with a more glamorous carrier. He'd have to check through his luggage as Hedges had advised, so he needed to find a secluded spot to do that first. On the floor below the check-in hall is a coffee shop. Not too many people. That would do fine. He ordered a small cappuccino conscious of the fact that his meagre resources amounted to less than fifty quid. That was all the money he had.

"Hope they've factored that into the equation somewhere, otherwise this is going to be a very short trip." He thought aloud. A young woman at a nearby table smiled at him when she realised he wasn't talking to her. He dragged his suitcase up on to a seat and sat down next to it. He went through all the pockets and compartments and felt through the linings and the lid for anything untoward.

He found nothing that would be out of place in a man's suitcase who was travelling to holiday on Lanzarote. He carefully placed his old Swiss army knife inside a sock and then inside a shoe. Satisfied that everything except his false passport, his assumed identity, and his sanity was in order he made his way to the check-in desk and told the first two small lies that would, according to the practical and reasoned side of his character, mushroom into a full blown criminal record. Yes, He was Roger Penrose and yes, he had packed his own bags. They had no issues with his passport, a brand new biometric version. Although he felt he must look guilty of something, the scanners and officious staff in the security hall didn't so he entered the retail temple that is the departure lounge with huge relief that he'd got that bit over and done with but also with a self-consciousness brought about by the irony that he's wearing thousands of pounds worth of clothes but he can barely afford to buy himself a beer. Four quid in change and a few coppers and literally two, twenty pound notes in his wallet which was all the ATM would let him have the previous night.

"Keep that for back-up." He said out loud. "Although I'm not sure what forty quid is going to back up exactly." Shaking the change in his hand wondering if it was enough for a beer, he stood in front of the flight message boards looking for his flight number before sitting on one of the many bench seats beside an overweight and balding man playing a game on his laptop. He had forty five minutes to wait before the gate number would be displayed.

A vibration and a quiet tinkling sound come from the inside of his new jacket. Pulling the small phone from his pocket he poked at the screen. It was a text message.

It read. **[Check upper left inside pocket. Text back OK.]**

The caller's number, a mobile phone, was displayed on the phone screen. *Getting closer* he thought. *Getting closer. I now have your number.* He played with the words for a moment or two. *Now your number is up. I am not a number,* before his mind tracked back to what the message actually said.

The inside left pocket on the jacket went up as well as down and was secured by a button and a loop of silk ribbon. He undid the loop and found ten completely fresh brand new, hot-off-the-press, five hundred Euro notes. Total five thousand Euros. About four thousand five hundred pounds sterling. Ten new notes measure less than a millimetre in thickness and therefore among the highest value to volume note in the world of cash. Astonished at himself for not noticing them, he immediately looked up and around hiding the money under his hands. A broad smile crossed his face. It had been a long time since he had had this kind of money about his person. Now he didn't feel quite so self-conscious.

"A little of the MOJO has returned," he said out loud to himself too loudly, causing the balding man playing pool on his laptop to turn away from his game and smile a 'Go on lad, you go for it' smile. Back with his internal communication system, *I'm beginning to like these people. Whoever they are.* He text back - **[Received with good grace.]**

There was a regular steward's enquiry at the currency exchange. Although it was perfectly legal currency they didn't want to just change it into smaller more usable notes so he had to make do with a hundred pounds sterling and the rest in Euros. The girl at the counter told him that they didn't see many of those notes. Apparently they are usually reserved for drug dealers and money launderers. Paul's conscience nudged him in the ribs and said 'Told-you-so.' Paul's conscience lost again though as he reasoned that a hundred quid will go a long way to helping him understand the style to which he is being paid to become accustomed. He headed to the bar. On his way he stopped and bought two tickets in a lottery to win a super-car. While he was drinking his Guinness, he pondered how aggressively he would have been questioned if the airport security had discovered the money on him. Was that perhaps another test? How innocent would he have looked when he told them that he genuinely had no idea that the money was there? The first pint of Guinness went down in four gulps leaving four rings on the side of the glass indicating gulp volume. He ordered another beer completely unaware that he had sat down on the barstool next to Hedges who's pulse rate rose significantly. Hedges texted Benson, who was watching from the balcony overlooking the lower floor and about thirty metres away. **[All going to plan so far.]** Benson texts back. **[Just keep it cool.]**

While drinking his Guinness Paul noticed but again paid little heed to a small pin the size of a five pence piece in the band of the baseball cap on the man sitting next to him on the barstool. *They must be getting popular*, he thought to himself.

Benson was calmly surveying the area from the balcony that surrounds the main concourse when his jaw dropped. He shook his head in disbelief. *There's no coincidences in this game.* Just arrived through the corridor from the security area was a tall red headed woman dressed and made up to be looked at. She was wearing a long flowing lightweight black coat, black suede boots and black leather trousers and a bright white silk blouse with ruffles down the front. She had a heavily made up face with candy pink lipstick. From his vantage point he could see that if she was dressing to impress she was succeeding. She was turning the heads of everyone she passed. She was dragging behind her a soft black leather case that seemed full to bursting. Benson tapped at his phone and put in the earpiece. He spoke softly into the microphone that was hanging from the earpiece. It would have looked, if anyone was watching, which as far as he was aware no-one was, as if he was talking to himself.

"Six o'clock. Don't turn around. You'll never guess who just walked in." He was still looking around checking no one was in earshot. Down in the bar Hedges fumbled with his own earpiece. He finished the last of the small coffee he was drinking and got up from the barstool. He turned out towards the middle of the terminal and walked toward the display of the fancy cars. He was looking down pretending to inspect them while scanning the area ahead of him looking for who Benson might be referring to.

"You a gambling man sir?" asked an earnest young man with a security pass hanging around his neck from a lanyard. Hedges took a moment to realise he was talking to him.

"Not today." He said with a gracious smile but continued circling the cars. The salesman followed at a nonchalant stroll. Benson came through in the earpiece again.

"Your one o'clock. Perfume." Hedges looked in the direction indicated but the salesman for the lottery tickets for the cars had sensed wrongly a prospective punter. He was almost at Hedges' shoulder again when, making him jump a little said,

"I can see you in one of these." Hedges, exasperated by the man wagged his finger for him to come closer. He whispered into the salesman's ear. The salesman quickly walked away.

"Woah, steady," said Benson through Hedges' earpiece, "Other side of the roundel." Hedges continued his slow walk and his jaw also dropped as he saw the woman. She may have clocked him looking at her but it wouldn't have made any difference even though he looked at her for too long. She was used to being stared at. She was holding a box of Chanel No.5. Hedges continued past her. He glanced at her bag for any information he could glean about the woman but there was nothing forthcoming.

"Is that...?" said Hedges into his earpiece.

"Believe it is, yes." Benson replied. "This is getting complicated. Why the hell do you think she's here?"

"Dunno," said Hedges, "but I've got a feeling our paths will be crossing."

"What's the connection do you think?"

"I've no idea but I can't say I'm surprised. Look the gate will be up on the screens soon. You keep your eye on Marta Hari and I'll watch our man. We don't want a bit of cash to go to his head."

A large group of people were standing watching the flight display boards near the entrance to the gates on one side of the departure hall. The EZY237 to Arricefi was saying -Please wait-. The flight was already half an hour past its departure time and no information was forthcoming.

The people in the crowd were getting restless. It was a busy time in the airport. Paul was standing patiently in front of the display screens looking up waiting for the gate number to appear..

The display board eventually showed the gate number and there was a rush towards it. The red headed woman in black appeared to peer at the screens a little longer before asking a man picking up his bag what the screen said. From where he was in the bookshop Hedges gathered that he had told her what the gate number was. *Short-sighted.* He said to himself. *Too vain to wear glasses?*

The boarding gate was a ten minute walk away and another queue had formed. The hard core travellers were in the process of going through the gate as speedy boarders. That left the rest of them. It looked to Hedges like it was going to be a full flight. Plenty of families and groups of lads going to Lanzarote. There seemed to be a small commotion up ahead in the line. It had been split in two.

Benson who was nearer the front could see the woman with the red hair remonstrating with the staff.

"I don't care about the fifty bloody quid." She was saying loudly, "I just need this bag on the plane."

"But madam." the attendant was saying, "If it won't fit in there." She pointed to an orange steel cage, "It can't go on the plane." The red-headed woman tried stubbornly to stuff the bag into the steel cage but it was never going to go. The attendant on the left desk continued to check the boarding passes of the other passengers. Benson walked past holding out his boarding pass and passport for inspection. Six more passengers did the same before Paul arrived. He had been watching the show also.

"Excuse me," he said to the attendant. "I don't have any hand luggage. Don't suppose I could help could I?" The red headed woman looked up at Paul from her position of attempting to wrench the now firmly stuck bag from the steel cage. Hedges, who was only a few behind in the queue decided to get a bottle of water from a vending machine and let the passengers behind go in front of him. He'd be obvious if he got to the other side of the desk and had to loiter. The attendant was unmoved.

"I'm sorry Sir." She said with a false smile. "The rules clearly state only one piece of hand luggage per passenger on the aircraft. It's a full flight, Sir." Paul knew better than to try to argue the toss.

"Look." He said to the woman with the red hair. "Let me help. Have you got something in there you can give to me?" He pointed to the bag that was still wedged in the orange cage. It took all of his strength to pull it out. The woman with the red hair adopted a 'damsel in distress' look.

"I put my handbag in there at the check-in. They said I could only take one piece. I'm not being funny but I'm not really used to this."

"Don't worry." He said, "Neither am I. Take the handbag out and give it to me. I just need to carry it onto the plane." She didn't hesitate in obeying. She crouched on the floor, scuffing the toes of her very sharply pointed boots and carefully unzipped the case. She took care, maybe as all women would in not revealing the contents of the case in their entirety and extracted a handbag at least half the size of the original case. It was black leather with a big brass buckle. She handed it up to Paul.

"You asked." He said underneath his breath but too loudly.

"Sorry?" She said looking up at him and zipping up the bag again.

"Nothing." He said. The woman with the red hair pushed the bag back into the metal cage and it slipped in easily enough. She performed a victory salute by holding her arms in the air and hissing out the word 'Yes'. Paul stood back a little surprised at this as the attendant scanned the boarding card. The woman with the red hair scowled at the attendant like an angry cat as she passed. They walked down the ramp onto the air-bridge and joined what was now the back of the queue to board the plane.

"Forgive me," said Paul as they stood there in embarrassed silence. "You don't look like a holiday maker."

"What does a holiday maker look like?" she replied.

"Not like you." He said. "More…" He whispered as he pointed to a couple with two young children. All were dressed in shorts and brightly coloured plastic shoes. "More like that."

He saw a smile creep across her face. Her demeanour had changed though from damsel in distress back to an obviously default position of a business woman with a high regard for herself and little regard for others. She nodded and against one of her own rules spoke without needing to.

"I'm working actually. Listen. Thanks for that." She motioned with her head back toward the gate desks. He detected that she was not that interested in any more conversation. He caught himself wondering what kind of man would put up with a woman like her.

"Working?" He said. Ignoring her unspoken instructions. "What do you do?"

"Facilities Management." She said. Her body language now explicitly telling him to leave her alone. The queue was nearing the end of the air-bridge and the entrance to the plane.

"What does that mean?" He said, knowing she didn't want to talk as they boarded the plane together and the steward checked again their boarding cards. He knew she knew he knew.

"It means I get things done." She said as she strode away from him up the aisle.

26

Five hours later Paul Finch walked through the arrivals gate at Arrecife International Airport. A tall tanned guy in a bright green and yellow striped jacket was holding up a card with Paul's new name on. Still not used to his new alias, he walked up and down the line of waiting drivers three times before remembering he had a new identity. He made himself known and the tall guy insisted he carried Paul's bag to the waiting car despite Paul's protests. Paul was not used to having his bags carried for him.

The tall guy led him to a car parked outside. Paul got in the back seat as the tall man put the suitcase in the boot. His nagging conscience was getting the upper hand again and his mood had swung around from being positive and excited to being negative and doubtful. He hadn't the slightest notion where he was going or what he was supposed to be doing and the carefree side of his nature was losing the battle against the reasoned and rational one. Since earlier that morning he had been the star in a feature film of his own imagination but the flight, the Guinness at the airport and several little bottles of whiskey was now causing him to feel queasy and the novelty of the whole experience was rubbing off.

They drove out of the airport and very soon were haring along an almost empty two lane strip of black tarmac that stretched for miles ahead of them. A huge setting sun glowed on the horizon in the distance casting an eerie light on the desolate landscape of black volcanic rocks and sand either side of the road.

Presently, they passed a distillery a saw mill and a cheese factory before turning into a palm lined road. The sun dipped below the horizon shortly before they drew up to a gated driveway. Three hundred yards in the distance was a single storey building. The signs told him he was being delivered to the Moridaira Hotel and brewery. He pinched himself. The car pulled up to a glass roofed entrance, lit with flaming torches. There were three smiling faces waiting. The door of the car was opened and he heard his new name again.

"Good Evening Mr. Penrose."

The reception of the hotel was luxurious in its decoration of aged timber panelling and old furniture but the staff of handsome young men who were the welcome committee provided a certain easy charm that Paul was both familiar and comfortable with. Costas, the chief it seemed of the welcome committee, asked if he would like a cool water or a glass of white wine.

"Did I see a sign saying this is a brewery?" Paul asked. "I'd kill for a cold beer." Costas was at first confused but smiled as he worked out the idiom. As Paul signed the register Costas appeared with a frosted glass of cold beer.

"Mmm." He purred as he took a gulp. "Hair of the dog. Just what the doctor ordered."

The receptionist handed him a credit card sized key. "Your office has supplied all the details we need, Mr. Penrose. Just charge anything you like to the room and it'll be taken care of. Oh and I have a package for you." She produced a Federal Express box the size of a briefcase and placed it on the reception desk.

"We'll have it sent to your room, shall we Sir?" asked Costas.

Paul is warming to his character now and nodded.

"Yes. Thank-you."

"If you'd like to follow me, Sir, I'll show you to your suite."

Costas nodded in the direction of a narrow corridor and began to walk. Paul followed. The narrow corridor opened out into a sumptuous lounge where the cushions on the many beautifully upholstered couches and arm chairs looked as if they had been blown up with compressed air.

"This is the Lansdown Room, Mr. Penrose." The large room was bright and cool. Three huge oil paintings on the three main walls depicted rugby scenes. The dominating colours being the emerald green and white of the Irish national side.

"The owner is a bit of a rugby fan Sir." Costas waved a hand towards the paintings before pushing open a grand set of French doors revealing a gravelled courtyard again lit with flaming lanterns. He motioned Paul through and followed after him. Costas was in no hurry and continued at a strolling pace.

"We serve breakfast here this time of year, Sir. The air is particularly clear around eight. The temperature hits about twenty five by nine."

At the far end of the courtyard he pointed through more French doors to another tastefully decorated room.

"The dining room is through there, Sir. Will you be dining with us tonight?" Paul was temporarily thrown by the question. He'd really not thought that far ahead.

"Err… Yes. Thank you. Yes I suppose I will."

"Cocktails in the bar, Sir, from eight." Costas looked at his watch. "Oh! You've missed that Sir. Feel free to dine whenever you like though, Sir."

They turned into a passage lined either side by high dense hedges that opened out into a formal garden the size of a tennis court. At the far end of which was a building that appeared to be a scale model of the big main house. They approached the front door of the building and Costas inserted a key card and the latch clicked as he opened the door. Inside was a hallway containing a leather sofa and a heavy section wooden table topped with a three foot tall vase of chrysanthemums. By the table were Paul's bags and the Fed-Ex box was sitting next to the vase of flowers. Costas opened a walnut door inlaid with satinwood. Paul couldn't help running his fingertips over the surface and casually inspecting the workmanship as he passed by it. He was trying desperately and unsuccessfully not to look overawed. The room was open plan and luxuriously decorated. A huge bed was on one side of the room opposite more French doors. Through the doors Paul could see nothing but a black void. Costas approached the doors and pulled them together before pulling the heavy curtains also.

"The moon's not up yet, Sir. But wait for the morning to take a look out here. It'll take your breath away."

Costas winked at Paul. "There's nothing except the Atlantic Ocean between us and America, Sir." He paused while Paul looked around. "I'll leave you to relax Mr. Penrose." Costas bowed toward him and lingered. Paul took a few seconds to understand, not recognising his new name again, that he was waiting for a tip. He pulled out an untidy wad of notes from his trouser pocket and gave one to Costas. He had no idea how much it was.

"Thank you. Sir, see you shortly for dinner then." He said and left Paul alone in the room. Paul strolled around the huge room a few times. He looked at his watch as he took off his jacket.

"God I'm knacked." He said out loud to himself and jumped on the bed. Before long he was asleep. He was disturbed by the tinny sound of a mobile phone ringing. Ringing and ringing. *Oh! God will someone answer that phone,* He thought through a half sleep before he realised the noise was coming from his own newly acquired mobile. He looked at his watch before answering.

"Damn," he said to himself. "Two hours." He pressed the accept button on the cover in anticipation of speaking to someone else who was party to this escapade but was disappointed. An automated voice, at least he thought it was an automated voice was telling him that this was his wake up call. Then as he was resting his head back on the pillow the text message alert sounded. He noticed there had been four more sent while he had been asleep all reading, OPEN THE BOX. It took a moment or two for the message to sink in. He jumped up from the bed and walked to the lobby. He picked up the FedEx package and took it back to the bed and ripped open the outer packaging to find a plain brown cardboard box. Inside was a small laptop computer, a power cord and a white envelope. Inside the envelope were a set of expensively printed business cards. Roger Penrose – Rare Books and Periodicals. The cards included an address in Chelsea, London, his new mobile phone number and a Landline number. He immediately went to the phone on the desk and asked the receptionist for an outside line. He rang the number on the card. After three rings a woman's voice, who he could swear he had heard before but couldn't quite place, answered.

"Good Evening. Penrose Rare Books."

"Hello." Said Paul making it up on the spot. "I've arrived safely. Talk when I'm back in the UK."

"Hello, Mr. Penrose. This is Harriet. And do you mean for me to tell Peter you've arrived safely?" Said the voice on the other end of the phone. She sounded like she had something in her mouth.

"Sorry about that Harriet. Yes. Let him know will you."

"No problem Mr. Penrose. See you soon." Said the voice.

He put the phone down on its cradle.

"Mmmmmm." He said to himself out loud scratching his chin. "Interesting. Very interesting indeed" then he turned to the laptop and hurriedly opened the lid. The laptop was in sleep mode so fired up immediately and a pop up window asked him to connect the power lead. There was a power socket behind the desk. As he was crouching to plug in the power cord, he noticed a car key fob attached with Velcro to the underside of the desk. He pulled it away from its fixing and placed it on top of the desk. *Odd.* He thought.

"Maybe it's someone's spare," he said to himself but thought no more of it.

A page of text appeared on the laptop.

> **Roger Penrose. Your email address is R.Penrose@me.com and your cover is as a rare books and periodical dealer visiting the Island because you've heard that the owner of the hotel is in possession of some rare copies of Private Eye magazines. The owner's name is Tom Gates. He is a wealthy hotelier and landowner and will be glad to talk to you. He may or may not be in residence in the hotel tonight. If he is not, the hotel is also his principle place of residence-his home. So if he is not there for dinner today, he will be there tomorrow. We don't envisage you having any**

problems recognising him. The reason you are there is to observe and to report back anything that you may find peculiar. Anything relating to the behaviour of Tom Gates. Your contact number is the one on your business card. The receptionist at the office, and your personal assistant is Harriet. Your partner in the business is Peter. Report each day at six in the evening and if nothing significant has occurred just tell Harriet that everything is fine. Ask for Peter or ask Harriet to get a message to Peter to call you if anything important happens. You will be able to access your regular business emails via the hotel WIFI at Rogerpenrose@me.com. Sign in with your email address. Your password is DOVETAIL. When you have read and understood all of the above it is imperative that you delete this document and empty the recycle bin. This must be done before you leave this machine anywhere unattended. Please leave this computer on the desk with the top upright at ninety degrees when you are not using it. Ensure that the power cable is always plugged in and that the wifi is set to on.

Paul read with care the single page of text and deleted it. He looked at his watch. The time was 10.10pm.

"Still, missed cocktails at eight." He said to himself out loud. "Better get cracking." He pulled off all his clothes and highly uncharacteristically hung them in the wardrobe in the vestibule. Naked, he unpacked his suitcase. He found three more pairs of really good shoes including a brown suede lightweight loafer made in the traditional way with a proper sole and heel, four more shirts in understated but beautiful cloths including a shantung silk, three more pairs of trousers of what appeared to be the same design and cloth as the one he was wearing but in three different colours one of which was a bright white and two more jackets, folded in a way he recognised with the sleeves on the inside so that they wouldn't crease too much having been packed in a suitcase. The fold worked too. One of the jackets, bright pink linen with blue silk lining was the one he'd wear tonight. He hung it together with a pair of the trousers on a clothes hanger in the bathroom and turned the shower full on hot to steam the creases out. *All these beautiful clothes*, he thought. *He'd better make the best of them. And all of the labels where they were supposed to be. On the inside.* He gave the shower five minutes and rehung the clothes on a valet stand in the cool air by the French doors. A light breeze was billowing the curtains. There were all sorts of grooming products and tools in the bathroom. He made use of as many as he could and emerged fifteen minutes later feeling invigorated. He put on the clothes he'd selected and with the key card, the phone and his Swiss army knife in his pockets stepped out of the door into the garden looking forward to what the remains of the evening might hold. Halfway up the garden path he was stopped in his tracks by the scent from a blooming Chinese Jasmine. He stood breathing in the scent for a few moments before picking one of the star like blooms and sticking it into the button-hole in the lapel of his jacket.

He arrived in the bar-room and was greeted again by Costas. He was a little disappointed to be, except for Costas and the barman, the only one there. He plotted up on a bar stool.

"Sir?" Asked the barman who was wearing a fixed half smile that seemed to be his only expression and was shining a huge wine glass with a teacloth.

"I'll have a beer." Said Paul.

"Certainly. Sir. Would you like our own? We have other bottled lager if you prefer."

"No, No. Let's try the home brew. If it's cold it'll be just fine."

"It's cold Sir."

"A pint of that then."

The Barman took an old fashioned dimpled pint pot from above the bar and poured the pint.

"Just what the doctor ordered." Said Paul again after taking a large gulp.

"Begging your pardon Sir." The barman replied.

"No No, just saying very nice. Everything good." Paul nodded at his beer.

The barman's expression did not change.

"Very good sir." He said.

Paul took a good look around the bar for the first time. In the corner by another set of French doors that led he knew not where was an upright piano and hanging above that by their necks were two acoustic guitars. The first was a six string Guild. It was pushed away from the wall slightly by its bulbous shaped back. The second was a very rare nine string of unknown make. Another flurry of excitement ran through him. He'd seen one of these before. A long time ago though. This one appeared well worn. The fretboard had indentations in the wood only on the first three frets and the body was well scratched from vigorous strumming. He was about to ask the barman if he could take a look when the redheaded woman he had helped-out on the flight walked into the bar. She nodded at him acknowledging the fact that they were both guests at the hotel. The expression on her face suggested that she expected to be looked at and that she would be offended if she wasn't. He nodded back and mumbled,

"Hello again," and then so only he could hear, "Things are looking up." Then two, by his new standards, scruffy men strolled into the bar as if they owned it. One of the men, judging by the clothes he was wearing, could have been American.

27

[**They've gone into dinner together. Not part of the plan. Instructions please.**]

Benson typed the text into his phone.

"Could we have a bottle of your best Champagne?" Paul said to the waiter even before they had sat down. Mary gulped back what remained of her vodka and tonic. "I've told you all about me," he said. "Tell me about you."

"If I told you that I'd have to kill you." She said with a smile. The waiter appeared again without a bottle.

"Excuse me Mr. Penrose Sir," He said bowing. "I am sorry for disturbing you but there is a telephone call for you at the reception. The caller says it is urgent." He stood waiting to show Paul the way. Paul raised his eyebrows. "Do apologise Mary," He said rising from his chair.

"Won't be a mo." He turned back to the waiter.

"Don't forget that Champagne," He said as he followed the waiter to the reception. A walk of a couple of minutes.

The receptionist handed Paul a phone handset.

"Mr. Penrose. Harriet here. Sorry to disturb your dinner. Peter has asked if you could meet him urgently at The Flat Club. It's a mile down the road and a short walk into the village. There'll be a car waiting." Before he could reply the phone went dead.

"Sir, Mr. Penrose, Sir. This way if you please."

Costas was there directing Paul through the entrance doors where a car was waiting with its passenger door open. Paul, bemused got in the back. The driver could have been the same one that brought him here but it was too dark now to make a positive identification. They drove in silence for five minutes and arrived at a dusty car park. There was a bright crescent moon in the sky now. The driver stopped and Paul got out. The driver got out also.

"This way please." He said. They walked down the narrow cobbled streets, some little more than passageways and having passed a few bars all seemingly full of holidaymakers his guide directed him into a smart place buzzing with loud music and happy customers. Almost all of them seemed to be pretty young women.

"I'll be waiting for you up at the car." The driver said with a polite bow and disappeared in the direction he had come from.

"Roge, mate... How the hell are you?" A tall slim man with shoulder length blond curly hair in his early thirties was standing in front of him with his arms outstretched welcoming him. He looked him up and down, a big smile on his face and his head cocked to one side.

"Nice clobber man." He said in his south London accent as he strode forward. He rubbed the cloth of Paul's jacket lapel between his thumb and forefinger then pulled him into a big hug.

"Roge, man." He repeated. "Don't tell me you don't remember." He winked an almost indiscernible wink as he pushed him slightly away still holding onto his shoulders.

"Gaz, Man." He pointed at himself.

"Gaz," Said Paul nodding his head. "Of course."

"Listen, man," said Gaz. "Pete's at the back. On the terrace. It's quieter up there. You go on up. I'll send some drinks up. Beer, Yeah?"

"You're good." Said Paul out loud but to himself. "You're very good."

Paul made his way through the crowded bar. All of the barmen were good-looking boys with big smiles and were serving drinks at a frantic pace. He walked around the dance floor weaving his way past pretty young girls in summer dresses.

You're too old for this place he thought to himself.

Heady stuff though and Paul was liking it. He found himself thinking that just forty eight hours previously he was drinking stout in a pub in Pimlico and would shortly have been going home to heat up some baked beans.

He reached a short staircase and found that maybe he was not too old after-all. All sorts of bohemian types were sitting around up here. Gaz was right. It was quieter but not much.

Gaz reappeared at the top of the steps with a pint. "Here you are mate. Enjoy. He's over there, look." Gaz pointed to a corner of the terrace and led him over. A man was sitting at the table who he recognised. The American from the hotel. He was dressed differently in an old fashioned but new looking cream safari suit and a Panama hat. He got up from his seat as Paul approached.

"Roger." He said as if they were friends. "Sit down will you. See Gazzer's already sorted you out with a drink." He turned to Gaz and with another wink palmed across some notes. Gaz didn't look at the notes, just slipped them into the pocket of his white linen trousers.

"I'll leave you two to reacquaint." Said Gaz and disappeared through the tables and back down the stairs.

Benson immediately changed his attitude.

"Roger. I know this must be very confusing for you and you've probably got a load of questions. We were not supposed to meet. At least not just yet." Paul considered carefully the man opposite him at the table.

"Do I know…" Paul tried to speak but as he did so Benson raised his hand to stop him.

"I'll get straight to the point." Said Benson. "The woman you were having dinner with…"

"About to have dinner with." Paul corrected before Benson could raise his hand again.

"The woman you were about to have dinner with," he continued, "Is a very dangerous woman and on no account are you to tell her why you are here." Paul's curiosity, for the moment at least was stronger than any fear Benson might have been trying to instil.

"That shouldn't be too hard," he said, "As *I* don't know the reason I'm here." Benson nodded.

"You know why you're here, Paul." He said reverting to Paul's real name. "You're a rare book dealer looking for a deal. Have you told her you want to meet the owner of the hotel?" He gestured with his head in the general direction of where they had come from.

"So is that why I'm here then? The laptop. It was from you?" Said Paul. Benson ignored the question.

"What did you tell her, Paul?"

"I told her I was an eccentric millionaire just getting away from the London winter."

"No you didn't. What did you tell her?"

"Look… Who are you?" said Paul.

"Call me Benjamin."

"No, not what do I call you. What is your name?"

"Peter then. I'm Peter. Your business partner, remember." Benson knew he didn't sound convincing. "But that's not important..."

"Yes it is. It's very important. I told her the truth. Like I like to do most of the time. I told her I am a penniless, well very nearly, carpenter looking for a bit of adventure. I have to say I don't think she believed me. I don't blame her. Penniless carpenters don't wear this kind of gear," he pointed at his jacket, "and don't stay in the most expensive hotel in the Canaries."

"Tricky beast. Truth." Said Benson. "Did you mention you replied to an ad in Private Eye?" Paul is bemused. He took a long slurp from his beer and put his elbows on the table.

"Is that particularly significant?" He asked with his head turned to one side slightly.

"Well did you?" Benson's tone is brusque. Paul now sat back in his chair. Benson noticed an expression in his eyes he had not seen before. *Why would I have seen it before,* he thought, excusing himself. *I've never really met him before this evening. You get to know a lot about your subjects in this game but you never really get to know them. The first time I have been within a five foot circle of this man was this morning in the car.* The expression he noticed now was one of anger. Tempered, controlled anger but anger all the same. Paul wasn't that good at hiding it even if he thought he was. Benson calmed a little. He could tell that he would be compromising the situation if he were to let Paul kick off. A little bit of him liked what he saw though. Perhaps Jill was right. Perhaps this looser might have balls. He raised his hands in deference. Paul continued.

"I'm not complaining. This little fiasco suits me just fine. I've been given?" He looked to Benson for agreement on the word. Benson shrugged.

"I've been given," Paul continued, "a few grand to have a bit of fun. No explanations needed. No explanations wanted…"

There was a commotion in the lower bar that stopped Paul mid-sentence. The sound of breaking glass and young girls screaming would normally indicate a fight breaking out. Paul tried to continue talking but Benson was out of his chair trying to see what was going on. Paul calmly drank from his beer as if nothing was happening. It would all blow over in due course. Paul glanced up at Benson who was looking more than a little agitated.

"Paul." Said Benson. "Have you got the phone on you?" Paul tapped the breast pocket of his pink jacket.

"Yeah." He answered, still appearing as if fights happen all the time in the bars he goes to. Benson sat back down quickly.

"Listen Paul. Listen please. The men that have just come into the bar… believe me that I don't know exactly who they are but I know they are not punters. When I go downstairs there…" He pointed to the steps to the lower bar, "You slip over this wall." Benson laid his hand on the white stone wall they were sitting next to.

"What?" Said Paul, suddenly annoyed again. Benson had to use a shock tactic. Otherwise the party for this brave or stupid or whatever he was rookie could be ending very soon.

"Paul. Please. Slip over this wall without being seen. The drop's only six feet behind here. If you don't you may die here tonight."

Paul's demeanour changed instantly. A bar fight he could cope with. This could not be something to do with him, surely. He saw the earnestness in Benson's face. Although he was trying to appear calm the fear rising up in him was showing in his eyes. Paul obeyed and got up to look over the wall that was waist high on their side. The drop looked a damn sight more than six feet but it was down to a narrow cobbled alleyway set at a steep angle.

"Go!" Said Benson. "Keep your phone to hand and walk slowly up. Keep going up. You'll come to the car park. Do not be seen." Paul downed his pint before slipping as silently as he could, over the wall. For some reason he cringed at the damage he was doing to his beautiful new clothes. He hung on to the top of the wall for a second or two before letting go. Thankfully the cobbled street was just six inches below his feet. He patted his breast pocket again to check for the phone. All good. As he walked up the hill he could hear the commotion rising back on the terrace. Where the hell was he going? He walked on up the hill. The crescent moon was casting a decent light before him. After two hundred yards the alley forked. The lights and the music that had followed him up the alley had now dispersed into the night. He was alone. His heart was thudding in his chest. Or was it just his heart. No it wasn't. The phone was vibrating in his pocket. He pulled it out and started pressing the screen. He was not familiar with the touch screen but soon got to the reason why the phone was vibrating. A text message.

Reverse the jacket. Go to square.

Paul read the message through three times and ignored its instruction as he walked nervously up the cobbled path. Along the cobbled pathway were doorways. Doorways that presumably led into houses. They were all quiet. He could hear that round the corner there might be another bar or club or something where there might be people. People who he could mingle with and not be noticed. He stood for a moment to catch his breath and thought that maybe he was a little drunk. He felt a little light headed. He started to count through the drinks he'd had. Two pints in the bar before he started talking to Mary, then three pints before they decided to eat. Plus the one he'd just had. Adrenaline was also in his system so for the moment this wasn't a problem. But he must keep the adrenaline where it was so he started jogging on the spot in one of the doorways. At the end of the alley, the lights were brighter. He could see the shadows of people walking by. *Look natural*, he thought. *Act normal.*

He was about to walk casually up the fifty meters or so toward the source of the lights at the end of the alley when his mind was cast back to the hotel room. All the clothes seemed as well made on the inside as they were on the outside. He checked the inside of his pink jacket. It was neatly lined in blue slub-silk. A knowing smile fought its way across his anxious face.

"They haven't, have they?" He said out loud to himself. He took off the jacket and turned it inside out. *They have.*

He put the jacket on again and he was transformed into an altogether different person wearing this time a blue jacket. The alley was quiet except for the competing muffled bass lines of music from various bars. All-together they made a low rumbling sound. He was still nervously panting and was sweating heavily. He walked up the alley towards the sound and light. If whoever it was who was looking for him, was looking for a man in a pink jacket, then the disguise might work. As it was the light in the alley was too dim to discern any colour. Everything just looked grey. He would have to get into the light and mingle with other people. The alley appeared to open out into a wider street where there was plenty of light and sound and people. As he approached the end of the alley a man appeared mainly in silhouette. Paul glimpsed a reflection coming from the man's shoes. Like the reflection from a high visibility vest that cyclists wear. It was three white stripes. They blinked at Paul. The man's back was turned to Paul but he was obviously searching around. Fear temporarily incapacitated him and his arms and legs remained rigid for a moment. He slowly calculated his options. The man saw him, took a double take and whistled an odd bird call with his thumb and forefinger. Paul remained stock still. The right thing to do, maybe, he reasoned excruciatingly slowly, would be to continue walking towards the man. Maybe he would have been right but instead he turned tail and ran back down the alley. Two men followed him. He could hear the running footsteps and little else.

    He ran hard not knowing where he was going. He did not turn around. He ran as fast as he could on the cobbles, sliding around corners and taking whatever path appeared to be the easiest. Judging by the sound of their footsteps they were only a corner or two behind him and they were gaining. The fear was sharpening his mind but that only had the effect of making him realise that he had very few options. There was a series of thuds behind him and he heard the sound of a struggle. He also heard a metallic clunk and skid as if someone had dropped or had thrown a heavy metal object onto the cobbles and it had skidded along. The sound of chasing footsteps had stopped but he didn't. He wanted to put as much distance between them and him as he could. He ran and ran through the maze of cobbled alleyways. He eventually arrived at the open space where he had started. The driver was sitting on the bonnet of the car in the moonlight smoking a cigarette and was startled as Paul emerged from the alleyway. The driver flicked the cigarette away as if for some reason he shouldn't have been smoking. Paul took a moment to compose himself and glanced behind him. Nothing. Not a sound except for the usual. He jogged toward the car. He was soaked with sweat and breathing so heavily he had to stop a moment with his hands on his knees. Still shaking with fear, he managed a smile.

"Could we get out of here?" He said to the driver who attentively opened the back door. Paul jumped in.

"I couldn't pinch one of those fags, could I?" He said making a smoking mime with his fingers. The driver was not sure what Paul was talking about. Paul pointed at the cigarette packet. They arrived back at the hotel twenty minutes later. The short journey had calmed him a little but he furtively looked around before getting out of the car. He had asked if they could drive for a while before going back to the hotel. He sat in the back of the cab with the window wide open smoking the cigarettes that the driver provided. When they arrived back, Paul walked past the eerily quiet reception. A smart young women with a pony tail and glasses was staring at a computer screen. She appeared to be intent on completing some task or another, the computer screen reflecting in her glasses. She nodded a greeting as he walked by but quickly resumed her endeavours. Paul walked towards the bar which was now empty of customers. No staff either so he walked behind it, found a glass and poured himself half a tumbler of whisky and threw in a hand-full of ice from a stainless steel fridge. He gulped back half the whisky and walked onto the terrace.

Still no-one. He looked at his watch. 2.15am. *Shit, where did all the time go. Where did all the people go?* He felt around his jacket pockets but could not find his key card.

He realised with a stamp of his foot and a grimace to himself that the card must have fallen out of his pocket when he reversed the jacket or when he was running for his life. He cursed, what did he call himself? Benjamin or Peter or some-such. Why did he make me do that? *Like the colour of my jacket is going to throw thugs like that.* He made a mental note to bring him to book whenever... or if ever he saw him again. A couple of things occurred to him.

One. He could get into his room all-right by asking the receptionist for another key card. *But what if whoever was chasing me found the key card. They'll know exactly where I am.* He decided he had to go back. He checked the phone in his jacket pocket. Nothing. No calls or messages. He walked back to the girl at the reception who was still staring at the computer monitor. She smiled again as he approached noticing the large half full tumbler of whisky. He slipped off the rather obvious blue silk jacket which had suffered from his excursions earlier and handed it across to girl. "Would you mind looking after this for me?" He asked.

"Certainly Mr.. Penrose." She replied taking the jacket from him as if this was perfectly normal. He left the tumbler of whisky on the reception desk and walked towards the glass doors that swished open for him. The night was warm and there was no-one around that he could see. There was only one road out of the hotel and he started his walk. When he'd been driven earlier, he'd not really paid attention to the route they had taken so he was not at all sure where he was going. The walk took less time than he thought and he arrived at the dusty car park at the top of the village. He wished he'd paid more attention before.

There was an alleyway going down that he thought he recognised. Walking slowly and deliberately he tried to retrace as best he could his steps. The crescent moon was still providing enough light. The lack of any street lighting allowed his eyes to adjust to the light and it was surprisingly easy to make out details in the shadows. As he walked further downhill on the cobbled alleyways past old wooden doors and iron gates leading into dark courtyards he could just make out the bass sounds of a club or bar still wafting through the night air. He recognised a corner he had turned earlier. A curbed semicircle of earth held the roots of another jasmine plant, its white flowers closed a little in the darkness. He sniffed the blooms and knew then that he had been past this spot at least. But which way now? He could have come from or continued on in any of five different directions. He peered up each of the alleys in turn looking for anything that might give him a clue as to where he had been. He walked randomly up the widest of the alleyways and saw a little white rectangular shape sitting on the black cobblestones a few yards ahead of him. He let out a little whistle as he picked it up and looked it over.

"*Let's get out of here.*" He said out loud to himself. Which way now? He remembered deciding to go down when he was here before. He was being chased then but it was coming back to him. He walked slowly down what became quite a steep incline at the bottom of which was a low wall, painted white. He remembered this also. The cobbled stones beneath his feet were slippery as if they were polished. *How did I run on these?* He said to himself. *It's easier to run though.* He reasoned with himself. *Centre of gravity further forward, or something like that.* He was ten yards away from the low wall. He was gingerly stepping along, more conscious of his footsteps than he should have been. The leather soles of his shoes starting to skid. He realised he had been treading in some black liquid, like used engine oil. He lifted up his left foot to see if he could see what it was. He was mostly concerned with ruining the shoes. As he cocked his leg behind him his other foot slipped again in the black liquid. There was more of it than he had first thought. He tried to steady himself but with both feet on the ground he started sliding toward the low white wall arms outstretched like a surfer. He automatically crouched as he went. He held out his hands and came to a halt, his torso tipping over the curved top of the wall. He saw as if it were perfectly normal a pair of eyes peering up at him from six feet below. As his mind tried desperately to rationalise the situation fear took over his body again. His breathing automatically quickened and his hands started to shake. He crouched on his haunches behind the low wall. They were still here. They had been lying in wait for him. He crouched where he was for a few seconds while he weighed up the scene. It was deathly quiet. The only sounds he could hear were his own heartbeat and waves lapping onto a beach somewhere near. *They'd be making a noise.* He reasoned with himself. *At least some noise. It's silent. I'd hear something, surely.* He slowly straightened up and peered over the wall again.

The eyes were still gazing up at him reflecting in the moonlight. He could make out the silhouette of a body in the dimness. It was all tangled up in thorny wild brush. As his eyes adjusted further to the shadows he could see a wide black gash under the chin. He had never seen a dead body before but he instinctively knew that that was what he was looking at. He thought his heart could not beat any faster or with more force but it seemed to as he was about to turn away and just get the hell out of there when he saw six feet further down the slope, sticking out of thick gorse a leg with a training shoe at the end. The same training shoe he had seen earlier that evening. Three white stripes reflecting in the moonlight. He turned away and started to run down the hill. The fear he felt stopped him from worrying about his footing but *yes* he thought. *It is easier to run.* The downward incline levelled out briefly and the path turned to the left and finally uphill. Paul continued running up the incline thinking that soon he would come across something that he was vaguely familiar with. The ground levelled out again and he found himself walking now and trying to regain a semblance of calm, along a tarmac road. To his left and way below was the Atlantic Ocean the moon glinting on its surface. He remembered none of this but the hotel, his relative safe haven was overlooking the ocean and unless he had passed it running around the lanes which he doubted, or if he had become so disorientated that he was walking in completely the opposite direction to the way he should be going, he should come across the hotel soon. It was impossible that he was walking in the wrong direction, he reasoned to himself. The Ocean was on his right as he came here and it was on his left now. It seemed like an age, making him seriously question his judgement several times, but soon enough he recognised the lights of the hotel entrance. He headed towards them going off the road over dusty black sand. When he reached the entrance gates the lights showed up what a state he was in. He'd guessed the black liquid was blood but he'd not imagined the mess it had made of him. He looked like he'd been in a knife fight and hadn't done too well. He couldn't go through the main entrance. He looked at his watch. Four AM. The dawn would be surely breaking soon. He needed to get back to his room and sort himself out. Let alone get some sleep. He skirted around the side of the hotel past tennis courts and a swimming pool and into his own private garden. He slipped the key card into the slot and a green light blinked on the lock. He quietly slipped inside and gently closed the door behind him. He stood up against the closed door for a few seconds with a partial sense of relief.

"*What the hell just happened?*" He whispered to himself. "*What the hell just happened?*" He pushed himself away from the door and went straight into the bathroom and turned on the shower. He stepped under the stream of water still wearing the clothes and turned the temperature of the water up as high as he could bear. He stood there washing anything he could off the clothes. The suede shoes would be totally ruined. As for the shirt and trousers, they might survive. When he was happy that the blood was washed out as far as it could he undressed and flung the clothes into the shower tray, squirted some more soap on them and washed himself as he continued to knead soap into the clothes with his feet and toes. The clean-up must have taken him half an hour. He took a thick towel from the rail and started to dry himself off as he walked along the corridor of the suite towards the bedroom. The sun was just starting to come up and the light was seeping into the room around the perimeter of the drawn curtains. For the third time that night Paul had the wits scared out of him. He was towelling his hair dry with the only towel he had brought out of the bathroom when he heard the click and saw the light from one of the bedside lamps. With the towel held around his head he turned slowly and faced the bed. He pulled the towel down onto his shoulders. Mary was lying on the bed in front of him under a single sheet.

"Won't be a mo." She said in a mocking attempt at Paul's voice. There was anger and mirth in the phrase. He couldn't help thinking she sounded slightly mad. Paul stood there with his mouth open. She had the sheet pulled up over her. She looked him in the eye for a few seconds then let her gaze obviously fall to his groin. She then let her head drop the same number of degrees and lifted her eyebrows as if looking over the top of glasses. She threw off the sheet revealing her naked body. On her thigh was what looked like a lipstick mark in the shape of lips. She reversed the movement of her head, sharply flicking her chin forward and upwards, beckoning him. She reached with her left hand upwards to the bedside light and switched it off. The light creeping in from around the closed curtains had increased somewhat even in those few seconds. It took a few seconds more but then Paul could easily make out her figure lying in the bed. He let the towel drop to the floor and walked toward the bed where he lay down by her side. She wasted no time on preliminaries and rolled on top of him. She sat there for a moment or two grinding herself onto him with her hands on his chest. She leaned further forward until her hands were either side of his head. Her left hand slipped under the pillow.

Paul suddenly panicked. He was still piecing together the events of the evening and his mind was coming up with all sorts of scenarios. Who is this woman? A facilitator.

She gets things done. His body had gone through the motions without consulting his brain. What made it worse was that she seemed to be searching for something underneath the huge pillows. He was about to throw her off when she sat upright. He could see her black silhouette in the dim morning light. She was holding up a little square foil package.

"Best not be takin' any chances." Said Mary.

28

Paul woke from a deep sleep. The blackout curtains had done the job as well as they could of keeping the sunlight outside the room. It couldn't be mistaken though. The halo of light around the edges of the drawn curtains was screaming to get in. Paul glanced at his watch. For some reason it said it was past one o'clock. In his just-woken state nothing was making sense. For a moment or two he was sure that he had been dreaming and that thought comforted him. He made to turn over and go back to sleep when the reality of what had been happening caught up with him. He threw off the sheet that had been covering him, flung his legs over the side of the bed, stood up and strode towards the windows and pulled the curtains roughly apart. The sun flooded into the room. He had to cover his eyes with his arm so strong was the contrast in light. Still covering his eyes he pushed the handle in the middle of two French doors downwards and pushed them open. He walked slowly outside onto a narrow iron and timber balcony that stretched the width of the room, a distance of maybe thirty feet. It was only perhaps three feet from the French doors to the heavy iron balustrade. He looked out towards a sparkling blue ocean. His eyes were slowly adjusting to the bright sunlight. Still shading his eyes though, he could make out a sail-boat in the distance halfway between him and the horizon. He scanned the extent of the horizon from left to right. There appeared to be nothing else there.

"I like this." He said to himself out loud. "I could get used to this." Still with his eyes peering at the far horizon and still with his left hand shading the afternoon sun from his eyes he stepped forward a pace and placed his right hand on the black iron balustrade. The balustrade was hot. It was becoming quickly too hot to hold onto. For the first time his eyes dropped to the line of the balustrade and with a reflex action jumped backwards banging into the half open door. He couldn't believe what he was seeing. He had assumed that he was on a level with the ocean. He approached the balustrade again and peered this time downward. The ocean seemed a mile below him. He was perched on an iron balcony built into a column of rock that started in the Atlantic Ocean below and went straight up. Straight up for he couldn't guess how many feet. It was dizzying looking down over the edge. He heard a sound from inside the room and realised he was naked. He walked confidently back into the room, it was his room after all. His eyes were blinded again briefly while his irises adjusted to the contrast. He blinked his eyelids shut. When he opened them he jumped back again. Costas was standing in front of him. Costas made a loose fist in front of his mouth and coughed into his hand. With his other hand he handed Paul a white towelling robe.

"I do apologise Mr. Penrose Sir. Your colleagues have been very worried about you. Your mobile phone has not been operating and the house phone is off the hook."

Paul glanced over towards the bed. It was a mess. One of the bedside lamps was on the floor and yes, the phone that had been sitting on the bedside table was on the floor, the receiver lying beside it.

"You've taken in the view I see Sir. Spectacular isn't it." Continued Costas.

"Yes. It certainly is." Said Paul as he pulled on the towelling robe. "Just how high up are we here?" Costas nodded and smiled a knowing smile.

"About sixty five metres." Said Costas. Paul nodded his head and let out a whistle. He wasn't quite sure how high sixty five metres was. He tried for a moment to convert it into feet but gave up before he reached an answer.

"What time is it?" He said instead.

"Just coming up to two o'clock." Costas replied.

"What day is it?"

"Saturday, Sir. Your friends have asked me to ask if you would join them for lunch in the courtyard, Sir."

Paul walked back to the balcony and looked over and down. He was dizzied looking down. He could hardly bring himself to look and he instinctively and unnecessarily crouched a little.

"Isn't this dangerous?" He asked. The pitch of his voice got higher with every word.

"Not if you stay on this side." Said Costas with a deadpan expression.

"Yeah right." Said Paul flaring his nostrils and nodding. "Tell them I'll be there shortly would you."

"Certainly, Sir." Said Costas as he turned to leave. Paul searched through his mind as to where the mobile phone might be. He thought that maybe he hadn't taken it out of the jacket pocket. *Wait. Where was the jacket?* He knew he'd not thrown it into the shower tray with the rest of the clothes. Then it came to him. He'd given it to the night receptionist when he left the hotel for a second time to look for his room key. He picked up the phone from the floor and dialled zero for the reception. A woman answered.

"Yes, I hope you can. Yes. This is…"

He paused for a second trying to think what to call himself. "This is Roger Penrose in room…"

He hesitated again. He couldn't remember the room number. *That's if the room even had a number.*

"Yes, this is Roger Penrose. I left a jacket at the reception late last night," he paused again and nodded. "Good, thanks. Listen. Could you check to see if I left my mobile phone in the…"

He paused again briefly.

"Oh really. Ok. Well sorry about that. I should have turned the sound down but I don't really know how to. I'll come along shortly and pick it up." Again a short pause.

"Could you? That would be grand. Would you just ask them to leave it on the chair by the mirror. Thanks. I'd be much obliged."

He rang off and went to the wardrobe and opened the doors. The sight of the clothes hanging up caused a tiny little bit of excitement to run through him. He pulled out another jacket, another pair of trousers and a shirt and placed them on the unmade bed. He placed a pair of loafers on the carpeted floor then went through to the bathroom where he expected to find the clothes he had attempted to wash the blood from the previous evening. The bathroom though, was as if he'd never been in it. He briefly questioned himself. Which bit was he dreaming? He let the towelling robe fall to the floor and stepped into the stone clad shower. He turned on the water and stood beneath the powerful stream for a minute or two. He finished his ablutions and returned to the bedroom to dress. The crumpled jacket had been returned by the reception and he fumbled around for the phone. He touched the screen and found there were a dozen or so text message alerts.

They were all from two numbers. One of them he recognised from the previous day. He threw the phone down on the bed and picked up the trousers. Simple electric blue linen. The shirt was a white cotton. Nothing special at first glance but a great handle. He was pulling on the jacket when it occurred to him, this would be the point in his daily routine where he'd think about what needed to go into the various pockets, his little Swiss Army penknife was in the trousers that were in the shower tray. He cursed himself briefly. He'd had that penknife since he was fourteen. He shook his head to release the thought and it was replaced by a sudden and real desire to get out of the room and into the sunshine. He realised he was also starving hungry. He put the phone in the inside breast pocket of the jacket and the key-card in the side pocket of his trousers. He was about to walk from the bedroom to the entrance hall when he noticed the laptop on the desk. The lid had been closed. He also saw that the little key fob, which he was certain he'd placed directly by the side of the laptop was no longer there. He opened the lid of the laptop. A tiny orange light on the front edge blinked a few times and then stayed on. There were too many questions. Too many little inexplicable incidents. He'd wait though. Who was he going to meet now? Whoever it was he'd be looking for answers. He walked past the Jasmine plant and stopped to take in a deep breath through his nose enjoying the scent. The walk to the courtyard was a winding pathway lined with beautiful plants and green hedges. He'd been led this way the previous evening when Costas had showed him the room and he had walked the same route back when he'd gone to dinner. *God that seemed like a long time ago.* It was dark then.

Although there were lights along the way, a whole new world had now appeared. Peaking through gaps in the flora he could see the ocean curiously covered in white horses even though the day appeared calm and warm. On the other side, over a hedgerow just slightly taller than he was, a black mountain, the summit surrounded by white wispy clouds. He was in two minds. He was walking quickly. Maybe because he was hungry and frankly there were few pleasures he'd prefer to a fillet steak and a glass or three of country red wine.

Maybe he was excited about the idea of finding out about what was going on, whatever it was he caught himself doing a London walk. But he wasn't in London. He was on a tranquil island in a luxury hotel. He had nothing to rush for. He made a conscious effort to slow down. To slow down and observe his surroundings. By the time the sentiment had reached his limbs he had arrived at a set of eight steps that led up onto the courtyard. He stopped for a moment. He could hear the sound of the guests above him enjoying their afternoon. He was glad that he'd checked himself. He walked very slowly up the steps and was so glad to see at the top of them, in full view of the entire courtyard a friend. He was drawn again to the white flowers of another Jasmine and he poked his nose into a bloom. He was certain that although the gesture was a reflex, it hadn't gone unnoticed by the lunching terrace. He'd perhaps expected that the terrace would go quiet briefly as he made his entrance but that didn't happen. Most of the lunching couples and families were unaware of his presence but not everybody was. Benson and Hedges were sitting at one of a collection of tables under the shade of a gnarled old olive tree. Paul, not wanting to stand for one second and give the impression that he was not in complete control, had began to stroll on the gravel path. He wished he'd bought his expensive sunglasses with him then no-one would have seen the furtive almost desperate look in his eyes when he realised he didn't know anyone. He walked past the table where Benson and Hedges were sitting when he heard a familiar voice.

"Roger. Roger Man. There you are. Come 'ere you old wolf you." Benson strode up to Paul like a polar bear, his arms wide. Just for a second Paul looked the other way but then thought he understood the game. He mimicked Benson which made Benson raise an eyebrow and they embraced in a hug.

"Sit down, won't you?" Said Benson as they left the embrace. "This is a friend of mine." Paul reached slowly across towards Hedges to shake his hand, a look of realisation spreading across his face.

"And who are we today?" Said Paul. Hedges almost blushed. He hadn't realised that they had been rumbled and he and Benson, foolishly now come to think of it hadn't discussed the matter of which false identity they were going to use today.

"Marks and Spencer?" Paul continued as he sat down. "Jack and Jill, Lambert and Butler?"

"I'm sorry for the subterfuge, Paul." Said Hedges as he stood over the table to shake his hand and glanced an affirmative nod towards Benson. "It just so happens that I have been given the nick name of Hedges and his," he gestured towards Benson. "His name is Benjamin or Benny as some people call him. We got the stupid name when we worked together on a job a few years ago."

"Why Hedges?" Said Paul. Before Hedges could answer, Benson butted in.

"Because he likes to hedge his bets."

They were all being polite but as they all sat down

Paul, with a big false smile on his face, beckoned toward both Benson and Hedges with the forefingers of both hands.

He dropped his voice as if he were whispering.

"Gentlemen. Some answers please. Who are you? What do you do? Why Me?"

Hedges could see that Paul was growing impatient.

Benson however, couldn't.

"We work for a number of clients in the field of security." Benson said while ever-so-slightly sucking his teeth.

"That's bollocks." Said Paul raising his voice to a normal level. The volume was enough in the calm surroundings to allow everyone in vicinity to hear him.

"If someone doesn't tell me a little about what is going on here I shall have to re-evaluate my position. Strange things happened last night after I met you." The volume of Paul's voice lowered again.

"How did you know those men were going to chase me down." Now turning into an angry hiss, "And why did you kill them?" This seemed to change the look on the faces of both Benson and Hedges.

"I didn't..." Began Benson. Hedges held up his hand to stop Benson mid-sentence.

"Hold on Benny." Said Hedges in a calm but stern voice. "Hold on. Tell us exactly what happened Paul. Exactly what happened."

At that moment the three men were chilled by a floating breeze that blew through the courtyard causing all the other luncheon guests to slightly lower their voices. The result was a period of near silence that lasted for just a few seconds. Mary had walked up the steps that Paul had just emerged from and had caused this little anomaly in atmospheric conditions. Only the very young would have not been interested enough to gaze perhaps surreptitiously towards Mary. And there was no-one under the age of twenty one lunching on the terrace. Mary was not dressed inappropriately or gaudily. It was not her clothes that attracted attention. In fact no single thing about how she looked would have drawn a comment on its own. But something had caused the wind to change. Something. She walked along the gravel pathway between the tables just as Paul had done earlier but with a different sense of purpose. Her gait was slow and measured. The expression on her face was a mix of welcoming smile and standoffish indifference. She walked on slowly crunching the gravel on the path until she arrived at where the three men were now sitting. Benson and Hedges had both, without realising, shrunk slightly in their seats as she approached. Neither of them had wanted to be noticed and they were both hoping that she would play the game and leave them alone. Mary wasn't playing their game though and approached their table directly. Paul immediately stood. He was closest to the gravel path but his location was not the reason why he stood. He wanted to ask her to join them but the body language of Benson and Hedges could not be mistaken for anything other than outright hostility. Mary took both of Paul's hands in hers and to a chorus of slight blowing out through pursed lips of the lunching, now audience, she kissed him slowly and delicately on the lips. Benson and Hedges, following a protocol that neither of them knew the origins of and completely disagreeing with even if they did, were beginning to stand awkwardly. The kiss went on for a while and ended with a momentary silence as the audience expelled all the air they had in their lungs. She turned to them and spoke as if they were small boys. She proffered her hand.

They both held out a hand towards her.

"Hello boys." She said as their hands met. Both Benson and Hedges smiled a totally convincing and yet wholly insincere smile. First her face moved towards Benson. She kissed him on the cheek very close to his ear and whispered breathlessly as she did it.

"One Nil." Before she turned to Hedges and did the same. She spent a little longer whispering into his ear.

"Needs must as the devil drives I suppose?" She ended it as a question and as she drew away, her eyes glanced downwards and towards Benson. Hedges was immediately smitten with the precision with which she had judged the situation between them. The whole introduction seemed to have been conducted at the pace of a slow moving dream but in reality had taken seconds. Mary turned back to Paul. 'When you've done talking business with the boys here,' she said not even attempting to hide her opinion of them. We're over there darling. She pointed to an empty table set on its own on a crenelated portion of the terrace underneath a white canvass awning with elegant red rope trimming.

She crunched away on the gravel pathway. Everything returned to normal. Hedges' phone vibrated in his pocket. He picked it out and swiped the unlock command. A little circle appeared to rotate before it turned into a video picture. Even though it was a small screen, Mary could be clearly seen walking around in Paul's room. She didn't actually appear to be doing anything. She was just there. The video saw her open a wardrobe door, spend a moment or two gazing inside then briefly sitting on the bed. It lasted for thirty seconds before she got up to leave. The words attached to the video were. **More arrivals. Be prepared.**

"You need to see this." Said Hedges. He tapped the screen a few times trying to replay the video.

Paul ignored Hedges playing with his phone, and nodded at them both as he got up to leave.

"Thanks guys. We'll pick this up later, Yeah." He pointed at Benson and Hedges in turn as if he wanted agreement.

"Yeah?" He repeated, nodding his head towards them. "Catch up later!" He walked as nonchalantly as he could towards where Mary was sitting on the special terrace. His own phone vibrated in the breast pocket of his jacket. He left it were it was.

A waiter brought Benson and Hedges some menus but before he could leave Benson ordered drinks for them both.

"Shit!" Said Hedges presently, too loudly and spluttering into his wine glass. Through the main doors to the terrace, twenty meters from where they were sitting Roland Garret strolled into the afternoon sunshine. There were perhaps only four more tables vacant and he spoke to a waiter and was directed to a table not three meters from where they were sitting. Before he sat down Garret leant over to Benson and Hedges and turned the bottle of wine so that the label was facing towards him.

"What's the Claret like gentlemen?" He said.

'Good." Said Hedges nodding and taking a sip from his glass.

"Mmm. It's fine," said Benson. "Just fine."

Roland Garret looked at them both briefly. They both looked nervous or guilty or both he thought. He put it down to two Englishmen who did actually recognise who he was. He was right of course. They did recognise him but not on account of his political significance. He nodded cordially to them both and went to sit down. The waiter was still holding out a chair for him.

"I'll have a bottle of that." He said to the waiter pointing at the bottle in front of Benson and Hedges.

"Does he know?" Said Hedges under his breath and dipping his head slightly.

"Does he know what?" Said Benson.

"Who we are?"

"He can't." Said Benson. "More importantly does he know she's here?" He indicated across to where Mary and Paul were sitting. The awning was partially obscuring the table.

"Have you got any idea what is going on Benny?"

Normally when Hedges asked Benson a question regardless of whether he knew the answer or not Benson would try and make it sound like he did. On this occasion Hedges was pleasantly surprised with Benson's frankness.

"I know precious more than you do Hedge old-boy. You're the one that reminded me not to ask questions. Let's just do our job." He said pouring more wine into Hedges' glass.

"I've never really been quite clear as to what our job is Benny."

"We are here to help in any way we can. Listen. As far as I can make out, this is the end game. The story that our friend Ian is apparently writing, I think started many years ago and I think it is coming to a conclusion here."

Here he goes. Thought Hedges.

"Benny mate. Tell me something I don't already know. It was the thirty year thing we..." He couldn't bring himself to say steal. "We copied. It's obvious this all started thirty years ago. How old do you reckon Garret is?"

"I know how old he is. It's in his file. He's seventy two. He'd have been forty two thirty years ago."

"You are a true genius Benny Boy."

"No Really. He's the only one here who is that age. He must be part of the original story."

"Not anymore said Hedges. Don't look now. To your right."

The man in the creased-linen-suit entered the courtyard through the same doors Garret had come through. With him were two other men dressed in the uniform of the trade. Black suits and ties and white shirts. They looked distinctly uneasy as they eye-balled their respective sides of the courtyard. After speaking to the maître d' he was led to one of only three remaining tables. The two men in black followed closely behind. As they walked to their table, the ambient noise created by the assembled guests didn't seem to change as it had done for Mary. It was as if it is difficult to make that kind of thing happen when you try too hard and the man in the creased-linen-suit looked to be trying too hard.

"A little over the top don't you think." Said Hedges.

"I wonder if he knows something we don't."

"I reckon he knows a whole load of stuff we don't. Now there are two people here that are old enough to have been actually involved in anything thirty years ago."

"Yep. Whoever else is here that is involved, is involved in another way."

Benson was tapping at his phone.

"Think Ian is going stir crazy. I'll bet he won't be able to do another day with only room service and Jill yakking away in his ear." The waiter approached them.

"Gentlemen." He said cordially. "Are you ready to order yet?" Neither of them had even considered the menu.

"Sorry." Said Hedges. "Can we have another few minutes."

"Certainly, Sir." Said the waiter. "I'll be back shortly. Take your time. It's a beautiful afternoon."

"I wish they wouldn't do that." Said Benson quietly when the waiter was out of earshot.

"Wish who wouldn't do what?" Said Hedges.

"Waiters weren't so familiar."

Hedges blew out slowly through his mouth, shook his head slightly and closed his eyes.

"Benny mate. Do you know what year it is?"

They both started to look at the menus. Which wasn't too hard. There were comparatively few choices.

"Will you look at this." Said Benson in a high pitched voice and in a passable Irish accent.

"Salt Beef and Potatoes. I've just gotta have some of that."

"Whoa." Said Hedges. "Eyes left again." Martin and Sarah had arrived. They were being directed to their table.

"Who's the woman?" said Benson.

"I think she's the police woman who he called up about the other day." Said Hedges

"Sarah Quinn." Said Benson

"That's right." Said Hedges

"She's apparently a sharp one. Hope he knows what he's doing."

"Just follow the orders. Don't let on we know him unless he lets on first."

"Has he seen us?"

"Don't think so yet."

"But he knows we're here right?" Benson had to take a little time to answer this.

"He should do," he said slowly, "but then we were sent to work undercover."

At that Benson's phone vibrated. He glanced at it.

"Talk of the devil." He said. He read the text message.

"'He wants to see me now, urgently. In the office." He smiled at Hedges and got up from his chair just as the waiter returned.

"Sorry." He said. "Just need the little boy's room. Order me the salt beef will you Hedge old man." He left Hedges with the waiter.

Martin returned to his table first but after more time than it would generally take him to just relieve himself. He sat down opposite Sarah. The look on Sarah's face was pure intrigue. Like she was dying to know the gossip.

"They're working on this." Martin said in a hushed voice.

"Martin," said Sarah. "About three hours ago you said you'd tell me all you know. In the meantime we've been shopping, done some seriously intense driving and been shot at. Now we sit down to eat lunch in the most serene of settings that you say you've never been to in your life before when remarkably there are people you know here who you have to visit the toilet to see." The look on Martins face was apologetic.

"Sarah. Ok." He said. "That was Benson."

Benson got back to the table where Hedges had been nonchalantly keeping an eye on the various contingents.

"What did he have to say? Said Hedges.

"He was genuinely surprised to see us. I told him who the client was but it still didn't seem to make sense to him. He'd been shot at earlier by someone in a black Chrysler." Hedges' eyebrows raised ever so slightly.

"How would you get a car onto Lanzarote?" He asked as he pulled his phone from his pocket.

"I don't know." Said Benson. "Ferry from Gibraltar or somewhere in Morocco I suppose. Maybe Casablanca. It won't be the same black Chrysler as the one in London you ejit. There's more than one black Chrysler."

Hedges was tapping away at face of his mobile phone.

"There's more than one black Chrysler," he said, "but unless you've been dropping softballs around the place that have the same mac address as the one you put in the car outside Jill's house, the same Black Chrysler is within a five hundred meter radius of this phone." Hedges waved the phone in a three inch arc just above the table as he held it between his thumb and forefinger.

"Are we missing something Hedge Old Boy?" Said Benson scratching his chin as the waiter brought their salt beef.

"Listen!" Said Benson after they had both taken mouthfuls of food. "How many cameras did we put up around here?"

"Three." Said Hedges.

"Can Ian see all the tables?"

"Possibly." He said. "The only one he might have a bit of trouble with is the one our boy is sitting at with Marta Hari. They put the awning up after I put the cameras in."

"Watch out." Hedges said. "Incoming."

Through the tall French doors Greg appeared. He was brushed up and shining. Hedges smiled. He liked and respected Greg even though he could be incorrigibly patronising belligerent and stubborn. The waiter led him down the gravel path towards where Benson and Hedges were sitting and continued on a little as Greg stopped.

"What the fuck are you wearing on your feet?" Said Benson.

"Correspondents." Greg shot back turning his head sideways. "I wouldn't expect you to understand Benjamin. The people here have tried to create a place of sophistication and hope with real materials and ingredients and you dear Benny boy repay their attempt to make your life a little less ordinary by turning up wearing clothes designed for use on a sports field." Greg turned towards Hedges.

"How are you Hedge?" Nodding towards him. Hedges sniggered as Greg moved away towards Roland Garret's table.

"Mr. Garret, Sir." Said Greg proffering his hand. Roland Garret had watched the exchange at the table close to him out of the corner of his eye. He was still stuffing food into his mouth as Greg approached. Dutiful politician that he was he dragged the napkin up from the table and chewed furiously to get the food out of his mouth. He half stood to accept the handshake. He thought that maybe he'd met this man before but he couldn't quite think where.

"No Sorry." Said Greg. "Don't get up. Just want to say love your work on foreign policy. Inspired." Roland Garret shook Greg's hand half sitting half standing and when their hands parted, Greg looked towards the waiter who was standing a few yards ahead.

"So sorry. I'm with you now." He said as the waiter led him to the last vacant table.

"That was Benson." Martin continued. "He and the man he is with work for me and sometimes use the office here back in the house. Hedges is the other man's name." Sarah took a moment or two for the words to sink in. She was facing in the direction of Benson and Hedges and was studying them.

"I didn't actually know that they were here on this job."

"Wait a moment." Interrupted Sarah. "Benson and Hedges? Really?"

"Really." Said Martin. "I know it's childish. The fat balding one is Benny Wright and the slighter one is Terry Hall. His nickname while we were in the nick was Hedges because he never gave a straight answer. Ironic really because Hedges never does anything without a chess players consideration for the consequences. The idiots in the prison saw it as him just hedging his bets."

"What were you in for?" Asked Sarah bluntly. She was expecting prevarication but Martin seemed quite comfortable telling her the truth. She was still not entirely convinced though.

"It was a while ago. More than twenty years. I was twenty years old and I was running a scam whereby I'd put ads for wannabe actors in the papers pretending I was a talent agency. I asked for a twenty pounds registration fee promising castings. I was inundated with replies to the extent I couldn't handle the sacks of letters containing cheques. The rented virtual office in Park Lane gave me notice to leave suspecting nefarious goings on. The law eventually caught up with me and I was sent down for a year. Served six months."

"And what did they do?" She indicated towards Benson and Hedges.

"Benny was sent down for banking fraud. He started working in the back office of a trading bank in the eighties. Within a year he had set himself up in the exchange as a broker in direct competition. He 'stole' several of their bigger clients. He probably did nothing illegal but the bank found irregularities in his trading and used their power and influence to hire better lawyers than he could and he was sentenced to a year of which he served six months too."

"And the other one. Hedges?"

"Hedges is ex-army. His training was in firearms. After ten years in the front line he transferred to the Communication Corp. What used to be called Signals. There he became, over a period of years a hacker. The army taught him all the cutting edge technology. They bought into it big time. He had one of the highest security clearances possible. He left the army in 1990. He was caught hacking into the DVLA database to remove the record of a drink drive conviction and sentenced to a year. He served six months also."

Sarah was silent. Just listening.

"Then there is Greg."

"Greg?" Repeated Sarah.

"Greg is the bloke who just walked past. The one who stopped as he walked past Benson and Hedges and then Garret. The one wearing the two-tone shoes."

"Okay." Said Sarah slowly. "He's in on this too. Is he?"

"Yes." Said Martin. "He sells clobber in the town where I live."

"He was also in prison with you." Said Sarah.

"Yes. He was in for fraud to. He swears he was just a victim of a smarter businessman than him and that he is innocent. But then they all say that."

"So that's your lot. The people you know here. About…" Sarah theatrically looked at her left wrist which didn't actually have a watch wrapped around it.

"About twenty four hours ago you were about to reveal why an elderly Libyan man living in St Johns Wood being shot by the same type of bullet that was used to fire at you revealed so much."

"I've told you I was adopted. I did some investigations years ago into who my real father was. I don't know why. I was happy as I was. Anyway I came up with the name of David Crane. He was apparently killed in nineteen eighty four by a car bomb. They were driving it to London but it went off as they were on their way to the ferry port. He and the bloke he was with were both killed although no body was ever found. Not that a body would be found if it was sitting on top of a car load of Semtex when it goes off. I could find very little about him in the public records.

"Oddly this is where Greg comes in. He has this crazy little hobby if you like. A more cynical man it would be hard to find. It's not that he is a conspiracy theorist or anything like that. He just thinks that the state just lies according to its own needs. See he thinks that the state is a kind of self-fulfilling prophecy. Because everyone in it is party to it, it becomes just what it says it is. People don't want the politicians to tell it like it is. They want their employees to lie to them because the truth is too hard to bear and when it goes wrong and everyone is so surprised that it has they have someone to blame."

Sarah shook her head.

"Sounds like a load of old bollocks to me. He fancies himself as some kind of philosopher does he? How did that help you to find your father?"

"He has made it his business over many years never to be the victim of circumstance again. When he was in prison he used the time to study his particular interest. Greg can get to the bottom of anything. However, shrouded in mystery and clouds the inventors make it. Bear in mind I'm not talking quantum mechanics here. This is generally stuff written by workaday civil servants watching their backs. The language they use is designed to appear to say something but in fact says nothing. Point I made at the beginning is that you, we are party to that. We are accomplices. We are complicit."

"How?"

"Because we let it happen instead of speaking up against it."

"And so how…"

"Greg turned his anger and resentment into a service for others. Greg uncovered my father's name. You don't just have to know where to look you have to know the language. Greg became multi lingual."

"And so how," Sarah paused, "What do you know about the shootings?"

"You said the bullets were unusual because they were thirty years old. No-one would use thirty year old bullets surely unless they had a reason."

"And what do you think that reason might be."

"Well it wouldn't be to cover up the crime would it? No. It would be done expressly as a clue."

"A clue for who?"

"Maybe me, Maybe you, I don't know. I think that bullet was never intended to hit me. It was just to get me interested. It has to be from the Libyan IRA arms from 84 and it has something to do with my father."

"Paul." Said Mary, in a compressed voice that was straining to remain civilised as Paul approached the table. "Sit down." Paul dipped his head below the awning and smiled.

"Glad you said that." Said Paul. "Cause I was just gonna stand there like a lemon otherwise." Mary's face had changed from being gracious and all accommodating to being slightly fierce. There was a bottle of wine on the table that had been half drunk.

"Mary Dear," Said Paul as he dutifully sat down. "Why is everyone treating me like a…" He thought for the word he wanted to use but decided that perhaps that wasn't the most appropriate one. "Like… Like some kind of idiot." He gave her no time to respond. "What happened last night?" Mary's transformation from Femme fatale to Irish Lass was now well underway. It actually never took much. She shrugged her shoulders.

"Any port in a storm." She said. Paul shook his head.

"It wasn't so bad was it?" Said Paul smiling. "But that's not what I'm talking about and you know it. No. before. In the town."

Mary shook her own head. She was doing a good job and Paul was almost convinced that she was telling the truth.

That was until he saw her glance over his shoulder. She watched as a man wearing two tone shoes, white trousers and a stripped blazer walked towards the table Benson and

Hedges were sitting at and stopped to talk. She couldn't disguise her agitation when the same man also stopped at the table Roland Garret was sitting at. Her expression turned.

"Paul, how much do you know about why you are here?"

"My name is Roger Penrose and I'm a rare book dealer."

It occurred to Paul as he was talking that he had never told her anything other than this and yet she had called him Paul as far as he can remember back. As if reading his mind she said,

"I can see it has just occurred to you that I have only ever referred to you as Paul."

"Am I that obvious?" Said Paul.

"Pour yourself some wine Paul," said Mary, "and order another bottle. You need to know this."

Paul was already filling up both their glasses.

"Why are you so interested in the fellah in the fancy clothes?"

"Was I that obvious?" She said. "Don't worry. I'll get to him. Do you have any idea who or what I am?" Said Mary. Paul shook his head and looked around for a waiter.

"No." He said.

"And you have no idea why you are here?"

"None."

"I had a phone call out of the blue about three weeks ago from the fat man over there." Mary pointed discretely in the direction of Roland Garret. "Do you know who he is?"

"Just assume I'm going to keep saying no." Said Paul.

"It's Roland Garret. Government minister of state for Northern Ireland and ex IRA Terrorist."

Paul glanced over in the direction Mary was indicating.

He first nodded his head back and forth and then shook it slowly.

"I've heard of him but no. Still nothing I'm afraid."

"That call was closely followed by a call from a man named Ricky Starr."

Paul's eyebrows raised a little. "What, The Ricky Starr. Of Starr Media?" Mary nodded.

"I kind of work for him."

"How can you kind of work for someone?"

"Thirty years ago or more, Roland Garret and my father were in the same unit of the IRA. My father was killed by a British Army ambush. Garret was supposed to be in the squad that night but mysteriously wasn't there. For years everyone thought that this was just the way the cookies crumbled. That is until recently."

"What happened recently to change the way you see it."

"It's not the way I see. It's the way it was. And all documented in black and white by the British Government."

"Ok. I understand even less now."

"In 1985, there was a secret government enquiry into a huge arms smuggling operation by the IRA involving Libya. Among the people involved were Roland Garret who was a commander at the time and your father." Mary waited and watched Paul's face carefully.

"You must mean the father I never knew. My real father, the father that adopted me and brought me up was a good man."

"Yes Paul. I mean the father you never knew. He was working for both sides."

"So how do you know this?"

"The transcripts of the secret enquiry were due to be released to the public. Roland Garret asked Ricky Starr if he could arrange to have them digitally deleted."

"And he said yes?"

"He said he could supply the labour and the relevant expertise if he were given enough information."

"Labour and relevant expertise?"

"Yes. Odd as it may seem your boys over there nearly completed the job."

"What was the job?"

"To erase any record of the inquiry."

"Surely that can't be easy and anyway there must be paper copy backups. Weren't they just cutting off the leaves of the weed?"

"It's not easy and yes there were archived copies. According to my sources..." Started Mary. Paul butted in.

"Can I just stop you there Mary. Can I ask that we continue with this in a spirit of trust and mutual respect and cut out the police-speak bollocks. According to.. insert actual persons name here please."

"According to Rick Starr then." She said as if she were a teenager.

"So how does Ricky Starr know so much?"

"Starr, if you can believe it, runs Roland Garret's public relations. He told me that the records were first rendered into digital form in two thousand and four. Garret came into his first bit of power around that time."

"Why does Garret feel so worried by these records?"

"Because if or when they ever come out he will first loose his status, then his money and then his life. There are still many people who would love to see him out of the game."

"You included I suppose."

"Yes, me included."

"Why? What did he do?"

"He forewarned the British army paratroopers of the raid that my Papy was in on a rail depot which he didn't turn up for in which my father was killed and then blackmailed your father into murdering his friend by threatening his young family. Is that enough for starters."

Paul nodded slowly. He was taking his time assimilating the information.

"Not that I'm doubting what you're saying for one moment." He took a big swig from his glass and waved at a waiter. When he caught the waiter's eye he pointed at the bottle. The waiter understood and went to fetch another.

"You've just introduced relations I didn't know I had."

"Do you want to know?" Paul considered the question as if no could have been a possible answer.

"Yes." He said. "But forgive me. I'm trying my best. Why would Garret employ those jerks to hack into a government computer if there were copies of the same report sitting in vaults somewhere in some mysterious government archive?"

"He'd had all the archived copied destroyed. Systematically."

"How do you know all this?"

"Your friends over there." She was playing with him now. Paul didn't rise to it just yet. "Your friends over there managed to get into a government level security data centre. Garret would have got them cleared because you just can't normally do that kind of thing."

"Now stop again." Said Paul. "Do you actually know that or are you just making what you do sound more glamorous and difficult to a mere Hokey from Miscokey like me to make you look better?"

"What? You think that it might be easy to get through the doors of any government protected facility."

"No. I wouldn't imagine it would be easy. But those two did. So they must have had help."

"Garret gave them the green light. Anyway. They went in and erased the document. All 1500 pages. Including graphic photo evidence. I was asked by our friend Ricky to act as an insurance policy. Apparently, in this branch of the intelligence community…"

Paul's shoulders involuntarily bumped up and down…

Mary ignored him,

"There is a protocol in these circumstances to make a copy first of anything you delete on a hard drive. Even though you have to use complicated software to cover your footprints up to the scene of the crime. Your friends did as expected and made copies which I stole from them on a rainy M4 as they drove back towards London. Ask them and they'll deny it because it's like getting mugged by a girl. They had two data sticks. So good at this were your friends that no one stick contained the whole document. The first held the first half or so and the second held the last half. I only managed to get hold of one of the sticks."

"That seems quite sensible to me. If I was robbing a bank and had to stash the loot until the heat died down I wouldn't stash it all in the same place."

"Well whether this was by luck or judgment remains to be seen. But I have to hold my hand up to what happened next." The wine came and the waiter filled both their glasses.

"So I had one out of two data sticks and when I got them back to my own computer it took me twenty minutes to get past their security. They went on and on but eventually I found the piece I was looking for. Roland Garret ordered the murder of my father. They were supposed to be friends, Paul. This was three months before the arms haul was seized by customs in the channel. Papy suspected that Garret was playing for the other side and confronted him. Garret denied it of course but that same night Papy got killed. Your father comes onto the stage in act two. He allegedly was the man who fixed the boat carrying the arms so that it got caught but it didn't actually say that in the part of the report I had. I phoned someone at this point."

"Who did you phone?" asked Paul. She pointed over to the man in the creased-linen-suit and his two bodyguards.

"He runs a security firm now. Back then he was a field operative for whoever was paying the most money. Technically he is the reason you are here. He is the reason those men last night were looking for you. They were here to kill you."

Paul shook his head again and took another slurp from his glass.

"I'm gonna have to leave off this stuff. You're expecting me to follow this."

"Yes I am Paul. Nothing is ever simple. You know that. If I hadn't called that man and told him what I knew none of us would be here." Mary looked as if she were about to cry.

"I've caused all this because I jumped to a conclusion. I didn't read the last part of the enquiry."

"I'm very sorry Mary." Said Paul "But I still don't understand a word you are saying."

"Roland Garret has been a slimy bastard and he caused the death of my father. If I'd have left it alone when I learnt of the details then he'd have got away with his pathetic crimes. As it was I opened up a can of worms. I called that man and sent him some passages from the report. That was enough to start a chain of events that has begun to culminate here."

Paul was listening as intently as he could but his was not the sort of brain that processed information like this.

He was also under the mistaken illusion that if he drank some more, the red wine might unlock a channel of understanding that had up to that point been blocked. He took another big slurp of wine. Mary continued.

"Be a little careful with that." She said.

"That's a bit calling the kettle black." He replied.

"Anyway what about you?"

"I can handle it." She said. Paul didn't like her suddenly.

"So can I." He said and took another although smaller than normal gulp from his wine glass. "So what chain of events is beginning to culminate here?"

"The vultures are circling." She said dramatically.

Still not completely convinced that she was not just being a bit dramatic Paul raised his eyes slightly. Mary's posture straightened.

"I'm getting the impression, Paul, that you are not taking me seriously. You must remember last night Paul… You survived an assassination attempt."

"Well let's talk about that." Said Paul, his own back straightening a little. "I was about to have dinner with you last night when I get called out to a bar in town and meet that…" he couldn't think of an appropriately polite but derogatory word, "that Benson fellah. Shortly after I arrived it all started to kick off. I get chased around dark alleyways by a couple of geezers until oh, they stop. Someone had killed them. I must admit they looked dead when I went back shaking with fear to look for my key card." Mary's upper body bobbed up and down.

"So that's what you were doing," she looked at him and slurped from her wine glass. "Wise move actually. I'd have done the same.

Although I wouldn't have dropped it in the first place." Paul shrugged.

"Why were they waiting for me and why did Benson lead me to them? And I'm forgetting. Who the fuck were they?"

"They weren't waiting for you there Paul. They were here. Last night Benson and his crew, and there are a few of them as far as I can make out, must have thought that you having dinner with me was a no no. So Benson went into town and met you in that bar so he could warn you about me. The two guys that chased you were here first and they followed you. I'm not sure how good their surveillance is but someone was watching. They told Benson that those two men were following you. I went straight to my room when you left and then followed them into town."

"Why would Benson need to warn me about you?"

Mary smugly grinned and shook her head.

"You really haven't cottoned on have you? I'm a facilitator Paul. I get things done."

"Here we go again." Said Paul. "I don't know what that means."

"I really didn't want to have to spell it out Paul. I kill people for money. Roland Garret has paid me a lot of money to get rid of your father. You know. The one you never knew."

Paul took another large slurp from his glass and sloshed the wine around in his mouth trying to make sense of what Mary was telling him.

"So it was you with the two last night?"

Marry nodded.

"Brace yourself Paul. They were hired hit men working via various sub contractors for the Liberian Government. They are the most vindictive. They are a mafia really. They'll kill anyone associated with their target before they kill him. Last night they'd been hired to get rid of you."

"Oh Shit." Said Paul as he put his head in his hands, his elbows on the table. "I thought I was beginning to understand." His phone made an urgent tinkling sound. This time he picked it out of his pocket and tapped the front. A video image appeared. The same image that Hedges had tried to show him earlier. He watched it through then tapped the phone again to replay it before turning the phone towards Mary. He said nothing as she watched the clip.

"So." She said when it had finished.

"So what were you doing?" Said Paul.

"I was just coming to get you."

"How did you get in?"

"Paul." She said, not liking having to answer these questions. "I was trained in black ops by the IRA. A hotel door is not going to pose a problem." She held up a key card similar to his. Paul tapped his pockets.

"It's not yours." Said Mary. "It's a master key. I paid the receptionist an amount she couldn't refuse. She's getting married next year."

"How do you know that?" He said incredulously.

"She told me Paul. What do you think I'd done. Pulled out her fingernails?"

Paul swirled the wine around in his glass. They were both silent for a few moments.

"I replied to an ad in a magazine." He said eventually. "Anyone could have done that."

"I'm afraid you've been hoodwinked, Paul. They've had you under surveillance for some time. They know about your mild obsession with Private Eye. The Ads were put in expressly to lure you in."

"Why didn't they just ask me to come here?"

"Because they thought you'd say no."

Paul nodded in agreement.

"You're not the only one." Said Mary. "There are others."

"What others?" Said Paul. "You don't mean those two jokers do you?" He motioned towards where Benson and Hedges were sitting.

"No. I don't." She said. "I mean others of your family."

Paul was beginning to feel uncomfortable. He had indeed been hoodwinked into this and she was right. He wouldn't have come if he'd have known.

"What others of my family?" He said. Mary considered prevarication but decided against it.

"Your half-sister Jill is here. I don't know where yet, I haven't seen her. She's here with a man called Ian. He was apparently a writer once. They are trying to turn this story into a book."

"Wow." Said Paul, nodding gently trying to understand what he was being told.

29

Paul and Mary were the only two people still in the bar. Lunch had come and gone without any incident much to the surprise of at least half of the lunch guests. Mary's eyelids were taking longer and longer to complete the cycle of a blink. To the point that for short periods at a time her eyes were actually closed. She was leaning forcefully on the bar with her elbow and her other hand held a tall glass containing ice and a clear liquid. Paul was sitting next to her on a bar stool. Both his hands were clasped around a half-full pint glass. He appeared deep in thought.

They hadn't spoken to each other for a few moments. Paul woke Mary from her approaching state of temporary hibernation.

"So what do you think will happen next?" He said.

Some part of Mary's brain was still wide awake and she answered immediately.

"On this occasion," she said, "we have to react to whatever is thrown our way. It's apparently peaceful at the moment. We don't want to provoke anything. That's not the way it would work in the military. You're always supposed to be as proactive as possible. Never let the enemy have time to think. Always take the battle to them."

"You think there is going to be a battle?" Said Paul.

Mary turned slowly towards him and grimaced.

"Do you not believe me, Paul. Do you think I'm making it up? Remember last night."

Paul didn't want to think back to the previous evening and had so far got through most of the day by pretending it hadn't happened.

Mary had spent a good deal of time earlier in the afternoon explaining that he was in mortal danger and that he shouldn't let the peaceful and sophisticated surroundings lull him into thinking all was well. She had already killed two men. How? He didn't know and didn't want to find out. She'd then casually met him in his room afterwards and seduced him and had appeared today as if nothing had happened. As if reading his mind she filled in the blanks.

"I'm telling you Paul, it was you or them. You should be thanking me you're still here. Anyway, what happened afterwards is only natural."

"Only natural?" Paul repeated. His voice a higher pitch than normal. He had suddenly got himself worked up a little. God it hadn't taken much. He thankfully recognised it happening and blew a long breath out through pursed lips.

"Only natural?" He said again this time the tone was a request for information. "Please elaborate."

"Yes." She said. "It takes two to tango Paul. However much you like it or not it's a link between life and death. It's what hunters would do. They'd…"

"I'd rather not think about it if you don't mind." He said.

Mary was not going to let him get away with pretending that he was an innocent party but thought again as she was gathering herself up to further berate him. *No.* She thought. *He is an innocent party.* She was wrestling with conflicting and foggy thoughts when two men came into the bar.

"I've got an idea that things are going to liven up around here." She said quietly as Ricky Starr and Tom Gates, known to anyone who would have been acquainted with them thirty years ago as Eamonn Boothe and David Crane, looking a little bedraggled, walked up to the bar. David greeted the tired looking barmen familiarly and ordered himself a large beer. Ricky nodded when David asked him if he'd have the same.

"Sorry Paul." Whispered Mary, leaning in towards Paul, "I wasn't expecting them to come in here. Like this." Paul looked puzzled.

"What do you mean? Like this. Who are they?" Mary retracted back on her barstool and hesitated. She'd come too far though.

"The shorter fellah is the owner of this place." Said Mary. "That is the man that Garret paid me to..." She couldn't bring herself to finish the sentence so Paul did it for her.

"Kill?" He said in a voice that neither of them was sure was loud enough for the new arrivals to hear. Mary didn't react to him. "Who is the other fellah?" finished Paul slowly. Mary could almost hear the cogs of thought turning in his head.

"He's Ricky Starr." Mary waited to see Paul's reaction.

He appeared to be unmoved.

"Funny," she said. "I've never met him before. I thought he'd be taller." Paul was trying to listen to the conversation the two men were having, what of it there was, but was just out of earshot.

"So I've been brought here under the pretence of talking to a father that I've never known about rare issues of Private Eye and you've been sent here to kill him and we're sitting here on barstools chewing the fat as if that scenario is perfectly normal?"

"Paul." Said Mary. "Forget Private Eye."

"Why have I been brought here then?"

"You are here for your own protection."

"That seems odd. It's more dangerous here."

"If you'd have stayed at home, Paul, you'd have been dealt with by now."

"What do you mean?" He said disbelievingly.

"I mean it Paul. I know these people. They'd have got to you."

"Why with all the stuff about Private Eye then. If it was so terrible why didn't someone just tell me?"

Mary shook her head.

"To be honest," she said. "I don't really know. Your file said you were stubborn so recommended that you should be lured here under some pretext. They knew you collected Private Eye."

"My file." Said Paul. "I have a file?"

"We all have a file Paul. Some people have more than one."

David Crane and Eamonn had their heads together sharing some kind of secret. David Crane turned towards Mary and Paul. He walked over to where they were sitting slouched on their barstools and introduced himself. He noticed that they were both pretty drunk.

"Good evening." He said.

'God,' thought Paul as he swivelled on his bar stool. *'That voice is familiar.'*

"I do hope you are enjoying your stay." Continued David Crane. Both Paul and Mary tried as best they could to straighten their slouched bodies.

"My name is Tom Gates. I have the fortune to be the owner here." He held out his hand firstly to Mary who was suddenly at a loss but composed herself surprisingly quickly.

"Mary..." she hesitated momentarily. She couldn't possibly use her real name. Even if she was being over cautious. She was searching through her foggy mind for an appropriate surname then thought that he would know it anyway as it would be the name she checked in under and the name on her passport. She thought she'd gotten away with it. Just leaving it there hanging like that.

"Mary." She said again. David was still shaking her hand expecting her to add to her description of herself. When he realised that she wasn't going to say a different word he smiled and offered his hand to Paul. Paul had had a moment or two to prepare and was forthright. He overcompensated for his inebriated state though by talking too loudly. Like a child in a school play with one line to say he said it with confidence thinking he was annunciating every syllable.

"Good evening Mister Gates. My name is Roger Penrose." He said. The name seemed to flick a light switch on behind David's eyes. He held onto Paul's hand and a broad inquisitive smile spread across his face.

"Mr. Penrose. I'd heard you were coming. I believe we have a shared interest."

"I believe we do." Said Paul sneaking a brief glance towards Mary.

"Look," said David. "I know it's late but let me get you a drink. I can imagine you're not in the mood for talking business right now but hey if you're a Private Eye completest you can't be all bad."

David realised that he may have made a mistake by using the word completest. He thought it was the kind of word you use when you've been informed. Briefed. Which of course he had. Paul didn't notice. At least not immediately. His subconscious mind worked more thoroughly than his conscious one but took more time about it.

David nodded at the barman and pointed to the glasses in front of Mary and Paul.

"D'you mind me asking," said Paul turning slightly and not waiting for an answer. "That guitar on the wall there." He pointed towards where two guitars were hanging on the wall above the piano. "The one with the odd number of strings. What's that all about?"

David was unbalanced slightly by the question but actually loved it. "Oh that old thing." He said and glanced over to where Eamonn was sitting. Eamonn had swivelled too on his bar stool and was unashamedly sitting open bodied facing them. He held a nearly empty pint glass in both hands between his legs. He was about to call over to Eamonn when he too double checked himself and with his hand in the air said nothing for a fraction of a second before saying,

"Ricky. Ricky come and join us." He waved theatrically with the hand that was already in the air. Ricky didn't need him to ask twice. Out of the four people that were party to this exchange, not one of them was unaware of the fact that there had been flaws in the way it had been conducted given that it was as innocent as it was pretending to be. Each one though, for different reasons loved the drama, the deciphering of the non verbal, The Game. And each one of them for different reasons, maybe, wouldn't give away the deceit. They all knew that to trespass across the imaginary line they'd created would result in an ugly fight at least. So no-one did. Ricky sidled over to where they were standing. For a multi billionaire media mogul he was strangely ill at ease. To begin with he behaved like a polite sixteen year old boy would when being introduced to his parents' friends.

"Hi." He said, offering his hand to Mary. He was completely aware of who she was, and what power she wielded because of her lack of respect for other people's rules. He had never met her before now though and was awed and disappointed at the same time. Mary took his hand and drunk as she was held it between her strong, very unfeminine fingers. She almost pinched her thumb down into his hand.

"Rick." He said. She looked hard into his eyes for some kind of signal that, and she knew it wouldn't be an obvious one, that said he understood but no such signal was forthcoming. Ricky pulled his hand away from Mary's grip and waved across towards Paul. Paul grasped his hand as if he were meeting a mate in a pub.

"Were you christened Ricky?" asked Paul.

"Not exactly." Said Ricky.

"Richard then." Said Paul. "Should I call you Richard?"

"You can call me whatever you want." Said Ricky. "I'm never really sure who I am myself." David interrupted them and drew Paul's attention.

"Do you play?" He asked, pointing up towards the guitars.

"No." Said Paul. "I just remember seeing one like that somewhere.'

"You do though." Interrupted Mary, shocking all of the three men. David couldn't help himself. He got off his stool and walked to where the guitars were hanging on the wall. He picked the bulbous backed Guild from the wall first and before handing it to Ricky strummed the six strings with a familiar chord.

"I always keep them in tune." He winked at Ricky as he passed him the guitar that he had not played for more than thirty years. Despite his reservations, his inabilities as a guitar player, his total focus for the past thirty years on not this, he put the guitar across his knee, fingered a couple of chords and picked single notes, one at a time.

"Come on Man." Said David as he reached up on the wall for the other guitar. David immediately started playing a song as if he had done exactly this yesterday. He went from strummed chord to strummed chord, melodic as hell.

"Hold on here." Said Ricky after a while. "Are we supposed to be playing together now?" David stopped his performance and looked at Ricky. After all that they had been through in the last few days he was right. They would have to play together. Mary, noticing an odd tension between the two men piped up.

"Anyone a Van Fan?" As she stepped up to the piano and lifted the lid. "In case you're wondering' G C D in the verses and an E-minor in the chorus finishing on D. Yeah."

She banged away at the old upright piano like a pro. It was only when the other two joined in that she eased off. It took a verse or two for everyone to feel at home. Mary stopped thumping the keyboard and the guitars could be heard. First David. He seemed to be practised. Mary started singing. As soon as the song starts the musicians stop rehearsing. Paul stared open mouthed at the woman who had altered his life in so many ways in the last forty eight hours. He was a seasoned consumer of alcohol. To the extent that he had to justify himself sometimes in a way he knew was pushing the boundaries but she was keeping up with him every step of the way. She had only yesterday saved him from being murdered, shagged him senseless in the meantime and was now singing a tune with the two men that seemed to be the architects of all this.

"Half a mile from the county fair…" She sang, "and the rain came pourin' down. Ohhh the water."

"Ohhh the water." The two old men joined in with a decent harmony, eyes flicking between each other, constantly checking.

Paul had heard the song played before but he'd never heard it sung by a woman. The three of them played an extended version that went on for ten minutes or more. When they finally ended with a flourish all four of them were smiling and applauded the others. They sang some more together. Each of them suggesting a simple song they knew from way back until finally Ricky was the first to break.

"That's me done everyone." He said standing up and hanging the guitar on the wall behind the piano. "I'm too old for this these days. I need my beauty sleep." None of the others objected too much.

"Goodnight then Old man." Said David shaking Ricky's hand. "You know where you're going don't you?"

"Yes." Said Ricky. "No problem." He shook Mary's hand first.

"Pleasure." He said. "We should do this again." Mary looked intensely for a clue. *'Did he hold my hand just a bit too long?'* She thought. Ricky turned to Paul. "See you soon I hope." He turned and walked out towards the reception.

"I'm done too." Said David finishing the last of his beer and standing up from the stool to replace the guitar next to the one Ricky had put up. Mary closed the lid of the piano.

"Well it's been a pleasure Mr. Gates." Said Paul.

"For me too Paul. Please call me..." He hesitated again. "Call me Tom." They shook hands. David Crane could see no glimmer of understanding in Paul's eyes. *'Surely he must know.'* He thought. *'If he does know who I really am, he's a cool customer.'*

"What room have they put you in?" He said as their hands parted.

"The Atlantic suite." Said Paul.

"I'm glad of that." He said. "It's the best room in the hotel. To be honest I often stay in that room when it's not booked. But that's not very often these days. Waking up to that view is a pleasure few things can match. Come." He said. I'm in a room nearby. "We'll walk together." Paul shrugged and slid off his barstool.

"And where are you Mary?" Said David.

"Just over the other side of the gardens." She said. "Not as palatial as the Atlantic suite."

"All the rooms have a hidden secret though." Said David. "Have you found what yours is?"

"No." Said Mary intrigued. David winked at her as he took her hand and kissed her on the cheek. He turned away. He had used this little trick many times before with guests.

'What on earth does he mean?' Thought Mary. She leaned forward to kiss Paul. As she did so she whispered in his ear.

"See you later." Paul wasn't sure if this was a question or a statement. He suspected that she wasn't asking him though. David started towards the tall French doors that were still wide open. There was no breeze at all. The air was still and warm. They walked together over the gravel path that Paul had walked down earlier in the day. He was drunk and a little unsteady on his feet but he felt that the last hour had sobered him up a little. They walked around past the Jasmine flowers. The path from there to the door to Paul's room was maybe twenty yards.

"Paul." Said David. "I just know she is going to ask you what the secret is in your room." They approached the door and Paul took out his key card. "Let me show you quickly what it is." Paul opened the door and walked inside the lobby. David followed and closed the door behind him. The lights were on in the main room.

I didn't leave the lights on. Thought Paul. David was strolling along the corridor to the main room.

"This area was originally inhabited by early humans thought to have been blown here on the wind." He said, completing the sentence as he entered the room. The man in the creased-linen-suit was sitting on a white leather couch by the wall.

"Was it really?" He said. "And by the way. I thought you'd never fucking finish. What is it about you Irish and a singalong?"

"Hello." Said David unruffled. "Are you a friend of Paul?" He said this just as Paul appeared at the doorway to the room with an escort of a big shaven headed bloke in a too-tight cheap black suit. They both stood there. The shaven headed bloke, his head cocked slightly to one side, held his hands together in front of him just a pace behind Paul. David nodded to himself. As another black suited shaven head appeared from the bathroom. Paul looked across to the desk hopefully. The laptop lid had been closed.

"Do you know these men, Paul?" Asked David.

"No." Said Paul. "But they were at lunch earlier."

David held out his hand towards the man in the creased-linen-suit. He was playing ignorant only he knew exactly why these men were here.

"My name is Tom Gates." He said.

"Is it now?" Replied the man in the creased-linen-suit refusing David's hand.

"Are you sure about that? Listen," he said. "I want to get this over and done with. It's a spot of luck that you're both here. I'm only supposed to do you Crane." He wasn't looking at either of them. "This is a bit of buy one get one free. I do like a bargain." He had got up from the couch and was walking over towards the French doors leading to the balcony. He pulled the curtains. Paul assumed that the man in the creased-linen-suit was talking to him.

"You two will have had a fight that will tragically end in you both falling to your deaths." While he was talking Paul thought he heard the slightest of clicks come from the hallway. Unfortunately so did the shaven headed bloke in the black suit who was standing behind him. The shaven headed bloke turned and walked back towards the hallway and the front door to the room. Presently thudding sounds came from the direction of the front door. Thudding sounds that everyone in the room heard this time. The man in the creased-linen-suit had pulled open the curtains and had opened the French doors. The smell of the sea filled the room. He turned quickly as he heard the noise and indicated with a flick of his head to the second shaven headed goon to go and investigate. The second man drew a gun from inside his black jacket and tentatively entered the passageway where the noise had come from. The three men remaining in the room stood still in anticipation. Paul was fairly certain what was happening. He recalled the sight of a leg sticking out of the gorse bushes with the stripped training shoe attached to it and the man's dead staring eyes. He wasn't reckoning on that second fellah's chances. There was indeed another couple of thumps. Then all the lights went out. Somebody had withdrawn the key card that controlled the lighting. David heard movement in the direction of where both Paul and the man in the creased-linen-suit were standing.

When the lights came on again the positions of the three men who were left had changed. Mary, if it was Mary who had been the cause of the thuds in the hallway had not appeared. David was standing by one of the French doors.

"You're in a bit of a corner now." Said David with a slight smile on his face. The man in the creased-linen-suit was now standing in a corner of the room. David and Paul could have just stood aside and let him run out but they stood their ground. The look on his face indicated that he realised that the tables had turned in the last few seconds and that his position was not that advantageous any more. In all the information he had received about these two men though, nowhere had it said they were in any way fighting men. That didn't seem to compute as the man in the creased-linen-suit made the slightest of movements and both David and Paul countered by covering any path that the man in the creased-linen-suit may have considered taking.

"Don't be foolish." He said with as much gravitas as he could muster. "You're an old man." It didn't work though. David picked up an orange from a fruit-bowl on the table.

"I'm an old man?" Said David. "Just as well. I think I've got a score to settle." Said David. David held up the orange. "I've seen this done in the films." He said.

"And I was never sure about it working."

"What working?" Said the man in the creased-linen-suit.

David threw the orange hard towards the man in the creased-linen-suit. As David had suspected he might the man reached up and caught it with both his hands in front of his face. David and Paul Crane saw clearly that his left hand was missing a little finger.

"What do you know? It does work." Said David turning to Paul who was standing with a bemused frightened, but still a little aggressive expression on his face. Paul, not knowing what the hell he was talking about nodded in agreement. David slowly paced towards the now sweating man. David was surprised to see the extent of his transformation into a quivering wreck. He was indeed an old man but David had kept himself fit. Something inside him had kept the anger of this moment hidden for thirty years. He deftly punched the man square on the nose. Blood flowed and the man quickly held his hand up to his face. David punched again in the middle of his stomach and he fell forward. David twisted him around and pushed hard over the side of the balustrade. The man screamed an almost feminine scream as he realised what was happening. He grasped for life at the rail of the balustrade as he went over. He managed to get first one hand then the other to the balustrade rail.

"Jesus." Screamed Paul. Emerging onto the balcony.

"Let's get him back. You've made your point I think." David put a stern hand to Paul's chest.

"He was going to kill us, Paul. Never mind why for now but he'd have shown no mercy."

"But..." Tried Paul. David was having none of it.

"Paul. Please. Trust me." The man in the creased-linen-suit was kicking and screaming hanging on to the balustrade. He was trying desperately to raise a leg up so that he might clamber back to safety but he was too overweight and unfit. David crouched to his haunches and looked at the struggling man through the iron bars that formed the railing as he kicked and buckled.

"Keep yourself calm now Marvin. You'll wear yourself out with all that shouting."

"Help." He shouted as loud as he could.

"I've thought about what I'd do at this moment for thirty years and do you know there have been short periods during those years that I have felt more charitable than others. This isn't one of those moments though." He reached into his inside jacket pocket and pulled out a Swiss army knife.

"That's..." Started Paul.

"Yes sorry Paul. I was going to return it to you. I sent this to you for your fourteenth birthday originally." He flipped a blade from the knife and thumbed the edge.

"This is getting out of hand Mr. Gates." Said Paul.

"Please give me back the knife." An ever so slightly annoyed tone entered David's voice.

"Please stop calling me Mr. Gates, Paul." David readjusted his position so he was face to face with the reddened and petrified face of the man in the creased-linen-suit.

"My name is David Crane." He said as he roughly cut the buttons from the sweat and blood stained shirt that was stretched around the torso of the man hanging from the balustrade.

"You are..." started Paul as David Crane pushed the edge of the knife against the man's chest and carved a semicircle the size of a saucer. "What the hell are you doing?" He continued as blood started to trickle down towards the screaming man's waist.

"I'm settling a score, Paul." He said. "Now do calm down Marvin. We wouldn't want you to lose your grip. You too Paul. I wouldn't want you to lose yours either." David turned the knife around and held the familiar red case between the forefinger and thumb of his right hand level in front of him. Paul had already lost his grip.

David steadied himself again and lifted his left hand slowly towards Marvin's face. He bluntly pushed the thumb and forefinger of his left hand into Marvin's right eye. Marvin's reflex was to tightly shut his eyes. David prised his eyelid open and held the blade a few millimetres away from of his eye.

Paul wasn't sure if he understood what David Crane had just said to him. He wasn't sure if he was up for being party to this regardless of what the man hanging over the balcony had done or who David Crane was. Father or not.

"Mr. Gates." Paul shouted defiantly and purposefully as he grabbed David's shoulders and pulled him backwards. The heat and tension of the moment caused the crouching David Crane to totter backwards as he pushed himself upwards into a standing position. This in turn pushed Paul who banged against the wall by the French doors. He ricocheted back again towards David. Neither of them intended to fight but to a casual observer, that is what it looked like they were doing. They, almost as one, fell back towards the balustrade. David, while trying to steady both of them, cut through the skin of the flabby and tired left hand of the man in the creased-linen-suit. His screams intensified as he was left holding the balustrade with three fingers and a thumb. David Crane pushed Paul back towards the wall away from the railings as the man in the creased-linen-suit released his grip on the rail.

30

Paul couldn't stay in his room that night. Not having just witnessed a man practically pushed to his death from a millionth floor balcony by a man he'd just met who purported to be the owner of the hotel and who could also possibly be his father. He'd paced around the room wondering what he should do, hyperventilating and talking to himself in a high pitched voice before a text came through on his phone from Mary giving him a room name and some directions. For some reason, and it frightened him a little that it had, Paul was glad she'd summoned him. Tom Gates or whoever he was, had left him to it. Inexplicably just left. Killed a man and nonchalantly as you like just said goodnight.

"Goodnight Paul." He'd said. "I have to go. We will meet again." He'd said while he shook Paul's hand with an iron grip. "I hope I'll be able to explain."

Dear Guests,

A black and gold printed card was delivered under the door to Mary's room that following morning. It was hours before either Paul or Mary noticed it. They had practically passed out. Paul was mentally and physically exhausted. Mary reluctantly turned over in bed soon after Paul had arrived and flopped down next to her. Sleep took hold of her quicker than she thought it would.

"Dear Guests," Mary read out loud as Paul was still in a half sleep. His eyes slowly opened. In his half sleep he was dreaming of walking a dog along a peaceful country path.

"Dear Guests," Mary repeated having read the rest of the invitation in her head.

"You are cordially invited to join us in the Lansdowne room this evening for dinner. The entertainment will be the amazing Da Vinci, the world-famous magician who will make you question your existence and your sanity. He might even make you disappear. Cocktails at six."

In Paul's dream, the dog had started to drag him along faster than he wanted to go. He couldn't let go for fear of losing the dog but he was finding it hard to hold onto the lead. He tried to think where he had found the dog but he couldn't.

"They've hired a turn." Shouted Mary finally pulling Paul out of his dream. She was genuinely excited.

"I love magic."

"Who's in so far?" asked Jill as she slunk into the room and sat down next to Ian at the open laptops. She was wearing a long black evening dress and her short blond hair had been recently coiffed. She looked pristine and lovely. "Your boy and Mata Hari are there." He said.

"She's on her third Margarita already." He pointed at one of the screens. A wide angle view of the Lansdowne room.

"And there's these characters over by the doors." He moved his finger across to two men sitting by the French doors looking distinctly out of place. They were sitting bolt upright in two of the four seats next to each other at the table. Ian played with the zoom control and the picture went to a close up. Both of the men looked as if they had been in a fight. The first was wearing sunglasses but it was evident that he had a very bruised face. The second was sporting a cut and swollen lip.

"Do you know who they are? They look like they've already been at work. They've got to be players?" He said glancing for the first time at Jill. "Do they look innocent or... Wow. Look at you."

He leant back to get a better look.

"You look..." He searched around for the most appropriate word.

"You look fantastic." Jill smiled in appreciation. Ian stared at her for a few moments before he returned his attention to the screens and panned a camera around the room using the touch pad on one of the laptops. Two more men that they had never seen before were sitting drinking iced water on a table by the wall under the oil painting of a rugby match. Opposite them and towards one end of the room, a stage, eighteen inches high had been erected.

"They have to be players, surely." Said Jill.

Ian nodded.

"Listen Ian," said Jill. "Why don't you come in with me tonight? Get out of this room. You've been stuck in here for nearly three days."

"I've nothing to wear." He said. "I'd look ridiculous. Look at you. I'd stick out like a sore thumb." Ian's eyes were still locked onto the screen. The tone in his voice was saying he'd like nothing more than getting out of this room and having dinner with Jill but he had a job to do. Jill produced a large heavy paper carrier bag from beside her. Ian had been too preoccupied to notice when Jill had come into the room.

"Well we can easily solve that one." She said holding the bag up. Ian couldn't help a broad smile.

"You are…" He searched again. "You are good. You are very good." He said.

"Well you didn't think I'd expect you to sit in here all the time did you. Come on. Get yourself ready. I'll watch the screens."

The previous afternoon Martin had drunk too much wine to drive back to his house. Sarah was no better so they decided to book a room. Neither of them had expected it but a room had been reserved in Martin's name. She was still not convinced she had the whole story but she was happy with how it had gone so far. She knew that catching monkeys was a slow process. They'd asked for the bill. The waiter returned with a silver tray containing a black card.

"Sir, your meal today is compliments of the owner." Said the young waiter. "He has asked me to thank you for coming and has said to give you this." He offered the tray to Martin who took the card that was on it.

"Can you tell him that it was most appreciated." Said Martin. "Is the owner here?" He said. "I'd like to thank him myself."

"I'm afraid not Sir. I don't think he's back from a fishing trip."

"So how…?" Martin started but thought better of it.

The waiter made to leave but loitered momentarily before turning back.

"I hope you don't mind Sir, he said, but is that your red car parked outside?"

"Yes." Said Martin with a smile on his face.

"Is it a Ferrari?"

"A 246 Dino." Said Martin.

"Just that I've only ever seen one like that before on telly."

Martin smiled and nodded his head. The waiter, only a young man. Smiled and nodded as he backed away from the table.

"Better than a puppy." Quipped Sarah.

Martin smiled holding the black card away from his eyes to read it.

"Appears we've been invited to a show tomorrow night."

Years ago Roland Garret had learned to tie a bow tie.

He'd been embarrassed into doing so after an evening in a gentlemen's club that he was anxious to join. The group of men he was with had chuckled politely to themselves when Garret had innocently told them that he had been to Moss Bros' to hire his. Although at the time he was hardly able to afford it he had gone out the next day to Saville Row and been ripped off the price of a months rent for a distinctly ordinary shawl collar evening suit. A set of instructions had come with the bow tie but he couldn't make head nor tail of them. He was eventually shown a trick of how to tie it by a sophisticated lady who he employed to keep him company when he thought it more appropriate to attend an engagement with a female partner. As soon as she told him that the knot is the same knot as the one you use to tie your shoelace, he had understood. He was never asked to apply for membership at that particular club however. After that though he would wear his dinner suit whenever he got the opportunity even when the occasion was not necessarily suitable. This was one of those occasions. A dinner in a good hotel where the entertainment was to be a cheesy magician. Frankly he wanted to get the whole thing over with. He'd like to have this whole irritating little problem go away and get home. Still he thought as he pulled the knot together round his thigh, just above the knee,

Food's good. Wine's good. We will make hay while the sun shines."

A waiter led him to a table in the middle of the room.

He ordered a straight whiskey with ice before he sat down. Sarah and Martin had arrived shortly before he had and she was watching him. She'd noticed him the previous afternoon. The waiter returned with his whiskey on a silver tray. With it was a rolled up magazine tied with a red ribbon. The waiter put both the glass and the rolled up magazine on the table in front of Roland Garret without saying anything. Garret sat still for a few moments, his head cocked slightly to one side, staring at the rolled up magazine. He looked up and around him suddenly. Sarah was lucky she wasn't the first person he looked towards otherwise he might have caught her staring intently at him.

He obviously didn't see anything untoward. He picked up the glass first and drank all the whiskey he could through the ice. Then he picked up the magazine and untied the red ribbon. He smoothed the magazine flat, turned directly to a page towards the back and slid out a piece of paper a quarter of the size of the open magazine. He looked up for a waiter and pointed at his glass.

"Could you get me another one of those please and would you have a pen or a pencil?"

The waiter left and returned a short while later with another silver tray. He put the whiskey down first and then handed Garret a ballpoint pen. Garret spent fifteen minutes or so comparing the loose paper with what was written in the magazine and making notes. He looked at his watch and then around the room again narrowly missing Sarah's intense staring for the second time. He slid his heavy bulk around the horseshoe of leather banquette and got up to leave. He stuffed the loose paper in a jacket pocket but left the magazine sitting open on the table. Sarah watched as he hurriedly walked out of the room. A waiter quickly cleared the table.

"Excuse me a moment." Said Sarah to Martin who was idly perusing the menu. "I need the powder room."

"Ladies and Gentlemen."

A voice came from nowhere and was everywhere. A man's voice, low and modern. The lights in the Lansdowne room started to dim. Over a period of thirty seconds the room became pitch dark. The audience of diners, having been lulled by the rich food and the continually flowing alcohol, were, to varying degrees excited, nervous and downright fearful of the darkness.

"Ladies and Gentlemen." The voice said again this time with a heavy dose of reverb. So much reverb in fact that the words were beginning to repeat on themselves. The show had begun. The room became darker and darker to the extent that there was no light at all. Behind the heavy damask curtains that had been drawn over the windows was a blackout blind that had been built into the window frames.

The human eye only adjusts to low light conditions when there is some light to adjust to. In almost all circumstances there is some light bouncing around somewhere. Only when all sources of light have been removed does it become technically dark. The Lansdowne room then was technically dark.

After a long theatrical pause, a single dot of light the size of a pea appeared above the black stage and moved around in an apparently random manner.

"In the beginning there was one." Said the disembodied voice. The audience was focused on the tiny light as it was the only light in the room. The single pea sized light split into two and they started to move faster and further, even above the heads of the audience.

"One became two." The voice continued. "Two became four," it said as the lights split again. Four tiny lights were now swirling around the room. They continued for a few moments before they all seemed to follow a similar path. They created a circle about three metres in diameter. A circular trajectory parallel with the floor. They split again into eight tiny lights and the spinning circle of light that looked now like one thin beam moved from the middle of the room to over the stage. The lights span around for a moment then began to descend to the floor while the diameter of the circular path became slowly smaller. As the lights reached the floor the diameter of the circle was maybe two feet. They were indiscernible as single dots of light. It was now just a ring of white light sitting six inches from the floor. It span there for a full minute. A sudden flash, like a flash from a camera lit up the entire room. The flash lasted for a fraction of a second but it was enough for everyone in the room see everybody else. The only thing that appeared to have changed was in place of the ring of tiny lights stood a figure in a long cape and wearing a wide brimmed hat and a white Venetian carnival mask.

"Please welcome Da Vinci." Said the voice as the room was dark again. The audience applauded more enthusiastically than was anticipated under the circumstances. As the applause started so did a hissing sound coming from behind the heads of each member of the audience. A slight scent of lavender filled the air.

31

From a small aluminium aerosol can, Greg sprayed a fine mist into the air above each of four tables that had descended into a space twenty feet below the Lansdowne room. The space was an exact replica of the room above.

"Just stay seated for a moment longer if you don't mind?" Said Greg to the occupants of the four tables as one by one they awoke from a light sleep. He flicked a remote control in his pocket that released a circular metal ring around the chairs that was holding them firmly in place.

"Is everybody with me?" He asked. They all now seemed awake and to different degrees were looking around with questioning looks on their faces wondering where everyone else in the room had gone. Everyone in turn nodded or gestured that they were awake.

"Firstly, I'm sorry for all the theatrics. For those of you who are still not with the programme completely I'm sure it'll all become perfectly clear in due course."

Greg then put two small metal canisters on the table in front of Paul and then four canisters each on the tables in front of Benson and Hedges, Jill and Ian and Martin and Sarah.

"A word of explanation." Said Greg. "It is not right that a magician should give away his methods. For reasons I have yet to understand I have been asked to transport you down here and separate you from the other guests at the party. They will still be asleep." Greg squirted an aerosol into the air. Everybody was obediently sitting watching and listening to Greg as if the performance was continuing. Which it was to a degree. This was as odd for Greg as it was for the remaining audience members. He'd been asked to separate them from the others so they could have a little 'strategy meeting'. He didn't mind too much though because at least for a short while he would not be interrupted. He'd say as much as he could before someone cottoned on that this was no longer a performance. When that happened it would be more difficult to keep control.

"Don't go overdoing it with this stuff." Said Greg "and remember this is not an exact science. These little bottles contain two different compounds that I am very proud to announce are the result of years of painstaking research. The first," he held up a bottle with the word SLEEP written on the side. "As the name might suggest, is for putting your victim to sleep." He then held up another bottle and pointed at the word WAKE. "And this, and I hope you're ahead of me here, is to wake your victim having previously put him or her to sleep. I used this one," he said holding up the SLEEP bottle again, "to send you all to sleep upstairs earlier. It's a hell of an illusion don't you think. Press the button here and spray directly into your victims face. The dosage depends on how long you want to disable them for and their body mass index. Unlike some of our other products," Greg threw the thinnest of glances towards Martin who was sitting quietly with his hands on the table in front of him, "this one is made from natural ingredients. The chemistry affects the body's own sleep triggers." He put the bottle down again and picked up the other one. Sarah, having noticed the hint of a connection between Martin and Greg flicked

Martin an angry look and broke the silence that had unknowingly, to them, been imposed by Greg.

"Is this legal?" She said loudly and like a union shop steward quickly followed that by, "And is it dangerous?"

Greg nodded towards Martin in a way that communicated his disappointment that he was being asked this question.

'Shouldn't this have been dealt with?' He asked Martin with body movements and eyes alone.

'She is beyond my control.' Answered Martin using the same code.

"Although attempts have been made," Said Greg, at this point remaining loosely conversational and non-combative, "to conform to the rigorous demands of both the American and European agencies whose remit includes making qualitative judgements on issues they have a limited understanding of, as of this moment, no the compounds contained in these containers are not strictly legal, but then using the same measurements lavender oil would not be legal either. As far as the safety aspect goes, I'd like to address this. An overdose is almost impossible. A small amount of the spray will induce almost immediate sleep. But the subject will wake within minutes. Probably, depending on things like body mass, age and addiction to alcohol." Greg glanced again at Martin. He was enjoying himself again.

"This is part of the act," Martin whispered in response to Sarah's predictable reaction. "Don't be too taken in."

Greg waited a moment for them to finish their brief dialogue and even nodded in their direction before he carried on. Martin made a mental note to punch the pretentious prick squarely on the nose the next time that the opportunity arose but as if reading his mind and with an almost indiscernible smirk but a smirk all the same Greg said,

"Never a good idea to shoot the messenger." He continued.

"A bigger dose will put the subject to sleep for long enough to trick them into thinking that it's sleep time. We all sleep more or less eight hours in twenty four so it actually isn't difficult to simulate the conditions when this occurs. But is it safe? Well what is safe? Is driving your car safe? Is drinking alcohol safe?"

"Save us the lecture Greg." Benson piped up and pointed a finger upwards. Greg looked at his watch.

"What you need to know about these little bottles is that they can give you an advantage. It's up to you what you do with that advantage. Guns tend, and I mean tend to shift the advantage, and with advantage I mean the balance of power, but that only happens when only one of the sides has the gun. Sometimes this is a good idea. When only one side has the gun. It means all parties remain alive. Alive to fight, to debate to influence to educate, another day. We have all been taught what happens when two sides have similar power, similar perceived advantage. They annihilate each other eventually. They kill each other's young people." Greg paused.

"I'm banging on." He said. "Sorry. Look. This stuff is safe. It's safer that carrying a gun. It won't, unless you are very clever compete with a gun for sheer power but power as they say is worth nothing without control. See these little canisters as little tins of control." Everyone was silent.

"Oh." Said Greg as he handed out more of the little canisters, "They are CFC free. Now if you all don't mind I'm going to run through how we would like things to go from here." There were no objections.

"You may have noticed when we were all upstairs earlier," he pointed towards the ceiling. "Roland Garret has left the building. He received a coded message earlier that told him to rendezvous with David Crane and Eamonn Booth. Known more recently and probably to you," He made a sweeping motion with his hand towards his audience. "As Tom Gates, the owner here and the media mogul, Ricky Starr. Before that meeting happens," he looked at his watch, "In about an hour, we have to keep that lot up there occupied and avoid getting ourselves killed."

Greg pulled a remote control from his pocket and pushed a switch. The painting of the rugby match that was hanging on the wall turned into a huge display screen. It showed a wide angled view of the upstairs room. Greg handed the remote control to Ian.

"As you can see." Said Greg. "We still have four different threats to deal with. Top left." He glanced over towards Paul. "Mary Wilks. Perhaps the most lethal of the bunch now freelance and employed directly by Garret to eliminate David Crane."

"Excuse me," interrupted Paul. "I think she's had some bad press here. She's not on their side. Her father died 'cause of Garret."

Greg stopped what he was saying for a moment and a questioning expression moved across his face. He continued.

"Ex IRA, trained and adept in judo, quick with a knife and…"

Paul piped up again.

"Sorry." He said. "She's on our side." Greg ignored him and continued on.

"Trains anyone who will pay in firearms, explosives and poisons."

"Is no-one listening?" Said Paul. "Whatever it is she was, she isn't any more."

Greg looked at Paul nodded his head and continued. He was going to finish what he was saying.

"Theatrical credentials are excellent. Has an, in my opinion, overly inflated sense of theatre in that she leaves her victims with a pink lipstick kiss. Anyone who receives…"

"I'm telling you she's not that person anymore." Said Paul louder this time.

"Please Paul." Said Greg, with an irked tone. "I'm just telling you what I know. Make of it what you will." Greg turned deliberately towards Benson and Hedges.

"Anyone who receives the pink kiss of death from Mary Wilks and is still alive should consider themselves extremely fortunate." Benson wanted to say something but didn't. Hedges squirmed in his seat and blushed. Greg turned back to Paul.

"I imagine you would like the opportunity to deal with her."

"Yes I would." Said Paul. "I told you she's on our side."

"Whatever." Said Greg and pointed at the screen again.

"Top right. The woman with the black hair and red lipstick. What is it about the women in this game? They've almost got to advertise. Sandy Lane. Lithuanian. Trained by the Israeli secret service. That alone normally proves too much for most of her conquests. The rather dull looking man she is currently asleep on is her decoy. He doesn't know it but he is a sacrificial lamb to the slaughter. It was a tactic that became well used after the war. Men you see," he glanced at all the men. "Men you see, always have an inflated opinion of their position in the great hierarchy of all things and this among countless other reasons…"

Sarah piped up again.

"Are you one of those men Greg?" Martin tried to stop her but she continued.

"Do you have an inflated opinion of your position in the," her voice changed into a sarcastic mimic, "Great hierarchy of all things?"

"I can't say that I don't, Detective Inspector. I detect a note of defiance in your voice."

"I don't like the patronising way you are talking to us."

"Well I can't help that." Said Greg as he moved closer to where she was sitting and lowered his voice but not so the others couldn't hear him.

"For whatever the reasons you are sitting in a cave beneath a room where at least three known, possibly more, professional assassins are sitting fast asleep. They are a highly motivated bunch who have all come here to kill a member of your party." Sarah tried to interject but Greg slowly shook his head as he continued.

"I don't care." Said Greg. "My advice to you, and you absolutely do not have to take it, is to listen to what I am saying and not the way I am saying it."

Sarah huffed. She didn't look to Martin for support because she knew she wouldn't get any. Martin hoped that she wouldn't and was sitting scratching his chin looking down at the table.

"Where was I?" Said Greg. "Yes. Just bear in mind that the fate of this fellah is very likely to be very different from the one he imagines." He pointed again up to the plain looking man asleep with the black-haired woman with the red lipstick.

"They are working for the Liberian Government. Well, Liberian government is a contradiction in terms. One single man in the Liberian administration that against all the odds has managed to retain some power over the last thirty years. He is a gangster and as such represents the most serious of threats."

"Now you are kidding." Said Paul. "Am I the only one here who is wondering if that sleep stuff was just sleep stuff?"

"Paul." Said Greg slowly. "Have you not read the dossier?"

"What dossier?" Said Paul.

Greg nodded to himself three or four times as if connecting the dots. He looked around the room. No-one looked him in the eye. Greg moved a little closer to Paul.

"Paul." He said. After a short pause, "who is that?" He pointed at Jill.

"I don't know. I did think I'd seen you before," he said nodding politely towards Jill, "but I wasn't sure."

Jill smiled at him an embarrassed smile. It wasn't just an embarrassed smile. It was apologetic. Paul saw it and added some numbers together. He was nodding his head again and staring as it slowly became clear. He pointed at her.

"I remember you now." He said. "In that silly bar." He looked around the others. He pointed at Benson and Hedges unable to come to a conclusion.

"So." Said Greg. "Everyone here knows what is going on except for Paul. Is that right?"

No-one said anything for a moment or two. Then Sarah spoke in her defiant belligerent tone.

"I don't know what's going on either."

"Yes you do." Said Martin.

"Martin." Said Sarah twirling a finger round and round. Her voice was angry. "Do you really think you told me everything you knew? Did you read this 'dossier'?"

Greg came to Martin's rescue.

"Now calm down everyone." He glanced at his watch again. "For the sake of the greater good I am now going to lay out the facts of the case so that Paul here, and you Sarah, are on an even playing field. We are gathered here on account of an impending family crisis so I'm not going to mince my words. You Paul, your half-sister Jill and your twin brother Martin here," Greg pointed at Jill and Martin in turn, "are here because your father is about to be scapegoated for something he didn't do thirty years ago and you three are in danger of being punished for the sins of the father, so to speak."

The fact that this was news to Paul showed on his face. It was as if there was too much to compute. Too much information. Paul started to shake his head as he stared into the middle distance. A moment or two passed as Greg waited for the revelations to sink in.

"And Father." He said. "You said my Father." Said Paul.

"Yes." Said Greg. "The man who owns this hotel is your father. Greg went silent waiting for this information to sink in.

Everyone in the room was silent waiting for the reaction from Paul. He'd met this man for the first time the previous evening and after a drink and a singalong he'd pushed a man to his death over his hotel room balcony. His face was displaying the varied and mixed emotions he was dealing with.

"Why…?" he said. Greg drew breath to answer what he thought was Paul's question but Paul raised his finger. "No, No." He said. "Why didn't someone just tell me?"

"I didn't know you Paul." Said Jill. "We were afraid that you wouldn't come if you knew the real reason why we were here. Our information suggested you wouldn't want to get involved."

Paul's face turned a little redder.

"Your information." He nodded to himself. "It was you. You said 'Why don't I have a shower and get ready?' You'd couldn't have known that I hadn't had a shower already. You've been watching me. Who supplied your information?"

Jill was trying to put a brave face on the exchange but the look on her face was of regret.

"I'm sorry Paul." She said.

"I'm not sure he still knows the real reason he is here." Benson piped up.

"Why don't you tell him Jill? Why don't you tell him that he's been chased down by assassins because you and your boyfriend want to write a book." Hedges put his head in his hands.

A smile gradually morphed onto Paul's face. He looked first at Martin and then at Jill. A moment passed and the smile disappeared. He got up from the table and walked the three paces towards where Martin was sitting. Martin didn't know what to expect and looked up. They were two feet apart. Paul stood there. Expressionless. He lunged downwards with his arms held out wide and embraced Martin in a hug. The hug lasted longer than either of the two men thought it would. They both closed their eyes. No words were exchanged. Paul then walked the few paces across to where Jill was sitting with a tear in her eye. Theatre ran in the family she thought to herself. Paul did the same thing to Jill as he had done to Martin.

"I'm going to want to know all about the book." He said into her ear. While he was embracing her. "I'm a writer myself you know." As he retreated he winked.

"I know." She said and winked back.

"Right." Said Paul. Turning to Greg. "You seem to be the one who's in command." He stepped towards Greg and felt the material of his cape.

"Nice bit of schmutter. What do we do now?"

"Thank-you Paul. At last someone has seen sense."

He looked at Ian and flicked his head to one side. Ian pressed a button on the remote control and a room plan appeared on the big screen. With a red laser pointer he outlined the perimeter of a large square that filled the screen. Inside the square were a number of other shapes and symbols.

"Some of you may have noticed that the room we are in," he gestured with his arm, "is, when all the blinds are closed an exact replica of the room upstairs. The tables you are sitting at are divided into quarters and each one of the legs is in fact a rather hefty hydraulic ram. The chairs, you'll notice now that I'm telling you are really quite comfortable aren't they? That's because they have been designed to hold the occupant in a certain position. No allowance for slouches. So we have the ability to raise or lower any member of the audience at will between the two spaces. I can see now," He nodded towards them all for agreement, "Yes I can see now that you are beginning to understand the fun we can have with this arrangement when used with this stuff." He picked up a can of Sleep.

"But I know what you're thinking. Tell me if you're not. You're thinking that this is one hell of an elaborate set up for one gig. Well a quick word of explanation. The owner here believes in magic. I, with a little help from my friends designed this elaborate set up so that the owner could indulge his beliefs." He waved a hand towards Ian again and after a brief pause the big screen zoomed into a smaller area. He flicked his red light pointer towards a black rectangle on one side.

"This is the stage. It too has a small circular hydraulic lift that enables the host, me in this case, to travel between the spaces." He moved the pointer three tables back from the stage and looked at Paul.

"This is where Mary is sitting, Paul. She is your responsibility and we'd like you two to deal with these two." He moved his pointer towards another circle three tables away. He gestured again towards Ian and a picture appeared. The woman with the bright red lipstick was sitting upright her chin on her chest and her black hair covering her eyes. Her companion was in a similar position opposite.

"You've had the briefing document." He stopped himself. "No you haven't have you." He looked at Jill and tutted and raised his palms questioning.

"Do you have a copy?" Jill shook her head, flustered.

"No. I don't." Jill looked across at Benson. Benson was examining his shoes.

"Paul." Continued Greg. "If you think you have the measure of our Mary there, she'll know all about her."

"We'll be fine." Said Paul. "Leave them to us."

Benson who up to this point had just kept quiet sitting opposite spoke up.

"Do you really think that's a good idea? She's a trained assassin and he's just a…" He struggled to find a word.

"Just a what?" Snarled Paul. "Just some overweight fantasist prick who's about to discover what it feels like to have his bollocks rearranged by a size eight loafer."

Half of the assembly raised their eyebrows. Most of the others smiled inwardly to themselves. Hedges couldn't help an audible grunt of amusement.

"That was unfair, Paul." Said Greg. "He's only a bit overweight. This is your job, Paul. OK. That's the end of it."

Greg pointed at the screen again with his pointer.

"Martin and Lady Sarah. You've had a run in with these two already. The black Chrysler was airlifted into Lanzarote on Monday. Only the Americans would do that. This in new info. This fellah has come out personally to oversee this. He is sitting in his car. His two oppos' are here." He pointed at the screen again at two men sitting in the same upright position their hands neatly folded in their laps and their chins on their chests.

"I'm fairly certain you can take the fight to them."

"Benson and Hedges. The Stan and Ollie of the trade. You lucky pair. These are your targets." Greg pointed at the two men dressed in black sitting at another table.

Hedges sat running his hands through his hair, his elbows on the table.

"Now everyone above thinks we are in a magic show." Greg continued. "All those people here are after Tom Gates also-known thirty years ago as David Crane. We need to hold off these people for as long as it takes for the meeting I mentioned earlier to take place, as I said, without actually getting killed ourselves. Don't ask me what the purpose of that meeting is because I don't know but I'll know when it has been completed. Apparently, so will all these other nasty people. You are decoys. They'll follow you because they think that you know the whereabouts of David Crane. You'll give them the impression that you do know."

Greg looked at his watch again.

"It gets dark quickly here. We have about an hour of daylight left to do this. Either way it will be done by nightfall."

There was a flurry of questions but Greg ignored them and pressed a button on his remote control. The metal safety rings slowly slid around the waists of everyone. Greg stepped onto a disk in the floor of the stage and pressed his remote control again.

32

"Katy," shouted David. "Can I do this?"

"Sure Mr. Gates. Go ahead. You be skipper."

"We need to get going," said Eamonn. "We've a rendezvous."

"He'll be fine." Said Katy.

"I know he will be."

"So what's the fuss?"

"Katy darling girl." Said Eamonn as he was making his way below down the companionway steps, "Could you just give that incredibly generous nature of yours a day off and tell him to just do as he is told. I'll be down below for a bit."

"We saw a huge old grey smoker heading out there." Called Nana as Eamonn disappeared.

"That'll be Garret." Eamonn's voice came from below. "He'll have to wait for us. Now come on let's get going."

They performed the manoeuvre of departing the birth in the marina as if they had been doing it all their lives. They made open water in only a few moments. Katy at the helm checked her position on the plotter and pressed the buttons that simultaneously hoisted the main and the foresail.

"Twelve knots dad." She shouted down. "We'll be at those coordinates in seventeen minutes. Straight up on a south westerly."

Eamonn reappeared at the companionway hatch and although it was the same Eamonn that had gone down below earlier it didn't look like it. He had attached a small rubber prosthetic nose and a donned a ragged haired brown wig. He was unrecognisable as the

Eamonn they knew. Katy and Nana's expressions told David that they'd seen this before.

"And who are we today dad?" Asked Katy.

Eamonn smirked.

"You know how I like to remain incognito sometimes." He said as he looked around him before glancing at his watch and returning to the lower deck. The wind was behind them and although they were speeding along all was relatively calm on deck.

"Let me know when you see anything." Shouted Eamon from below.

"What was that?" Asked David. "Does that happen a lot?"

"We're not sure if dad's not going a bit daft in his old age." Said Nana sounding more serious than David thought she would. They didn't have to wait long before a grey steel ship came into view in the fading evening light.

"That big grey smoker dead ahead dad. They look like they're waiting."

Eamonn was up on deck again. A faint smile was obvious on his face.

"Gather round crew." Said Eamonn. "Here's what I'd like to happen. Head straight for the target under full sail." He pointed quickly towards the grey ship.

"Two hundred foot away after they have got panicky on the radio, tack hard to port, then immediately hard to starboard and drift alongside. Do not under any circumstances collide with a Spanish navy vessel otherwise a diplomatic incident that has had no preplanning whatsoever will ensue and we will be properly in the shit."

"That's what we did to win the Cowes race Dad. That should be a breeze." Said Nana.

"That was three years ago in a forty footer." Said Katy.

David wasn't sure what they were talking about. He was looking at his arms and trying to work out the port and starboard thing. He hoped no one would notice but Katy, ever the schoolmistress, never missed.

"Don't worry Mr. Gates. It takes a while. Take the forward winch and I'll tell you what to do. They may look a long way away but they're not. I reckon we've got three minutes."

Katy wasn't far wrong. Down below, the radio, which Eamonn had directed into the cockpit speakers calmly began to transmit a message. The radio operator's accent sounded like it was from Liverpool.

"What's Paul McCartney doing on the radio?" Said Katy.

"Yacht Babydove, yacht Babydove, yacht Babydove. This is SNV Relampago. Switch to channel 39 and respond. Over."

Eamonn who was up in the cockpit now shook his head in response to the silent question from the other three that said, 'Shouldn't we answer?'

As Eamonn predicted the radio operators voice grew slightly more frantic as evidenced by the rise in pitch. This, despite the seriousness of the situation made everyone smile.

"Yacht Babydove, yacht Babydove, yacht Babydove. This is SNV Relampago. Switch to channel 39 and respond. Over."

"Dad?" Said Nana nervously.

"Yacht babydove, please alter your course. We are a large vessel and as such find it difficult to manoeuvre." Said the Liverpudlian.

"Yeah right." Said Eamonn. "With the engines in that thing they can go wherever they want. Ready about." He shouted.

"Ready," Katy and Nana shouted in unison. David manned his button mouthing the word slightly behind the girls.

Katy pulled the wheel hard down with her left hand.

They performed two more tacks one after the other and presently with little commotion but a great deal of nervousness on David's part gently drifted into a position twenty feet away but alongside the matt grey painted ship whose deck was a full thirty feet higher than the deck of the Babydove.

"We regard your conduct to have been reckless." The same Liverpudlian voice came from the loud hailers of the boat. Four uniformed young seamen, two holding coiled sheets stood to attention along the deck. A slightly more elaborately decorated and older man appeared from a double sliding door on the side of the ship and then Roland Garret stepped into view still dressed in his black dinner jacket.

From the deck of the Babydove Eamonn nodded an unspoken command towards Katy and she calmly stepped down below.

Roland Garret took the little handset that was at the end of a coiled wire from the hand of the man in the uniform. Without any elaborate introduction he pressed the button on the handset and spoke into it.

"I have reason to believe that you are harbouring a fugitive from British Justice."

Eamonn moved to behind David Crane. He whispered into his ear.

"Just stand on the side deck there. By the jack stay."

David turned quizzically towards Eamonn.

"What are we going to do?"

"Trust me." Said Eamonn and grabbed David's elbow.

"Mr. David Crane." Said Garret through the loud hailer. "Will you please make yourself known to us."

A weird voice came from Eamonn as he tightened his grip on David's arm. A pair of handcuffs appeared from nowhere and were deftly clipped around David's wrists. David had no time to struggle.

"You bastard." He whispered into Eamonn's ear.

"I think this be the man you be lookin' for Sir." Said Eamonn in a silly voice. "Drop down your gangplank and he'll be yours for the takin'."

David could hardly believe his ears. Open mouthed he attempted to catch Eamonn's eye but Eamonn was having none of it. He pushed David hard towards the gunwale. The boats had been drifting closer together. The opening on the side of the hull of the Navy ship was three feet higher than the deck of the Babydove and six feet away. Two crewmen dressed in white lowered a gangplank. It scraped around on the deck of the Babydove as the two big boats bobbed about on the water. Eamonn pushed David up towards the gangplank. The uniformed Spanish Naval officer and Roland Garret were watching in a detached governing manner. Eamonn made another push and David stepped up onto the wobbly gangplank. No-one noticed Eamonn turn his head slightly while looking Garret directly in the eye. Eamonn was holding onto David tightly. He appeared to be waiting for something. Garret picked out his own mobile phone from the inside breast pocket of this dinner suit and tapped the surface a few times. Seconds later Eamonn felt a vibration come from his own phone that was tucked into his trouser pocket. He let go of his grip on David. As soon as he felt

Eamonn relax his grip, David lunged towards Eamonn but as if anticipating the move Eamonn stepped deftly backwards. David missed him completely and fell for the third time into the Atlantic Ocean. The cold water paralysed him and he sank downwards quickly as if he were being pulled. It was close. Too close he later thought. He was about to give up. Give up this stupid fight. Let them win. Then he had the feeling of being pulled downwards. In fact he was beginning to charge through the water. He could make out the hulls of the two boats above him. The Babydove dwarfed by the vast grey ship. Seconds later an arm held him from behind and a mouthpiece of an aqualung was thrust into his mouth. His eyes had by reflex become tightly shut and as he tried to open them he saw nothing. The water was clear but the light had faded to the extent he couldn't see a thing.

He automatically started inhaling and exhaling into the mouthpiece of the aqualung. He really wasn't trying to work out if he was alive or dead. If this was real or a dream.

His hands were suddenly free except one of his arms was being dragged away again. He could feel a vibration coming from the now cut handcuff. His other hand was pushing the mouthpiece of the aqualung into his mouth. He could feel a metal bottle of air banging at his legs as he was drawn along. His ordeal continued for three minutes or more. The thought that stopped him from letting go, and for a moment or two he really wanted to let go, let go of everything, was that he was not alone. Someone was doing this. Someone was helping him. The dragging stopped and he was drifting. He was impressed with himself suddenly. Perhaps he would survive. His breathing was regular. He felt a hand on his shoulder. He didn't jump. Nothing was going to scare him now. He felt a rubber band being pushed down over his head. He instinctively held his head down and displaced the water with air before pulling the face-mask over his eyes. He looked around trying to work out what was happening. He could see a dim yellow light some distance away, he couldn't tell how far. Then a moment of shock. It was as if he was looking into his own eyes. Katy was treading water in front of him holding up her thumbs. David nodded and did the same. She strapped the oxygen cylinder to him then grabbed him tightly before yanking smartly on the cord that had been pulling him along before. This time as two they sped through the water. It wasn't long before the temperature of the water increased.

33

With the slightest hiss, Paul, secured by the thin chrome ring around his waist rose up through the ceiling and emerged back seated next to Mary who was fast asleep.

He couldn't help but smile. The thin metal ring that served as the seatbelt retracted into the seat. He was seated at a quarter of a table and chair section. He could see now how the table could be split into four quarters. Each a quarter of a table and chair section on its own.

The three other quarter sections had remained on the upper floor. The lights were slowly getting brighter. The other tables all rose slowly to their original positions. Greg appeared in his cape.

"Ladies and Gentlemen." He said without the entertainers flourish and without the aid of the amplifier as the main doors to the room opened.

"Just as we rehearsed Ok? The waiters will be in in three minutes." He pointed at Paul and covered his face slowly with a black theatrical sad face mask mounted on a short stick. Paul picked up the aluminium can marked 'WAKE' and sprayed it in the direction of the sleeping, very slightly snoring, Mary. Nothing appeared to happen. Mary didn't stir. The rest of the room were looking on despite Greg telling them to act unconcerned. Paul turned his head ninety degrees towards Greg and dropped his head as if he was looking over the top of reading glasses and slightly shrugged his shoulders. Greg twisted the mask slightly away from his face revealing an outwardly calm expression betrayed by ever so slightly flaring nostrils and bored eyelids. He lifted an arm and mimed pressing the top of an aerosol can. He leaned forward and held his finger down over the top of his hand as he closed his eyes for three seconds. Paul watched him and nodded in understanding. He pointed the aerosol can at Mary's face again and pressed down the button on the top this time as if he was spraying insect repellent. Mary's eyes flicked open without any other part of her body moving from the rigid position that it had been held in by the high backed chair. She took in the surroundings in a half second flat but made no unconsidered move. She moved her head to the left as far as it would go then panned right.

"What's going on Paul?" She said under her breath and without her lips moving.

"We are at a magic show." Said Paul. The others were just beginning to talk among themselves but Mary felt like she had a spotlight on her.

"Why are those people asleep?" She said, still calmly but with a tinge of anxiety. "And what are those." She nodded towards the little aluminium cans on the table.

"I'm going to have to be quick." Said Paul, his voice a hushed whisper. "They've been drugged." he said lifting the can with the word 'sleep' on the side, "With this." Mary nodded in apparent understanding.

"So they managed to do it." She said. "Did it work?"

"Seems to have done." Said Paul. "You've all been asleep for twenty minutes or more. We've been down there," He pointed to the floor.

Mary looked slowly round the room at the various guests. None of them now were looking over at her. There were still three tables where the occupants were fast asleep.

"What do you mean, they've managed to do it?" Then he thought better of it. "No never mind. Later."

"If everyone knows who everyone else is, why aren't they gunning for me?"

"I've convinced them that you are on our side. That you could help us."

"What makes you think that?"

"Because you are and you can."

"I'm not on anyone's side, Paul."

"So what? I was wrong to say that was I? Does that mean you won't help?"

"I didn't say that either. What do we have to do?" Paul detected a tiny bit of capitulation. *You've just got to do it her way* he thought to himself. He didn't wait. He had an inkling that she'd like what he was going to say next.

"See that woman over there with the jet black hair." Paul nodded across the room. Mary looked over and slightly raised her eyes.

"What?" He said.

"Nothing." She said shaking her head. "Go on."

"She's a deadly Lithuanian assassin sent here to get to David Crane through me. We have to lead her and her sidekick a merry dance until they get the word to stop. That is after we've woken them up." He picked up a can of Wake and shook it.

"Who told you that, Paul?"

"He did." Said Paul, pointing towards the stage. Greg had gone.

"You remember. The chap with the fancy clothes and two tone shoes." Mary was nodding.

"Yes. You knew him didn't you? When he walked onto the terrace yesterday?"

Mary ignored his question.

"Paul. Shes not Lithuanian. Her name is Sharon and she comes from Essex. You can practically smell the botox. Her MO is standard honey trap but if you ask me she is well past her sell-by. We've worked together. She's cheap. All I'll need to do is pay her a bit of cash. Don't worry leave it to me. Is that all we've got to do?"

Mary picked up the can of Wake. She looked around again and this time clocked some swift turning of heads.

"They are waiting for us." Said Paul. "As soon as we start they start." Mary looked over towards Benson and Hedges.

"Are they supposed to be looking after anyone?"

"The big fat chap and the skinny fellah all dressed in black."

"Those two are pros." She said. "I hope they know what they're letting themselves in for. Come on. Let's get this over with." Mary slid around the leather seats with the can of Wake in her hand. Paul slid around the other way. She brushed down her skirt then turned back towards Paul.

"It's OK Paul. I'll handle it. You wait here." Paul slid back onto the leather seat to watch the show and wondered if the waiters would be in soon. As if to answer his unspoken question, waiters started appearing from the main doors. The room went back to what it had been like before the start of Greg's performance. Mary had slid around the table and was sitting very close to the woman with the jet-black hair.

Benson, anxious to get on with proceedings, was pushing himself up from the table seconds after he saw Mary walk over to the woman with the jet black hair.

"Wait." Said Hedges. "We need to…" But it was too late. Benson picked up two of the four aerosol cans sitting on the table and walked directly over where the two men, who were their targets, were sitting, heads dropped to one side, fast asleep.

"Benson." Hissed Hedges as he too rose from the table.

"We need to have a plan." Benson sprayed the aerosol directly into the faces of the two sleeping men. He then stepped around to the front of the table put the cans in his pockets and waited. The two men gradually woke. It was is if they had been in a long and deep sleep. The bigger of the two men stretched like a bear and yawned. The skinny one seemed to recover his faculties a little faster. He was obviously very confused. All the more so when Benson waved at him, a little wave consisting of four side to side movements of his open palm.

"Hello again." He said and as he did so walked briskly to the double doors. Hedges was peering through the crack in the door.

"Why did you do that?" Hedges asked calmly. "What's the plan now? You really didn't think that through did you?"

"I haven't a clue." Said Benson. The two men were gathering their thoughts together and trying to figure out what had just happened and what was going on.

"I've got an idea." Said Hedges. "Go out front and try and find us some transport. I'll be buggered if I'm running around in this heat. Make sure the engine is running. I'll keep them in the dark for as long as I can. As soon as they see me they'll be after me. We really should have thought about this before we woke the buggers up." Said Hedges

"I agree." Said Benson. "But we didn't."

"No Benny. You didn't." Said Hedges.

"Go on. Let's see how good you are." Hedges turned back to look through the crack. Benson strolled away towards the main entrance. Hedges casually looked behind him to see Benson slowly walking away from him as if he were on a Sunday stroll.

"Oy." He hissed again towards Benson. Benson turned back with a questioning look on his face. Hedges held his palms out towards him.

"Don't spare the fucking horses man." He hissed again giving him a shooing motion. Finally Benson broke into a trot. Hedges turned back to look through the crack of the door. The two men were obviously agitated but also seemed bemused and disorientated. Without a warning Mary had sidled over to where the two men were sitting. This had the effect of making them appear even more confused. She offered her red finger-nailed hand to them which they both gingerly shook in turn. Hedges glanced over to Paul who had a distinctly anxious look on his face. The woman with the jet black hair was bizarrely sipping from a cocktail glass that a waiter had brought to her table. Her companion was still asleep. Hedges couldn't see the state of the American operatives from his vantage point but he could see Martin. Sarah was not at the table. Where the hell was she? He thought. He surveyed the scene for a minute. He was glad for Mary as he couldn't think of what he would have done if they'd have got up straight away and chased him. It would have been a proper fist fight in the dining room and he'd be sure that Benson wouldn't be getting himself involved in that.

"Boo." Said a voice behind Hedges. Hedges jumped a foot in the air and turned to see Sarah standing there.

"Looks like you got a bit previous. And you two being the pros and all." She was smirking. *Does everybody think this is a game?* Thought Hedges to himself.

"Your chum Benny told me to tell you he's ready when you are." She flicked her head towards the open front entrance perhaps thirty meters away.

"Thanks." He said. "You scared the… you scared the life out me." Sarah turned and walked back through the double doors into the dining room mouthing the word 'Sorry'.

Hedges turned back to look through the door jamb. Mary was still there in front of the skinny man and his hefty sidekick. He watched as the skinny man shook his head with a disgusted expression formed from only his nose and mouth.

He looked as if he'd smelt something bad. Both the men dressed in black got up from the table. Hedges turned and ran towards the entrance. It took a moment for his eyes to adjust to the evening daylight. A glance backwards and he could see the two men appear from the double doors of the dining room. Hedges heard Benson calling him anxiously.

"Hedge mate… Over here." Hedges was standing waiting for him fifty feet or so away on a machine that he'd only ever seen before in pictures. An off road Segway. As Hedges ran towards him he shouted.

"Benson. You are an idiot. I am never going to…"

The loud crack of a gun being discharged went off behind him.

"I didn't know they'd have guns." He shouted out loud to himself.

"No-one told us they'd have guns." He ran faster towards where Benson had started to move slowly forward on his machine.

"I said get us some transport." Shouted Hedges.

"I did," Said Benson moving his feet apart on the aluminium platform between the two fat wheels. The two men, even the larger one were surprisingly agile and appeared to be keeping up. Hedges wasn't slow either and he was running alongside Benson when another shot rang out.

"You're going to have to hop on old boy."

"We'll crash and burn and then they'll shoot us."

"No we won't. Just jump on."

Hedges was angry frightened and tiring. He quickly weighed up his options. There appeared only to be one of these and that was to jump on the machine. He grabbed Benson's shoulder. This had the effect of pulling Benson slightly backwards. The machine sensed this movement and slowed quite suddenly. Benson compensated for this by moving his weight forward. The machine took this as an instruction to increase speed. This oscillation continued through several cycles. During which time they heard another crack from the gun.

"You are going to have to bite the bullet mate." Shouted Benson as he drove the machine along the dirt pathway formed by a multitude of walkers over the years.

"Just jump on and grab hold of me. Let me drive. Hold me as tight as you can and just move with me." Hedges wasn't sure but a bullet seemed to ricochet on the handlebar of the Segway followed quickly by the now familiar cracking sound. *They are either not very good shots,* he reasoned with himself *and I'm still alive because of that or they are very good and they don't actually want to hit us. Why have they got guns?* He thought. His mind went back to what Greg had said and he remembered the little cans of sleep Greg had given him.

"We need to get away." Shouted Benson. "Now."

The thought of grabbing hold of Benson and putting his life in Bensons hands did not sit squarely with him, neither did the thought of having to get too close to that flabby body but there was no choice. Now or never. While running at full tilt he looked down at the eight-inch square platform of ridged aluminium between Benson's feet that he had to jump onto. He lined himself up directly behind Benson running at a frantic pace. Another crack from the pistol was the motivation he needed and he skipped up onto the plate and wrapped his arms around Hedges' bulk. The immediate effect was to push the weight of the load forward. A Segway is designed to take the weight of one person. It would be true to say that that could vary considerably but the Segway is controlled by microprocessors. Microprocessors, despite appearing to be able to think still as yet can't. So there are upper and lower limits programmed into them which define the weight of a human being. The combined weight of Benson and Hedges exceeded the upper limit. So the machine accelerated to its maximum output. The high tech electric motors that drive the wheels are very efficient but the torque required to instantly do this was beyond their operating parameters so they gradually over a period of three seconds reached maximum speed. The terrain directly around the hotel was unfamiliar to both Benson and Hedges so it was by far more a matter of fortune than judgement that the path they chose to follow did indeed lead to the high road that travelled along the cliff top.

They emerged much to their relief from a worn dusty pathway through a lightly forested area onto a black tarmac strip. Hedges leant slightly backwards and slowed. Hedges relaxed his grip slowly and carefully. For the first time they seemed to be moving in the direction they wanted to go and in a relative state of equilibrium. They were both pulled violently out of their state of calm after the storm by a 1965 red Ferrari Dino drop-head passing them doing what must have been in excess of a hundred miles per hour. No sooner had they recovered from the back and forward oscillation initiated by the shock wave that the little relatively aerodynamic Ferrari produced, it started all over again except really rather more violently as a much less aerodynamic black Chrysler Voyager went screaming by them apparently in hot pursuit.

After they had rocked back and forth several times for the second time and the two cars had roared off into the distance. The low volume whirring sound of the electric motors in the wheels of the Segway, the sound of the fat tyres rotating against tarmac warmed by the evening sun and a gentle breeze floating in from the sea were the only sounds that Benson and Hedges could hear except of course for the nagging sound of a single pot 500 cc four stroke petrol engine so often found as the power unit of choice on motorbikes built for trials through mud and rocks, in the distance. It wasn't that far distant though and was getting louder and louder behind them. They could both hear it.

"How come Benny," Said Hedges into Bensons ear, "They can, as if by magic get their hands on a trials bike and we are, like a couple of amateurs are twos up on a fucking teenagers toy?"

"I'll have you know that Segways are…"

Hedges stopped him short.

"I don't care Benny. You make stupid judgement calls and one of these days they are going to be our downfall."

The sound of the trials bike was getting closer. Hedges knew they couldn't outrun them. He pointed to a trodden down track that led back down off the road through the trees.

"Pull over there," He shouted in Benson's ear and Benson complied without a word to Hedges' surprise. Hedges looked behind him to the road as they dropped down from the tarmac ribbon on to the dirt again and pointed at an exact spot.

"Stop there." He commanded. Benson did as he was told and as the machine came to a stop they both stepped off.

"I've got no idea what you think this will achieve," said Benson as he surveyed the road. They were standing just yards from dense undergrowth. Hedges stuck his finger in his mouth and held it briefly in the air.

"I'm sorry mate." Said Hedges. The sound of the motorbike was getting ever closer.

"Sorry for what?" Said Benson as he turned around to face a spray from a little aluminium canister. Benson flopped to the ground. Hedges flipped the Segway onto its side next to him and swiftly went through Benson's pockets and pulled out four more little aluminium cans. He made no attempt of disguising his tracks through the dust into the trees. Within a few seconds the mid tone drone of the engine working at its long stroke high torque low rev high power full speed dropped first to a recurring asthmatic back cough to a putt putt putt of the engine idling. Hedges stood still behind the first tree he had come to. He tried to remain as still and as silent as he could. He could see both the men. The larger of the two was driving. Which surprised him. He had underestimated the big lad. But then he reasoned, in this game you don't want to be carrying passengers. Everyone has a skill at something. He looked at Benson. Fast asleep in the dust by the Segway. They were alike, he found himself thinking. That man and that machine. More form than function. More promise than delivery. More style than substance. He flicked his head back into the moment. He couldn't think of a sentence in which the words style and Benson could be used except...

'Stop.' He almost said out loud. But fortunately didn't. The big lad who he'd thrown the dart at in the hospital, god it seemed like months ago, had silently been given the job of standing over Benson. *Please don't wake you oaf.* He said to himself. He could see a gun held nonchalantly downwards. God though it was a gun. The skinny bloke, gun drawn, was following the tracks towards the trees. Stepping carefully, but as Hedges noted not that carefully toward him. He thought again about what Greg had said. About power and control. This man thinks that because he has the power, he has a lethal weapon and is prepared to use it, he has control. But does he have the power? Hedges once again stuck his finger in his mouth and held it in the air. There is not a time or place on the Canary Islands when a wind of some description is not blowing. In comparison to the average wind speed of the Island, today was a very, very calm day. But the air was moving all the same. The skinny man was warily making his way down the dirt path following the tracks that Hedges had made. Hedges held his two cans of sleep up into the warm breeze that was travelling in the direction of the skinny man. He pressed the buttons and the contents of the cans wafted towards the skinny man. The effect was almost immediate and better than Hedges imagined it would be. He watched as the skinny man's eyelids blinked slowly three times before closing and then his knees buckled under him and he slumped to the floor just as Benson had done. He could see through the trees that the big fellah saw his comrade fall and that he was going through the process of making a decision about what to do about it. Obviously fearing that history was going to repeat itself he looked first at the idling motorcycle on its side stand and then at his comrade lying fast asleep in the dust. He waved his gun in the direction of first one then the other as if this would help him decide. Moments passed and he decided on his next course of action. In an accent that Hedges could not quite put his finger on, somewhere between Welsh and South African, the big fellah pointing his gun directly at Benson lying on the ground, shouted towards the undergrowth where his friend was lying.

"Come out with your hands up or I shoot your friend."

Just for a brief moment Hedges mind wondered. He wanted to shout back 'where' and call the fellah's bluff but he didn't. No it was his turn to wonder what to do next. He considered squirting some more sleep into the air and letting the breeze take it across to the big lad but ruled it out thinking that the distance would be too big and the stuff would become too dilute by the time it got to him to have any effect. He raised his hands slowly above his head and stepped out from his hiding place behind a tree.

"Don't shoot," he called lamely, thinking that it was unlikely anyway that the fellah would. *But you never know* he said to himself. After last time he'll be doubly cautious. Hedges could see him now. He was standing astride Benson as if pinning him down but he wasn't pinning him down. Benson was lying on his back snoring like a hog. Hedges could see that the big fellah was unsure of exactly what to do next but got back to his job.

"You know where Crane is? We have no interest in you or your friend. We are here just for Crane."

Still stepping ever closer to the big fellah and with his hands still raised above his head Hedges said,

"Hey listen. Sorry about the other day in the hospital."

"I owe you for that." Said the big fellah with a renewed anger in his voice.

"I should just shoot you both now."

Hedges edged further towards him.

"Just stop right there." He said, waving the gun. He looked this time as if he were more confident. "Where is Crane? You tell me now or I shoot your friend."

"Ok." Said Hedges holding up the palms of his hands.

"Ok."

Just as he thought he'd run completely out of options he stepped a pace backwards and a grin slowly crept across his face. The big fellah kept his position and slowly shook his head.

"Stay exactly where you are or I shoot."

Hedges looked over the man's shoulder and nodded his head slightly in some unspoken agreement.

"You think I fall for that?" Said the big fellah.

Hedges shrugged but kept looking over the big fellah's shoulder.

"I was born at night." Said the big fellah. "But it wasn't last night."

"Where have I heard that before?" Said Hedges as Ian deftly grabbed the man's hand that was holding the gun and sprayed a good amount of Sleep into his face. Ian helped the big fellah sink slowly to the ground next to Benson.

"I heard the shots." Said Ian. "Thought you might need some help. You know you just went round in a big circle. The hotel is just there." He pointed through the bushes. "What shall we do with these two?"

"I don't know." Said Hedges as he bent down and picked up the pistol. He threw it into the undergrowth then went back and picked up the gun the skinny fellah had in his hand. He threw that too into the bushes. He went back and looked down at Benson.

"He could of got us killed."

"He could have." Ian agreed. "But he didn't."

A tinkling sound came from the inside of the big man's jacket. Hedges leant down and picked out a mobile phone. The phone was an older model with a small screen the size of a big stamp. The text message on the screen was in a foreign language. Hedges shook his head and handed the phone to Ian.

"I've no idea what that says. You any clue?" He said. Ian took the phone and looked at the text. He too shook his head.

"No. But give me just a moment." He said as he pulled his own smart phone from his pocket and started tapping at the screen.

"I'm tempted to just leave him there to sleep." Said Hedges, nodding down towards Benson. "He's less of a liability."

"It's Romanian." Said Ian looking at the screen on his phone. "It says *Mission Aborted*" He too looked down at Benson before walking towards the still idling trials bike. "I've got one can of this." He held up a can of Wake as he grabbed the handle-bar of the trials bike and swung his leg over the saddle. He tossed the can towards Hedges. Hedges looked at the can for a moment and then down at Benson.

Then he stepped over towards Ian sitting on the trials bike, put a hand on his shoulder and swung onto the pillion. Ian pulled in the clutch lever, kicked up the stand, tapped it into gear with his foot and they roared off in the cloud of grey dust.

34

"There's four more bundles up there." Said Martin as he climbed down the loft ladder holding a stack of magazines wrapped in polythene and taped up with parcel tape. He took them through into the kitchen where Sarah was sitting at a heavy wooden refectory table, turning the pages of a Private Eye magazine. A small pile unexamined on her right and a taller pile that she'd carefully scrutinised on her left.

"I think these are too early." She said as she continued to carefully flick through the pages.

"These all seem to date from the late seventies. Look, do you remember this?" She held up the magazine she was examining and turned the cover to face Martin. It was a picture of Lord Lucan. "Do you recognise this?" She asked.

"No." Said Martin. "Should I?"

Sarah shook her head.

"No." She said with an absent mind. "Not really. Lord Lucan killed his children's nanny mistaking her for his wife. He mysteriously disappeared the night it happened. He was never seen again. He was apparently helped to run away by his rich London socialite buddies. It's always the same. One rule for them and one rule for us."

Martin pulled the second bundle of magazines up onto the table.

"I remember now. It was never proved he did it though." He said, his tone just slightly annoyed.

"No." Said Sarah, looking at him with questioning eyes. "It never was."

When she'd finished looking at the first bundle, she pulled the second towards her and pulled at the packing tape. She took out the top magazine.

"This is more like it." She said looking at the date in the top left hand corner.

"December 2nd 1983." She read out loud. "This is about a year before that boat was caught."

Martin turned around and trudged back towards where the loft ladder was sticking out of the ceiling leaving Sarah looking at the magazine. She'd turned it over and was examining the back page. He was half way up the ladder again when Sarah called up in her police voice.

"Martin. Come and see this."

Martin stepped back down the ladder. Sarah was at the table gazing at the open magazine. A white piece of paper was sitting on top. She had involuntarily taken a slight push back on her chair and her face was lit up with excitement that belied her voice.

"What have you got?" Said Martin. "You look like you've lost a penny and found a pound."

Sarah pushed the magazine carefully away from her before reaching onto the newly opened pile, grabbing another and turning to the back pages. Another piece of white paper appeared. Sarah was shaking with excitement.

"But they're just bits of paper Sarah. If there was something written on them it's not written on them anymore."

Ignoring what he was saying, Sarah looked around her.

"Do you think he'd have a sun lamp or something like that in here anywhere?"

"Why?" Said Martin.

"These are fax messages. We don't see them anymore but the same thermal paper is still used in receipt printers and credit card machines. The chemical reaction caused by heat that creates the black printed impression degrades over time. Quite a short period of time actually. But the impression can still be seen under ultra violet light. A sun lamp or one of those disco tubes that made your teeth go white."

Martin had perched himself on the edge of the table. He had moderated his breathing purposely so that he remained calm.

"I know you are a woman of the police species," he said. Sarah's jowls dropped and stayed dropped a moment as she shook her head.

"But," Martin continued, "tell me just why you would know that?"

"Martin." Said Sarah, obviously irritated and gathering her thoughts.

"Martin. We've had a nice time over the last week. I can't say I haven't but you're not the only one in this room with a brain and if you are going to treat me like a moron you can..."

She was stopped in mid-sentence.

"I'm sorry." He shouted. They were silent for a moment. Martin was the first to speak.

"How do you know about that stuff with the printer paper?"

Sarah considered her options. He didn't appear to have listened to her. But he still had something she didn't want to lose.

"I know this because when I used to file expenses claims half the receipts had faded away. The bean counters cut those out of the payment. Being the champion of justice that I am I fought them tooth and nail for the fourteen quid that it amounted to. I got forensics to help me out. Fact was it was simple. Ultra-violet light brings out the original like it had been written in lemon juice. So get me a sun lamp and we'll get to the bottom of this stuff."

Martin looked at her intensely. Sarah held his gaze.

Martin broke first and walked to the window behind Sarah and twisted the slim aluminium pole that closed the venetian blind. He took his phone from his pocket and flicked upwards on the screen. Bright light emanated from the back of the phone. He tapped the front a few more times and the colour of the light changed. He smiled at Sarah.

"What can you see now?" He said calmly.

Sarah stared at him, a smile creeping across her face.

"Something much more interesting." She said. "What kind of man has a phone with an ultra-violet light on it?"

"A man like me." He said. "It's a 20 dollar Chinese fix. I got it off eBay."

Martin nodded towards the white piece of paper and Sarah looked too. Lines of letters and numbers filled the page.

35

"Good morning Mister Garret Sir. Lovely to see you again." Said Greg as he sat down next to Roland Garret on the Thames Clipper. Unusually for Greg he was dressed in a plain grey suit that didn't even seem to fit him too well. Today, Greg wanted to just blend in. He didn't want to be noticed.

"God." Said Greg quietly after a moment or two. "I just had a pang of Deja Vu. Do you get that? You know, when you think you've been somewhere before. Like in another life."

Roland Garret had no choice but to grin and bear it.

The Thames Clipper was half full. They were on the eleven fifteen shuttle from Westminster pier. Greg had followed Garret on to the boat. Garret was visible angry. His face was reddening and his expression wasn't attempting to hide his mood. As Greg spoke he twisted a smart phone between his fingers in front of him.

"Where's Starr." Said Garret ignoring the phone.

"He's asked me to let you know that he won't be around much anymore." They reached the London Eye dock and the boat cleared of passengers. Greg's voice lowered.

"Are we going to be a good boy now and sit there very quietly while Gregory tells you what to do next?"

"I don't have to listen to this." Said Garret as he tried to rise from his seat.

"You do." Said Greg as with a sleight of hand the smart phone changed into a tiny silver data stick. This time Garret paid attention.

"What the fuck is that?" He said.

"It's a memory stick." Said Greg. Garret immediately made a grab for it. Greg did not try to stop him.

"So now you have it." Said Greg. "It's all there this time." Garret was on his feet again and was stepping over Greg towards the aisle. Greg held up the phone again.

"I just have to press this button here," Said Greg. "It'll send a text to all your friends saying you don't want to talk to me."

Garret still didn't listen. The boat was crossing the river towards the embankment pier. A short queue of people had formed in the aisle waiting to get off. Garret stood waiting there obviously fuming. Greg made a show of dialling a number on the phone. After a few seconds he started to speak into it.

"No. He wouldn't listen. No not yet. Thought I'd just ring and make sure. Yes I told him. No he didn't seem to care. Yep. I didn't get a chance."

"Ok, ok," said Garret and reluctantly and angrily sat down again.

"Oh. Look. Got to go. He's just seen the light." Said Greg into the phone.

"This had better be good." Said Garret.

"Oh don't worry about that. It is. Can you swim?"

"What kind of question is that? I'm over seventy years old. Do you think I'm about to go jumping into the water or something at my age?"

"That's exactly what you are going to do."

"I don't know what Starr is up to but please get to the point so I can go home."

"I suppose that is the point Roland. You don't mind me calling you Roland do you?" Garret didn't answer.

"I'll take that as a yes. Yes. That is the point Roland. You aren't ever going home." Greg pulled four sheets of white paper that had been folded into thirds from the inside pocket of his cheap grey suit.

"There's a certain irony here." Said Greg. "That stick you've got. That tiny little thing that holds so many secrets. It's only got about half the enquiry transcripts on it. Not that that should concern you really because you are hardly mentioned. Not just in that bit but the whole report. It hardly mentions you. How funny is that? You did a good deal at the time Roland. Got to give you that."

Roland was staring straight ahead. He had gone quiet.

He looked to be doing some complicated mental arithmetic involving negative numbers. Greg continued.

"Now, better than that but if none of this had happened, the record alteration stuff I mean," he winked a theatrical wink which Garret still staring resolutely forward ignored, "If none of that had happened the report would have surfaced and the one man whose life would have changed dramatically for the second time would have been, drum roll for effect," Greg tapped his fingers on the arm rest, "your friend and mine David Crane AKA Thomas Gates AKA your scapegoat." Greg emphasised the last two words by slightly raising his voice and slowing down on the delivery. He was looking to see if there'd be a reaction from Garret. There was no discernible movement of his body except he was blinking more slowly than before.

"Crane drowned." Said Garret. "In the Canaries. I witnessed it myself."

"Yeah. That's right. Crane is dead. So this whole thing should just go away. Right?"

"Right." Said Garret. "So why are you harassing me?"

"I'm not harassing you Roland, I'm helping you stay alive." Greg was now tapping the papers he had been holding on his knee.

"For pities sake man. Enough of the fucking playacting. Just tell me what you got." Said Garret. Greg was jogged out of his performance. Garret was right. He was revelling in his discomfort and that wasn't strictly playing the game.

"I'm sorry." Said Greg. He suddenly sounded like a different person. "I've overstepped the mark. You're right. I'm just the messenger." They were passing under Blackfriars Road Bridge.

"Blackfriars." He said. "Look. These papers." He unfolded the sheets of white paper and waved them in the general direction of Garrets fixed stare. "I'm sure you know but they are copies of original messages you sent to peoples various about twenty-nine years ago. To be decoded in the small ads in Private Eye. Now although we are fairly certain that they'd have difficulty standing up to a British court of law with all its liberal get out clauses for," He paused. "No I'll say it. For people like you. We are absolutely certain that presented with this evidence your countrymen will not think kindly of your actions."

Garret lifted a finger that stopped Greg talking.

"Who's 'we'." He asked.

Greg thought for a moment. This was a question he hadn't anticipated.

"David Crane, Eamonn Boothe, their respective families and me."

"Why are you so interested?"

"That's not important." Said Greg. "Let's just say I believe I have an understanding of the difference between right and wrong and that these are difficult concepts for both small children and powerful men."

"You pathetic little prick." Said Garret. "You know nothing."

"I was beginning to have pangs of regret. You know, self-doubt." Said Greg. "But I don't anymore. Listen. It's like this." He looked carefully at his watch. "I'm not even sure why they are going to all this trouble to keep you alive. If it were up to me I'd just let your old mates have you or I'd lie to you about there being divers in the water. We just went under Blackfriars Bridge. This boat will turn at Canary Wharf and make a return journey and travel between the first and second pontoons on that side."

Greg pointed at the bridge. "As it does so you'll be standing on the rear deck and you'll jump overboard. Just let yourself sink down." There was no more theatrical asides from Greg.

"And you think I'm going to do that do you?"

Greg touched the face of his smart phone.

"Yes I do but don't worry." He said pointing out towards the Thames.

"This way, you'll not actually die. That is unless the divers that are waiting for you in the water either fail to pick you up or are indeed not there at all." He held up the phone so that Garret could see it.

"My next meeting will be with this fellah." Garrets face went pale.

"Now you'll be knowin' who he is now won't you." Said Greg in his best northern Irish accent.

"This way." He wagged the white papers in front of Garrets face. Garret could clearly see the decoded messages. "This way. You will."

They passed under Blackfriars bridge. A Starr Media outside broadcast van was parked on top.

36

In the Green Room of a television studio in north London, Ian Whitting paced nervously up and down by a table laid with refreshments. He was booked to be a guest on the Charley Westbrook Chat show, an hour long show that airs live at primetime on Saturday nights. Half an hour previously the room had been occupied by two middle aged, well dressed men with American accents and a young woman wearing a hugely revealing dress and the highest heels Ian had ever seen. Still in the room and presumably waiting to perform were a group of seven young lads who were in a boyband. They didn't look nervous at all but Ian was almost visibly shaking. He hadn't bargained for these nerves.

Jill had just come into the room despite the protestations of an assistant director. She had tried to calm him down and was now sitting calmly herself on a big sofa leafing through a copy of Hello magazine. Ian had clocked most of the young lads. He'd made a snap decision about each of them. One of the lads approached him and he questioned himself briefly. He'd missed this one. He made his assumptions quickly. No brains, No talent just a good looking young lad. As they all were. His friends were giggling. Ian made yet another mental note to try to stop doing this. When he was actually in the army and was under the greatest of strains in combat or enemy territory it paid to judge harshly any given situation. As long as you erred on the side of caution then you remained alive. This is what made him into such an effective albeit blunt instrument.

Civilian life calls for a little bit more finesse though. He shouldn't have judged those kids. He simply did not have enough evidence.

"Excuse me Mr. Whitting." The young man sounded as if he was talking to his teacher.

"Hi," Said Ian. "It's Ian ok. Sorry I should have introduced myself. Frankly I'm a bit nervous." The kid's face took on a serious look and he shook his head.

"Don't be," He commanded. "Any man that has laid low in a sewage ditch for twenty four hours to avoid being caught by the Iraqi army and lives to write it down shouldn't be scared by a TV camera."

As he said this he moved his head slightly forward.

His mates were poking each other and farting. Ian was taken aback. Jill heard what the kid had said and her eyes were peering upwards over the top of the magazine. The monitor in the room showed a guest, the young girl in the high heeled shoes riding around on the back of one of the smartly dressed American men who was on all fours on the floor. The other guest, an actor known for his action-adventure films was cracking a bull whip. The audience were screaming and whistling with delight. An assistant director poked his head around the door.

"One minute Mr. Whitting. Please remember, this is going out live."

"Thank you." Ian replied. "Yeah. Thank you for that."

He was still standing close to the young kid.

"Did you read the books?" He asked.

"All of them. My dad was there." He said. "In ninety-one. After you though. He was with the Royal Fusiliers. He wasn't lucky like you. He never came back."

"We're ready for you now Mr.Whitting." The Assistant Director said and this time waited expectantly.

"Yes. Of course." Said Ian and moved to go then turned back to the young lad.

"What's your name?" He asked matter of factly.

"Harry. After my dad." Ian could see and hear on the monitor the host introducing him. The two men and the woman had gone. *They obviously take them off stage a different way.*

"Later in the show, Ladies and Gentlemen, we have for your delight and delectation, performing their new single, Tea and Biscuits." Charley Westbrook grimaced at the audience, "I mean what's that going to be about," The audience, encouraged by the floor manager waving a card saying 'Laugh', thought this was hilarious, "just back from their record breaking tour of America, yes, N'sing are in the building."

Wild screaming came from a large part of the studio audience. Charley, after a period of smugly nodding his head and making various facial expressions finally, again with the help of the floor manager, gesticulated with his palms downwards towards the audience and the audience quietened.

"But before that," he said, "can I introduce to you a man you will not recognise but whose name you will definitely know. Ladies and Gentlemen, this is very exciting for me because I'm a big fan. Revealed for the first time publicly and this is an exclusive for this show ladies and gentlemen…"

"Mr. Whitting." Said the Assistant director anxiously.

Ian stepped towards the door still looking at the kid.

"How old are you?" There was not a hint of pain on the young lads face. Just a big innocent smile.

"Nineteen." He said. Ian turned his body and began walking towards the stage with the Assistant director. His head was still turned towards the kid.

"You'll know him as the author of a series of books from the worldwide bestseller Bog Rats to the even more successful The Western Connection… Please give a warm Charley-Westbrook-Show-welcome to," He paused briefly for effect. "Ian Whitting ladies and gentlemen." He shouted this as he led the audience with enthusiastic applause.

Encouraged by the Charley's introduction and again by the floor manager frantically waving a card with the word Applaud on, the audience started to clap and whistle enthusiastically but not as fervently, Ian thought, as they had done for the other guests.

"Good luck." Said the assistant director with a kindly wink as he ushered Ian onto the set. As Ian walked on he glanced behind him to see Jill and the young lad from the band standing watching him. He turned again towards Charley who was leading the applause and they shook hands. The audience were still clapping but the noise they were making was more Woman's Institute than rock and roll. He didn't mind.

"Won't you make yourself comfortable?" Said Charley motioning towards the huge yellow velvet sofa. Ian went to sit down and the Charley took up his position behind a fashionably designed desk. The applause subsided.

"Well well," said the host "The elusive Ian Whitting. So why now? Why have you decided to show the world who you are… now?"

There was a silence for a moment. It probably didn't last for very long but Charley and the floor manager started to panic.

"The new…" Started Charley but to his great relief was interrupted by Ian.

"I'm not really sure." said Ian uncomfortably. Charley expected him to continue but he paused again as he glanced into the wings of the set where the assistant director and Jill were standing watching with the young lad from the band. Jill and the assistant director had very concerned looks on their faces. The young lad from the band caught his eye and gave him a thumbs up sign.

"No." Said Ian. "I am sure. I don't want to write war stories anymore." Charley nodded.

"The new book is certainly something of a departure in terms of style." He said. "But they weren't really stories were they? All of your books have been more, well accounts haven't they?"

"They were." Said Ian. "But they glorified it. Made it all sound worthy but it wasn't."

Charley knew that his show was prime-time light entertainment. It was no place for what he thought he might be about to hear. He touched his earpiece momentarily but he let Ian continue.

"I've come to realise that we live in a world," Ian paused again and glanced behind him to look at Jill. There was a horrified look on her face.

"In a world of misery corruption and hate and at some meagre level I have in the past contributed to that misery rather than help alleviate it."

Jill's head was now in her hands.

"Wow." Said Charley who was wondering who it was that booked this madman. He tried to get things back on track.

"I mentioned the departure in style of the new book, perhaps I understand now. Could you give us a short synopsis of what it's about?"

"I couldn't bring myself to write about misery and hate but I thought I'd write about corruption. The book is really about love and friendship and forgiveness in spite of all the corrupted minds that get involved."

"I can't help but ask the question and I don't want to put a spoiler on it but something happens towards the end that has an uncanny resemblance to events that happened in London a few months ago." Charley had a big smile on his face indicating to the audience that he was being sarcastic. "Looks like you had some insider knowledge there."

Ian smiled.

"I can assure you Charley that it's pure fiction. You know what they say, any similarity to persons living…" Ian suddenly took on a new persona. He started to play the game as he shifted in his seat.

"Any similarity to persons living." He repeated, "Or dead…" He said the last word actually turning towards a camera and raising his eyebrows slightly, "is purely coincidental."

37

Roland Garret awoke from a deep sleep with a thumping pain in his head. As he slowly came to his senses he looked around the sparsely furnished room. He was lying on a hospital bed. The room was lit by grey daylight coming in through a small window. The window was set quite high in the wall. His foggy eyes were looking around for something that was familiar to him but there was nothing he recognised. His headache was getting worse. He noticed a cord hanging from the ceiling with a red plastic triangle attached to it. He pulled. Presently he heard the sound of a door unlocking and a burly man and a young woman appeared at his bedside.

"Mr. Bingham." Said the young woman in a lilting southern Irish accent. "Can you hear me?"

Roland opened his eyes and saw the two figures dressed entirely in white standing at his bedside.

"Mr. Bingham," repeated the young woman. "Can you hear me?"

"Course I can." Said Garret in the most officious bark he could muster in his pained and weakened state. "Where am I? And for goodness sake give me something for the pain in my head."

The young woman turned to the burly man and spoke into his ear. The man left the room.

"You're home Mr. Bingham. You're home."

"This is not my home." Garret almost shouted which made the pain in his head worse "And why are you calling me Bingham. My name is Roland Garret and I'm a British Cabinet Minister."

The door of the room opened again after the turning and clicking of locks. The burly man appeared with a stainless steel tray. On the tray were two small plastic cups, one containing little white pills and one containing water.

Next to the cups was a buff coloured envelope.

"Of course you are dear." Said the young woman in a deeply patronising manner. "Of course you are." She pressed a button on a hand-set attached by a curly cable to the bed and Roland's upper body started to rise. "You'll be able to have a chat with Winston in the room next door later." She picked the little cup that contained the pills from the tray and passed it to Roland who weakly took it and swallowed back the pills. She then passed him the little cup of water. He drank it all down.

"Your friends have asked us to give you this when you woke up." She picked the buff coloured envelope from the tray. "You've had a trauma, Mr. Bingham. But you'll be right as rain in a week or so. Then you'll be able to meet the others. Would you like me to open it?" She motioned towards the envelope.

Roland had exhausted himself. He nodded slowly and the young woman tore open the envelope. She pulled out a copy of Private Eye with a picture of a diver on the front and the headline 'Environment minister visits Somerset' and placed it on the bed in Garret's lap. He picked it up and his eyes rose to the ceiling and a questioning expression formed on his face.

"Are we in Somerset?" He asked.

"Oh no Mr. Bingham." The young woman said with a hint of a laugh.

Garret slowly turned the pages towards the back where, as he expected a piece of paper fell out that had lines of numbers printed on it.

"Could you get me a pencil and paper?" He said, too tired to fight and almost politely to the young woman. The young woman turned again to the burly man who took a small reporters pad from the top pocket of his white tunic and handed it to Garret.

"We'll be back again at dinner-time. Best you get rest." Said the young woman before she left the room. The burly man sat on a chair by the door with his arms crossed and a blank expression on his face.

Roland deciphered the message.

26-15-111-110 J-113-29-317
41-15 511-113-28-121 219-113-321 212-17-332-121
219-113-321-110 11-15-38 510-113-42-121.
11-113-38 41-15 210-27-16 210-119-12
123-613-116-112-31-13.
18-11-518-12-17-19 12-113-117-221-511-211 & 26-11-114-15-114
114-28-111-16-120.

Dear John,
We hope you like your new home.
Now we are
all ghosts.

Eamonn Boothe &
David Crane.

(First letter of each word comes from section 1 of the ads.
Second letter from section 2
Third letter from section 3 and so on
Each letter is separated by a hyphen.)

Printed in Great Britain
by Amazon